PALM, CLEAR, FIRE, SHIFT, FIRE

Setting the bottle down, I raised my glass in my left hand, signed for him to pick up his glass. He raised it in his right hand.

"I propose a toast," I said, "to a couple of inches."

"I don't get your drift, Mister." Simmons stiffened. His eyes narrowed down to slits.

"Two inches left, you'd have blown my head off."

The cantina fell stony silent. Then I heard my three friends behind me move away from the bar.

"Two inches left, I'd have blown your head off, saved myself the trouble of arrestin' you for murder."

Simmons and I stood facing each other holding drinks in the air. His right side hugged against the bar and his gun was pinned to his side under the bar. My gun hand hung free. I remembered fighting Bustos, using the bar to protect my side from his knife hand. The man who outlived this lead swap would be the man who could survive the most lead poisoning.

Simmons threw his drink at my face, ducked left, slapped for his gun. Before it cleared leather my shot smashed into his chest. I laid the hammer back as the Colt bucked back in my fist. Reeling backward, Simmons brought his gun level.

We crushed triggers at the same time.

"Eli Waller, plagued by defeating experiences from the Civil War, finds himself working as a New Mexico cowboy to escape his personal demons. Challenged by the territorial governor to bring gold train robbers to justice, Waller out thinks and out shoots his adversaries. Haley uses skillfully described action, in depth perception of his characters and beautiful landscape description to braid an exciting tale into a fine novel."

——John Dunklee, author of *Genevieve of Tombstone*

*   *   *

"Authentic and powerful! One man tracking fifteen seasoned killers with two women on his mind, a vengeful Latino brother trailing him."

——Jean Henry, author of *Escape on the Wind*

*   *   *

"*DURANGO GOLD* is a humdinger of a tale. Mike Haley presents an action-packed story of a cowhand turned lawman who trails a robber gang to hell and back. You won't want to miss the ride!"

—Matt Braun, author of *Deathwalk*

To Jano Haley

and his love for the Southwest.

DURANGO GOLD

By Michael C. Haley

Cover illustration by Dean Kennedy
Jacket design by Image Corp

Published by:

Poncha Press
P.O. Box 280
Morrison, CO 80465
SAN: 253-3588

Copyright© 2000 by Michael C. Haley
First Printing 2000
Printed in the United States of America

ISBN: 0-9701862-0-7
Library of Congress Number: 00-134914

DURANGO GOLD

By
Michael C. Haley

Poncha Press
Morrison, Colorado

CHAPTER ONE

Red Charney kicked the door open, stomped out on the kitchen porch of the big house carrying the coffeepot and two empty Mexican clay mugs in his fists. He looked over at the corrals and hollered, "Eli!"

I flinched and ducked behind the shoulder of the gray stallion I had just roped and tied to the snubbing post. Red had a habit of offering a cup of coffee before he gave out tough jobs. I considered his coffee routine a decent gesture, but mostly a warning of trouble to come.

"Hey, Waller! You deaf?" Red bellowed directly at me this time.

"A minute, Red!" Why me? Irritated, I threw my saddle on Gray, cinched it up tight. Gray could stand and blow while I had coffee. I'd work him over after that. We had his "first-thing-in-the-morning bucking routine" to do yet. We'd fight to determine if Gray worked for me today, or not.

Wondering what the hell Red had in mind, I strode towards the porch. I liked riding for the VR brand, but didn't care much for extra chores or obligations. Brush popping wild cattle wore me down sometimes, but hadn't killed me. Cow punching was decent work. I had chosen it for now. Other than that, I preferred to be let alone.

"Mornin', Red." I stepped up on the porch, touched the brim of my hat.

"Mornin', Eli." Red poured two steaming cups. He wasn't one to spit and whittle, socializing before a morning cup of coffee. He spoke his mind right off. "I want you to ride over to the

1

land office in Santa Fe an' pick up some documents for the VR." He handed me coffee and looked me in the eye. "They're important papers, Eli." He gave his words time to sink in. "Then ride on down to Corrales. There oughta be cattle buyers down there pickin' up herds from the fall roundup. Find out if you can make a contract for one thousand head at fourteen dollars. We'll deliver December first." Red dug a fist in his pocket, came up with a couple of nuggets of brown sugar, which he offered.

I declined the sugar by not reaching. A break from the current roundup sounded good. Why had Red picked me to get the contract for the VR's cattle? Maybe he remembered the time I read a couple of legal documents for him. I blew on my coffee to cool it.

Red wasn't one to give away much. I wondered if there was more to this job than he let on. Still, an extra chore for Red sweetened by a drink in town, a poker game and a visit with those dark-eyed, Santa Fe señoritas had some appeal.

"Fine with me, Red." A little too much enthusiasm enriched my voice.

Red looked at me sideways over his mug. Under his bushy roan mustache the corners of his mouth creased, hinted at a wry grin then turned stern. "Don't be takin' your time over there, Waller. We got cattle to catch and move. You'll be needed here." Red gulped his coffee. His brow furrowed either from scalding his gullet or from remembering something. "Pick up the mail when you're in Santa Fe."

Red grabbed the coffeepot off the railing and turned on his heel to get after his day. I thought he was a good foreman, usually easy to work for, knew cattle and how to run an outfit.

Like most men in the West, he did not talk about his past. Cookie had told me that Red came to New Mexico from Texas in '59. During the war he had served out of Fort Marcy in Santa Fe, been in the fight over at Glorietta Pass. After that, the VR hired him as a hand. Red earned the foreman's job because of hard work and savvy.

Cooling the rest of my coffee, I stood alone on the porch and gazed south down the valley towards Cabezon Peak. I owed Red. He hired me back in '67 when I'd come wandering in, needing work. It hadn't bothered him that I had been a Reb. The last two years since I'd taken a bunk here had rolled on by without much to interrupt the routine. I worked cattle and rode through the seasons, seeking only peace and quiet.

Seemed to me Red had just given me time off, rather than a job. I almost smiled at my good luck. My stride had a lively bounce to it as I headed over to the bunkhouse, until I looked up at the ridgeline east of the ranch. The first snow of the season had dusted the high country last night, powdered the slopes down a quarter of the way. Winter wasn't far off, could catch me up in the high country, give me hell.

Considering the weather, I bet and chose anyway to take the straight-line route to Santa Fe over the mountains. To hedge the bet, I figured I had better pack my fleece vest and reminded myself to pick up a new winter coat in Santa Fe. Then my mind wandered over the rough terrain I meant to cover.

I'd ride due east over the San Juans and pass through the Valle Grande and Bear Canyon in the Jemez Mountains. The Valle, fine, high up meadows, commanded a visit if I came close. The first time I saw the Valle, I wanted it, even though I had no hopes of ever owning it.

From Bear Canyon I would drop down into the Rio Grande Valley, stop at San Ildefonso Pueblo, then ride on to Santa Fe. From there an easy ride took me on down the Rio Grande to Corrales. As I stepped into the bunkhouse, I pulled my traveling saddlebags off the wall peg, shook out the webs and dead bugs.

I stuffed my other Navy Colt in the saddlebag, assembled my tack. Long knife, a flask of black powder, some caps and shot came out of my war bag. I preferred to travel light, but there was a handful of things I liked to carry in my possibles bag, just to add some comfort.

Pulling my rifle off the rack, I checked the caps and loads. The Colt, a five shot revolving rifle, had not been converted to fire cartridges yet. One of these days I'd have the money and find a smith to bring the rifle up to date.

Taking a last look around the bunkhouse, I pulled a book off the shelf, *Plutarch's Lives*, to read by the campfire. Since I was going to the post office in Santa Fe, I paused long enough to scribble a letter to my younger brother in Virginia. I told him I'd send money when I could.

I hung my gear on the corral gate and turned to Gray. He rolled his eyes at me, snorted, tossed his head. Gray was about the only decent, unclaimed horse left in the corral. The rest of the good stock went out with the boys earlier.

Gray got left behind because he was new to the *remuda* and few of the hands would put up with his bad habits, wouldn't pick him for their string. I had discovered that Gray ran fast, had bottom, would do for a long ride. If I could, I wanted to work him out, claim this strong horse

4

for my string. I figured we better have our go-round now and get it over with. If I won, I'd work him all the way to Santa Fe and back.

First thing every morning, Gray's act was the same. I knew the routine. I jammed boot to stirrup, grabbed rein and mane, swung into the saddle. Digging in my heels, I went to bronco squeezing as Gray reared. He threw his head up high to rock back on his haunches. He jumped into the air to shuck me off over his rump. I heard my backbone crackle like snapped green beans as he leapt high. Gray felt strong today. Midair, he kicked his hind legs straight out behind him to punish me, had I fallen too close behind. Pissed that I'd survived in the saddle this long, Gray ducked his head between his legs, stuck his bill in the ground, landed stiff legged to pitch me over his head. I stuck to him.

Crisp, fall air made Gray feel feisty. The big horse kicked up the dust and put on a show. He was trying to make a name for himself. He hoped I'd quit him and he'd gain fame and have the day off. He cat-backed, swapped ends, crow-hopped.

Sometimes bucking paid off for him, but not today. I worked him out, settled him, dismounted, and snubbed him to the post again.

I noticed we had drawn a couple of spectators who swapped their bet money before they turned to get after their chores. I tied my trail gear to the saddle and regretted not getting a bet down.

*   *   *

Mid-morning, I heeled Gray out of the dense, ponderosa pines, crested the San Juans, and looked over into the Nacimiento Meadows.

We both sucked in the vanilla-scented air cooked up by the hot sun off the pines, with a touch of rock dust added. I let Gray rest from the steep climb.

We had reached high-up country, rolling grass parks fed by rambling streams. A gang of elk grazed not more than a half-mile away. On the slopes, aspen trees quaked golden leaves in a light breeze. Last night's snow still lay in their shadows and drove me to worrying about getting through the mountains before the next storm hit.

Swinging in the saddle, I could see off to the west, maybe a hundred miles, the air was so dry and clear. The sky, deep, dark-blue, seemed bottomless like a calm ocean. I shivered and admired the country around me.

The headquarters of the VR lay hidden in the pine and fence-post oak of the foothills below. East, Santa Fe lay maybe seventy miles over the volcanic mountain country I meant to plunge into. Seven miles south of the VR, I could see the irrigated farms around Cuba. A hundred years ago, bean farmers and sheepherders built homes on the flats below the foothills where the Rio Puerco watered the arid land.

John Young was building his new hotel in Cuba. Young had a contract with the stage line that ran from Santa Fe to Bernalillo and planned a new route on up through Cuba to Durango. The stage wasn't running the second route yet, or I'd have taken it and saved myself from the dangers of the ride over the rough, game trails ahead.

Shoving my worries aside, I gigged Gray into the meadows. Fresh signs of cattle pocked the mud of the stream bank. When I returned from Corrales I'd come back and round them up.

I felt guilty about rousting them out of this lush, cow heaven, but that was what I did for a living.

*   *   *

Late in the day, I rode on to the San Diego Grant north of Jemez Pueblo. In the bottom of the broad canyon that cradled the Jemez River watershed, I heeled Gray through river willow and thorny red berries and crossed the stream that smelled like sulfur. Riding up the slope, below the canyon walls, through pine and fallen chunks of tuff cliff, I came to the hot spring. Finding no one around, I decided to camp.

Now I'm no fool, and my plan for the day had worked out fine because the spring offered a place to enjoy, and enjoyments were scarce in my life. About two hundred yards up the side of the canyon above the Jemez River, hot, sweet water gushed from under rocks into a waist-deep pool.

Indians left altars, feathers, and fetishes as totems of their regard for the spring as a holy place. Maybe they believed the waters healed. Well, Sir, I had to agree the place was charmed, as I lowered my saddle sore body into the hot water. The hard ride just melted out of me. My spirits grew calm and happy. I intended to soak until I turned to soup.

With only nose, eyes, and hair above water I gazed down the canyon through rising steam. Cliffs rose high beside me to the east. The low, evening sun tinted the buff white of the tuff cliffs to blood red. My eyes feasted on the steep walls of color and early evening shadows. Memory conjured the square sails of tall ships, pink in a misty, Caribbean sunset.

I reckoned I had pushed thirty or more miles over rough country, but the saddle pounding had been worth it to have the luxury of a soak in the spring.

A full moon would rise above the cliffs by about ten, but descending darkness drove me to make camp and care for the gray stallion. Looking like a prune all over, I dragged myself out of the pool, stomped boots on to wet feet.

I don't make a habit of wandering around unshucked, save for my boots, but the spring had heated me through like a steam boiler and the cold air felt invigorating as it dried bare skin all over me.

I picketed Gray on good grass down by the stream and gathered up dry firewood.

Suddenly I heard a moan that made my hair stand on end. Twisting toward the sound, I realized I was without my gun, or anything else but my boots, for that matter. I moved to cover behind some bushes and almost stepped on an Indian, lying face down. In the twilight I could see his blood.

The Indian moaned again as I rolled him over. He took one look at me and his eyes glazed over. He passed out. I guess it would be a shock to anybody seeing me nude and prune-wrinkled up like that, but I took offense.

The young buck weighed maybe a hundred and twenty pounds. I carried him up to my camp by the spring and washed him off. I found two bullet holes in him. He had lost a lot of blood. I patched him up best I could with what I had in my possibles bag.

Figuring if the Indian came to I should be a might more presentable, I put on my hat, shirt, and pants, buckled on my pistol. Feeling the weight of responsibility descend on me again, I built a fire, put coffee on to boil.

I had time to wonder what the Indian boy's story was, as I waited for the coffee. I had not heard shots. They would have echoed up and down the canyon. Still, I kept an extra eye out for Indian trouble.

As I poured coffee in my tin cup I noticed the boy had opened his eyes. When he saw me look at him, he started sign talking by pointing down the canyon then pumping his arms and legs like he was running, even though he lay flat on his back. It must have hurt him to pump so hard, but he meant for me to understand running, not walking. He kept mumbling, "Jemez, Jemez."

"Jemez. I'll take you there." I pointed down the canyon and nodded vigorously. He pumped his arms like he was running again and pointed to his chest then his mouth. His signs made me think about a tale I heard about Indian message runners. Campfire stories told of some messengers that could run fifty miles without stopping. Seems the pueblos up and down the Rio Grande Valley sent the runners to each other with secret messages about their pagan rituals. This boy had a stringy, lean runner's body.

Hell, I was guessing at the meaning of his sign language. What was clear, the boy was in a hurry to get to Jemez Pueblo, enough to jar open his wounds to convince me.

I pointed at the boy's wounds and jerked my chin up in a question.

He held up two fingers then pointed at me. Then he pointed at the high heel of my boot. I nodded that I understood he meant two white men. He made two shooting motions with his hand, pointed at his wounds. Then he passed out.

Pounding leather all day long over rough terrain, I had been looking forward to lying around my fire and reading the book. Now I had a near-dead boy on my hands. Jemez Pueblo lay down the canyon about twelve miles south out of my way, but I could not leave the boy here to die.

Even in daylight, the trail down the canyon was treacherous. I decided to wait for the light of the full moon. This damn detour to Jemez would cost me an extra day. Red had told me not to dally around on this trip. My coffee tasted bitter as I rustled up grub and waited for the moon to rise.

*   *   *

The orange, full moon touched the rim of the hills to the west. A cold breeze rustled dry corn stalks in the field by the stream. A single dog barked as I approached Jemez Pueblo. Riding into the pueblo in the dark of night, holding up a half-dead boy in front of me, might cause a stir. I was surprised when no other dogs joined the first one in sounding the alarm.

I had come to this pueblo before, once to deliver cattle, once to contest ownership of a range bull. The Jemez Indians had seemed civilized for the most part. I had left with the impression that they did not like Anglos, but that the Spanish Padres had brought them Christianity. I didn't expect big trouble, but I rode into the plaza with care.

"Hello! I need help!" I called out.

A door opened and an old Indian, wrapped in a gray blanket up to his nose, stepped into the dimming moonlight. He sized me up, then came over to inspect the boy. The old Indian called a couple of times over his shoulder and two more men came out to help him. They signed for me to wait and carried the boy inside.

The old Indian returned with a Spanish Padre beside him. The padre stood tall on bare feet, a skinny man with a hawk nose and rotten buckteeth. He said he ran the mission at the pueblo and spoke fair English. I told the padre what I knew.

The old Indian listened to the padre's translation and then disappeared again. When he returned, he handed me a leather pouch and said something to me. The padre explained that the old man had thanked me, that I had done the pueblo a great service by returning the wounded message runner. I would be an honored guest when I returned sometime. Then abruptly the padre and the old man left me sitting on my horse and went back inside.

I stuffed the leather pouch in my saddle-bag and rode out of Jemez Pueblo thinking this was strange doings for the middle of a night.

Who had shot the boy? Why? The questions rattled around my tired brain briefly as I sought a place to picket Gray, drop my saddle and sleep. Some men hunted Indians like game animals. Few white men drew a distinction between the warrior tribes and the docile Pueblo Indians. Most likely the boy had run up and surprised the men who then shot him. Perhaps the boy had seen something the men wanted to hide.

I was too tired to speculate on the Indian's problem for long. My thoughts turned to my own business. I had to get to Santa Fe to fetch Red's documents and Corrales to make a contract. Hell, one day out from the ranch and I was already running a day late.

*   *   *

I rode out on the south rim of the Valle Grande in early afternoon. A trout stream twisted and ambled invitingly through the middle of the huge meadow ringed by forested, mountain peaks. Good grass grew for cattle, but the land was high up, and you had to move the herd before October or lose it to hard winter blizzards. Magnificent as ever, the place created a yearning in me. I wanted to own the Valle.

Red told me once that the Cabeza de Baca family owned the Valle by original grant from the King of Spain. The grant covered a hundred square miles ringed by the mountain peaks I looked at now. Much as I wanted the land the mountain peaks fenced, I was just a cowboy with no money and few prospects. The war had taken everything from me and left me hollow. Yet here was land that triggered a need I had not felt for a long time.

I had given up wanting things after the war. Maybe in the lonely nights I dreamed of a good woman and a place of my own again. Lately I had stopped dreaming. The farthest I thought into the future now was to the end of the job at hand. Strong and in my prime, I was not going anywhere but to Santa Fe and Corrales for Red. I was resigned to being a good cowhand and not much else. Still, I admired the Valle.

I camped on the east rim of the Jemez Mountains, looking into the Valle Grande behind me and the Rio Grande Valley ahead of me. The evening sun cast light across the Rio valley to the Sangre de Cristo Mountains. Fresh snow on the distant peaks reflected brilliant scarlet across forty miles. This evening spectacle had inspired the

Spaniards to name the range the Blood of Christ.
I could see why.

Because of the detour to Jemez Pueblo I
had not reached San Ildefonso like I planned, but
this was a fine place to camp. I appraised the
whole world from up high on the ridge. Eagles
must feel like this when they fly high.

One of these days I would have to ride over
those distant peaks into the Pecos watershed. On
the other side lay Mora and south lay Las Vegas.
Taos was to the north, this side of the range. A
few years back, the last of the trappers had come
to rendezvous at Taos. "Those were the days",
some said. I had met an old trapper once who
called them, "the shining days, when pelts was
gold."

At the south end of the Sangres lay Santa
Fe, a hard day's ride away. Further south I saw
the Cerrillos Peaks. Almost due south, Sandia
Peak rose up from deepening evening shadows.
Corrales lay down that way. Seemed a body could
see forever from up here. I could not believe I
could look at a place now, from here, but it would
take me three day's hard ride to get there.

Astounding!

I soaked up the broad views in the last
few minutes of dusk. In this clear air, golden
daylight fell off to dark quickly. I had a fire to
kindle and a horse to rub down. Maybe later on I
would start reading the book.

Still, reluctant to fold up and put away
this huge map spread out all around me, I stood
watching the country turn orange, and then fall
into deep purple shadows.

*　　　*　　　*

From the northwest into Santa Fe, the trail narrowed down leading off the bluffs. My timing stunk. I fell in behind a burro train hauling bundled *piñon* firewood and kicking up dust that rose like smoke off a forest fire. Hot, sweaty, and tired after a four-day ride, I gathered my weight in burro trail dust.

The clock in the window of the bank indicated four when I rode into the plaza behind the shuffling wood haulers. I beat the dust off my clothes with my hat, but the effort did little good.

Burro Alley dust had the best of me. A bath, fine Mexican food, and a drink were what I needed. My mind just naturally turned to hot Mexican food when I smelled the *piñon* smoke that hung over Santa Fe. That unforgettable light pungency, not sweet like cedar or sharp like pine, set my mouth to watering, invited me to a warm hearth, a table with candlelight, and a pretty serving girl. I forgave the *piñon* wood haulers for the dusting they gave me, thanked them for the perfumed air.

The VR kept a running account at La Fonda. Across the street from the bank and just off the sou'east corner of the plaza, the two story adobe hotel offered the best rooms in Santa Fe. The desk clerk checked me in and stopped scowling when I ordered hot water for a bath. Soaking in the tub wasn't anything like boiling in the spring, but it broke the burro dust loose.

I pulled my long black coat from my duffel, put it on over a clean shirt and stepped in front of the mirror. The band of pink forehead skin, between the borders of my tan hat line and chestnut hairline, stuck out as an ugly feature in contrast with the rest of my sun-baked face. I clapped my hat on to cover the pink forehead that branded most cowboys and surveyed my six-foot frame. When I caught the glint of devilishness in those green eyes looking back at me from the mirror, I judged I was ready to impress the señoritas that had been on my mind for the last couple of days.

However, being of a mind to get the job done first before unwinding, I headed over to the land office to pick up Red's documents. A closed sign hung in the window, but I talked a sour-looking clerk into opening up and digging out a bundle marked for the VR. He didn't say anything, just handed the bundle to me with a scowl, pushed a receipt in front of me to sign, then showed me out the door. I heard him lock the door behind me as I stuffed Red's important documents under my arm inside my black coat.

I had forgotten that city folks kept hours. The post office was locked up for the night. I found the postmaster out back, cinching up his saddle, and persuaded him to open up since I was from out of town. I stuffed six letters in my pocket and thanked the postmaster as I handed him the letter to my brother. I headed back to my hotel room with a jaunty bounce in my stride. Finished with my chores in town for Red, I felt free to enjoy an evening in Santa Fe.

While putting the documents and letters in my saddlebag, I noticed one letter addressed to me, apparently from Virginia. I couldn't tell for sure. The envelope was battered and smudged. The writing did not resemble my brother's hand, so I decided to read the letter later and stuffed it in with the rest. Besides, my thoughts ran to that first drink. I locked my room, strolled through the lobby, stepped out into a cool, fall evening and headed for the plaza.

Local women, their heads covered by black shawls, carried bundles or baskets and gathered in the plaza to swap the day's gossip. Shopkeepers, finishing up the business of the day, locked their doors. Six rough-looking teamsters, getting wound up for a night on the town, whooped it up, laughing and slapping each other on the back. Under the portal of the governor's mansion, a dozen Pueblo Indians displayed trade items on colorful, woolen blankets. A pair of rich-looking *caballeros* loitered under an ancient cottonwood tree, smoked cigarillos and waited for the señoritas to promenade. A handful of soldiers marched, two abreast, towards the cantina on the west side of the plaza.

I hadn't seen this many folks for a long time. I paused to watch and soak in the local society. Santa Fe was a poor town, compared to other places I had seen, but it could stand up to any town when compared to the variety of characters. I felt at home in this adobe village.

When chores were done, I was one to cut myself slack and kick up my heels. The war had taught me that death always hovered close by. I carried scars to prove I had cheated death. The scars reminded me to revel when I had the option. So when the time came, I was among the first to whoop it up. Here was a rough-and-ready town and I meant to have me some fun.

Poker was my game. I liked the mix of people, chance, and skill. Besides, poker was usually profitable for me and I could use some free spending money. I always felt the need to spend money when I got to town, and I needed a winter coat and a new pair of boots. I decided I would gamble for new boots tonight.

Besides being fun and profitable, poker could be dangerous. I had seen games explode in an instant gun battle with men left dead all around, some of them innocent bystanders. Thinking over the risks a bit, I decided not to go back for my gun. I had my long knife in my belt under the black coat. I felt sufficient.

There had to be a poker game going on somewhere, but the need for that first, dust-busting drink pulled me across the plaza towards the cantina. I wanted to find a Mexican beer maker Pete Montoya had told me about.

Pete, a hand at the VR like me, was a local, knew his way around. One night sitting herd, we had talked about beer. Seems we both had a taste for it. Pete knew about a brewer named Rivas and swore by a tall, cool Rivas to wash down the worst trail dust. Information like that was easy to remember. I could taste beer. My step quickened.

Something caught my eye. It was the same thing a hunter experiences when just a glimpse registers that he has seen his prey. My feet had already stopped walking and all thoughts of beer and poker had vanished.

Just for an instant, I had seen the face of the most beautiful lady in the window of a polished, black carriage that pulled into the plaza. Then a curtain had been drawn to hide her face. I wanted to see more of that beauty and calculated where the coach would stop. I planned to be there as a close-up spectator.

The coach appeared to be swinging around the plaza to the front of La Fonda. Turning in my tracks, I could be there to greet it in a few casual steps. I wanted to see what a little chivalry might get me.

I timed my steps to push just in front of the man reaching to open the coach door. I heard him grunt angry Spanish words, but paid him no mind.

When I opened the coach door, it was like lifting the lid off the box where the sun was stored. Everything else around me disappeared as I looked into brilliant sparkling green eyes. I offered my hand to assist her and I felt her gentle touch warm my heart. Perfume, light, sweeter than the *piñon* scent in the air, conjured an image of her dabbing it behind her ears and along her slender neck, exposed beneath piled, black hair, held up by a tiara that reflected the sun's last, red rays.

Lightly, she glided to the ground, adjusted her skirt over dancing slippers. I knew this graceful lady had just captured my heart. I bent to kiss her hand. I must have said something right because she gave me a flashing smile, warm, friendly, inviting. Suddenly I felt like a boy suffering his first bout of cupid's cramp.

Next thing I knew, an old lady screeched Spanish in my face, jabbed me in the ribs to push me away. Then both women were whisked away by a scowling *caballero*. I was left standing stunned.

I knew I had been on the range with stringy cattle, a long time away from women, but I also knew I had been treated to a touch of five-and-a-half-foot-tall, well-proportioned heaven just then. I wanted more of this lady's presence, but I had not moved quickly enough to introduce myself properly. She was gone.

Most likely from her dress, she had arrived to meet friends for dinner and a party. As I turned to head across the plaza to the cantina, I resolved to find her later. There might be music at the party and dancing with this beautiful lady appealed to me.

Maybe after a Rivas beer, Mexican food and poker, I could round out my evening on the town with her on my arm. My spirits rose. Cupid's cramps and anticipation mixed into a strange feeling in my chest that I could not put to words. It seemed like Lady Luck hovered above my right shoulder with her hand on me.

Stepping into the cantina, I paused to let my eyes adjust to the light, dimmer than the dusk outside. The noisy crowd jostled, three bodies deep at the bar, well launched into an evening of raucous fun. The crowded tables would sport poker games after the evening meal had been served on them.

I jostled to the bar and waited for the bartender, an old alkali who still showed considerable strength in his shoulders and forearms. He could handle whatever trouble this job brought, was my guess. He worked his way over as he lit another oil lamp, poured another dram for the gent next to me.

"Rivas beer!" I slapped a coin on the bar.

"He don't sell it here. Has his own place," he jerked his thumb over his shoulder. "Maria's, 'bout four doors west from the southwest corner of the plaza. Can't miss it." He looked me over then winked the eye with the scars over it that proved he'd been over the trail a few times. "I don't blame you none, Mister. Good beer, when he has it."

Maria's place was entirely different from the cantina on the plaza. A man could socialize here with the bright-eyed girls who sashayed among the tables. The soldiers I had seen cross the plaza lounged here with their collar buttons undone. Working folks, who had come to unwind, lined up at a long, hand-carved, wooden bar. Guitar music drifted from the fingers of a young man, shadowed in the far corner of the large, perfume-drenched room.

"Rivas beer, if you have it." I grinned back at the smiling woman behind the bar.

Luck was with me. Maria pulled a bottle from a box of ice brought down from the mountains by wagon. I fairly puckered when the beer poured, all headed-up and frosty, into the mug before me.

Pushing back from the bar to arm's length, I planted my feet and lifted the cold mug.

"To the Irish Sergeant," I toasted and chuckled at the memory of Irish. He had soldiered with me in the war. He had served in the north African desert in another army before he came to die in Virginia.

Irish told me once that when he died, he wanted to come back to life as a camel. He explained that being a camel he would have three feet of throat for a beer to flush and cool. It had been months since I had toasted the sergeant. In case he hadn't made it back to this life as a camel, I would cut the dust from a hundred lonely trails for him now.

The first long gulp paid off. It made my eyes water. Pete Montoya was right. Rivas was a beer to linger over. A Mexican dinner might have to wait a bit because the Rivas tasted rich, like a dessert, and I favored having dessert first tonight.

I couldn't imagine how cold water with bubbles and malt could feel so good. This beer had the taste of brown sugar in it, and I would bet there were raisins in the recipe. A dark, amber glow pleased my eye. I admired the beer against the lamplight a moment longer, then enjoyed a second, deep swig.

Savoring the Rivas taste, I put the mug down. Then I noticed the guitar music had stopped and the cantina was almighty quiet except for a hushed but excited babble. I turned from the bar to see what had changed the atmosphere. Everyone in the place looked at me and another man, who stood with his fists on his hips glaring at me. I focused on his dark, brown eyes, pinched close together over a hawk-beak nose.

The *caballero* staring me down stood short, stocky, and richly dressed in black. His vaquero jacket, which fit snugly on broad shoulders, had fine, silver wire woven into it. Silver *conchas* ran in a line down his tight pants legs and over his boots. He wore a broad sombrero in the fashion of the rich Mexican families around here. Hunched by the bar, just out of arm's reach, he seemed to smolder like a hot coal ready to hiss at any drop of cold water.

The *caballero* did not wear a gun. A finely tooled, black, leather belt and holster, with a silver-handled pistol in it, lay coiled on the bar beside him. He deliberately moved away from the pistol. His placing of the gun on the bar must have drawn everybody's attention. Those close around us had pulled back and were waiting expectantly for something to happen.

I had been so intent on that damned beer I had missed the whole proceedings. I took a better look at his face and didn't recognize him. Under his clenched jaw, I saw the veins in his neck pulse with hot blood. I felt the cold chill of death pass through me. I had seen this kind of anger before. It usually led to killing.

MICHAEL C. HALEY

"Nobody touches my sister," he hissed. With a slow, steady hand he removed his sombrero, tossed it over by the silver-handled pistol. "A pig like you?" he taunted. "Never!" His steel-hard eyes, turned black now, snake like, locked on mine. *Hijo de puta!* he jerked his chin up in a challenge. "I will teach you some manners."

I almost turned back to my beer on the bar. Maybe, if I paid no attention, this cocky bantam rooster would go away. I had seen too much killing in my lifetime, and I wanted no more of it. Besides, I hadn't been dallying with any ladies, not yet anyway. Perhaps he had the wrong man. Instead, I stood firm and I kept him in my vision like I would a rattlesnake I meant to step around.

Something warned me. I jerked hard away from the flashing streak of light. Turning instinctively to my right, I sucked in my gut as I watched the slashing blade merge with my black coat. Pain seared my side. Blood stained the knife. I looked up in time to see his fist coming. Too slow, I thought. I'm too slow. I heard my teeth clack as his left hook connected.

The white flash in my brain buckled my knees. Falling backwards saved me from his back-slashing blade. When I hit the floor, I rolled toward him, kicked his knee.

Off balance, he reeled in a limping jig and butted up against the wall.

I had just enough time to get my feet under me and fist my long knife. Cold sweat popped out on me. As I shook my head to clear it, I realized this hombre struck fast like a rattler and he meant to kill me.

I circled to the right and touched through the rip in my coat to the cut in my left side. Fingers came away sticky with warm blood.

"Back off, Son-of-a-bitch!" Quickly I searched the crowd to locate who else I might be fighting. No one moved in the room, but I heard men making bets, and not on me. "What t'hell's the matter with you?"

His lips twisted in a snarling grin then split open, uncovering stubby, tobacco-stained teeth. "You kissed my sister." Disdain hardened his words. "For this kiss I will cut off your lips before you die, *pendejo*."

"You'll die trying," I threatened and feinted a stab at him, but I didn't feel confidence. Regret filled me. I had been foolish not to fetch my gun from the hotel room when I had thought of it. I wasn't sure I could kill this knife fighter.

"Bustos Sanchez'll die of old age." He laughed. He lunged, lightning fast.

I sidestepped.

Anticipating my move, he shifted quick as a cutting horse, sliced another slash, left side between first and second ribs. Two cuts now, bleeding considerably.

Flinching from the sting, I stabbed, missed, noticed my clumsiness when the joint in my shoulder popped. I'd never missed by that far before!

The pistol on the bar loomed large. I thought about circling to it, noticed the thong still locked on the hammer.

He'd cut my heart out before I get the gun free of the holster.

He saw my eyes cut to the gun, register disappointment. Bustos laughed triumphantly.

I hadn't fought a crazed man for a long time. I felt how slowly I moved. I needed an edge, didn't have one. Fear cursed me, blamed me. Fear knew I was about to die.

Bustos attacked.

I leaped back.

He ducked in under my slashing blade, sliced another cut into my left side, between second and third ribs.

My counter-slash split the empty air he had just danced through.

The man's a butcher! Carving me up like a slab of roast beef.

Time slowed way down, like before in the trenches, when rifle and bayonet were too cumbersome, when it got down to killing with knives. Time slowed for me so as to delay having to meet Death. Well, Sir, Death stood right here, now, toying with me. As my blood drained out, cold fearlessness flowed into me.

The same timeless, fearless feeling had saved me in the war when all I could do was lunge forward, slash and stab, knowing I had to kill anything standing in front of me. I had learned in those times all I needed to know now. Attack to kill, or be killed.

I felt weak, maybe too weak to kill Bustos. Time and blood were running out together. I circled left up against the bar to shield my carved ribs. The move forced Bustos to strike high over the bar. My knife hand remained free to maneuver.

I attacked slashing viciously, jabbing, stabbing, always thrusting forward.

Bustos stumbled backwards, surprised. He expected to whittle me at his pleasure. Recovering, he parried and dodged my slashes and thrusts. His legs danced the formal steps of saber training. Then he lunged, counterattacking full force for the kill.

I sprung forward to grapple. In close was the only way to kill him.

My blood on the floor gave me the edge when Bustos charged. His boot slipped in my gore. He missed my belly but sunk his knife to the hilt low in my left side.

I grabbed his wrist in an iron grip, kept the blade from moving in me. I stabbed at his heart, hit his breastbone without penetrating his chest.

He jerked down hard. His knife cut free of my flesh.

It felt like my backbone had been yanked from my body. In a gray haze, I slumped to the floor, still gripping his wrist. I yanked him against me as I fell, stabbed my knife deep into his heart this time. I twisted the blade with all my last strength. He fell, jerking and thrashing, on top of me.

Through the pain and gray haze, fading into unconsciousness, the regretful part of me rasped, "Bustos and I die of old age. Too soon."

CHAPTER TWO

"Get up! Get up and fight! Fight until you die!" a staccato bugle commanded urgently from way off in the distance.

"Force your men to fight 'til bullets strike'em dead," the colonel ordered. "Your wounded, too. We need that extra effort from 'em boys to win, an' it's hell to die in'em damn field hospitals. You order your men to die! Now! To win!"

I could not move to follow his orders. Too many had died already. Too many. I lay crushed under their mangled, bleeding bodies. The smell of blood and rot made me twist away, retching. My soul rose up out of my body and looked back at the corpse lying there. A shaggy, black wolf tore at the body. His teeth snapped at hot guts up under the rib cage towards the heart. To escape rending fangs, the live body jerked.

That ripping spasm yanked me out of the nightmare.

I felt suddenly that I had escaped the dream, but pain kept me jumping in a haze between the wolf in the nightmare and a vague memory of a shiny, slashing knife. Flinching again to duck a ghostly knife thrust, I came more awake to the real pain in my side. Sharp now, pain drove my hand to my left side to fumble over a sticky bandage. It was my own blood that I smelled.

"...damn, field hospital." My dry mouth mumbled the words.

"You ain't in no hospital, though we been nursin' you four days now," some voice said from far away, like it came from inside a cave.

"Who?" came out of my mouth. No other part of my body moved.

"It ain't no wonder we ain't met, what with you layin' around all the time passed out." Irritation tainted the statement. Then the voice added, "I'm Beckett." From closer up he said, "Thought we'd lost you a couple times, Boy."

Memories failed to come to mind to connect with reality. My eyes opened and began trying to focus on shapes in front of them, maybe a ceiling. Deep roaring filled my ears, but I heard my voice say, "Get up!"

"Ain't no need to rush. You ain't goin' no where 'til Moore gets back." Beckett's voice sounded threatening, close now.

I did not venture to move my head to look for Beckett. Another shot of pain and I might lose the headway I seemed to be making towards consciousness.

"What happened?" I groaned hoarsely.

"Well, Sir, you boys went to killin' each other off an' damn near got the job done." He spit before he asked, "You remember anything, Waller?"

The sound of that name triggered memories. Shadowy forms, grief, frustration brought panic to knot up my guts. A sudden fear brought questions. What battle is this? Goddamn, not again? Why can't I die and be done with this friggin' war? Prisoner? How does he know my name? "How...?"

"How come ya lived? Old Bustos let up on his half of the deal, but he shore as hell left his mark all over your hide 'ere. You killed him, gettin' your knife in his heart." Beckett's boots scuffed the wooden floor as he moved closer. "Hell of a fight, they say." He chuckled. "Folks're still talkin' 'bout you gettin' all cut up an' then killin' Bustos with one stab. Kind'a wished I'd seen it." Beckett hocked up a gob, spat. "Doc run over to Maria's soon enough to sew you up 'fore you bled to death. I never seen such patch work as he done on you. Regular quilt-like. Ya hungry?"

I turned my head towards the voice slowly. Beckett and a deputy sheriff's star came into focus behind iron bars. "I'm prisoner?"

"Sort of custody for your own protection," Beckett said reaching for a ring of keys on his belt. "You bein' out of it, laid up, Sheriff Moore felt he better save your ass from Patricio Sanchez." Beckett unlocked the cell door. "You done kicked a wasp nest, Mister," he chuckled again. "That Sanchez family has three more sons tougher than Bustos." Stepping into the cell Beckett added matter-of-factly, "That Patricio's a known killer. Does the dirty work for the family. They say he's a cruel man, good with knife or gun."

Aware of another feeling in my guts, I asked hopefully, "Got food?"

"Want anythin' special?" Beckett turned to walk to the door to call a small boy to run the errand for him.

"Beef'n beans, coffee'n two Rivas beers." It took no effort at all to decide on the beers. It took effort to talk.

A man, wearing a sheriff's badge on his left shirt pocket, elbowed Beckett out of the door way and stepped into the jail office. "How's he doin'?" He jerked his chin in my direction.

"He's awake, Sheriff Moore." Beckett pulled a blue rag from a back pocket, blew his nose, mopped snot out of his top lip whiskers.

"Go tell the governor he's awake," the sheriff ordered Beckett. After Beckett left, Moore walked over to me, stared down. "How you feelin', Waller?"

I tried to look good by sitting up, but changed my mind. A flood of new pain almost knocked me out. I knew some tricks to stop pain, if I could only remember them. "Tolerable," I said, with little conviction.

I decided to take my time and work up to moving around. Opening and closing my hands, like a baby, seemed to get feeling back into my arms. Moving my toes, I began to collect myself. Coyote came to mind. A Navajo medicine man had told me that no matter how badly coyote was smashed up, he could pull himself together, if he could find the tip of his nose and the tip of his tail. I backhanded my nose clumsily, asked, "When do I get out of jail?"

"Any time you want, after the governor sees you," the sheriff said while he appraised my condition. "I think you oughta stay put 'til you can stand and shoot." The sheriff pulled out a pocketknife and went to work on a split thumbnail. "Beckett tell you Bustos' twin brother, Patricio, has his men watchin' you? You can't move that Patricio won't know it. He means to kill you."

"No." I could move my arms and legs better now.

Moore pocketed the knife, pulled out his makings to build a smoke. "I got no cause to hold you. Witnesses all said it was a fair fight. The Anglos say Bustos deserved killin'. The Mexicans say it was a duel of honor."

He licked the paper and rolled it tight. "To the Mexican's way of thinkin', you was rude, but they respect the bold way you introduced yourself to the Sanchez girl. They call it *macho*." He offered me the *quirly* and dug in the shirt pocket behind the badge for a match. "Most of them think it would've been justice for you to die. They figure it won't be long before Patricio takes revenge. The vaqueros're giving ten-to-one odds you don't last the month." Moore used the newly repaired thumbnail to strike the match. He held the fire for me.

I took a drag, choked off a cough to save wrenching my side. "How'd you bet?"

The sheriff snuffed out the match, shrugged, and turned his back on me. He walked over to the desk and got after some paper work.

I sat up, tried to get over being dizzy, when the boy returned with my dinner of beef and beans, coffee, Rivas beer, apricots, and a couple of apples. I had not thought to ask for the fruit, but I knew it would help me heal.

Wonder if I'll get to finish my Rivas this time? The first gulp tasted better than before and, unlike the Irish sergeant, I was alive. The beef was rare, the coffee hot, and I could feel the alcohol. I decided to save the other bottle of Rivas to take to Pete, if I lived long enough.

I began to believe I could stand up. I had my feet on the floor. About that time, the office door pushed open. Sheriff Moore, standing by a cabinet, wheeled and stood facing the door, pistol in hand, before the door was half-open. I had never seen anyone get a gun into action that fast.

"Hello, Tibits. Come on in." The sheriff rolled his pistol over his trigger finger into his holster. "Your patient lived despite you," he grinned.

"Sheriff Moore." Tibits eyed the sheriff's holstered gun. "A might jumpy today? I can give you something for your nerves. "

I would have to remember to ask the sheriff about that fast gun action later.

Tibits peeled the bandage off my side. The damage did not look good, although the sewing was artful. Tibits must have had field hospital experience during the war. He sewed with the same, new stitches invented to close the stumps of amputees.

Black and blue, my side still oozed a little blood from one cut, but with no evidence of pus. There were three, long slashes and the one V-shaped cut, where Bustos had stabbed and cut downward. He had laid back a flap about two inches wide and four inches long. The bottom of the V cut ended below my hipbone. It would be a while before I wore a gun belt.

"Don't go movin' around much. You tear loose those stitches, lose much more blood, and you'll die." Doc sprinkled some powder on the wounds and bound me up. "The light-headedness ought to pass when you build up some new blood. Rest and you ought to pull through." He cocked his head, contemplating. "I'm surprised there's no infection. Bustos' knife must have missed your intestines. Lucky, I guess."

I didn't feel lucky. "Put your bill on the VR account over at the hotel, Doc." I tried not to groan as I lay back on the cot.

"It'll be fine to get paid for a change." Doc tipped his hat and left.

Laying there, I could feel the food working on me, giving me strength. I might try standing up later, but first, some sleep.

*   *   *

"Waller!" Sheriff Moore yelled to wake me up. "The governor's here."

Yellow light filtered through the small barred window into the cell to announce evening time. I smelled *piñon* smoke again and thought of the Mexican dinner, poker game, and señoritas I had missed. I felt hungry again.

Suddenly I remembered I was in Santa Fe on a job for Red and needed to get to Corrales. What the hell day was this? Had Beckett said they nursed me for four days? I calculated I had been gone from the VR eight, maybe nine days all told. Red would be looking for me to return tomorrow or the next day. I only had half my job done. Then I felt the sharp pains in my side that meant more delay. My mood turned miserable.

The sheriff unlocked the cell door and stood there with a medium-sized, blonde, curly-haired gent wearing a black, string tie and coat. I had never seen him before.

Moore introduced me to the governor of the Territory of New Mexico. I missed his name because my full concentration was required to sit up. I planted my feet on the floor and pushed upright to stand. Seemed to be the thing to do for a governor.

What's he doing here? Could I keep from passing out? I managed to remain standing, but I had to hold up my pants. I could not bear the pain of tightening my belt. Next soldier I saw, I would buy the suspenders off him.

The governor sized me up, and then turned to the sheriff. "I want to talk to him privately, right?" Moore and Beckett left the jailhouse.

That worried me some. Every time an official had talked to me privately, I had come out on the short end of the stick. I decided to sit down to hear the bad news. Besides, I felt sick and dizzy and didn't want to puke on the governor's polished, black, English riding boots.

"Mister Eli Waller, from the VR ranch, right?" the governor's tone deepened my worry. "Up until '63, you captained a ship, became a famous blockade runner, right?"

I nodded and wondered how he knew about my past.

"After '63 you served in the infantry, then transferred to cavalry. Made colonel by field promotion, right?" His eyes drilled into me.

"With the casualties we suffered, they promoted anyone standing close by. How'd you get my history?"

"Major Watson was in Maria's cantina the other night. He recognized you from the surrender at Appomattox. Watson says you were on Lee's staff at the end, right?" He did not pause for me to answer. "Watson claims that you were a Reb hero from a very wealthy, Richmond family, right? Are you this man I'm describing?"

"That's me." A warning went off in the back of my mind; this was no friendly visit to ask after my health. I waited for the governor to continue and hoped he wouldn't ask 'right?' again. Nodding my head so often had increased my dizziness.

"Major Watson commands Fort Marcy here. He's very familiar with a problem I have and suggested you could be of great help to me, right?" The governor reached into a breast pocket and pulled out an envelope. Handing it to me, he continued formally. "You are hereby commissioned by me and the territorial judge as deputy marshal of the Territory of New Mexico."

I looked the governor in the eye, handed him back the envelope, and said, "No, Sir. I'm just a cowboy now."

"I need you to work in secret for me," he continued, as though I had said nothing. "My problem's protecting the gold shipments from Durango to Santa Fe, right? Come late September, snow blocks the passes between Denver and Durango, so the gold's shipped through here, right? The first shipment left Durango last week. It never got through to Santa Fe, right?"

I had stopped responding to the governor's false questions, but I interrupted to say, "I'm not..."

The governor flashed a hand signal to cut me off. He turned to stare out the little window into the growing darkness outside. "One of the guards lived long enough to drag himself to the settlement at San Ysidro. Before he died he said they'd been attacked northwest of there, right?" He turned and jabbed a finger at me. "That's your territory, south of the VR, right, Waller? It'd be easy for you to scout around for me while working at the ranch, right?"

"No, I..."

"This commission gives you the power to bring the criminals in dead or alive." He flipped the envelope into my lap. "Just me, Major Watson, and the judge know of your commission. You will take it, right?"

Wrong! I had no intention to take up arms! Warring lay behind me now. Finished. Forgotten. I had run long and hard to escape the bloody past that had ruined me. Anger at the governor's prodding welled up, but gave way to weakness and despair.

Hell, after the whipping in the war I'd tucked tail and fled west with no hopes, no dreams. I'd meant to lose myself, to become a nobody on a far out ranch, away from people. I found peace and independence at the VR. I craved the open spaces, the clear air, the dry heat of this arid country and wanted nothing to do with the affairs of men. Cattle were my business now. The work was dangerous, but not because of men shooting at me.

Besides, unlike the governor's description, I was a failure. I lost my last ship, with a rich cargo on board, bound for the South. I did poorly as an infantry officer. I learned to survive war's hell, but hundreds of my men died by my orders. After my regiment was decimated, I was saved from courts marshal by an old family friend. He knew my family had owned fine racing stock before the war and ordered me to cavalry to save my life from the tribunal. I failed my men in that command. Casualties in my troop ran as high as seventy percent. I accomplished my orders. But after the war, when guilt and shame brought perspective, I swore never to pay that high a price in blood again, for anything.

Was the governor crazy? He could see I was in no physical condition to go hunt outlaws. The fight with Bustos showed how slow my reflexes were. I was one step behind until the end, and that had come too damn close to disaster.

Was the governor desperate? He could figure out that I was out of the habit of solving complex problems. It took no skill at all to outfox a long-horned bull. I'd told the governor I was a cowboy and that was what I meant to keep on doing.

"No, Sir. I won't take the job." Sitting down on the jail cot made it hard to stand firm, so I handed him back the envelope to make my refusal look official.

"Well, Sir, let me put it to you this way, right?" The governor, not daunted by my refusals, sounded like a poker player with two aces in the hole. "I'll give you a choice, right? I'll pull my men off protecting you from the Sanchez brothers right now and leave you in the soup. Or, I'll get you away from them and give you a chance to heal and survive, if you take the job." He handed me the commission again. "Right?"

I held a losing hand. I would not survive a day on my own against killers in my present condition. If I took the job, some outlaw would kill me sooner or later. All the governor offered me was an edge, some more time to live.

Damn that pretty girl's face in the window of the polished, black coach. Damn Bustos! If he hadn't cut me up so bad, I wouldn't be weak and in this bind. Damn the governor for taking advantage of me when I was beat up and down.

I stuffed the commission into my shirt pocket. "Like a steer, I can try. How do you plan to get me out of town, Governor?"

The governor smiled like an amateur winning a big pot. "I'll make the arrangements, Marshal Waller, right?" He left the jail abruptly.

Despair rolled over me like a thick fog. The job for Red in Santa Fe was half done. I still had to deliver the land office documents to him. I had no idea when I might get to Corrales and make a cattle contract. No telling when I'd make it back to the VR. There was no way to get a message to Red. And being this late would piss off Red something fierce anyway.

I'd seen Red lose his temper, go on the prod before. No one around him was left standing after. Bunged-up as bad as I was, he'd have the right to fire me, even if he didn't lose his temper, because I was worthless for working cattle with my side all cut up. I saw my job at the VR slipping away in the bleak fog of despair.

To boot, I'd killed Bustos in self-defense and now I had a family of hard men bent on killing me for revenge. I didn't even know what they looked like, let alone how to defend myself. I couldn't strap on a pistol. And my body felt about as strong as a fresh-dropped calf. I imagined my body lying dead, back-shot in some alley.

On top of all that, I had a commission from the governor in my pocket that made me a warrior, a hunter and killer of men. More than likely, he'd turned me into an easy notch on some outlaw's pistol butt. And covert, undercover at that, a spy! What that meant? All on my own, I had no help coming from anybody. The governor had turned me loose into trouble I couldn't even imagine yet.

I hated it, wounded, this damned body letting me down. I could see no future through the pain. This cowboy was doomed!

My legs began jerking with the need to run from my troubles, but I couldn't even stand up.

CHAPTER THREE

The army wagon bulked, then pitched over rocks, lurched and jolted in the ruts of the trail from Santa Fe to Bernalillo. Inside, gunnysacks full of corn, wheat, and beans jostled and slid for the newest low point in the wagon bed. On top of the bags, I fought for position against a side of beef, salted but rotting anyway. The governor's plan to get me safely out of Santa Fe was killing me.

When I told the governor I had business to get to in Corrales, he arranged with Major Watson to send a shipment of army supplies down to Bernalillo under escort. Riding in the back of a covered wagon on grain sacks seemed, to the governor, like a secret and comfortable way to transport me away from the Sanchez brothers. Battered, blistered, and bleeding from my side again, I had a belly full of the governor's protection.

Dobbs, the soldier I bought the suspenders from yesterday, also had a quart of whiskey hidden away. He'd made me pay top dollar for the bug juice. I had tried to ease the pain in my side by staying drunk. Now the whiskey bottle was empty. My head ached with hangover. Preferring to die in my saddle from the wounds, or the hellish hangover, I bolted from the wagon when the troop stopped for nooning. I demanded Gray.

I called Dobbs over and told him a little bit about Gray's bucking routine. "I bet two dollars you can't line the stallion out for me so I can ride him."

"Hell, ain't a horse in the world I can't tame." Dobbs took the challenge, puffed out his chest and asked around for more bet money.

Old Gray pitched Dobbs, forked end up, over his head, into the dust and stared the cavalryman down. I pocketed Dobbs' two dollars and felt a little better about the rotgut whiskey deal.

Gray only needed one win a day. I crawled up into the saddle and he stepped out into an easy walk.

Mid-afternoon, smoke rising above Bernalillo pointed out where the town lay up ahead. A sizable settlement on the Rio Grande, to the north of Corrales, Bernalillo had been the capital city of the New Mexico Territory some years back. The army supplies were meant for the small garrison there that rode patrol on the Camino Real to El Paso.

Bernalillo was as far as the governor's protection from the Sanchez brothers extended. However, the governor had written out a blank requisition, which allowed me to take whatever I needed from army supplies for my own protection and the deputy marshal job. The governor had not specified a limit on his account.

I felt like a kid with a silver dollar in a candy store as the sergeant showed me around the army warehouse. If the governor meant for me to protect myself from the Sanchez clan and fight outlaws, I aimed to meet the threats well armed and equipped.

The sergeant showed me a Colt .44 Army, 1860 model that the armories had altered to fire cartridges. The old ramrod and lever had been removed and an ejector had been added to the right side of the barrel. The new rig loaded cartridges faster than I could load my old cap and ball Navies. I took two of the new Colts and a couple hundred .44 caliber cartridges. I would need practice to get the feel of the new weapons.

The new Winchester Arms Company had a modified Henry magazine rifle they had sent out West a couple of years back. The troopers I'd come to Bernalillo with carried them now. With the Henry lever action, better than a Spencer, the Winchester loaded shells automatically into the chamber from a long, tube magazine. The magazine held fifteen, .44 caliber cartridges. It tripled the firepower of my Colt wheel rifle. I pulled a Winchester off the rack, laid it by the Colts.

I requisitioned blankets, shirts, pants, equipment, a duster, the whole kit. The governor was paying. My limit was set by what I thought Gray would carry. I figured I was evening up the score with the governor some. And if I got killed, I wouldn't appear to be too shabby.

I tossed a good pair of boots on the pile I had accumulated and told the sergeant to write it all up. Admiring my new wealth put a grin on my face, the first one since I'd come to after the fight.

While the sergeant scribbled, I inspected the first Gatling gun I'd seen. The Gatling would have changed the conduct of the war, had it been manufactured earlier. By late '63, early '64, I had figured out that the massive frontal assaults by thousands of infantry in ranks were doomed to failure. Firepower had grown too wicked. My voice to staff couldn't overcome traditional tactics. The Gatling would have changed the tradition in a single day of battle.

The war spawned invention, particularly when huge profits could be made. Lethal inventions, like brass cartridges, the Gatling, and the lever action Henry, had come into production late in the war. Had they come earlier? The killing had been efficient enough. I felt the old pang of guilt. My family had profited early in the war from the manufacture of weapons.

Sore as I was, it took three trips to haul my supplies out to Gray. I had talked another trooper into bucking Gray out this morning in exchange for the two dollars I'd won from Dobbs. I didn't like the look in Gray's eyes as I tied the extra load on him. I gambled on Gray and climbed aboard. He had won his morning bout and stepped right out with the new load. At a slow walk I headed him out of Bernalillo for Corrales.

Uneasy, I worried that the Sanchez's spies might have seen Gray led out with the army supply detachment and followed me to Bernalillo. Even though it hurt to ride, I would feel better with more distance between whoever might be following and me. If I rode the foothills above the river, I could watch my back trail for a while. If need be, I could run for the cover of the trees along the bank.

Corrales lay a mile ahead when pain, fatigue, and late afternoon overtook me. I'd ride into Corrales come morning to look for cattle buyers. I found a place with grass, in the cottonwoods by the river, and hobbled Gray. Pulling my rig off him, I let it all fall by his feet. Right there I rolled up in my army blankets and fell into deep sleep.

*   *   *

Early sunlight jabbed through my eyelids to wake me. My body felt stiff all over. The butchered side itched and ached, but the deep pain had eased up some. I lay still, letting life flow into me slowly.

Startled suddenly by the memory of where I was, I looked around for what might be threatening, listened for what might have awakened me. I did not find anything to fear around me in the woods, but in my guts I knew I had to fear waking up too slowly, groggy, in a stiff, sore body with slow reflexes. In this condition I was easy pickin's.

Guilt got on me. Counting this morning, I'd been gone so long, Red would be thinking I had run off and got married or been thrown by my horse and died of a broken neck somewhere. To his way of thinking, both were equally bad fates. There was nothing I could do about running late. I'd just have to get on with the job I'd promised.

I reached out of my blankets to pull sticks and brush together to build a fire. Gray snorted at my laziness. Usually before I bedded down, I gathered kindling and set the fire and coffeepot up for morning. Then all I had to do was strike a match come sun up and catch another nap until coffee boiled. Last night I hadn't felt up to the chore.

After four cups of coffee strength seeped back into me. I began to sense my surroundings again. A light frost melted into dew on the grass. Sparrows darted among the gold leaves of the cottonwoods. Sandia Mountain loomed up from the valley to the east. The deep-blue sky stretched off forever to the west. The crisp air smelled good with a touch of campfire scent in it. I lazed around.

I delayed breaking camp to head for Corrales because there was the "first-thing-in-the-morning bucking routine" with Gray to handle. I didn't trust the stitches in my side to hold up to much bucking, but I had to do something about Gray. He was my ticket home.

I poured another cup of coffee and sat up with my back against a tree to contemplate Gray's bucking act. Halfway to the bottom of the cup I got an idea and reached for my lariat. I rigged a line from bit to cinch that snubbed Gray's head down low. I loaded him up with saddle and gear and climbed gingerly aboard to test my idea.

Gray tried a couple of times to throw his head up to rear, but met with a nasty jerk on the bit from the snub line instead. If he couldn't get his head up and rear, he couldn't start his bucking act. Gray pranced sideways, tugging at his bit in confusion for a minute. Not being too dumb a horse, he discovered real quick that I had put his act out of business.

I don't know why I hadn't thought up the trick sooner. Probably because I had enjoyed the bucking routine before Bustos changed my ways. I left the snub on Gray as he ambled towards Corrales until I was convinced he had forgotten about his bucking routine for the day.

Corrales had long been used as a trailhead for gathering herds of cattle and sheep. The Rio Grande supplied water, and plenty of grass grew all around for holding the herds. Matter of fact, there were a couple thousand head of stock spread out right now. My prospects of finding cattle buyers appeared to be good.

A dozen, adobe buildings, flat-roofed *jacals* mostly, lined a dusty road. I caught a scent and followed my nose. I tied Gray in front of what appeared to be a saloon. A faded sign over the door still had "oon" readable on it. The smell of fried eggs seemed to be coming from this place. My stomach growled, hungry as a spring bear.

"Any eggs left?" I asked the fat Mexican woman who came from a back room to slouch on one foot behind the rough plank bar.

"Five, Señor." She held up a hand with her fingers splayed.

"Fry 'em all for me with beef, beans'n chili," I requested with a wet mouth.

I sat down at a table by the fly-specked window to survey the street, a couple of wagon wheel ruts running in front of the squat adobes. Nobody stirred outside that I could see. Turning my attention to the man sitting across the room, I asked him if he knew of any cattle buyers in town.

"There are four of us in town." He spoke with an eastern accent. "If you are interested, we are all offering fourteen dollars a head for three-year-olds or better. That is a high price, My Friend."

"I'm interested." The price was higher than the last time Red had sold cattle. It must have been a bad year for ranchers south and east of here. Or maybe they were trail driving their herds northeast to the new railheads.

"How many head do you have, Sir?" he lifted his coffee cup and gestured that he wanted to join me.

I pointed at the chair across from me and pondered his opening bid. Red's price was fourteen dollars a head. With the opening bid at fourteen I wondered if I could get more. Maybe Red would give me a bonus if I made him some extra money. With a bonus I could send my brother, John, money to help out in Virginia.

The fried eggs and the buyer arrived at my table at the same time. The eggs got my attention, and he seemed patient.

"My name is Sam Bartlet, from St. Louis." He had waited until I washed the last egg down with coffee. "You look like you have been over a rough trail. What brand do you ride for?"

"VR," I said, putting down my cup and leaning back from the table.

"I haven't seen that brand around here. Where are you holding the herd?"

I was about to give him an answer when three men pushed into the saloon and looked around. They spotted Bartlet and came across the room to hover over the table.

"We have a seller here, Gentlemen," Bartlet said to them. He asked me with a jutting chin and a sweeping hand if his friends could join us.

I began to feel like things were running a little too smoothly here. I had just arrived and I had all four buyers in town corralled at my table. I needed to find out just how lucky I was.

"Sit down, Gentlemen." I waited for them to settle then added, "Mr. Bartlet's just offered me fourteen dollars a head, sight unseen. Says that's the going price around here. How about it?"

"That's about it," the short, fat buyer with a scraggly mustache said. "It's been a pricey year, but there's plenty of stock to choose from. Take it or leave it." He looked satisfied with himself. His two companions showed no interest in the proceedings and started a side conversation while they waited for the coffeepot to be brought to the table.

I thought a moment then addressed Bartlet. "Sounds like you've got the fall market covered." I took my clasp knife from my pocket. "I have a December delivery in mind, one thousand head."

All four men perked up. Cattle buying was easy in the fall when most ranchers made their roundup. Ranchers wanted to avoid the winter kill and they flooded the markets with stock. The price was driven down by the over supply. A December delivery was another thing altogether.

Come December, buyers sought out cattle for the Mexican markets, the Indian agents supplying the reservations, and the military. By then most ranchers had sold out or had driven their cattle to range to manage on their own over the winter. A herd was hard to find in winter. A December contract was a rare thing, and a thousand head at that.

"I'll give you eighteen dollars a head for three-year-olds and over, delivered here by December tenth," Scraggly Mustache offered eagerly.

Bartlet sized me up as I whittled a toothpick off the lower edge of the wooden table. Here I sat, a wore-out-looking cowboy, smelling of sweat and campfire smoke, and needing a shave. I had no herd to inspect. For all he knew, I was just another drifter making conversation. I pocketed my knife.

I kept my eyes on Bartlet, ignoring the short, fat buyer. I bet that Bartlet had his system set up so he could move a herd south to El Paso, hold it until fresh meat became scarce in late winter. It was risky business moving cattle in winter, but from here south along the Rio Grande, snow cover was rare until January. If Bartlet had twenty days of fair weather, he would make a bundle. I put wood to the plugged gap between my teeth.

Scraggly Mustache had shown his hand. He must believe he had his risk covered. But there was something about him I didn't like. I decided not to deal with him unless I had to.

Bartlet leaned forward in his chair, elbows on the table, palms up. "I can only offer you seventeen dollars a head. I shall have to buy feed in El Paso and run the risk of bad weather between here and there."

"Done at seventeen dollars," I said, "and the cattle'll be here December first. That'll give you an edge on the weather."

Scraggly Mustache slammed the table with his fist. "That don't make no sense a'tall! You just give away a thousand dollars, Cowboy. Hell, you don't make that much in four year's wages."

I flicked the toothpick at Scraggly Mustache's boot, but otherwise paid his insult no mind as I finished up the details on the December contract with Bartlet. We shook hands on it.

My business done here, I headed out of Corrales, turned towards home finally. I felt pretty good about the cattle deal, had made three dollars a head more than Red required. Maybe there would be a bonus for me after all.

More than likely, the extra money I had just made Red might save my job at the VR. There was no way of telling for sure. A lot of things had to happen before the dollars met the cattle at Corrales.

Even with the contract in hand, the problem now was getting the herd to Corrales by December first. That would take day and night work for all hands and the cook. Beat up as I was, I didn't feel up to the work. Red said he could deliver a herd by December first. I doubted it strongly, at least about me being there to deliver.

Gray pranced light-footed, felt like he wanted a good run. I held him to a jiggle. The day was young yet. A good ride today and a long day tomorrow, I would be at the VR if my wounded side held up to the pounding.

*   *   *

The terrain stretched out ahead, mostly flat and fast, broken up some by deep erosion. Heat waves made the horizon wobble like reflections on water. I had chosen a beeline route to save time and to stay off the usual trails. I feared an ambush by a Sanchez brother.

A hawk hunted overhead, circling, riding the wind currents without flapping a wing. West in the distance, Mt. Taylor rose up sharply off a flat skyline. A man riding in this vast country had too much time to think. I started worrying over my troubles.

A herd of a thousand head of cattle had to be gathered and delivered. That many cattle might be spread over a thousand square miles. That meant a hell of a lot of riding in rough country and brush popping in scrub oaks on the mountain slopes. Every head had to be roped, thrown, and branded. The herd had to be trail-broken and driven over ninety miles through wind, rain, maybe snow. A good cowboy could get killed doing any part of the job. A beat-up cowboy was a pure liability.

Bustos' knife work on my side would make roping and branding very painful for a spell. It might take weeks to get back to my strength so I could put in a good day's work and earn my keep.

I scratched absent-mindedly at the edge of one of the slashes, which itched like I had seam squirrels. I hated the idea, but Red would probably order me to wrangle the *remuda* and help with the chuck wagon and wreck tub.

Up ahead, the outcropping of boulders, perfect for an ambush, made me leery. I approached keen-eyed. Whether the Sanchez brothers followed me or not, they had me spooked and running scared. I hadn't feared another man in years. The feeling didn't set well with me. I loosened the Winchester in the saddle boot beneath my right knee and reined Gray to pass the rocks in a wide circle.

I pondered the fear that knotted up my shoulders and neck. Maybe I felt fearful because I was wounded and weak, couldn't fight hand to hand, couldn't wear a gun belt and pistol and therefore had to shy away from trouble, or worse, hide from it. Maybe Deputy Beckett's description of the three Sanchez brothers, all tougher than Bustos, loomed too large in my imagination because I had no real knowledge of the men. Fear made me twist in the saddle to study the country I'd passed through. I hated having to watch my back trail, never knowing when trouble might strike.

I had no idea how to handle the Sanchez problem. Two miles further down the trail, I still had no ideas. Even though the breeze cooled, sweat trickled down my temple. I lifted my John B., backhanded my brow, and combed fingers through damp hair. Well, one thing I could do was keep a pistol handy.

I pulled one of the new Colts and a box of shells from a saddlebag. Then I reconsidered and put them back. I wasn't used to the new Colt and it made no sense to add variables to a shooting situation. I dug again to the bottom of the saddle-bag for my Navy Colt. My old Navy was dependable.

Gray became a little spooky, with all my thrashing around on his back. I noticed it, called a break and stepped out of the saddle. I still held my pistol because I couldn't figure out where to carry it. I couldn't put it in my waistband. Pants pockets were too shallow for the long barrel. In desperation I finally dumped the gun into the pocket of my duster.

Suddenly I started laughing at myself. Physically weak, scared, confused, and overwhelmed by troubles, I was flapping around in the breeze, sheets to the wind, out of control, off-course. No wonder Gray was spooked. I had the dithers, as my mama would say. I felt ashamed, on top of being out of control.

A long drink of water seemed to pull me together, settle me down a might. Then anger flared in my guts at the way the damn governor had blackmailed me into doing his dirty work. He had condemned me to death because hunting outlaws would lead to gunfights. Hell, I couldn't fight. I had to carry my pistol in a damn pocket.

My eyes roamed the horizons looking for my killers, or seeking help that I knew wasn't there. Then my shoulders slumped, as if under intense pressure from above. My chin hit my chest as anger turned to hopelessness. I had lost the solitary life I sought and was doomed to failure and death, the way I felt things were shaping up.

Gray snorted, pawed the ground eager to move out. I tied the canteen to the saddle and mounted up. Maybe, with some luck, I could get on home and deliver the documents to Red. At least I'd have one damn job done and some of the pressure would be off me. Slumped in the saddle, head hanging low, I dealt with the pain in my side caused by each step Gray took as he plodded northwestward.

*   *   *

Gray needed a rest. Carrying me and the extra load of gear, he had covered a lot of ground. I spotted a rise up ahead and decided to top it, rest, and look over my back trail.

From the crest I could see back four or five miles over the country I'd passed through. I dismounted and let Gray graze. Using the field glasses the governor had bought me, I searched the terrain for a quarter hour. I saw nothing disturbing, but decided I ought to get the feel of the new weapons, just in case trouble followed me.

A draw lay the other side of the rise with grass for Gray and a bank for me to shoot into. Against the bank I stacked up rocks in the form of a man's head and shoulders. Thinking about making a better target, I retrieved the governor's commission, shucked the official document out of the envelope, folded it down small, and stuffed it in my shirt pocket. I ripped the envelope open and pinned it to the bank with a couple of twigs to make another target. Then I rode Gray down the draw about a hundred yards where I dismounted. I hobbled Gray, eased the cinch, and pulled the Winchester from the saddle boot.

Squirming sorely to ease into a prone position, I let my breathing settle down, then drew a bead on the envelope and squeezed off four rounds. I liked the touch of the two-pound pull on the trigger.

I spotted my shots through the field glasses and adjusted the sight a hair to the left with my pocketknife. The next shot centered the envelope. Three more bullets pierced the envelope in a tight pattern around the center hole.

I rocked back on my knees charily, leaned on the rifle to push up and stand. Then I took a quick shoot at a rock the size of a head. The boulder exploded. The Winchester had a natural feel in my hands. I loaded it up all the way, including a round under the hammer, and slid it back in the saddle boot.

Sadness came with the thought of retiring my old Colt rifle to the gun rack in the bunkhouse. She had been the winning argument in some bad situations a time or two. The new Winchester was the superior weapon by far. Made me think, the old Colt rifle and I had become obsolete as warriors, both with limited capacity now.

My butchered side ached from the kick of the Winchester. The dull roar filled my ears again. Rather than cinch up and climb into the saddle, I walked to ease my stiffness and led Gray to about fifty feet from the targets. I pulled the new Colts and then opened another box of .44's from the saddlebag.

The Colts balanced in my hands. I had become an expert shot with either hand before the war, but, for lack of need, had become rusty with my left hand. I noted some awkwardness and resolved to work out the kinks. Some warrior I was!

Sheriff Moore came to mind, and how fast he had drawn his gun back in the jailhouse. He wore his gun low on his hip. I wore mine, military style, on the belt, waist high. The front of Moore's holster was cut down maybe an inch-and-a-half. The muzzle could clear leather faster. I would cut a new rig first chance I had, and practice that fast draw as Moore had called it. Now, all I had was a pocket to hold my pistol.

I squeezed off a shot to feel the pull on the trigger. It felt heavier than what I was used to. I had filed my Navies down to fire with a half-pound pressure on the trigger. That way I did not have to make allowance in my aim for a hard squeeze of the fist. All I had to do was point and let her buck back into the cradle of my hand.

I fired another shot and noticed the Colt was fast between trigger and fire. The cap and ball system seemed, in comparison, to smolder a bit between trigger and fire. I would have to master the change in the timing for a snap shot.

Seemed like the hammer sat up a little higher than on the Navy model. It was easy to hook a thumb over, but slightly out of position for my old habit. Loading the Colt was a breeze.

I lost interest in shooting all of a sudden. Fatigue took me over like a cloud shutting off the heat of sunlight. I felt weak in the guts, stringy-muscled, and had a long way to go yet to get to the VR. Seemed like my time would be better spent in the saddle. I put the new Colts away and left my Navy stuffed in the duster pocket.

Gray pranced, ready to go, when I cinched him up and climbed aboard. I glanced at the targets on the bank as I turned Gray to the trail. I appreciated the quality of my new weapons, but felt bad, too. Guns were for killing. The smell of gun smoke had brought back the memory of dying men, the screams of wounded horses.

Like it or not, I was back in the killing business. Damn governor! Maybe I'd just send the commission back to him. I shook my head and snorted in disgust.

I topped the rise again and watched my back trail with the field glasses. Be damned if I didn't catch a movement, then spot a rider about a mile back and heading my way. I couldn't tell at this distance if he wore a Mexican sombrero.

Could be a stranger, aimed to ride a straight-line route northwest, like me. My guts told me otherwise. I figured I better find out. I lopped Gray off the rise, headed south, away from my route to the VR and started covering my trail where I could.

Hiding my trail would cost me more time, but I had to know if the stranger meant to ride on by, or turn to hunt me.

CHAPTER FOUR

I woke up feeling mean. Night had another hour to go before it gave way to light. Darkness intensified the cold, gave me the deep shivers. I couldn't build a fire to cut the chill or boil coffee for fear of being shot. Hell, I didn't have water to boil anyway.

I ached all over, more than anywhere else, from lack of sleep and yesterday's hard ride. All day I'd kept Gray hugging hills, scrambling in rocks, and crawling the bottoms of arroyos to try and shake the hunter off my trail.

"Don't buck with me, Gray." I held the tall stallion by the bit and tied the snub line. "I'll shoot you before your hooves hit the ground. Swear to God!" I mumbled the threat with a thick tongue in a parched mouth over cracked lips.

Hell, I knew I wouldn't shoot my horse. The walk home was too long. But I felt angry and Gray was the closest dog around to kick. Besides, I wanted Gray to believe I would kill him if he bucked. I wasn't sure he hadn't figured a way around the snub line trick so he could run his bucking act. I stepped up with some trepidation, then clamped my legs around him like a bulldog's jaws around a bone.

The threat must have convinced the stallion. He stepped right out into his easy walk. I yanked the slipknot on the snub line at the cinch and let him have his head.

In the dark I let Gray pick his way through the low sage and clump grass, then I heeled him down the crumbled side of an arroyo. When we hit the bottom of the deep ravine I booted him into his smooth run and galloped northwest up the arroyo headed in the general direction of the ranch.

The pounding of the gallop hurt my side something awful, not like the ripping pain of the wolf, more like rats gnawing at my flesh. Pounding leather was no way to heal a wound, but running was better than dying from a bullet in the back.

Stronger than the pain in my side or the hunger in my belly, I felt rage burning in my guts. The killer stalking me played with me like a bobcat with a claw-hooked bunny. He could have killed me yesterday night. After I'd spotted him I tried to hide. I thought I had shaken him off my trace. But late in the night he snuck up where I slept, drained my water on the ground and left eight spent .44 cartridges by my head.

The son of a bitch could have slit my throat, pissed on my body and been done with his revenge. Instead, he'd scared the piss out of me. I'd run all day yesterday, spent a near sleepless night in the rocks. And I ran from him now and choked on my anger.

The safety of the ranch lay another hard day's ride northwest of here. I doubted that Gray could make the run without water soon. I had doubts about making it myself, but I wasn't doing the work Gray did. He was a stayer at a quick pace and I bet he could run faster than most horses when he had a mind to. He felt like he had settled into his work, but I feared he would wind down sooner, rather than later.

I reckoned my hunter would take his shot at me in the light of day. That way, he could enjoy his toying with me. I meant to get some distance between us in the dark. His water trick had me softened up for the kill and he knew it. He might trail along behind, letting me wear out my thirsty mount trying to hide my trail like yesterday. I aimed to run straight for home, no hiding this day.

First light began to fade the stars in the east. Fear tied a tight knot between my shoulder blades. Cold air bit at me. In the dim light I saw frost crystals glint on the rocks and deadwood in the dry, stream bed of the arroyo. I wanted to lick up that moisture. My tongue grated over chapped lips with no spit to moisten them.

Gray seemed to be holding up okay. But he had failed me the other night. I'd found a hidden place where I could sleep well protected. I had camped without a fire and had picketed Gray near me where he could act as sentry. I figured, like any mountain horse, he ought to know how to stomp and snort to wake me if danger came around. Danger slipped in and out of my nest. Gray and I both slept through it. I could have been killed. I still felt like shooting Gray.

Gray stumbled. I eased up on him. Chances were good I had put some distance between the hunter and me. "Don't let me down, Gray."

The sky, a turquoise strip above the high banks of the arroyo, warned that the sun would rise soon into a hot, cloudless day. Riding up this deep gulch gave me a trapped feeling, but I knew I'd be hard to see in the deep shadows. The man hunting me had little chance for a long shot.

"If it hadn't been for Red, I wouldn't be in this fix," I heard myself mumble at Gray. I winced as the words split a crack in my lip. What blood I had left after spilling most of it on Maria's cantina floor was drying out. Delusions rambled in my brain. A night, a day, and another night without water took their toll.

I shook my head to clear it. "If it hadn't been for Patricio..."

It had to be Patricio Sanchez hunting me. Nobody else I could think of was so cruel or so driven by hate as to risk sneaking into a man's camp and draining his canteens while he slept. It was suicide to try a fool stunt like that. Deputy Beckett had called Patricio a cruel man.

Or maybe the hunter, not so foolish, knew his prey was wounded, beat from the day's running and passed-out for the night. Patricio knew the nature of the wounds Bustos had cut into me.

Fool or not, whoever hunted me knew his tracking, all right, because I had taken care not to be found. He had done it and shamed me by walking into my camp, and taunted me by draining my water out on the ground.

Gray stumbled again. I jerked his head up to keep him from going down on his knees. Afoot, I'd be a dead man even if I wasn't shot. If I didn't shake the hunter off my trail, I'd run Gray into the ground trying to get away.

Shake him off my trail be damned! Wounded, tired, and sore, dying of thirst, no water, a worn-out horse and a son-of-a-bitch hunting to kill me? I had enough. "I'll kill him!" I choked at Gray.

I shucked the Winchester from the boot, dismounted, and ground-hitched the stallion. The arroyo I rode in had just turned off to the north. The hunter would be coming from the east. Gray would be hidden from sight. This bend in the ditch would have to do for my fort.

Boots slipping in the crumbling earth, I struggled up the bank of the arroyo, tried not to kick up a dust cloud. At the top I shifted a little to my right, stuck my head up over the bank behind a low sage bush. The early morning sun squinted my eyes. Using the sage for cover, I hid and studied my back trail through bloodshot, sand-gritted eyes. Nothing moved that I could see. The slanting sunlight glanced fiercely off rocks and sand, or cut deep shadows I could not see into. I was afraid to use the field glasses because of the angle of the sun, the possible reflections off the lenses. I let my eyes adjust and start to note details in the features of the terrain.

The arroyo cut through the bottom of a small valley. I could see about three hundred yards to the east, to the rim of the valley where the arroyo cut the skyline and dropped to another plateau. Most likely, I would see a bobbing head rise above that skyline as a rider approached. But the low sunlight might make that detail hard to see.

A few *piñon* trees dotted the terrain, but nothing else offered a hiding place for a man on horseback. Sage and *chamisa* grew waist high to a man, but unless my hunter crawled to Indian-up on me, the brush offered no cover. I was satisfied that I had an open field of fire. I hunkered down to watch, wait.

My head jerked around to look at Gray when I realized my hunter might be in the arroyo. It made sense that he would track me there in the dim light. I didn't like the thought of having to watch my flank, too. If my hunter came around the bend in the arroyo, it would be a close range shoot-out, with Gray standing exposed in the middle.

Fear tightened the knot between my shoulder blades and popped sweat into my palms. It would be awkward if I had to wheel to the right for a snap shot. I wiped my palms on my pants and bet that my hunter would stay out of the arroyo. Riding on top would be easier for him and he knew where I headed.

The low sun dimmed my eyesight, pounded a headache into the back of my skull. But my searching paid off. A small, black ball bobbed along the skyline and then stopped moving. I wiped my palms again, rubbed my eyes, slid the Winchester into position.

The black ball moved toward me, became a sombrero shape, stopped. Sure enough, my tormentor came along where I had expected him. Cautious, he paused in no hurry to expose himself to my little valley. Then he hunted warily as he rode the high ground beside the arroyo.

Gray snorted, pawed the ground, and pointed out to me that I wasn't thinking like a warrior yet. Not thinking ahead of the situation would get me killed! I eased down the arroyo bank and cussed myself for not doing earlier what needed doing now. I used my bandanna to tie Gray's nose and mouth so he couldn't whinny. Sooner or later he would scent the other horse. I didn't need him warning my hunter to my hidden position

Afraid of kicking up a telltale dust cloud, I crawled slowly back up the bank. When I poked my eyes over the lip to search, the hunter had disappeared.

Damn my lack of planning! I searched for the hunter and wondered what else I'd forgotten that could get me killed. Scared by my own unforeseen failures, I licked at my lips then gave up the futile effort to wet them. I couldn't distinguish the difference between dry teeth, gums or lips with my swollen tongue. I had no spit.

Sparrows popped out of a *piñon* tree, flitted away. I locked my eyes on that tree. The dark form of a horse and rider took shape through the tangled branches. My hunter had entered the little valley, had stopped to hide and hunt before he crossed it.

Easing the Winchester over the lip of the arroyo and into the shadow of the scrubby sage, I aimed at the side where I bet the hunter would emerge from behind the *piñon* tree. Three hundred yards was a hell of a long shot to make with any accuracy. I decided to let him advance.

Conscience prodded me suddenly with a sharp pain behind my eyes. I was no coward, yet here I lay waiting to bushwhack a man.

My way was to stand up to my enemies, seek Glory head on. Hand to hand, gun to gun, or the full, frontal charge were my tactics for fighting. But right now, I could not win facing another man with a gun. He'd kill me while I tried to yank my pistol out of my damn pocket.

Beat up, dying of thirst, nursing a used-up horse I had no choice but to ambush this enemy. Even with these excuses I felt low and cowardly. I cocked the hammer on the Winchester.

The shot I intended would draw first blood for this new rifle. It would be fired in shame. I hated the idea of it, but I told myself I loved living more and had to get on with this dirty work. The very words rang with cowardliness.

Sunlight glinted off the silver adorning the saddle of the man who had stolen my water and hunted me now. He rode a fine, black Arabian stallion and watched the arroyo carefully. His sombrero crowned the back of his head, shielded his neck from the sun behind him, cast his face in shadow. His broad shoulders reminded me of Bustos and this man wore the same black *caballero* outfit. The apparition startled me. Bustos was dead or so I had been told.

A few more steps and the hunter would be in range of an easy shot. Still, he was a stranger. How could I be sure he was a Sanchez brother? He might just be their spy. Unsure of what I intended, not wanting to kill another man, feeling like a coward, I hesitated, even though my guts told me that I looked at a rattlesnake that needed killing. Nobody would still be on my trail after all the circling around I had done, not unless he meant to kill me.

Besides, this hombre had declared himself with that cruel water trick. He rode for revenge, and sport. I had to end his deadly game here. I shifted my position to embrace the Winchester, heard my conscience say this is a dastardly way to end any man's life. Adjusting my aim for the glint of sunlight on the front sight, I squeezed down on the trigger.

Last instant, I shifted my sight from the rider's chest to his horse's heart.

The Winchester barked. The black stallion stumbled, then bucked. The *caballero* flew out of the saddle, landed on his face in the dust.

The horse kept bucking. The man didn't move.

I must have missed my shot with the new rifle and bushwhacked the man anyway.

Then the horse stumbled, fell to his belly and rolled on his side.

My legs twitched. I wanted distance between the man in the dust and me. If the man wasn't dead, he could jump up and try a rifle shot at me.

Then I saw the canteen tied to the saddle on the dead horse. I needed that water. But my hunter might not be dead. I could not handle a close-up fight to get the water. Temptation became irresistible. Bound up in frustration, burning for revenge I squeezed off another shot and exploded the canteen.

At least I knew the Winchester shot where I wanted it to, and I hadn't bushwhacked a man. If he was dead from a broken neck, that was a different matter.

Sliding down the arroyo bank to Gray, I ungagged him, swung into the saddle, and lit out up the arroyo. I stayed under cover for about a thousand yards before I topped out of the wash. I pulled the field glasses and looked back. The black Arabian stallion lay dead. The hombre had disappeared. I debated staying there to spot him. Better sense told me to get the hell out at a run. Maybe cowards thought that way to get them out of harms way.

I worried as I fled. It must have been Patricio Sanchez's horse I shot. All the evidence stacked up that way. If so, I would have to deal with Patricio another day. I had bought some time was all. But I hadn't become a bushwhacker. My personal honor was intact and that felt important to me. Yet I was running without a bark and with my tail between my legs.

The man I had unhorsed probably would not die for lack of water, but he would get almighty dry before his first drink. Thinking on it sort of eased up my own thirst.

Something Sheriff Moore had told me worried at the back of my mind. Then I remembered. The sheriff had said Bustos' twin brother, Patricio, aimed to kill me.

Relief flowed into me on a deep breath. I hadn't set some stranger afoot. I had brought Patricio to ground. I felt sure of it now.

Most likely Patricio would try to carry that silver-inlaid saddle out with him. Imagining that proud *caballero* walking in some place with a saddle on his back made me smile. My dry lips cracked, bled. For a minute I didn't mind.

*   *   *

Cool air moved across the land on a gentle breeze. Hot sun burned through it. My brain felt like an over-smoked ham, juiceless, salty. I couldn't keep a string of thoughts running in a straight line anymore. My guts knew I had to find water. Fast.

Gray plodded along slowly, head hanging down. He suffered. I thought about walking to ease his load. Then I thought about singing. I was too dry to do either. Something about singing warned me I was losing my mind. Even though I knew, it didn't seem to matter.

I slipped under the surface of the cool water, choked, fought drowning to get back to the surface for air. Next to me my ship, the *Croft*, burned, stern straight up, as she sunk slowly. Federal longboats prowled the water around me. Sailors shot the survivors they spotted in the water. I wished for the day I was twenty-one and my father had given me the *Croft* to command, not this day that ended my proud career as a blockade-runner.

Gray stumbled, stopped. I could feel his withers shiver with fatigue. I slumped out of the saddle and stood by him. I shook my head to shake out the delusion. My father was dead, shot in the Battle of the Wilderness north of our home, north of Richmond. I bet he died fearlessly, shooting all around him, even though he was sixty-five years old then.

The sun was frying my brain. This arid land that I loved meant to kill me, too, by hiding its water. I looked for what I needed and saw it up ahead. I pulled on the reins and started walking with Gray toward a hunch.

General Lee said, "We can no longer fight, Gentlemen. I shall surrender."

I felt like crying. All those men I'd ordered to their death. All good men, wasted! "We can... We must!" I muttered. Gray yanked at the rein at the sound of my voice.

"Easy, Gray. Over there, Boy."

I wombled down the side of the arroyo and turned towards the bank where the brush had piled up. I hobbled Gray and pulled my gear off him. I took my long knife from the saddlebag and stumbled over to the brush pile.

Picking up a long stick, I beat the brush to scare off rattlers then used the stick to dig. With knife, stick, and hands I dug a hole down about two feet before I hit damp sand. Sweating more water than I would probably get out of that hole, I dug another foot deeper. Exhausted I fell away and rested with my back against the bank of the arroyo.

Squinting at the sun, I guessed there were about three more hours of light left in the day.

By the time water seeped into my well it would be dusk. I thought about making a camp, but couldn't move. I stretched out my legs and passed out.

I dreamed of crossing the sea to England, learning to sail, attending the university, returning home to Virginia, racing horses, dancing with beautiful girls dressed-up for the ball. I stood at my father's shoulder as he gambled and won the *Croft*. I wept when I returned to the home place and saw it burned to the ground.

A chilled breeze woke me. The red sun scorched the edge of the horizon but failed to warm me. Gray pawed at the sand pile next to the well. I rolled over to look into it. Six inches of clear water, maybe three quarts, glistened in the bottom.

I scooped some in my hand and tasted it. Sweet water!

Gray snorted, pushed at my shoulder with his nose. I scooped water to him in my cupped hands. I drank a little more, then served him because he couldn't get his head down the hole.

I felt the water change my body, sort of thin out the screaming redness that burned behind my eyes, quench the heat in my guts, soften the starch that stiffened my muscles.

I dug my cup out of my gear and untied my canteen and slicker from my saddle. At the well I hollowed out a depression in the sand and lined it with the slicker. Carefully, I cupped all the water out of the well into the slicker for Gray and a little left over for me in the canteen.

There wasn't enough water to cure us of the thirst, but we were not going to die either. I sat back and slowly sipped another half cup as I watched the daylight fade away. This was the best tasting branch I had ever drunk, bar none.

After a bit, when I felt stronger, I kindled a fire to boil coffee. I reckoned that Gray and I could get to the ranch late tonight. With the water we'd had and a bit more seep in the well, we could make it to the Rio Puerco. From there we could make it on home. But first, Gray and I had to let the water do its healing work on us.

I poured my one cup of coffee and propped my back against the sand hill dug from the well. The evening had turned cold when the sun went out. My small fire took the edge off the crisp air. A nighthawk swooped overhead catching something that fluttered in the firelight. The coffee smelled good, tasted better.

I listened to the night sounds for a while to get the feeling of the place. Gray champed grass a little ways off. A cricket, seeking companionship, was the loudest singer. Then hunger rumbled in my stomach. I considered the jerky and corn meal in my saddlebag, and then decided against them. Too dry to chew. No extra water to boil.

Instead, I hauled my pipe and tobacco pouch out of my possibles bag. Sitting free, someplace out under the broad, starry sky, by a campfire, watching the coals glow, and enjoying a pipe suited me fine for now. I'd done it a hundred times before. I had survived this day and I had no desires for much more than this bit of comfort.

I was a cowboy plain and simple, I reflected as I stuffed my pipe. I wanted it like that, meant to keep it like this with no risks, no responsibilities, no way to lose it all again because there was nothing to lose. Yet, even though I sat here under the stars by a campfire, looking like a carefree cowboy, I felt all torn up inside. Appearances be damned, nothing else was right with me.

Staring into the coals, I was confused as to why I had hallucinated and dreamed of the past today. I hadn't thought of my father, Virginia, or the *Croft* for a long time. When I had arrived home after Appomattox, I found our properties destroyed. Brother John decided he would stay in Virginia and try to rebuild the shattered estates.

Broken, I just packed up, abandoned Virginia and headed to St. Louis. I caught the first wagon train traveling to Santa Fe and hired on as a drover. From then on I had worked hard to forget all my past. Then the damn governor had hurled my past identity in my face, used it against me to strong-arm me into working for him.

I hated the governor for the troubles he put on me. Hating him was okay. What confused me was my strong desire to abandon the job I'd been given. I did not believe I was a man to run from troubles. Yet, I wanted to. And I had been running from a man for the last two days, still felt like I had to run from the Sanchez trouble.

I shifted position by my fire to escape the confusion and melancholy that wanted to settle over me. The war had broken me, left me unable to challenge and contend by stripping away my identity and crushing my courage. I cursed the war as I tamped the pipe, burned my fingertip. Maybe it was just my knife wounds and weakness from thirst that had me feeling lost this way.

My mind drifted away from the dreams back to a memory of the months I had spent wandering the country around Santa Fe before I found steady work at the VR. I had taken to the VR right off. I liked Red. Over time he had turned me into a fair cowhand. But when I was asked to shoulder responsibility for other people, I always shied away. I just wanted to do my work and be free of everything else. I needed to be let alone.

Why? I did not believe I was a man to shirk responsibility, but that was what I did most of the time when I saw trouble coming.

Suddenly I snapped out of my reverie. My pipe fell to my chest and I slapped at live sparks burning pinholes in my shirt front. Responsibilities rained down on my head like hail stones. I had enough water back in me to set me straight, get my mind working again. I was no free cowboy, lounging around by a fire under a starry sky. I had documents to deliver to Red, a herd to gather and deliver to Bartlet, the governor's damn job, a carved side to heal, and Patricio would be hunting me.

So here I sat in the bottom of a wash with a tired-out horse and some personal gear. I hadn't achieved very much since the war, and I hadn't wanted to. All of a sudden I felt like I was under orders again, under the command of other men. I didn't like the feeling. Yet another part of me believed I had to finish what I had taken on.

To shake off the bad feelings and confusion, I walked out into the dark to take a piss and check on Gray. I looked up at my old friends, the stars. Mars and Aldibaron, two, fiery, red bodies in the sky, appeared over the bowl of my pipe. Mars, the warrior planet. Aldibaron, the red eye of the constellation, Taurus. The old bull of the sky had two red eyes, an unusual conjunction.

Orion would rise to rest on the horizon before long. I knew a hundred stars by name and could navigate by them. I had loved the sea, wished I were there now, instead of the mess I was in. Then I remembered the hell Captain Butler had put me through for two years as he forged me into a ship's Captain. I had survived, become strong.

I had captained the *Croft* at a profit for the family for the next six years. I could handle any crew, any port, and any sea. Those were glorious times as a young captain. What the hell had happened to change me to hate responsibility so? Where was my courage? Who had I become since I was Captain Eli Waller?

Come to think of it, the *Croft* probably still lay on the bottom where she'd sunk. She had carried a fortune in gold, meant for the Confederacy. Allowing for the currents in Chesapeake Bay, I thought I could find her. First chance, I would have to write Brother John and start a salvage operation. If we could get the gold off the bottom of the bay, we could rebuild the family fortune.

Suddenly stirred up I walked hurriedly toward my campfire. The salvage idea warranted more thought. Halfway to the fire, I realized I did not want to get involved in a salvage operation in Virginia. Enemies more powerful than I had driven me away and I had turned my back on that life and run.

I spun in my tracks to go catch Gray. The governor and his gold problem bore down on me. I had been delaying giving that situation any thought by rooting around in my memories.

There wasn't much to think on, just a few facts. Gold from the rich mines around Durango was being shipped south this time of year. Bandits killed men to get the gold. There had been a holdup somewhere north of San Ysidro and that was all the information I had. But it rankled me that I had become a spy again, undercover with nobody to help me out of a tight spot. All I had was a tin Marshal's badge. It wouldn't stop a bullet.

Four coyotes started a chorus off to the west, made me think of the wolf in my nightmare. I shuddered, felt the cold of dying on the battlefield. I thought of my fight with Bustos. It had been like other encounters with death, only before I had been a much better warrior. Now I was weak and no warrior at all.

The image of Patricio loomed in my mind. I had seen his face as he pitched over his horse's head. He looked like the wolf in my dreams, come to life to haunt me. He would continue to hunt me. I was sure of it. Next time he would be more careful, and more dangerous. I should have shot him when I had the chance. I wasn't even good at being a bushwhacking coward.

I did not believe I was a bushwhacker. I had nearly done it. Wished I had. Disgusted with myself, I knocked the dottle out of my pipe, and stuffed the pipe into my pocket. I didn't notice I was standing, stark still, in the cold breeze.

I wondered what Red was thinking long about now. A practical man, he would not send anybody out to find me. A search would be like looking for a twig in a flooding river. He couldn't afford to waste the time of another cowboy looking for me. Red would wait a couple more days and then send someone better to get the job done.

Most likely Red would forget about me until some word of my death filtered in off the rumor circuit. I wondered if he would be surprised when I wandered in alive. Probably not, knowing him. He would send me right back out to gather cattle.

I did not believe I was a nobody. Yet from a foreman's point of view, I was just another cow-hand to be paid low wages and used up on the job.

Maybe it was fatigue, or wounds, thirst, water, fear, rebelliousness or something else, but I felt worthless and on the edge of losing control again.

Fighting the overwhelmed feeling, I realized that what I needed to do was throw a rope on all the thoughts and feelings tearing me apart, snub them down one at a time, line them up and deal with them in a sensible way. Right now I felt like I had a head full of hummingbirds, and a gut full of snakes. I wasn't even a good cowboy! Hell, this worthless piece of shit was going to freeze to death in the breeze if he didn't catch up his horse and move out.

I scooped new water out of the well and split it with Gray. Then I saddled him. Kicking the sand I'd dug out of the well over the fire to kill it, I buried the life in this camp. But I carried my confusions, worthlessness and troubles out with me.

I awoke after a nap in the saddle to a flat, gray sky, low clouds moving fast from the south-west. The wind smelled wet. I did not like the prospects of riding at night in a cold rain.

I pulled Gray to a halt, dismounted and untied my slicker from behind the saddle. I went around in front of Gray so he could see what I was doing. The slicker always flapped in the wind and I didn't want a spooked horse on my hands. A spatter of rain began to fall and wet my saddle.

"Where t'hell's the rain when we needed it, Gray?" I pulled my hat down low, climbed back in the saddle and hunched into a cold, wet ride towards the VR.

*　　　*　　　*

Sometime after midnight, I watered Gray, turned him loose in the corral to roll and eat hay I forked for him. He had done his share on this trip. I would pick him again for a long ride, maybe add him to my string of working mounts.

It had stopped raining a few miles back and then turned colder. I turned up my collar as I walked to the bunkhouse where I dumped the rest of my gear.

Yellow lantern light glowed through the kitchen window of the big house. I wandered over to look for hot coffee. I found fresh-baked bread and apricot jam in the cupboard and sat down with them and the coffeepot.

Red wandered in looking like he'd just pulled his head off a pillow. "Thought I heard somebody ride up. You find a señorita, get married or somethin'?" Red scratched irritably at three-day-old stubble. "What kept you?"

Without answering, I pitched him the package from the land office along with the mail. Then with my healing tongue I caught a drip of jam just before it leapt from the side of the thick slab of bread.

"Well you're slow as hell, Waller, but dependable." Red casually tucked under his arm the items I'd almost lost my life to bring him. He said over his shoulder as he walked out the door, "You look tuckered out. We'll talk about the roundup an' drive first thing in the mornin'."

Looking into the bottom of the Mexican clay mug, I grunted, irritated. There had been a whole lot more to the job Red had given me last time I held this mug than he had let on. And it wasn't over yet!

CHAPTER FIVE

If I meant to live through my troubles, I needed to carry a pistol, and not in my damn pocket. Working a cattle roundup, a horse could spook and throw me. If my boot caught in a stir- rup, the only way to get out of being kicked or dragged to death was to shoot the horse, fast. More than that, I had in mind protecting myself from two- legged rattlesnakes, like vengeful broth- ers or gold bandits.

I searched around the tack room for the tanned leather I had seen here a while back. I wanted to make a holster rig for my new Colt. I had invented a way I could build a metal strip under the bullet belt, curved to lift the belt off my hip wound. I also wanted to build in the improve- ments I had seen in Sheriff Moore's holster.

Shadows flickered over my work as Red Charney darkened the doorway and cornered me in the tack room. "I come away last night thinkin' I didn't have the whole story," Red led off. "How're you feelin' this mornin', Waller?" Red looked me over carefully like he appraised a horse for sale.

"Passable." I had found the hide I looked for. "A man named Bartlet bought your cattle for seventeen dollars a head."

"Deliver December first?"

"Yes, Sir. I saw a lot of cattle sign up in the Nacimiento Meadows on my way over. Prob- ably a pretty good catch up there." I pulled my new Colt out of my pocket and laid it on the leather. Then I traced its shape with an awl.

"Take Stephens an' work the meadows. I'll tell 'em." Red turned to leave.

"Red?" I hesitated, unsure. "I got a lot goin' on all of a sudden."

I needed a place to work out of, and I needed people I could trust. I had known Red for two years and knew him to be honest. I thought about telling him about the job for the governor, then decided not to pull him into my troubles. Still, he was my boss and I needed to ask for some slack to work the governor's job while I continued to work for the VR.

"Let me take Pete Montoya and search for cattle up to the northwest of here. I think we can bring in a hundred, maybe two hundred head in a couple weeks."

Red turned around smartly. His neck flared red when he was angry. I had questioned his orders and his neck was flushed.

"I have some personal business to attend up in Durango. I'll take a couple of days out and slip up that way while we're workin'." It seemed to me that Durango was a likely place to start investigating the gold robbery.

"Your business is roundin' up my cattle, Cowboy! Where an' when I say." Red had his hands on his hips and his chin jutted out.

"Well, Red, there's another problem. I had a little fracas over in Santa Fe. There's an hombre huntin' me. He knows I ride for the VR. I'd like to work out and away from here. Let that gent cool off some."

Red's eyes narrowed, then he laughed. "I bet there's a damn señorita involved. I knew it." He didn't wait for an answer, dropped his fists off his hips. "Montoya's over La Jara workin'. Two weeks? You best be on your way." Red turned for the door again. "That the reason for the new-fangled Colt?" he said over his shoulder.

"Yeah. Thanks, Red."

Red left without mentioning the high price I had negotiated for him in the cattle contract. On the other hand, he hadn't fired me either. I felt relieved that he hadn't caught on yet to my being cut up and weak.

I shaped and laced the leather to make the holster, then bent the iron strip to fit under the bullet belt. When the whole rig was crafted, I buckled it on. The metal band worked to keep my wound from being rubbed raw. The holster itself hung below my right hip, putting the butt of the Colt almost at arm's length. I remembered to cut the front of the holster out about an inch-and-a-half.

The rig looked home-built but boxed the gun where I wanted it if I used a thong to tie it to my leg. I holstered the Colt and tried a couple of fast draws in the tack room where I would not be seen. The results surprised me.

*   *   *

Around noon I found Pete Montoya's camp at La Jara. Pete rode in soon after, driving twenty head of unbranded mixed stock. I helped him herd them into the temporary corral. It felt mighty fine to be back in the cattle business again.

The VR had a policy of letting the local people and reps from the other cattle operations look over what we corralled and cut out any stock they could identify as theirs. It worked well enough to keep peace in the region.

The VR claimed rights to everything within the territory bounded by a hard day's ride in any direction from the headquarters, except west. The west boundary lay out two days' ride. There were few people in the region to object. Most of them were bean farmers, like at Cuba and La Jara, who owned a few head of cattle.

Two, fair-sized cattle operations lay to the south, one north. They were no competition, and disputes were rare. I could see the time when this arrangement would change as more people settled the territory.

I built a fire, put noon coffee on, then got after digging a rock out of the frog of my horse's hoof. Over on the other side of the corral, Pete occupied himself mending his saddle while the cattle settled down.

Pete, a first class brush popper, had worked cattle for the VR for six years now. His family had farmed land in the Rio Los Piños Valley, just north of Cuba, for three generations. His tongue grew up on Spanish, but he spoke decent English. I considered Pete as close a friend as I had these days.

We had stood shoulder to shoulder in a couple of fights at family wedding dances in Cuba. Mescal flowed generously and things got to jumping at those shindigs, but the local hombres didn't fancy Anglos much. Something would trigger a fight, and the punching usually came around to me. Pete said he sided with me just to even up the odds, and because we both rode for the VR. His stand with me had cost him some old friends, and a couple of side teeth.

"Don't be drinkin' much of that coffee," I ordered in a way that made Pete pause mid-stride and frown. We were not in the habit of giving each other orders. "You'll ruin your appetite for this, *Compadre*." I offered the Rivas beer Gray had carried from Santa Fe. "Sorry it's not on ice," I grinned.

Pete moved faster than usual for him when he saw the Rivas bottle. "Amigo, this, for me?" He held the Rivas out at arms length, cocked his head and admired it. I could see his tongue sucking behind his pursed lips. Then we shook hands in greeting. "You did not drink this? *Qué milagro!*"

"It took goin' through hell to bring it," I said pouring myself a cup of coffee. "You're right, *Cuate*. It's the best beer I ever had. Figured you ought to have one." I stood back and watched his pleasure at the first gulp.

"I confess it," Pete gasped. "This brings me much pleasure." After two more gulps Pete asked, "What you doing over here anyway?" Pete sized me up. "What makes you walk so stiff, Amigo?"

"You know Bustos and Patricio Sanchez over at Santa Fe?" I squinted at him to gauge his reaction to the names.

"*Sí!*" Pete said earnestly. His body seemed to stiffen, stand taller as if at attention. "They are the sons of El Don Manúel Sanchez. He have the biggest hacienda in all of the territory." Then pensively he added, "He have the most beautiful daughter in all the territory. Dora Luz is a woman a man could easily die for. But she is my cousin." Pete paused to think, smiled. "Maybe not so close a cousin. You know this family?"

So her name was Dora Luz. She had been on my mind some, I would admit. Sore as I was from her brother's butchery, I still wanted to dance with her. I saw her eyes, her smile, and smelled her perfume. Now I had a name for the enchanting, troublesome woman. In just a few seconds, Dora Luz Sanchez had turned my head more than any other woman I had met. She had also caused me more pain than any other woman. That strange feeling stole over me again thinking about her.

"Pete, I killed your cousin, Bustos, in a knife fight. He interrupted me while I's havin' my first Rivas." I watched Pete closely, unsure of his loyalty here.

Pete finished his beer, used the back of his hand to dry and adjust his broad, black mustache. "That would be reason enough to kill him, Amigo." Pete paused and smiled the way some Mexicans do when they contemplate death. "You are a dead man, Amigo. That is why you mention Patricio and walk so stiffly?"

"Patricio's huntin' me for revenge." I put the frying pan over the coals. "Does he look just like Bustos?"

"*Sí.*" Pete grabbed my arm to keep me from reaching the food sack. "I will cook, Amigo." He let go of my arm, added, "As usual, *qué no?*"

"I haven't met him formal-like yet." I felt the relief that I had felt when I'd realized I had not stranded a stranger. "I shot his horse out from under him to keep him from followin' me home." I hitched up my gun belt.

"To kill a man's brother and his horse..." Pete trailed off into thought. "You will lose much sleep from now on. Patricio will not rest until he kill you." He threw a slab of bacon into the pan to hiss and fry. "I know him. He is ver' cruel, killed many men. If you have not met him, why do you walk so stiffly?"

"Bustos was faster'n me with a knife." I shrugged and changed the subject. "Red wants us to range up northwest and pull in strays. We'll head out when you're ready." I poured another coffee and waited for the bacon to brown.

Pete and his crew had already worked this side of the Continental Divide. They had gathered a hundred and fifty head, penned and ready, to drive to the Cuba valley where Red assembled the herd. The boys would head this bunch out tomorrow towards Cuba.

I roped extra horses out of the *remuda* for Pete and me. Rousting cattle out of the brush used up a couple of mounts a day. Considering it for a moment, I caught the pinto shavetail we used as a packhorse anyway.

Herding the mare with the stallions and geldings would bring trouble. But the VR's *remuda* had not grown large enough yet to afford a *caponera* for working cattle. We had to use all the horses we had for roundup, including the breeder stock. The crew would take their strings and the rest of the *remuda* back with the cattle herd.

On one side of the Continental Divide, surface water flowed to the Rio Grande or dried up trying. On the other side, water flowed west to the San Juan River or sunk out of sight in the arid sands. The cattle on the west side of the divide naturally drifted west, away from the ranch following water and grass. We would have to cover a lot of territory to find them.

Pete and I decided we would ride straight to Canyon Lagro and scout it for cattle. There, year-round water usually flowed. Then we would search Tapicito Canyon up to the Apache Reservation. After that we would turn due west and cover the area over to Huerfano Peak. From there we'd ride on up to the San Juan River and start to drive home what we had found.

*   *   *

Late afternoon of the fourth day we spent finishing up a holding pen just east of the San Juan River. Using an ax to cut brush for fences put some strain on my left side. The muscles would be sore from the work, but the skin had held together.

As evening came on, the air chilled off, promised a cold night. I built a fire. That was my job. Pete decided after one of my meals that he would manage all the cooking. He always carried homegrown chili. I had developed a taste for his cooking.

While Pete scrambled chili, beef, and beans over the fire he said, "Rivas!" He hung his head sheepishly for thinking out loud. "You sure you no have another Rivas in your saddlebag? It was a ver' fine gift," he added quickly. "But now you have the guilt for my feeling ver' bad. There is no justice if the world have only one Rivas to offer." He puttered around. Something else bothered him.

Maybe Pete's skittishness had to do with being in Indian country. The tribes were quiet in this area, as far as I knew, but I still kept a sharp eye out for trouble in Apache country. Stray bands of Apache, not broken to reservation life yet, still raided.

"Pete, maybe I have somethin' for you that's better than a Rivas." Going over to my saddlebags, I pulled out the other new Colt and a box of .44 caliber shells. I handed them to Pete.

"You ought to go well-armed. Patricio may catch up to me while you're around. Try it," I said, admiring the pistol in his hand. "You'll shuck that old cap and ball you carry when you see how fast this fires and loads."

Pete spun the Colt around his finger, palmed it, got the feel of it. He loaded the pistol and stepped out of the firelight into the dusk. He stood and stared, allowing his eyes to adjust to the dim light. Then he fired. I could not see where his shots hit, but I could see the gleam in his eyes.

"Thank you, Amigo." Pete grinned broadly, revealed his strong white teeth with the one big gap on the side. "It is a ver' fine pistol. But since you have mentioned cousin, Patricio, I think I will sleep ver' far away from the fire. He can kill two sleeping men as well as one." He shoved the Colt behind his belt. "You think he is around here?"

"Don't know," I said pouring chili beans into a tin plate, handing the pot to Pete. "I left him afoot south of San Ysidro." I squatted on my heels. "He may be raisin' an army of vaqueros, or he could walk in here blastin' away right this minute." We both searched beyond the firelight reflexively, then started chewing again.

"I have to ride on up to Durango tomorrow," I said with a full, chili-burning mouth. "If I'm not back in three days, start drivin' what you gathered back to the VR. I'll catch up and we'll work the country as we head in."

The stitches in my side itched like I was the feast of red ants. I pulled up my shirt and started pulling out some of the stitches by firelight.

Pete stared at my side. "Bustos cut the Triple Bar V on you, Amigo." He whistled through his teeth. "It is a thing to admire. The Sanchez family uses that brand at the hacienda down by

Las Cruces." He grinned, "You are the first animal I see with this brand that can shoot back."

"What do you know about the Sanchez family?" I needed information. I had learned long ago that the more I knew about my enemy, the better armed I was. Besides I might steer the conversation around to Dora Luz if I sounded casual about her. Pete held her in his dreams, too. I felt sure from the way he had said her name.

"Manuel Sanchez is *El Patrón*." Pete cut bacon at his mouth with his long knife. "His great-grandfather came from Mexico City, years ago, as the governor of Nuevo Mexico for the King of Spain. The old ones, before Manuel, took all the country as their own and have held most of it. Manual Sanchez is El Don of all *La Raza* of all the territory." Pete reached for the coffeepot and offered it with a gesture. "His son, Eduardo, is the politician now. He is representative from the territory in the Congress in Washington. Juan is the oldest brother. He run all the ranches from the hacienda at Cerrillos."

Pete paused to stuff his mouth and savor his beans and chili. "Bustos and Patricio, they do not like to work," he mumbled. "They are *Ricos*."

A horse snorted then stomped a warning. I slid out of the firelight, pistol in hand. Gliding through the shadows, tensed for trouble, I scouted the brush corral.

The bay stallion, with black main, tail, and three boots, attempted to mount the pinto mare we used for packhorse. Shying away from his attempts she stomped and snorted again. Relieved to know the alarm was just horseplay, I walked back to the campfire. The image of Dora Luz's face came to mind.

"Patricio was mean from the beginning." Pete settled by the fire, picked up the Sanchez story where he'd left it. "The family send him to New Orleans to study the law. He keep killing people in duels. He have to leave town. Patricio teach the knife fighting to Bustos. The knife is Patricio's favorite weapon. Some say he like to see his victims die up close." Pete sliced the air with his knife in mock battle. "You should think on this, Amigo." He stabbed a piece of bacon in the pan. "It is said El Don Manuel have six hundred men working for him. He holds lands from Taos to El Paso. He is a ver' powerful man."

Pete leaned away from the fire to escape the smoke. I had kept him talking so far. I tried to get him going again with a jerk of my chin, raised eyebrow and grunt.

"The son, Eduardo, the politician? He is elected by *La Raza* and sent to Congress to keep the territory from becoming a state. Texas is a state, *qué no*? I do not know if Arizona is a state. New Mexico, she is not, because of Eduardo."

Pete started cleaning up around camp. Apparently he had jawboned himself out. To my disappointment, he had not mentioned Dora Luz again. He rolled out his blankets and settled in for the night, well away from the light and warmth of the fire.

I turned from the firelight to let my eyes adjust to the dark. Shucking into my duster, I strode to the brush corral to take up the killpecker guard.

*   *   *

Wet snow on my face woke me before sunup. I reached out of my blankets to set fire to the kindling under the coffeepot. All my camps were marked by two fires, evening and morning. I would have to remember not to leave that signature anymore. There was no point in making it easy for some one to read my trace. I pulled the blankets over my head to stay warm, wait for coffee, and think about yesterday.

Before leaving our cattle camp for Durango, I had told Pete to practice with the Colt. I did not let on that I hoped he would back me up in a pinch. Maybe by now that was understood between us. I wondered if it was fair to involve him in my problems, but I needed allies. Pete would stand up when trouble came. I felt convinced of it.

The snow let up as the sun rose. I had been in the saddle an hour. I galloped Buck, the frisky bay stallion, north for Colorado and prodded myself to think about the Durango gold problem.

Most likely, the shipments left Durango at random times. The miners probably banked the gold until it built up and became too risky to keep that much around. Gunmen would be hired to haul the gold to Santa Fe. I wondered who else, besides the guards, knew when the gold was about to be shipped out?

The holdup of the shipment had occurred more than three day's ride south of Durango. How did the holdup men know it was coming or where it would be? No telegraph lines ran south between Durango and Santa Fe or Bernalillo.

Had the bandits followed along and struck when the opportunity presented itself? Were there inside men to tip the gang off? How many men were involved in the shipment or in the gang? Where could a gang hole up without drawing attention to itself? I had no facts to go on, but the questions took on a shape.

I cringed. I was the spy who had to find out the facts. No one else could help me. When the facts led me to the bandits, I would be alone to try to stop them.

Rolling my shoulders to shake off the fear that tightened them, I tried to figure how I would operate if I stole the gold. After about a mile up the trail I concluded for sure that I was rusty at strategizing. I'd make a damn poor bandit. And if I couldn't out-think the bandits, that made me a piss-poor marshal.

Back in the war, I had been good at anticipating the moves of the Feds. Armies operated in a fairly limited area. The rules of war were clearly defined. There were only so many options available when moving huge numbers of men to a battleground. Spies, outriders, and patrols gave me the information I needed to narrow the options down to the best attack or counterattack positions. I had been dead wrong a number of times.

Now I had to uncover a cold trail and piece together a tough problem. How had I done it in the war? Reluctantly, I dug back into old memories.

General Lee had ordered me to spy in Washington a couple of times in October of '64. The General wanted me to spread damaging rumors about Lincoln before the coming election. General Lee calculated that if McClellan got elected he could whip the new President and Grant. General Lee had observed that McClellan never attacked when he was General of the Feds. He calculated that McClellan would hold Grant back.

I dodged low branches and booted Buck up a broken slope and over a rise. I doubted spying in Washington was anything like corralling bandits in Durango.

Spying in Washington had been easy. My British documents and a decent English accent, left over from my university days at Oxford, had disguised me. I'd posed as a Yankee sympathizer, a merchant looking for arms contracts with the Union Army. I'd carried off the sham twice.

I doubted an Oxford accent would help me much in Durango.

Buck slipped on a patch of wet snow. I yanked his head up. He skidded on his rump down the backside of the rise. When we hit the flat I prodded him into a lope.

Maybe acting like I was someone different from who I was and going at the investigation from a side angle was the way to handle the situation. Studying on it, I decided to wait and see what developed in Durango. I needed more information.

It started snowing again mid-morning. Spotty, the storm dropped snow in one patch and let the sun shine where you could see it in another patch. The storm clouds drifted, confused and isolated. They worked to make it rain. A mid fall cold snap froze its efforts. I rode and watched nature work it out. She reminded me of a teen-aged girl trying to act like a woman, but not knowing how.

Around noon the snow shower let up and I needed a break from pounding leather. I hobbled Buck where he could paw up grass, then I built a fire. While beans and coffee heated up, I worked on my fast draw.

I did not fire any shoots. I wanted to get the feel of palming the gun, lifting it just enough to clear the holster through the notch I had cut in the front, and bringing it level to fire.

Practicing the motion slowly, deliberately, I let the feel of it take over my body. I increased the speed, but I never hurried the motion. I concentrated on getting the gun level every time.

Beans warmed my insides. Coffee lifted my spirits. My eyes feasted on the fine looking country spread before me. On this plateau, *piñon* and juniper had given way to ponderosa pine. What was left of the snow shower drifted off to the north. The sun shined here, sending brilliant sparkles every which-a-way. I admired the show, then decided to practice the fast draw again.

This time I set up a target. Rummaging around in my saddlebag for more shells, I discovered the letter from Virginia I'd picked up in Santa Fe. I stuffed it in my pocket to read later and turned to gun practice.

I'd seen gun play before, knew that the first shot had to kill. If it didn't, chances were excellent the other man's first shot would. Getting that first shot to kill was easy to talk about, but hard to do when you stood before a man who meant to kill you with hot lead.

The heart gets to pumping. The body gets jumpy. Fear can narrow eyesight down to a pinpoint. There was a balance between being fast into action and being controlled enough to shoot straight. Now was the time for me to put speed and control together.

Palm, pull, clear, level, and shoot. Three times I moved through the draw, slowly adding a

little more speed. My third shot winged the target. Three more shots pounded the still air. Two
bullets clipped the target.

I reloaded. This time I slowed up the action for the next round and put all three bullets
in the neighborhood of the target's heart. I began
to get the feel. Speed, control, and accuracy would
come with more practice.

A little way up the trail, I remembered the
letter in my pocket and pulled it out. I wondered
why I had forgotten about it for so long. Maybe
fate meant to spread out my hard times. The
letter brought bad news.

Sarah May McInroe had written the letter. Stuart McInroe owned the plantation south
of ours, north of Norfolk. Both our families had
been ruined by the war, Stuart killed. Widow
Sarah May and brother John had been courting.
John's last letter had mentioned her and stated
that he was seriously considering marrying her
when he got the estate reestablished.

Widow Sarah May wrote to tell me that
John was dead. Apparently he had been robbed
and murdered in Baltimore when he was up there
on business.

The news struck hard. Johnny had been
the hope of us all. He was the brightest, the hand-
somest of my brothers. Since he was the youngest, James, Zak, my father, and I had decided John
would run the properties while we fought the war.
Johnny had a kind but strong way of getting
things done.

Now Johnny was dead. The way my situation stacked up, some bandit would kill me. My
family was doomed. I stuffed the letter in my
pocket and rode on with my head hanging down.

I didn't mourn Johnny. I had run out of tears for the dead long ago. Still, a loneliness settled down over me, and I could not shake it. I stood alone against the world and felt totally cut off from the past.

I brooded about heading back to Virginia to find out what had happened, to seek justice for Johnny's death. Maybe he had left things working that needed to be carried forward. Maybe it was my job now to return to Richmond and start over for the family name. I could fight our fights in the courts and regain our properties. I could get the salvage job started on the *Croft* on the bottom of the bay to raise money.

But nothing in Virginia made sense to me anymore. I rode a bay stallion in the middle of vast, wild country. I rode for the VR brand. I had a job to do for the governor.

I grappled with the idea of the end of my rich tradition, the end of my family. We were beaten by the war, finished in the east by a murderer, and most likely I would be killed soon in the West by a spooky bull or bloody bandits. Then it would be all over for the Wallers.

Isolating myself in the moment, I had no past, no future. I didn't care anymore. I had nothing left to lose. I caught myself riding cock-eyed in the saddle. The tension in my leg put all my weight in the left stirrup like I was ready to dismount in a hurry. Why not bail out? Why go on?

CHAPTER SIX

Durango smelled of coal smoke from a smelter or maybe the steam engines used to lift ore and pump water from the mines. The stink of human waste rose off the muddy road. Miners and those that leech off the miners had thrown together wooden buildings between the road and the riverbank. Two stores, an assay office, a bank, and half-a-dozen saloons sported false fronts and gaudy signs. Hotels, boarding houses, tents, and shacks lined the other side of the road, and up a bluff.

I stabled Buck in the livery at the end of the road and decided to seek out a poker game. I wanted to make some money while I listened for information, got a feel for the boomtown.

I picked the brightest bucket of blood with the loudest music. Pushing up to the bar, I considered busthead, but asked for a beer. I stayed shut of whiskey as a rule. Whiskey either drove me to fight or put me to sleep. When the beer came, I had second thoughts. The news of Johnny's death and my sorrow needed obliterating.

The yearning for the solace of whiskey gave way to the need to do a job. Tired and sad as I felt, I had to keep my senses. The beer tasted decent, but didn't hold up against a Rivas. The Irish Sergeant would have been disappointed.

Over the top of the mug, I surveyed the saloon reflected in the mirror behind the bar. Then I turned to face a room full of rough men. Miners, peddlers, gamblers, a cowboy or two, drank and flirted with the calico queens. I saw no one I knew, wondered who I might have to arrest or kill in this crowd.

Three poker games offered me a choice. I began to watch the players at the table by the roulette wheel. I had found it cheaper to watch how a few hands played out before I sat in. Watching allowed me time to notice the tell-tale signs the gamblers tried to hide when they reacted to their cards. Then I could start counting the cards and figuring the odds to make the bets.

A tassel headed miner played to lose. He tried to buy the pots his low cards couldn't win. His stack of gold coins dwindled rapidly as the rest of the boys picked him clean. I ought to get in on some of that free gold before it dried up. I kept watching the players, especially the thin man in the black hat and vest.

Before he dealt the cards, he added an extra riff to his shuffle. When he dealt the hand he did not win, but the gent to his left did. I watched until Black Hat got the deal again. He stacked the deck professionally and his capper won a big pot. I started watching another game. I had no time to be cheated and I wanted no part of the shooting if the bottom-card mechanic got called out.

The gamblers at the second table played for low stakes, just having fun at cards while they got drunk and waited for the whore they had chosen to come back down stairs.

The third game looked ripe, but I had been standing around long enough and felt the fatigue of the long ride. I hadn't heard any information that was useful, as I'd listened to the conversations in the room. Tired, sad, and disappointed, I decided to find a bunk for the night.

*　　*　　*

I went to breakfast in the hotel dining room, if you could call it that. There were two long plank tables and benches. The dining room reminded me more of a bunkhouse. No one else was up yet, or they had already eaten and were about their business. I sat alone by the window for a while and watched the street.

Durango bustled. Wagons, carrying ore from and supplies to the mines, plied the road, churned the mud. An old prospector fought with two balky mules he loaded. Two women, wearing flower sack bonnets, went into the general store. The bank across the street looked closed, curtains drawn.

Finally a rough-looking, fat lady came into the dining room, stood over me, and glared impatiently.

"You have eggs?" I asked.

"That'll be five dollars," the fat lady grunted, "and by the look of it, you ain't got the money."

It was clear why nobody ate here. I made mention of the fact and walked out hungry. I would try my luck at the saloon.

Mining towns were expensive. Everybody had a get-rich-quick attitude. Five dollars for eggs? The fat lady lost her bet on me.

After steak, splatter dabs, and coffee I sat back to enjoy bear sign and another cup of coffee. The breakfast cost a buck, which was high. I cussed the cook mildly because the doughnut made up for it. I hadn't had one for a long time. This one had sugar and cinnamon dashed on it. While I savored the sweetness, I made a plan.

My first stop was the general store. I walked into a well-stocked room and started to browse around. The cinnamon bear sign had itched my sweet tooth. Growing up on southern cooking, I had acquired a taste for sugar. I filled a bag with horehound crystal candy and pulled a box of .44 shells off the shelf.

The storekeeper was a handsome-looking lady, which surprised and pleased me. Made me curious, too. This was a rough, mining town. She was probably the wife of the man who managed or owned the store.

I tipped my hat then dug for a coin.

"I'm new to Durango, Ma'am. When does the bank open today, Miss...?" I looked her in the eye. She met my eyes with a steady gaze.

Her face broke into a delightful, mothering smile, like she was looking at a helpless baby. "Why, today's Saturday, Mister. The bank won't open today unless someone brings in a load of gold." She accepted my coin.

Saturday. Hell, I had lost track of the days of the week. I paid attention to the passing of the seasons, but that was about it as far as I concerned myself about keeping a calendar.

Saturday night in town was another matter. It could be hell on wheels. The miners would come in to drink, fight, and spend the dust they had panned all week. Some would manage to get to church on Sunday, if they didn't get killed celebrating Saturday night.

"Anyway, the banker's out of town," she continued. "I think a shipment of gold went south yesterday." Suddenly embarrassed, she added, "Everybody's been talking about it."

"I hear a gold shipment was held up a while back. Is that right, Miss...?" I fished. She seemed talkative.

"It certainly was!" Her mouth tightened, "My husband, Benjamin, works our claim hard. We lost over six hundred dollars in that robbery. People can't figure out how it happened. The shipment went out with ten armed guards. All were killed." She scribbled in a ledger. "People have been mighty suspicious since. Some say it was an inside job. It had to be. Nobody knows when the gold's going out until the last minute. That'll be another penny, for the candy." She smiled again. "I made it myself."

One crystal, delivering its sweet taste, would last a long time dissolving in my cheek. I opened the bag of candy and took a crystal for myself. I offered her some. She took one, dipped her head to the side and flashed her eyes at me.

"What's being done to get your money back?" I leaned both elbows on the counter and gazed into her eyes.

"Nothing!" she scoffed. "The sheriff went with that first shipment south. He was killed and the committee can't find anyone who'll take his job. Charlie Patterson, he's the banker, he sort of runs Durango now as the mayor." She straightened a stack of folded shirts on the counter, arranged the candy jars next to me. "He rode out with the shipment yesterday. There were twelve well-armed men who went with him, as the rumor has it." She turned, distracted as two men walked in to the store.

"Thank you, Ma'am. Is there a tailor in town?" I asked as she moved away. She did not hear my question. I watched her and pondered. Durango might lose a mayor, the banker, and soon, to my way of thinking. The robbers had escaped, scot-free, after the first holdup. They would try again. Why did I have the feeling the shopkeeper's husband rode with the second shipment as well?

At least the dead sheriff, the possibly doomed banker, and perhaps Benjamin, her husband, were above suspicion as inside men for the robbery. If the gold robbery had been an inside job, the banker and owner of this store were unaware of it. No man, unless he was under binding orders in a war, would ride knowingly to certain death. It was clear from the massacre that the bandits would leave no witnesses.

I walked across the muddy road to the tailor shop thinking it was strange I had not seen anyone on the trail coming in yesterday. Perhaps the shipment had gone some other route, to give them an edge. Still, I had come over the logical trail to use between Durango and Santa Fe.

A party of armed men that large, probably with a wagon, would use the well-traveled route. That trail had been deadly for the guards of the first gold shipment. Maybe the leader of the second shipment figured a new route would work this time and the gold would get through.

I found the tailor in a Chinese laundry. I had hauled my long black coat along hoping to find a tailor in Durango who could mend the knife slashes Bustos cut in it.

The Chinaman said he could mend anything, even bullet holes. The coat would look good as new, guaranteed, and I could pick it up at noon before he closed shop.

"You lose any gold in the holdup a while back?" I acted casual.

"No me, Mis'er. You think I lich?" He turned and went into the back room. I heard Chinese spoken and then a burst of laughter as I walked out.

I had seen a doctor's sign hanging by the saloon. My stitches itched and it seemed a good idea to have my side tended. It turned out the doctor was the barber across the street. The gent who directed me to the barbershop swore that the barber was well respected for his skill with gunshot wounds and pulling teeth, but not so much for cutting hair.

I thought I might risk a bad hair cut because the barber might know what was going on in town. Seemed barbers were as good with gossip as barkeeps, and I could stand a shave and a haircut.

There were two customers ahead of me so I picked up an old newspaper, looked it over, and listened to the conversation between the barber and the man he sheared.

"I'll bet you five dollars there ain't no trouble this time. The boys've been tight mouthed about movin' the gold and there ain't been no strangers in town except fellers comin' in to mine gold." The barber seemed to speed up his clipping when he saw me come in.

"I won't take the bet. I got gold in this shipment. Can't bet against myself." The customer tried to keep cut hair out of his mouth with his tongue, and ended up spitting.

"It surely is mystifyin'," the barber continued. "There weren't no trouble shippin' over the mountain to Denver. Donaldson, now, he was a cagey sheriff, backed down from no man. They was either tricked or flat out ambushed." The barber shook out the bib. "That'll be two bits."

The room felt stuffy. I wanted to watch the street. I told the barber I would wait just outside the door until he could take me.

Ambushed? That took planning and inside information about the route. I leaned against the wall by the door so I could listen to the conversation inside the barber shop.

Cool, mountain air nipped my face. The sky could have been as clear and dark blue as in New Mexico, except for the pall of smoke that hung over the valley. Most of the snow had melted, except patches in the shade on the north side of buildings. The hardwood trees by the river had turned brilliant reds and oranges. I smelled fried food and rotting leaves as I stretched and warmed myself in the sun.

A mule train halted across the street while the muleskinner adjusted gear on a packsaddle. I walked over to him. "Which way'd you come in?"

He turned from the pack and squinted at me. "Come over from Aztec. The trail's passable, a little red clay mud after a wet snow."

"Anybody on the trail besides you?" I asked and offered a hand on a rope to help the muleskinner tie up the pack.

"Party of thirteen, heavily-armed men charged by mighty unfriendly like." Then he chuckled. "When I seen'em a-comin' I figured I's a goner. Looked like bad men. Hell, they just stormed on by with nary a word." He snubbed the knot down, thanked me with a jerk of his chin. "Looked like they's each carryin' a heavy load. All'em's leadin' a spare horse. Looked like they meant to travel fast."

"Hey, Mister!" the barber called. I thanked the muleskinner and turned to pick my way across the muddy ruts.

A sudden gust of chilly wind off the mountains pushed me back to the barber's shop. I understood why I had not seen the shipment. I came up the trail to the south of the Aztec road and missed them. With a fast moving troop like the muleskinner described, no wagon, individually mounted, able to scatter and fight, I began to hope maybe they would kill off the outlaws and my job would be finished. I liked the prospect.

"What'll it be, Mister?" The barber motioned me to the chair by shaking the white bib like a matador's cape at a colorblind bull.

"Cut and shave. Leave the mustache, and I want you to pull some stitches out of me." I settled into the chair and put my feet up as he rocked the chair back.

He started soaping my face. "Ain't seen you 'round town before, have I?"

"Rode in last night. I'm lookin' to sell cattle. Thought I'd see if there's a need for beef in Durango." I talked around his slapping soap brush. "The whole town's talking about some robbery and not much else. I's told to look up Charles Patterson about my cattle. Seen'im?"

"Patterson rode out with 'nother gold shipment."

"I thought he's a banker, not a professional guard. Who's guarding that gold?"

"Nest'a hornets, I tell ya'. All known men with a stake in the success of the delivery. I'd hate to be the bandit what met up with that bunch."

"I didn't find Benjamin over at the general store. He with the gold?"

"Him, the Mayor, Parkens, and ten min-ers," he said stropping the razor.

"Who rode guard on the first shipment?" I was beginning to feel right about asking more direct questions.

"Same's this time. All trusted men from around here." The barber pinched my nose and reached under it with the blade. I reminded him to leave the mustache. "We all lost friends. Good men each." He started shaving by my right ear. "Y'know, it's mighty puzzlin'. I ain't talked to a soul has any idea what's happenin'. I cut Mayor Patterson's hair day before yesterday. The mayor's runnin' the investigation what with the sheriff recently kilt. I asked him when he's here if he'd found anythin' out yet. He said there's absolutely nothin'. They hadn't even figured out where the holdup took place exactly."

The barber pinched my nose to attack my mustache again. I reminded him again.

He said, "I'm bettin' they get through just fine this time." He stepped back to size up the shave. Satisfied, he wiped around my ears and neck with a dirty towel. Then he got after the hair cutting.

I got to thinking that a boomtown like Durango always had a boss running things, on the other side of the law. The sheriff let the boss operate within certain limits. Boomers demanded their pleasures. The sheriff usually turned a blind eye, so long as there were no killings. Most times the boss knew more than the law about what was going on.

I asked the barber, "Who's boss of the sa-loons? Maybe he'll need beef for the winter."

The barber stepped back again and winked. "You askin' who runs the town? That'd be Sandy Thompson. Best girls, decent whiskey, if you're looking to relax a might. Stay shut of the poker. He's got card handlers workin' for the house."

The barber had a fair hand at pulling the stitches. He recommended I leave some of the stitches in the deep V cut. Said it would protect the wound should I have to strain or pull hard. I did not appreciate the admiration he expressed for the knife work.

I walked back over to the saloon where I'd had the cinnamon bear sign for breakfast. The noon crowd had not arrived yet. The bartender was sweeping up. I ordered a beer. He leaned the broom against the bar, moved to get the beer.

"Who runs Durango, My Friend? I don't mean the mayor and his committee." I set my beer down and watched the bartender carefully.

"Who's asking?" he said belligerently. His hands dropped below the bar.

"I'm new in town. Want to know who to step around." Both my hands rested on the bar. "Figured you'd know. Besides, I thought I'd see if he had any work he needed done, if you know what I mean."

He looked me over carefully. His eyes narrowed on my gun then he looked up. "You any good with that, or you wearin' that fast-draw rig for show?" He continued to study my face, tried to match it to a memory.

"I'm still livin'. Who's boss?" I bluffed.

"Sandy Thompson, big redhead. Hangs out at his other place, the Red Garter, over the other side of the hotel." He resumed his sweeping.

The Red Garter looked like any other saloon except for a dusty, red garter hanging on the corner of the mirror behind the bar. The mirror was the unusual thing. Mirrors had a way of being the first casualty in a bar fight. This huge mirror hung without a crack in it. Its unbroken surface indicated tough management.

I was directed upstairs to an office. Outside the office a burly man barred the door. His clothes stunk of stale beer and rancid beef, add tobacco smoke to the stink.

"I'm here to see Sandy." I reached for the doorknob. The big man knocked my left hand away agilely, powerfully. His quickness was a surprise.

I reacted from pure instinct, no thought. Instantly, my Colt lay in my hand, cocked, and the muzzle jabbed the big man's ribs. The big man's eyes widened and he raised his hands slowly out from his sides. I knew I had made a new enemy.

He opened the door slowly and without taking his eyes off me called inside. I backed the big man in front of me into the room.

"Mr. Thompson, call your watch dog off." I had a clear shot at both men. The bodyguard might take two bullets before his frame crumpled. Thompson three. He was huge without being fat. Red hair covered his head like a wild brush fire. Freckles made his ruddy face appear already burned over. His boiled shirt showed starch by its creases and the sleeves buttoned above hands with long strong fingers and polished nails.

"Easy now, Mister. Ben! Wait outside. Don't start nothin'." Sandy Thompson ordered.

Ben flamed red in the face and fumed. He turned slowly and left the room.

"Mornin', Thompson." I said it casually and tossed my tin badge on his desk.

"I'm Deputy Marshal Waller, New Mexico Territory."

"Kind'a out of your jurisdiction, ain't ya, Waller?" He sat down slowly.

"Depends. The crime's committed in New Mexico. I don't care where I find the criminal." I locked eyes with him and added, "It's not you I'm huntin'. I want information, and I know you run Durango."

Thompson reached slowly for a cigar box on the desk, turned it around and opened the lid towards me. "Cigar, Marshal?" His hands remained on the desk. I took a cigar with my left hand. As he reached for his, I holstered the Colt.

Thompson had been working on account books spread on the desk. He closed the books and leaned back, lit his cigar. Then he reached for the badge I had tossed on the desk and began to roll it between his fingers.

"A tin star gives a man a lot of power," Thompson drawled. "Gold dust gives a man a lot of power. I wonder which one'll win in the end, tin or gold?" He tossed me the badge. "What do I get for givin' information?"

"Peace," I said and bit off the tip of my cigar.

"You up here on that gold shipment holdup?" Thompson rose and went over to the window. Smoke curled from his cigar, seemed to bring the brush fire on his head alive. He appeared to be thinking, not looking outside.

"What do you know about it?" I lit my cigar, a fine-quality Cuban.

"It's the damnedest thing. I don't know nothin'. I've had my men on it. The lid's on tight, or else no one's operatin' out of Durango." Thompson turned from the window to face me. "I also need to know what's goin' on, Waller. Sooner or later the miners're goin' to turn their suspicions on me. I run the games, the whiskey, and most of the girls. That's the way I get the gold." He turned back to the window. "I don't have to steal it."

"The shipment that went out yesterday, know anything about it?"

"Nothin' beforehand. You can tell when a shipment's due to go out by the mood of the town. We had nothin' exact on the time or the men ridin' shotgun until they moved out. I've checked with my men and none of them report anything suspicious, no suspicious strangers, no change in activity, no overheard conversations. You think this one'll get through?"

I reflected, studied the evenness of the burn on the tip of my cigar. "I don't know. The robbery may be one of a kind. As clean as it was, I'd bet they try it again."

"Damnation! I bet the other way. I collect a lot of gold dust in my operations. Sent it out this time. I hope you're wrong, Marshal. What're you doin' about it?"

"So far, it's a cold trail. Seemed logical to start investigatin' in Durango. I've discovered nothin' yet. I'll head south and see if I can find where the robbery took place. One man survived long enough to get to San Ysidro before he died. I'll pick up there." I chewed on the cigar for a minute, thinking. "Thompson, I'm workin' under cover. I'd appreciate it if you'd protect me on that." I watched him calculate.

"Okay, Marshal, but you'll owe me for my silence, and I'll collect sooner or later." He sat down again, pushed the cigar box my way. "Take some cigars for the trail. If they get this shipment, you get my gold back. We'll call it even, if you do."

After a beer with Sandy Thompson, I stepped out of the Red Garter a little before noon. I stopped by the Chinese laundry. The coat had been repaired good as new, cleaned and smoothed.

I paid for the work and had turned to leave when the Chinaman said, "It is good enough to be bel'e in, yes?" He laughed.

I failed to see the humor in his question. Come to think of it, I did regard that coat as my finest outfit, poor as I was. I would probably be buried in it if I didn't die out on the range somewhere. The wolf of my nightmares flashed through my mind. Most likely, scavengers would beat the undertaker to my carcass.

I hauled my gear out of the hotel and headed for the livery. Questioning the owner of the stable produced nothing of interest. The stable boy had nothing to add. I told him to hold my horse for a while longer.

I wanted to have one more good meal before I hit the trail. I could not predict when I would have another one. I wanted to find some bottled beer because I felt an obligation to Pete. I wanted to prove to my friend that there was some justice in the world. Even if I couldn't bring him a Rivas, I could bring him more than one beer.

I went back to the general store to see if the lady storekeeper had any bottled beer there. She stood behind the counter adding up a miner's bill. I lazed around pretending to look at clothes and mining equipment; instead, I admired her golden hair and full figure. After a bit, the miner paid and left. She turned to me and her eyes flashed momentarily.

"More candy?" She smiled teasingly.

"When do you take your noon meal, Ma'am? I'd like to take you out for supper." I wondered if there was too much hope in my voice. I had no idea what I was doing asking a married woman out to dine. Maybe in the back of my mind I knew she would be a widow soon. Besides, I had a need to be around a woman like her, pretty, efficient, smiling.

She blushed, paused, and then flashed her smile again. "I can't leave the store unattended." She destroyed my hope. It must have shown on me because she added, "I baked a peach pie this morning. Join me in the kitchen. I'll put something together. My name's Ann."

Ann and I enjoyed a delightful lunch. We talked small talk. I had almost forgotten how to carry on a conversation about unimportant things. Ann's peach pie put another itch on my sweet tooth and I complimented her. She gave me a second slice with coffee. Then customers came into the store. Ann had to work and I had to travel. She smiled politely but with sparkling eyes as she saw me out the back door.

I had forgotten to ask Ann about bottled beer, but I found it at the Red Garter. I spent the last of my pocket money on four bottles.

As I rode out of Durango, which was heating up for a Saturday night, I groused around about this boom town having busted another cowboy flat, and without so much as a bad hand at poker or a kiss on the cheek. In addition, it had been a dead-end trip as far as the robbery investigation was concerned.

Still, my spirits rode high as I gigged Buck into a lope and thought about Ann's peach pie and warm, inviting smile.

CHAPTER SEVEN

Instead of traveling a beeline directly back to the cattle camp and Pete, I wanted to track the second gold shipment a ways. Maybe I could learn something useful to offset the time I had wasted in Durango. I turned the bay stallion down the trail towards Aztec.

The wind and light snow had worked to conceal the convoy trail, now a couple of days old, but here and there I could make out individual tracks. Just like the mule skinner had said, there were twenty-six horses, all shod, in the party. Each horse had a signature shoe print and gate. Thirteen horses were carrying heavy loads which told me the gold was divided among the riders. Tactically, that was a good plan for survival.

The convoy had rested the horses at a stream in a meadow off the main trail. The men had built a fire, eaten, and switched mounts. Lookouts had been posted. I followed boot tracks to a meeting, a congregation at one time of all the men around the campfire for a meeting or to receive orders.

My mind became cluttered sorting out all the details. I had dallied on the convoy trail long enough and felt a strong need to get back to Pete. I left the campsite with clear impressions of the trace left by fourteen of the horses and seven of the men. I reckoned that with the make-up of the convoy they had a chance of getting through to Santa Fe. My guts felt less encouraged.

I rode a compass line from the convoy camp to our temporary corral on the San Juan River. The country dropped away from the high mountains in a series of plateaus. I had to back-track out of a box canyon once. Bushwhacking through country without a trail had its risks. Trails came about because someone had already been through the troubles of finding the best way through the terrain. I figured I was lucky getting blocked only once.

I pushed on well after dark and then hit rough country. Wrecking a horse in the night on rocky terrain made no sense. I could see myself walking out with a saddle on my back, afoot like Patricio. I didn't want to look that stupid.

Rolling up in my blankets, I calculated I would make Pete's camp around noon tomorrow, well within my three-day limit. I had used up two days and learned very little in Durango. As I drifted off to sleep, I wondered how many cattle Pete had rounded up. I'd promised Red a couple hundred head by the end of two weeks.

*   *   *

I rode up to our brush corral at noon. Pete was gone. Sixty-five head stood in the pen or lay chewing cud. Most of the older stock bore the VR brand. Old Pete had been busy. His tracks pointed the way he had gone to hunt strays to-day.

It took a little while to clear the shallow ditch to bring water to the pen from the river. When I had finished digging, I traded horses and picked a different direction to hunt cattle. With half-a-day left, I might as well scrub the river breaks I'd just come through.

Before I left camp, I set a sign for Pete so he would know I'd been around. Then I tied two beers in a protected place in the river to cool and rode out into a sunny afternoon to round up stock.

* * *

Low clouds glowed blood-red on the bottoms from the horizon to directly overhead. Off to the north, tall thunderclouds rose up. Red painted their base, hot pink their middle, and the crowns of the clouds were still golden in direct sunlight. To the east, dusk had captured the clouds in deep purple-gray. The breeze nipped my skin and blew on by, as it always did just at sunset. I rode into our camp, worn out but satisfied. I herded twenty-six head of cattle in front of me.

Pete hunkered on his heels by a small cooking fire. The cedar wood smoke smelled sweet, pungently spiced with Pete's chili mix. I savored the tainted air as I penned the stock and hobbled my horse.

"Looks like you worked hard, Pete. Anything eventful happen?" I dropped my saddle by the fire.

"I killed Patricio Sanchez for you, Amigo." Pete grinned and slapped the new Colt on his hip. "With this fine pistol." He stirred the coals under his pot of pooch in his usual easygoing way. "Durango still there, or did the gold run out?"

"Durango's still rollickin' along," I said over my shoulder as I walked to the river to fetch the beer. I kind of hid them as I walked back to the fire. "Fine night for a beer, *qué no, Cuate*?" I teased Pete.

"It is not fair to tempt me, Amigo. You are cruel to give me only one Rivas and then to remind me of my poverty." The point of Pete's boot pocked angrily at a stray stick in the base of the fire. "I think you torture me. Remember, Amigo, I fix the chili. If you do not stop tormenting me, perhaps the chili will become too hot for your gringo tongue." Pete sounded a might pissed, like he had over heated sometime today.

"I'll tease your palate once more then, *Cuate*." I produced the beers.

"I hope you go to town often, Amigo!" Pete grinned, accepted the beer left-handed as we shook hands in greeting.

We drank. We ate pooch with chili in it, instead of sugar. Pete had added some kind of meat that I did not ask about. We planned how we'd move the hundred and ten head of cattle we had penned to Huerfano Peak where we'd pick up the search again. We estimated that by the time we got to Cuba, we would bunch maybe two hundred head to add to Red's herd.

Moving that many cattle would be hard work for two men. Until the cattle broke to trail, they'd tend to scatter. The next few days would be long and dusty, but it was work I took pleasure in doing.

One of us would have to be with the herd at all times. Pete and I would take turns sleeping and guarding the herd at night. During the day, one of us would ride point and the other push the herd from behind or ride flank. Point was the place to be, with no choking dust, out in front of the herd. You could admire the view up ahead. We agreed to trade off riding drag when the dust got too miserable to bear any longer.

Since Pete and I wouldn't see much of each other for the next few days, I broke out two of Sandy Thompson's cigars. We smoked into the evening, lollygagged, and told lies. "Did I ever tell you about the time when ol'..."

*   *   *

By the end of the fourth day of our drive south, we had gathered a hundred and eighty head total. Tapicito Canyon had not paid off. Canyon Largo had. We decided to hold up for the night, just north of Nageezi, where there was plenty of water and grass. We didn't think the cattle would wander much. Most of the stock was trail-broke by now, and the drive to Nageezi had been long and dry.

Pete and I agreed that we would take a break at Nageezi, rest up some. We figured we were halfway to the big herd in the Cuba valley.

I had told Pete about the other two beers, so he would have something to look forward to. Four bottles were all I could afford to buy when I left Durango. These last two would be it for both of us for a while.

I anticipated a sip myself. Beer always cut the trail dust with a bubbly kick, making the collecting of the dust worthwhile. I had collected a ton of it chasing bulls that bolted for liberty and headed for high brush, or taking my turn eating drag dust.

Pete poked his cooking fire. "Amigo, I see something ver' strange today." He rocked back on his heels and shielded his eyes from a flurry of sparks. "Maybe three miles north of the road to Cuba, I cut the trail of twenty, perhaps twenty-five horses. These horses are shod, run at the gallop." He set the coffeepot up. "I am puzzled who can this be? Is Patricio looking for you with an army?" Pete looked over the fire into the distance and scanned the horizon. "The Indians do not put the shoes on their horses, *muchisimas gracias a Dios*. Maybe these men are rustlers. I do not know what is the truth. What you think, Amigo?"

Apparently the second gold shipment had made it that far. It had to be them, and they were playing it smart staying off the road and moving fast. Whoever the leader was must have studied the cavalry tactics the raiders developed in the war, or invented them himself. So far, so good. I thought of Ann and then her husband.

"Pete, a few weeks back a gold shipment out of Durango headed for Santa Fe's held up. All the guards're killed." I opened the beer bottles, handed him his. "When I was in Santa Fe the governor asked me to look into the matter. That's why I went up to Durango." I held my bottle up in salute. "To your health, *Cuate*, and the Irish Sergeant."

"*Por Dios*, I see the robber's tracks?" Pete looked alarmed, but took his first swig.

"Nope. You saw the track of a second gold shipment. Least I think so. I'm goin' to ride up that way tomorrow and have a look."

"You work for the governor and the VR?"

"Uh huh." The beer cut the dust in my gullet.

"You work for the governor and the VR and you run from Patricio?" Pete whistled through his teeth. "You like to tempt *La Gloria*, Amigo!"

I didn't need reminding about my predicament. Patricio had been on my mind. I had been practicing every day on the fast draw. Two empty beer bottles would be my targets tomorrow.

I pulled a cartridge from my Colt. "Play you a hand game for the midnight watch, *Cuate*. You go first."

Pete lost the game and won the midnight watch. For now, we lollygagged by the fire, sipped beer and enjoyed beans, bacon, and some greens Pete had boiled up that tasted like spinach. He had found some wild onions he threw in the pot, too.

I asked him, "You ever eat cooked grasshoppers an' onions?"

"Are you kiddin', Amigo? Was that what we have the last time you cook?" He wasn't smiling when he asked.

We lazed around as long as we could, then I got up to fetch firewood. I stacked the firewood so I could lift it into the old fireplace without getting out of my blankets. I figured the habit of leaving two fires to mark my camp was broken. I was not about to break my habit of getting out of my blankets to a warm fire and coffee. Comforts just took planning.

Pete fell asleep by the time I had my kindling set up. I saddled up and headed out to lullaby the herd.

After rousting Pete about an hour after midnight, I lay back and let the tension and soreness run out of my body. Looking up at the stars, I let the voice in my head stop talking for a while and cleared my mind. Mars still haunted Aldibaron. Orion hunted overhead. Clear, cold air promised a frost by morning. I felt calm, no sense of past or future. I drifted off to sleep.

I had coffee boiling when Pete rode in just before dawn. "Catch a nap, Hombre. Then we'll head the herd south before I take off to look at the trail you cut up north. I'll catch up with you by noon."

"I sleep some in the saddle, Amigo. We eat and go now."

We got the herd moving. It appeared the cattle were going to trail along just fine. I broke away from the herd, waved my hat at Pete off in the distance, and headed back up Pete's tracks to the gold shipment trail.

*   *   *

The troop of riders had passed three, maybe four days ago. I followed their trail a mile or so before I recognized enough signs to become convinced that this was the gold convoy.

Each man constituted a mounted, armed unit carrying gold. With no wagon to protect, each man could scatter at the first warning of trouble and fight independently or join a group defense. With this flexibility, total loss of men and gold seemed to be less likely.

The success of the convoy depended on the caliber of the fighting men that made up the guard. Veterans from both North and South roamed the West now. Most had lost everything in the war and sought new lives mining or ranching in the West, like me. Most likely some of the miners riding shotgun on the convoy were hardened veterans.

While galloping back to Pete and our herd, I crossed the trace of a single rider. He held his course parallel to the convoy maybe half a mile out. I recognized the signature of one of the convoy horses I had come to know. So whoever commanded the convoy used outriders on his flanks and probably ahead which demonstrated his war experience.

I could not think of any other tactics I would add to this fast sortie. My confidence in their success rose. In fact, I became downright hopeful, once again, that the guards would destroy the holdup gang if they attacked.

I bunched up five cows hiding out in the bottom of a wash, in a motte of cottonwoods. The ancient, gnarled trees still clung to their golden leaves. The sun gleaming behind them made a shine like a dazzling display of twenty-dollar gold pieces. I felt like a miser admiring his fortune. The cattle did not want to leave their good fortune either. It took me an hour to get them bent right. I caught up with Pete and the herd after noon.

* * *

When we arrived at the Cuba Valley roundup, Pete's and my catch brought the VR herd to a little over twelve hundred head. We hit our fourteen-day deadline on the nose. That left plenty of time to drive the herd to Sam Bartlet at Corrales, ninety miles away, by December first. The cattle would arrive fat and trail broke.

Red told us when we rode in that the drive would start at dawn.

After evening chuck, I roped a horse from the *remuda*. My bad luck, I had drawn the first watch along with Johnson. We would spend the next four hours riding around twelve hundred head of cattle, talking, and singing to keep them settled.

Johnson worked hard, a smart cowboy, a quiet man except when he sang boisterously off-key. When he sang to the cattle, you wanted to be two counties away, at least on the other side of the herd.

Maybe I'd get four hours sleep before we started the drive at sunup. Hell, after Pete's and my drive from up North, I was broke to the long days of hard work, the naps in between.

Red walked up on the other side of the horse I saddled. "Evenin', Eli." Red checked the cinch on his side and nodded it wasn't twisted.

"Red." He looked a might worried. "What's on your mind, Boss?"

"Over to Cuba this mornin' word come up the trail that teamsters found thirteen dead Anglos about ten miles southeast of San Ysidro." Red pushed his hat back and scratched at a curly, red forelock. "Dead maybe two days. Hard to tell after coyotes and wolves get to a body. Looked like they'd been shot up pretty bad and stripped of their guns. Didn't find anything else. No mutilatin'." He paused to let the effect of his news sink in. "I'm telling all hands and the cook to watch for trouble. If Apache or rustlers come, fire three quick warning shots. I want all hands bunched to protect the herd." He turned to go.

I understood the threat in Red's bad news a different way. Red and the herd had no trouble coming. I did. So did the new widow, Ann, damn it.

"Red?" My tone turned him to face me. "I told you back at the ranch I had a lot goin' on? Well that massacre's probably part of it."

"You know somethin' 'bout this?" He squinted, drew his fists up to rest on his hips, jutted out his chin. His neck hadn't changed color yet.

"You and the herd are not threatened, Red. There's more to the bind I got into in Santa Fe with the gent that's huntin' me. The short of it, the governor has me blackmailed into workin' under cover for him." I pulled the tin star out of my pocket and flashed it so he could see it, but no one else.

"Sounds like somethin' Bill Connelly'd pull. How you tied into the massacre?" Red saw more talk coming so he pulled out his Duke of Durham.

"Put away the papers, Red." I reached into my saddlebag and pulled out the last two of Sandy Thompson's Cuban cigars. "You hear about a gold shipment robbery over by San Yesidro a few weeks back?"

"Gold out of Durango?" Red lit my cigar first. "That what took you up to Durango?"

"Um. The governor wanted me to look around. A second gold shipment left Durango just before I got there." I puffed up a cloud of blue smoke as I coaxed the Havana to burn evenly. "Red, it sounds like the second shipment didn't make it either. This robbery business is gettin' mighty serious, and I haven't found any evidence yet to give the governor." I watched Red suck his cigar to life and waited for his eyes to lift back to mine. "If you can spare it, I'd like to ride ahead down to San Ysidro, have a look around. I'll scout grass an' water for the herd an' get back to you soon as I find out somethin'."

Red calculated for a moment. "Thirteen men guard that gold?"

I nodded. "Looked at first like they had a chance to make it."

"It'd take a crowd to kill thirteen men." Red smoked, looked like he was thinking. "How's that left side of yours healin'?"

"Pretty fair, Red. I can do a full day's work."

"Well, let me know about the water and grass south of here." Red turned towards the chuck wagon. Over his shoulder he said, "You take care of yourse'f, Eli. I don't want to lose a good hand."

I thought of Ann as I rode out to my night watch on the herd. Living in the West wore hard on women. Mostly they followed their men blindly, ill equipped to survive this country. Oftentimes they found themselves marooned. The frontier had a way of killing off husbands. I wondered if Ann had received word of her loss yet. Feeling sorry for her put a melancholy edge on my singing to the cattle.

*　　　*　　　*

By mid-morning the herd was lined out and moving along, so I cut out to ride down to San Ysidro. It had rained most of the night. The wet weather killed any hope I had of finding signs at the murder site, but I needed to see the terrain. I wanted to know how thirteen armed, mounted men could be cornered and killed. Maybe I would get lucky and find something to report to the governor.

San Ysidro was not a town so much as a cluster of small, irrigated farms on the Jemez River. I rode to the adobe church, the center of social life in any Mexican settlement.

The priest was inside hearing a confession, so I talked to an old man doing odd jobs outside. He had heard about the killings, mentioned that old lady Martinez had doctored the wounded man from the first holdup. I found out where she lived.

Finished with his holy chores the priest came out to talk. "We have seen and heard nothing. There are no bad men in San Ysidro." The priest lifted his head to stare with deep eyes into the northern heavens. "Where could they hide? It is beyond me, My Son."

I asked about old lady Martinez.

The priest winced as if I had touched a sore spot on him. I heard his dislike for her in his tone. "She's an old *curandera*, good with herbs. She can deliver babies that live. She'll know more than me about what's going on in this village." He pointed to her house in the distance. "I hear confessions but she hears rumors." He turned and retreated to the cool gloom of his church.

I found Señora Martinez stooped in her herb garden. As I dismounted, I pulled a small bag from my possibles bag.

"*Hola*, can you help me, Señora?" I asked.

She studied me for a minute and motioned for me to join her on a wooden bench by her door.

"When I was a child, I had a nanny who cured with herbs." I handed her the little bag. "She learned healin' from her people back in Africa. Many's the time while I was growin' up she'd put that on my cuts." I watched her open the sack. "I doctored my own wounds with it to heal an' stop infection. Do you have any such mixture, Señora Martinez?"

She took a pinch of the healing powder, smelled it, and then touched a bit to her tongue.

I knew how to make the mixture, but could find the herbs by sight only. I did not know their names. Not to speak badly of Doc Tibits, but this powerful mixture had healed my wounded side quickly, when I finally came to and rubbed some of the powder on the cuts. I had used up most of my supply, needed more.

"I not know this. Where it come from?" She asked.

"I can show you a couple of the herbs in your garden." I offered.

She rose stiffly and we walked into her garden patch, wilted by a recent killing frost. I pointed out three of the five herbs I knew went into the mixture.

"There're two more plants I don't see here, Señora. One's the root of the moss you find in wet forests, on the dark side of dead oak trees. The other's the leaf that looks like poison ivy but isn't poison. I've picked the wrong one twice." The Señora looked at me to see if I was kidding her. I was not. We both chuckled.

"I have see the other plants before. How you to make this?" She was curious. Most good healers wanted to learn more to perfect their art. Or she was testing me.

After explaining the procedure I asked, "Could you make some for me? I'll pick it up in about a month." She nodded. I continued. "You're the one that helped the dyin' man a month or so ago from the gold robbery?"

"He shot." She held up three fingers. "I could do nothing. Even with this." She handed me back the pouch.

"What did he say before he died?" I hoped she would help.

"He dying, out of his head, you know?" She drew a circle in the air by her ear with a gnarled finger. "He say, 'Open ground, all at once, lightning, lightning.' Then he die." She paused, as if thinking, but did not add anything.

"Did he talk to anyone else?" I asked.

"No, Señor. It is all I know." She turned to go inside, then added, "Gracias. It is good cure you to give me. I have in one month. I pray you no need it." She crossed herself and stepped inside her *jacalita*.

With a couple of hours of daylight left, I decided to ride southeast from San Ysidro and scout around for grass and water for the herd and signs of the massacre for the governor. I did not find anything before dark, so I made camp away from the road.

After cooking for myself again it became clear why Pete took over the chore. At least my *jamoka* tasted black and strong. I sat back with a hot cup and thought about the robberies.

With the second massacre, the governor surely would turn all his attention to the problem. Maybe he would call in the army to handle it. I wasn't getting much done about it, but I discovered I was fascinated by the problem.

Who had the force to wipe out armed war parties? Where could such a force remain hidden? How did they know when the shipments were coming? How did they know where to intercept the shipments in time to attack? How did they remain unseen after the robberies? Was there some operator in Durango? What did the words, 'all at once, lightning, lightning,' mean?

*   *   *

The cold woke me. Frost covered me. I lighted my fire and waited in my blankets for hot coffee and the sun. The breeze let me know I'd slept down wind of something dead.

My thoughts turned to the dying guard's words, "Open ground."

The brush around here was not tall enough, was too sparse to hide a man on a horse.

There were no rock piles to hide behind. The land lay mostly flat, except for some arroyos and the mesas, the last fingers of the Jemez Mountains reaching out over the plateau. The mesas rose up too far north of the road for men to hide and then charge out to attack. There would be ample time for the attacked convoy to scatter or set up a defense.

The only way men could attack from open ground was to lay hiding behind bushes or low rocks with their horses hidden elsewhere. I had seen ambushers use trenches or covered pits, but those took time to dig.

Where was there an arroyo deep enough to hide horses and that cut through open ground covered by brush or rocks sufficient to hide ambushers? I flogged my memory to cover the ground around here. I could not think of such an arroyo, but I knew what I needed to look for in the terrain.

Coffee boiled. I hauled out of the warm blankets and started frying a hefty slab of the chuck wagon chicken I had taken from Cookie's larder. While I gulped scalding coffee and scratched at peeling scabs under my duster, I planned the day.

I was camped about halfway between Zia Pueblo and Santa Ana Pueblo, about four miles up ahead. After I looked around here some this morning, I would ride over to Santa Ana and ask around. Then I would check at Zia for information. I could scout grass and water on the way back to the herd.

I broke camp and rode to where the trail drops off one plateau and cuts down a steep grade to a lower plane. The view from the higher plateau stretched all the way to the Rio Grande Valley to the east. I could see the top of Sandia Mountain, behind Bernalillo to the southeast, and northeast to the Sangre de Cristo Mountains behind Santa Fe. Due north lay the buff and dried-blood-red mesas that started the rise into the Jemez Mountains and the Valle Grande.

About a half mile further on, an arroyo cut deep into the lower plane and drifted to the northeast to drain into the Jemez River. The land around lay flat. I was more than halfway from the high plateau to the arroyo when I found the fresh graves off to the side of the road.

It was the stink that rose off this burial ground that had bathed my bed last night. Whoever buried the bodies had hurried. A wagon sideboard, stuck in the ground, marked only one grave. "13 unknown," had been burned into the wood with a hot iron.

If the miners had been killed here, it made sense that the attacker's horses had been kept in the arroyo nearby. As I rode over to the gully to investigate, I thought about how I'd set up an attack.

The leader of the gold convoy would anticipate an ambush from the rocks along the trail down off the plateau. That was the only trail down. All the men in the convoy would have to ride down that way like through a funnel. The convoy leader, probably Ben Patterson, the banker, would send a scout first. Then he would send his men down one at a time, spread out. If nothing happened, he would assemble his men on the flat and move on, thankful for no surprises.

About the time the convoy reassembled, I'd attack it. I began to gain confidence in the theory I had contrived until I studied the natural places where the convoy might reassemble. There was no cover for an ambush and a charge out of the arroyo would give the convoy too much warning, plenty of time to set up a deadly defense.

I pulled up at the edge of the arroyo and searched for a place where horses could be held but not seen from the road or the plateau above. The location would have to be up the arroyo. I turned that way and started looking for a sign. The rain two nights ago had not helped me any.

A hundred yards from where the arroyo came closest to the road it cut deeply into the hill at the base of the higher plateau. There I hit pay dirt. Maybe fifteen horses, pawing the earth and stomping to discourage flies, had been held in a tight bunch out of sight in the hollow.

I memorized the distinguishable tracks including the boot prints of a medium-weight man. Both his flat heels were worn off on the outside, like he had walked a long way in those boots. I found a used-up Durham sack and ten *quirly* butts laying around. The wrangler had waited and smoked a considerable time.

There were no other signs in the hollow where the horses had been held. Back down the arroyo, south of where I had first struck it, I found the crumbled bank where the wrangler had led his herd up out of the arroyo.

I followed the trail and discovered where the bandits had assembled with the captured horses from the gold convoy. I guessed from the signs that this was where the robbers had packed the convoy horses and their own mounts with the gold and guns they had stolen.

Following the trail of a herd of forty horses ought to be easy. I cut a wide circle to pick up the trail but did not discover it. What I did find answered the question about how the robbers kept from being seen in a crowd, as Red had put it.

The best interpretation I could make, from the tracks that remained after the rain, was that the bandits had divided into five groups of three men each. Each group lead two horses carrying gold and three unburdened horses from the convoy. The five groups had then scattered in five different directions. That boogered my aim to follow the bandits.

The situation raised new questions. Would the five groups meet at some designated hideout? Or, were the five bands stashing the gold in five different places? The fact that the bandits split up, with each group carrying its own gold, indicated that the bandits were well-disciplined men and lead by an iron-fisted and crafty boss.

Or had the bandits divided the take and split up to make a run for it? If so, the governor, miners, and I had big troubles. The gold would be out of the territory by now, lost for good.

Abandoning the five escape trails, I rode back to the graves and searched the open area around the road. I figured the teamsters who had buried the Durango men had not moved the scavenger-ravaged bodies far from where they found them. I did not know what I was looking for, but I was mighty curious how the robbers surprised the convoy on open ground.

After half an hour of circling the area, I caught the slightest glint of sunlight off brass. A spent, 45-70 cartridge lay almost buried, next to a clump of low sage. I studied the clump. Something seemed different about it, but I could not puzzle it out.

Suddenly it struck me. The mound of sand that the wind normally blows from the southwest to settle on the northeast side of the clump lay on the southeast side. All the sage clumps around this one had sand piled by the wind on their northeast side.

Then I noticed a slight depression had been scooped in the sand, about the length of a body. The depression looked natural enough. I would have overlooked it if I had not noticed the cartridge and misplaced sand around the sagebrush.

The depression was no trench but was deep enough to conceal a man behind the natural looking sand heap and sage. The straight line of the depression pointed to the vicinity of the graves.

Careful searching revealed thirteen more hiding places laid out in a rough half circle around the location of the graves. The bandits had hidden on both sides of the road.

Each killer must have been assigned a single target, probably the man closest to him in the convoy. When the convoy reached a designated spot, or on some other signal, the ambushers must have fired all at once.

If the ambush had worked right, the men of the convoy would have been blown out of the saddle in one volley, two at the most. It would have been like being struck by lightning.

CHAPTER EIGHT

Too many men had died hauling and guarding gold. Durango had lost a sheriff, a mayor, a banker, a storekeeper, and a passel of miners that I knew about. Twenty-three men all told, killed for greed.

I had seen twenty thousand men killed at Gettysburg. Those men fought for a cause, for what they believed was right and just. The gold killings were different, murder for the sake of greed only. The thought made my guts churn.

I reasoned that, by now, the governor must have heard about the second holdup. He would send word to Durango to stop shipments until the bandits were caught. He had to do that much! I would advise him to order more lawmen into the field, maybe call in the army.

The bandits must be led by a seasoned, calculating military leader who knew how to use the terrain to his advantage. He must have learned his bloody art of ambush from the Apache. There were none better at it.

Any leader that could split his force and assemble it again had established stern discipline in the ranks, especially since each small group held substantial amounts of gold to tempt them. Gold had a powerful way of working on a man, made him itch to spend it, to be a big man in front of others. I wondered how long discipline would hold out over gold fever. I had to admire a leader with such discipline over his men.

A magician, the bandit leader could make his men disappear and reappear like magic. A genius at organization, he had created a very intricate scheme by which this all worked. The plan had to be complex and it must have taken time to set in place.

How did word of the shipments pass faster than the hard-riding convoy which left in secrecy? The ambushes took place more than a hundred and thirty miles from Durango. How could the point of intersection be known so accurately that there was time to dig in and conceal fourteen men for the ambush?

Who knew this country so well that the site of the ambush could have been picked so perfectly? There must have been men out scouting the area. They might have been seen, or left, some mark on the land.

Possibly the outlaws would not wait to strike a third time. They had taken a fortune in gold. It might be enough. Maybe the reason the band had split into five groups was to accomplish a getaway to the States, or Mexico. They might pick up the stashed gold from the prior holdup and ride out.

My guts told me otherwise. Their system worked too well. Why quit now? As far as I knew, I was the only one who knew anything about their numbers and how they struck. Yet I knew nothing about the rest of their operation or who I sought.

As I rode back to the herd, I became morose and angry. Why was I pursuing this gang anyway? There were thousands of square miles of territory the bandits could hide in. I had nothing to go on, really, and I stood alone, one man against fifteen, seasoned killers. This was a job for a posse or the army.

The fight with Bustos had made it clear how out of shape I was. I didn't want to be a warrior! I didn't think like a warrior anymore and didn't want to ever again. Hell, I just wanted to get back to Red's herd, my work.

I was angry because I knew that even if the outlaws were pulling out, I would have to follow and stop them. They could not be turned loose on the land. These men were cold-blooded animals, killer-mad. They had to be stopped, jailed, or killed. I had no idea who or where the killers were or how to stop them. But, I had been given the job.

I was confused because I rode for the VR brand and the governor. My job for Red right now was to find grass and water for the herd. Yet I felt compelled to get back to the governor, to convince him to order more men to help me stop the outlaws. Trouble was, I had no plan and nothing to go on but the way the bandits struck and what I guessed.

I rode towards the herd, but I could not stop thinking about the holdups. Perhaps I had an edge if the fifteen bandits had split up into groups of three. It would be easier to handle three men at a time rather than fifteen all at once. The truth was, I had no idea where to find even three of the outlaws.

What kept me thinking like I held a hand in this game? I wanted to work cattle and be let alone. I could turn my back on the whole she-bang. I might just tell the governor I had seen nothing when I saw him next time.

I topped a hill and saw the cattle camp. Red had held the herd two days northwest of San

Ysidro on the Rio Puerco. The cattle grazed on good grass and had plenty of water.

From the look of it, the boys had just finished branding and culling out stock less than three years old. Only a hundred head of stock had been cut from the herd. The cowboys had all been selective during the roundup. The cull would be driven south to winter on VR land.

I had missed the hard work, escaped the risk of being gored, stepped on, or kicked. Branding cattle was a battle. Two of our boys had lost fingers between the rope and the saddle horn from prior brandings.

As I rode up to the cooking fire I could see the boys were tired out. Fortunately, no one appeared to have been injured in this go-round. Before I headed out to ride night watch, I had a chance to talk to Red. I told him what I had seen and figured out.

"Cagey, mighty cagey," Red said. "What're you goin' to do?"

"Hell, Red, I've got no damned idea." Frustrated and angry, I rode away from him into the night. After a long day it was going to be a long watch, with too much time for thinking about a situation I felt powerless to do anything about.

*   *   *

Seemed like I had just rolled into my blankets after a cold night watch when somebody kicking my foot brought me around. I woke up to the glare of daylight and Red standing at my feet.

"VR sends cattle up to Jemez Pueblo every year. Sort of pays 'em back for the water we use. Keeps peace in the area." Red eyed me carefully to see if I was full awake. "Take ten head. Drive'em up'ere." He handed me a tin cup of hot, black coffee. "On your way back you can stop in at Zia and Santa Ana. Nose around a bit. Maybe the Indians seen somethin'." He walked off when I grunted assent.

Before I finished my coffee, the herd moved out. Cookie hadn't packed up the chuck wagon yet. A sour old man, but a fine cook, he stuffed some grub in a poke and handed it to me with a scowl. I promised him I would bring in fresh meat, if I saw game to shoot. My promise didn't change his mood any. My mood wasn't so good either.

I cut ten head, including a good bull, from the herd. The cattle, trail broke, did not want to leave the herd. They split and ran back, or balked, or stood head down shaking their hat rack, or pawed up a cloud of dust before they charged my horse. I had picked Rojo, a fine, roan cutting horse, from the *remuda,* and he earned his keep.

Finally we got the critters headed northeast, and settled into the trail to Jemez. It would take the day to get there, if I could keep the bunch moving along smartly.

I drove the cattle into the plaza of Jemez Pueblo late in the afternoon. The plaza was surrounded on three sides by low, adobe structures, except for a few two-story buildings with wooden ladders up the walls to the second floor. Everything was the color of the surrounding dirt. In fact, you could ride right by a pueblo and never see it, if you didn't know it was there. Long shadows etched the shapes of the buildings that otherwise blended with the earth they rose up from.

The plaza was empty. The whole pueblo looked deserted. Yet I knew the Indians were there. Smoke from cooking fires hung in the cool, calm air, though none rose from a chimney. A dog lazed in the last of the sunlight. Dogs followed their masters.

Perhaps the people were out somewhere preparing for a religious ceremony. I'd been told the pueblos in the area still held pagan dances, even though they went to the Catholic Church on Sunday. I wondered where the padre was.

I called out a few times. The only answer I got was a bark from the lazy dog. Leaving the cattle standing would be unwise so I called for assistance again. Finally an Indian appeared and headed towards me.

As he drew near I recognized the old Indian who had taken the wounded boy from me the night I brought him in. The old Indian recognized me, signed for me to wait, and then left. Pretty soon he returned with the padre I had talked to that night a month or so back.

Both men appeared nervous, distracted, in a hurry to get rid of me. The padre looked especially haggard and bent over, though he was a tall man. I told him the cattle were a gift from the VR for the pueblo.

The padre translated into the Jemez tongue. The old Indian thanked the VR in return. I knew he recognized me, but there was no mention of our prior meeting or the well being of the wounded boy. Both men made it clear the meeting was over by turning their backs to me and walking off briskly.

Looking back over my horse's rump as I rode out of the pueblo, I saw the plaza lay deserted again except for ten head of cattle just standing there, forsaken. It seemed mighty strange, this meeting.

I got to thinking about the meeting as I made camp among tall cottonwoods by the Jemez

River. The last time I had been in the pueblo, I had been told I would be welcomed back as a hero for hauling in the boy who would have died if I had not found him. This time the old Indian had not even been polite enough to tell me if the wounded man lived or died. The padre and the old man had made it clear by their actions that there was no room for small talk. I had left with a mouth full of questions. Didn't get one of them spit out.

Pueblo Indians may not be partial to Anglos, but I had brought gifts and had been rudely snubbed. Maybe I had interrupted some high spiritual doings. Maybe there was a sickness going around.

My feelings weren't hurt, but it had been a strange meeting for one that could have had some ceremony to it. I thought ten head of cattle, a handsome gift, deserved some celebration over. I had hoped to get to know some of my Jemez neighbors.

I remembered the pouch the old Indian had given me. It was still in my saddlebag. As I dug it out, I found the book I had pulled off the shelf to read on the way to Santa Fe. I had never opened it. Maybe I could start reading it tonight.

I put the book and the pouch on a rock by the campfire and started rustling something to eat. Cookie had wrapped boiled beef in a cloth for me, along with bone hard biscuits and an air tight of beans. I wished I had some of Pete's chili.

I leaned back against an old cottonwood with my feet to the fire. Relaxing, I drank strong hot coffee. For the first time I noticed I was not sore from the day's work. My left side did not hurt at all. Tomorrow, in the light, I would go after the last of the stitches in the V scab.

Maybe tomorrow I would try my gun belt without the iron strip in it, test how the hip felt under the belt. I had not had a chance to practice with the Colt when I was around the big herd. Tomorrow I would work on the fast draw some more.

As I pressed the heel of my hand against my hip to test for soreness, Ann came to mind. I wondered how she was doing. Was the general store hers now? Could she survive in Durango without a husband to protect her?

Ann was a fine-looking woman, smart, able, strong. I rejected the idea that she would have to turn to whoring to survive. Most likely she would sell the store, pack up and head east, back to relatives. I hoped her husband had been proprietor.

Thinking of Ann left a yearning in me. What would it be like to have a wife like her, to build a home, have children? I shut out the idea, cut the feeling off short. I was a cowboy, meant to land in a shallow grave and turn to wolf meat by some lonely trail.

I got up and dug a horehound crystal candy out of my saddlebag. I would have to figure out an excuse to get back up to Durango soon.

Picking up the pouch the old Indian had given me, I settled against the tree and stretched my feet to the fire again. The evening seemed to be turning a little colder.

A stick burned through, snapped, rolled in the fire, and broke free a fresh flame to skip over the coals. Dora Luz Sanchez danced into my mind. Now there was a high-spirited lady. I had only seen her once. Still she had a powerful effect on me. She would be one to tangle with. She had fire in her, hot Spanish blood. I got that hollow feeling in my chest when I thought about her.

Dora Luz could run a household of servants and have time to entertain guests. She could arrange parties and evenings with music. She was born to wealth, thrived in that life. She reminded me of the life I had once led when the South bloomed in its glory.

Sadness filled me suddenly. I would never have that life again. I wasn't about to get rich on cowboy wages. Dora Luz lay out of my reach. Besides, I had killed her brother. She probably hated me, if she thought of me at all.

Restless, I poked at the fire, then walked out to check the hobbles on my horse. Rojo pricked his ears forward, didn't seem to mind the company either.

The wind gusted up. The air smelled dusty, and wet with moisture. Low clouds blew quickly across the stars from the southwest and obscured half the sky. As my eyes adjusted to the darkness, away from the fire, I saw lonely cottonwoods reach away from the cold wind. Dried leaves rattled, some fell and blew into the deep shadows.

I gave Rojo the rest of the horehound crystal. He knew what sugar was. Picking up dead wood I returned to my fire. Standing by it alone in the night, I packed my pipe, lit it, and poured another cup of coffee. Maybe lonely was what I'd call how I felt.

Wrapping a blanket around my shoulders, I sat down by the fire. The tobacco and coffee comforted me some. The book lay by the fire, but I picked up the Indian pouch instead.

The pouch was made of leather, all one piece with no seams. I had seen bags like that before. Cowboys made tobacco pouches out of tanned scrotum. I always felt sorry for the steer that made the donation.

The pouch, old and soft, had Indian signs painted on it. Drawstrings with silver beads on the ends, about the size of double-ought buckshot, sealed the puckered mouth.

As I opened the pouch, a puff of yellow smoke escaped. The pouch was filled with pollen. The Indians used pollen in their holy ceremonies. I held a medicine bag.

More carefully, I studied the symbols. A faded, black circle divided into quarters by a yellow cross in the center. A brown snake, the color of dried blood, cut across the circle. Four small dots ringed the serpent's head, which extended outside the circle. I had seen similar zigzag serpents in petroglyphs over in Chaco Canyon, where the ruin of a huge pueblo lay.

In the cliffs around the ruin I had found hundreds of symbols cut in the stone. I had wondered what the stone carver meant to say. What had caused him to spend all that time chipping rock? Was it art he meant, or some important messages? I wondered the same thing about the symbols I held in my hand.

Six stone fetishes nested inside the medicine bag. Each was as big as a silver dollar. The first fetish was a flint bear with a turquoise bead tied to its back with sinew. Next was a buffalo, chipped out of white stone. The third fetish was an eagle made from clear black obsidian. I could see through it when I held it up to the fire.

I could not make out the fourth fetish, maybe a rodent, a mouse made from marbled river rock. The fifth fetish was a turtle made from sky-blue turquoise. The last spirit creature dazzled my eye when I blew the pollen from it. The stone caught the firelight and sparkled like a star-filled sky. Formed in mica, the shape of coyote emerged.

I had been carrying powerful medicine and did not know it. These were the possessions of a shaman, a medicine man, a wise elder. From what I had picked up about Indian beliefs over the last couple of years, I guessed I was holding the fetishes that represent the cardinal directions in a medicine wheel, used for healing ceremonies and creating the balance of a good life.

I set my pipe down on the book by the fire. If I remembered right, the color white and the buffalo were the symbols of the North. Blue or turquoise stood for the South. I had been given a powerful and valuable gift. Why had I been shunned at Jemez today?

Fascinated by the obsidian eagle I held it to the firelight again. Fetishes were supposed to give their owner the powers of the animal they represented. I wondered what powers the eagle could give me.

Eagles dominated their territory. They flew above the rest of the animals. Their eyesight was most keen. Flying above, they saw everything below and knew what was going on all around. When eagle struck, it was from above, sudden, deadly. Thinking on it, I could understand the eagle's attributes were valuable.

The mica fetish glinted, caught my eye. It had to represent coyote and not wolf. There was too much sparkle in the piece to be the gray killer wolf. Also, a small fleck of yellow, garnet maybe, had been placed for an eye and gave the fetish a mischievous character.

The way the old Navajo I knew told the story, Coyote was the prankster, the bothersome kind that plagues people's lives. He played practical jokes just to find out what would happen. He always circled out away from people, but sooner or later could not resist his curiosity and came in close to see what was happening and cause trouble with his questions. I put the fetish back in the bag.

I picked up the bear fetish again. Bear appeared to be slow in movement, but really was quick, powerful, and wise. Not much bothered bear as he went about his own business, guarded his own territory. He hibernated most of his life.

Bear reminded me of my love for warm blankets. Bear wisdom told me morning would come soon and I ought to prepare my morning kindling and get in my blankets now.

I put the medicine bag and the fetishes next to the book by the fire. The book, small, leather bound, struck me as a kind of medicine pouch full of paper fetishes that were meant to impart wisdom. The thought made me chuckle. Animal fetishes and *Plutarch's Lives*, both crafted by storytellers not so different from each other in their intentions. Before me lay two ancient paths to the good life.

I picked up the book, opened it to the middle, and turned the page to catch the firelight. "Timoleon," I read at the top. Down the page, "Great general...began to find his eyes fail, and awhile after became perfectly blind. Not that he had done anything himself which might occasion this defect, or was deprived of his sight by any outrage of fortune; it seems rather to have been some inbred and hereditary weakness..."

I shut the book, put it down because I did not want to contemplate tragedy. Tragedy, some inborn weakness later triggered by time or some event. For Timoleon, the tragedy was blindness, driven by the necessity of heredity. Necessity in its turn was the child of immutable fate, or some whimsical God. Ah, Greek logic. It shaped the Romans and infected us yet today.

In the romantic way I had contemplated the world before the war, the Greek logic of tragedy might have explained my fall into poverty and the end of my family bloodline. Fate made us choose the wrong cause and fight against a force we could neither defeat nor deflect. Or a whimsical God directed the war's progress and chose us as the losers because of some weakness in our character.

In truth, now, I didn't believe in either fate or God. There was just too much malice, mischance, accident, sometimes luck, in the world to believe in fate. As for God? The horror and devastation of the war disproved God's existence. I could not conceive of a God great enough, broad-shouldered enough to handle all the blame for such a bloody waste of life, such sorrow, devastation.

Yet, in a way, I was a tragic figure fallen past the glorious times in my life. By fate or by God I was a beaten man because of my choices and actions and because of the war. I was wounded, weak and in trouble because of my fondness for women. I had no identity, other than a cowhand lost under countless stars. My courage had turned to cowardice and I ran from troubles. I had no real desires to improve myself, no future to strive for, and no character. I had bad dreams and no imagination or vision to guide me. I lived day to day, did my job like my horse, Rojo, hobbled over there.

Hell, I could blame this existence on some capricious God or fate if I thought like a university sophomore. But I wasn't that green, rich kid anymore. Bullets, blades and blood had hardened me, proved that what happened to me rested squarely on my shoulders, not fate's, not God's. I had made myself who I am.

I knocked ash out of my pipe and reloaded it. The wind, gusting hard, working to blow in trouble from the southwest, howled lonely in the trees and blew out my match. I set the pipe aside and pulled my blanket tight around me. I sat staring into the fire and let only the movement of flames occupy my mind.

The coals formed a bear's snout and beady, glowing eyes. Bears were wise. They slept a lot and tended to their own business. I picked up the bear fetish. That was me all right. Come to ponder it, I had gone to sleep after the war to forget the killing and destruction, my defeats and weaknesses.

Four years! No, the war had actually wasted eight years of my life; four fighting to stay alive, four sleeping, dead to life. Eight years gone by like I was hibernating. I had nothing to show for the lost time. I was just a cowboy, hunkered down by another lonely fire. A man still licking his war wounds.

I picked up the eagle fetish in my other hand. Eagle could see clearly over vast distances. Because he could see what was going on all around, he could plan. Keen vision into the distance was the eagle's attribute.

Vision! Able to see into the distance. Vision, able to see into time, past and future! The revelation hit me like Bustos' left hook when it shot light into my brain. Vision, the ability to make pictures in my head.

The horror of the war had beaten vision out of me. Defeated, I had lost courage. Without courage I did not have the guts to deal with the visual memories of the war. To keep from going mad, I had forced myself to stop seeing those visions. I had not been smart enough, wise enough to save my ability to envision the future and had killed that skill when I blinded myself to my past.

I had hibernated to escape my visual memory, content to work hard as a cowboy with no future, just living in the present. Hard as I tried now, I could not imagine into the future much beyond the cattle contract date on December first. I had lost the skill to envision like I had lost the skills to fight. Without vision it was impossible to have future dreams, desires, goals, wants and therefore, successes.

A strong energy with the feel of lightning just before it strikes close by, prickled down my back, caused me to break a cold sweat. Some power seemed to come from the fetishes into my hands up my arms into my chest to circle my heart. Indian magic!

I dropped the fetishes like they were red-hot coals and clasped my hands together as if to choke away the magic. Instead of relief, revelation struck harder at my heart.

I could no longer hibernate to cut off my past and thereby sacrifice my future. I had to take what I'd learned from the past and mold my future with it. I understood clearly, head, heart and guts, that I could no longer just live day to day. I would die having never built a new identity. Or I would end my days working for other men who would use me up to fulfill their own dreams.

I must build a future for myself by dreaming about it, envisioning it in my imagination. I must dream the vision of my future until I felt compelled by it. Then the vision would draw me, guide me into the future towards its own fulfillment.

The revelation overpowered me. I jumped up and shook my body, like a stallion just rolled in the dust. In my mind's eye, I looked into a vast distance, my future spread before me. The image of Eli Waller was nowhere in that vision. I had to exhume myself from the past I had buried and fill the future with the dreams of the man I wanted to become. I felt compelled to move toward the future, not run away from the past.

I shivered all over, not from cold, not from fear. I felt excitement bring my chin up, squint my eyes, sharpen my eyesight. I felt curiosity quicken my mind and pulse. I felt power fill my muscles, settle my guts, untie the knot between my shoulder blades.

I piled wood on my campfire, stripped off my clothes, and went to the stream to plunge in. The cold water shocked me again. It seemed like layers of caked mud washed off me. I ran back to the fire and wrapped in my blanket.

As if I had just taken a deep breath after the wind was knocked out of me, I felt alive, expectant. I knew I had just escaped from my past into a new life. I had regained all my senses. I had vision again, and it felt like someone had just taken a blindfold off my imagination. I felt whole, complete, and powerful for the first time since the *Croft* had gone down. My backbone straightened as if relieved of the weight of a bale of cotton.

I stood looking into my future, a totally strange terrain. What do I want? Who do I want to become? The questions conjured no pictures yet, but I felt I stared opportunity in the eyes. I was no longer blind like Timoleon.

Who am I then? What do I have to work with? I am healthy again. I have skills, experience, education and training to draw upon. I am well armed, getting fast with a gun. Deputy Marshal. New Mexican, loving this arid part of the world. Outside of some tough jobs to finish, I am set up better than most for making a success of myself.

I heaved a great sigh and became aware of the cold of the night. Shucking my blanket, I dressed. A good night's sleep, and, in the morning? Involuntarily, I took a step forward. I left a broken-down, split-apart, troubled cowboy standing behind me.

Here, it felt good to be whole again, to have a future, to have something to lose.

CHAPTER NINE

Whatever weather the wind had blown in last night, it blew out by morning. There didn't seem to be any air, it was so still and clear. Looking into the sky was like staring down into deep, Bahamas water. You never saw that blue sky in the East. Even in my journeys around the West, all the way up to Montana, the sky was never this blue. It was warm for early morning. The day would be hot for this time of year. New Mexico was unpredictable like that.

I had broken camp, packed, and my horse stood ready to go. But this was as good a time and place as any for some gun practice. The cottonwood trees offered knobs and holes to shoot at. No one else was around.

I took a minute to modify my bullet belt by taking off the metal strip. Trying on the rig, I slipped my long knife under the belt where the deep cut lay. The knife sheath spread the weight and kept the edge of the belt from digging into my scabs on the left side. Moving and twisting my body uncovered little irritation. I cinched the belt up tight.

Striding over to the fattest cottonwood, I took off my army suspenders, the ones Dobbs sold me, and hung them on a head-high branch. I walked away and just left the galluses and the memory of a wounded cowboy, with his pistol in his pocket, hanging over there. I was done with that po'boy.

Drawing the Colt a few times for feel, I didn't fire. Palm, clear, level. I increased the speed. Turning to a cottonwood about fifty feet away, I picked a knothole heart high, drew and fired. I moved quickly, but concentrated on the feeling of the action. My shot was two inches low. I stepped to another position, drew and fired a little faster. The bullet struck an inch to the right. Moving before each shot, I fired ten more times.

My speed and accuracy improved. I could cover the pattern of the last six shots with a playing card. So, I had the movement and the accuracy. It was time to go for quickness.

Changing position in relation to the target, I drew for speed. I holstered the Colt, drew, and fired several times. I had nothing to compare my speed to, but I felt I had become faster than Moore, the Sheriff of Santa Fe. I was surprised at how fast I could get the gun into action.

The second rule of gunplay commanded that if your first shot didn't kill, you had better be there with your second shot. It was time to add the second shot to the flow of my draw.

My first shot came from low, down by my hip, just as the muzzle cleared leather. I did not waste time and motion bringing the gun up to eye level to aim, like I had learned to shoot a dueling pistol. I could shoot accurately from the hip now. It was time to add the second shot to the procedure; palm, clear, shoot, cock on the recoil, aim, shoot. I tried it, slowly.

I added a side step to the rhythm to avoid being an easy target. Palm, clear, shoot, cock while sidestepping, aim, shoot. The motions felt natural. I practiced maybe twenty times at a slow tempo, like dancing.

Then I upped the tempo of the dance as fast as possible, all the way through two shots. Both bullets struck close in my target. It felt like luck had guided my shots. I tried the whole routine again. Two more shots, on target less than an inch apart.

Patricio Sanchez would have to be hell-on-wheels to match my two shots. I would be a moving target. He might get a bullet in me, but I would have two quick ones in his heart.

I decided not to file down the Colt's trigger pressure. The two-pound pull gave me extra weight to balance the gun. I could use all four fingers to grip and aim without fear of firing too soon.

The old Navy cap and ball had never been brought into action this fast. Its touchy trigger was part of a different equation. With the new Colt, I had much more control, much more speed.

Using the white rag Cookie had tied the beef in, I cleaned and polished the Colt. I loaded the pistol and the twelve bullet loops in my belt. Then I inspected my homemade holster. It had formed to my body and did all I required of it. Finally, I checked the loads in the Winchester.

If Patricio didn't shoot me in the night or from the back, I would give him a battle. And I meant to. Satisfied, I stepped into the saddle and turned my mount towards Zia Pueblo.

As I rode I thought about last night and staring into the fire. I remembered the feel of the powerful magic in the medicine bag and fetishes. I still felt light and free of the horrible parts of my past. I felt healthy and whole. My future seemed bright and open before me. My spirits were up high, soaring overhead like an eagle.

I thought of the coyote fetish. If he was the troublemaker, I would be coyote. I had some personal business to attend to that would take being troublesome. It was time to go after Patricio and get this thing over with. If I could find a way of resolving his revenge without bloodshed, I would use it. But if it took another killing, it would be him that died.

Just as soon as the cattle drive got to Corrales, I would take time off and head up to Santa Fe. The governor needed a report. After that I would hunt Patricio. Maybe then I could finish a Rivas beer in peace at Maria's.

If the other two Sanchez brothers wanted in on the action, let them come. I felt the need to handle unfinished business so I could get on with what I wanted to do.

Last night, pondering my future before falling asleep, I had decided that I wanted to build a fortune here in New Mexico. I wanted a ranch of my own. There were plenty of wild cattle to round up. With work I could start a herd. Pete Montoya might consider partnering up with me.

I could use the pay coming to me after the roundup to buy cows and a good bull from the VR. There was land open for the taking just north of Mount Taylor, maybe over by Cabezon Peak.

I had pondered returning to Virginia where Johnny had tried to reclaim and gather our land and properties. He had wanted to get the farms and lumber business going again. His knowledge of shipping had been as astute as our father's. Johnny was dead. I didn't want to pick up what he left in Virginia. I was New Mexican now.

I had changed my mind and now thought there was merit in considering the salvage of the gold on the *Croft* in Chesapeake Bay. Maybe I could buy the VR or the Valle Grande. Hell, with that much gold I could buy half the Territory of New Mexico.

After the ranch became established, I might consider politics. I realized I was a United States citizen, but I still had not come around to the federal interpretation of the Constitution. I would work to keep the territory from becoming a state for as long as possible.

New Mexico might retain some autonomy for a while, as a backwash territory. Except in the narrow, fertile valley of the Rio Grande, this arid land did not attract farmers like those migrating to the prairies. This was good cattle country. I liked the idea of becoming a cattle baron and Senator.

I set my dreaming aside as I approached Zia Pueblo. The place didn't feel right. No Indians worked in the fields. No one gathered or cut firewood. As I rode into the plaza, one sickly dog barked a couple of times then slunk off. This pueblo was deserted.

I rode over to the old mission church and went inside. I could not find the priest, but I was not sure there was one at Zia anymore. The Indians of Zia held different spiritual beliefs from Jemez or Santa Ana Indians. That was why the Pueblo Indians lived apart instead of joining together for their common good.

A different spirit clan dominated each pueblo. There were differences in the languages. Still, it seemed strange that Zia and Jemez would be having secret ceremonies at the same time.

Maybe, the Pueblos were carrying on some ceremonial together with a third Pueblo and every one had gone there. I was not familiar with the Indians' ways yet. That was the only explanation I could come up with for why the Jemez and Zia were deserted.

*   *   *

When I arrived at Santa Ana, I had the same experience as in Jemez and Zia. No one came out of the pueblo buildings. I couldn't find a priest or any one else. The fields lay deserted. I felt like I had discovered ruins like those at Chaco Canyon, only Jemez, Santa Ana and Zia were freshly abandoned.

I quirted Rojo into a gallop out of the pueblo. I left with a spooky feeling haunting me. I was new to the territory, but three empty villages just didn't seem right.

I had delivered the ten head of cattle to Jemez for Red, but there had been nothing in it for me that would explain the gold robberies and murders. I had no explanation for the deserted pueblos. This trip was about as bad a bust as the trip up to Durango.

I laid in a course that would intercept the cattle drive and prodded the roan horse on a beeline for it. I would probably ride up to Cookie's fire after dark.

I worried over what I had seen, or rather had not seen, at the pueblos. The farms around the pueblos looked untended. Livestock grazed in cornfields that should have been harvested by now, but were not. I had smelled the smoke of cooking fires, but had not seen smoke rising from chimneys.

I would have to find somebody who knew the Pueblo Indian ways. Maybe they could tell me if what I observed was natural this time of year, or unnatural as hell, which was what I suspected.

Late afternoon I halted, started a small fire for coffee. As I reached for some twigs to feed the fire I found a flint arrowhead. I found them from time to time. This point, a couple inches long, was unbroken obsidian and showed fine workmanship.

Most likely, an ancient hunter had made his shot, but it had not killed instantly. His prey had run off to die unfound or had shaken the arrow out as it fled. Holding the arrow tip gave me a feeling of brotherhood with the ancient hunter who had roamed this land, maybe hundreds of years ago. It gave me a profound sense of history.

I wondered why the arrowheads I found always seemed to float up on top of the dirt. Seemed blowing sand would have hidden them all by now. Maybe the rain had undone the sand's work. I dropped the arrow point into my duster pocket and remembered the fresh meat I had promised to hunt for Cookie and the crew.

Taking the field glasses, I walked over to the rise to scout for antelope. Just before the crest of the rise I walked onto a dim trace. I stopped dead still looking at a track I knew. Studying the trail, I became sure that what I had found was the trail of three of the bandits.

The tracks were old enough to have been made around the time of the second ambush. It had rained since, but identifiable tracks had survived. There appeared to be eight horses, all shod. Three were not carrying a load. That could mean three riders and two horses carrying packs of gold.

Drinking coffee from my coffeepot as I rode, I followed the trail some distance. Where the group had stopped I found a clear track. One horse had pissed and another had stepped in the mud. The adobe print belonged to one of the gold convoy horses.

I sat in the saddle thinking things over. The trail ran from the direction of the ambush and headed in the direction of Jemez. Had the outlaws headed to the pueblo to trade the extra horses for food? Were they hiding out somewhere north of the pueblo?

I knew I had to get back to the herd. This trail was old and I had to leave it. Yet it kept me puzzling. Then I remembered the two men that had shot the Jemez Indian boy I had found up at the hot spring. I thought he had said there were two men that shot him and left him for dead. Were they two of the three men that made this trail? Or, were these the tracks of three more men?

Were two of the five groups of bandits hiding out in this area? When I had found the five trails leading away from the ambush, I had noted their headings, the directions they had taken from the killing ground. I mapped it again in my mind. Two of the trails had headed in the directions of the pueblos. This trail was heading for Jemez.

It seemed unlikely that there was any connection between the pueblos and the outlaws. The Indians were peace-loving people. I reckoned the direction of the trails towards the pueblos was coincidence. Still, I felt sure that one, or perhaps two, of the bandit groups were operating in this area.

Come to think of it, there was a small settlement north of Jemez Pueblo, Vallecitos, where five or six Mexican families lived. They ran sheep in the high country above there. I remembered seeing a couple of vacant adobes the last time I drove cattle out of that valley. Vallecitos might be a likely spot for outlaws to hide out.

The settlement lay at the end of a rough trail up a narrow canyon. No one would be coming or going but the locals.

I dallied a moment longer, trying to make up my mind to investigate Vallecitos and check out a theory or get back to the herd. Sensing my indecision, Rojo pranced, anxious to get going one way or the other. I turned his head towards Vallecitos and gave him the boot.

Red expected me back, but he'd told me to have a look around. There would be enough moonlight tonight to ride to Vallecitos and back to the herd by late tomorrow afternoon. I had left the herd trailing just fine and it could do without me for another day.

I added another thirty miles to my trip, but I felt urgency. I had a job to do for the governor and every day that went by made the job tougher. The theory I chased might be a wild hair, but I felt like I had to prove it out. I watched the ground for shod horse tracks as I rode.

Jemez pueblo still appeared to be deserted when I rode by headed for Vallecitos. Dark and cold outside, the Indians might be inside by their fires.

The moon cast enough light to allow me to keep pushing on towards Vallecitos. But it was too dark to track. I had no idea if I was still on the trail of the three outlaws. Now I road the trail of a hunch only.

The people of Vallecitos descended directly from the earliest Spanish conquistadors. Their ancestors had settled in these hills, maybe two hundred years ago, to farm and herd sheep. They had remained cut off from their Spanish heritage and had developed their own beliefs and culture.

Hard mountain people, they spoke little English, and would not take kindly to a stranger riding in at night. If the outlaws were there, riding into the valley would be foolhardy.

Moonlight sparkled off the creek that flowed out of the Vallecitos canyon into the Jemez River. Half a mile up stream the creek cut between two cliffs, the entrance to Vallecitos Valley. The terrain formed a natural barrier protecting the south end of the valley.

The cliffs were a perfect spot for a lookout, or an ambush, for that matter. I pulled up and camped outside the barrier and a couple hundred yards away from the stream.

I woke before dawn, cold and hungry. A fire was too risky. Taking the Winchester I scouted the barrier cliffs on foot and found the natural fort unguarded.

At first light I rode into the valley. Surrounded by high mountains, Vallecitos lay hidden and protected from the rest of the world. I saw the settlement about a half-mile ahead. I searched for tracks as I rode. There were none I recognized. I scouted off the trail in a circling pattern, like I was hunting for cattle. Cattle were my excuse for being in the valley.

I passed an abandoned house with the roof caved in. The rotten beams jabbed into the guts of the old adobe. The land around the ruin had been divided into narrow, carefully tended, irrigated fields. Perhaps a grandfather had died and his sons divided the land, in *partido,* I think they called it, each inherited parcel abutting the water source.

Up ahead I saw a farmer burning brush by the stream. I rode up to the warmth of his blaze. Touching the brim of my hat, I jerked my chin up in greeting, but stayed in the saddle. "*Yo buscando por las vacas.*" I was unsure of my Spanish, grinned like a kid to prove it. "*Estoy del rancho VR.*"

"My English she so-so. You in the wrong place, *qué no*? You come ver' long way for nothing." He leaned on an old, wooden shovel. An ax rested in the brush close at hand. His clothes were tattered, but he had a proud manner. "We eat the last cow from the VR some time pass." He laughed. "I owe you *una comida, qué no?*"

I stepped down, pulled out my coffeepot, and approached the burning heap. He watched with some interest. Then he turned and walked to a bundle on the ground. He pulled out a blue glazed tin cup and returned to the fire to wait silently for the coffee to boil.

*   *   *

The coffee made me feel better. "Amigo, I'm also lookin' for three Anglos. Have you seen three Anglos around here?"

He blew on his coffee, passed the hot cup from hand to hand. "You got the sugar?" He jerked his chin towards Rojo.

I fetched the old boy a horehound crystal. "*Tres hombres*, Amigo?"

"No. I am for sure. Like you, *Pistolero*, they are not welcome." He fell into silence with his cup of coffee.

I respected the old coot for his polite way of running me off after taking coffee from me. I finished my cup and rode out of Vallecitos.

Thirty, extra, damn miles to prove a hunch. It hadn't paid off. If the outlaws had not come this far north of Jemez, where had they gone?

I rode into the plaza at Jemez Pueblo and dismounted. I needed answers and I did not know when I would be back this way. If I interrupted some ceremony, the Indians would have to forgive an unknowing Anglo. If sickness infected the place, I had to run the risk. I meant to find out why the pueblo was deserted, maybe where the outlaws were hiding out?

I walked over to the door the old Indian had come from. I knocked. There was no answer. I tried another door. No answer. I was about to knock on another door when the padre appeared on the other side of the plaza.

He walked slowly, shuffling, head down. The hood of his monk's robe hid his face. I started towards him, wondered if he was ill.

"What's goin' on, Padre? I called to him as I strode across the plaza. "Where're the people?" The padre did not answer. "Are you sick?"

The padre lifted his head and exposed a bearded face. As he did so, he pulled a pistol from beneath his robe.

My Colt bucked in my hand by my hip as his gun came level and blasted fire. I danced left, winced at a sharp sting on my neck and fired again.

The padre's body jerked right. He fired a second shot into the air as he toppled over on his side.

I dropped to the dirt, rolled behind a *horno*, searched the rooflines, the doors. A second shooter could be anywhere.

My skin crawled as I imagined the smack of lead striking me from behind. I spun around, searched behind. I turned again to the padre.

I searched for movement, color, or an unlikely shape. I listened, but heard only the ringing in my ears from the thunder of the guns. The pueblo was as dead as the padre over there.

Then I felt the warm trickle under my collar. Bloody fingers came away from the inspection of the welt on my neck. Afraid to holster my gun yet, I fumbled with my left hand and teeth to tie my bandanna over the neck wound while I searched.

After more searching, I became convinced I was the only living thing in the pueblo. I gave up the protection of the *horno* and crawled over to the padre's body on the side, away from his gun hand.

This bearded man was not the padre I had met here before. I had killed a stranger who aimed to kill me. I wanted to know why he tried.

Seeking answers, I skulked over to the adobe the old Indian had come out of when I delivered the cattle. Gun in hand, I kicked the door back and bolted inside. The room smelled of sweat, smoke, grease, hides, but was empty of people. The coals in the fireplace felt cold to my fingers.

I barged through the door of the next home and found no one. I searched all the adobes around the plaza. All were empty, no fires on the hearths. Where could some two hundred men, women, and children be?

I ran across the plaza to the mission, the only place big enough to hold all the people. Standing to the side, I pushed the door open. I called for the real padre. Echoes from an empty hall were the answer.

I hustled back to the dead man and searched his pockets. Besides a pocket knife, I found nothing unusual, nothing that identified him. Then I found a pouch of gold nuggets stuffed behind his belt. I took it.

If this was gold from the Durango mines, the assay office up there might identify it. I doubted that the dead man was one of the bandits. They ran in bunches of three. No one had backed this man up in the shooting spree. The dead padre was apparently alone. I could not explain his attempt to kill me.

Unable to find anyone to answer my questions, I could do no more in Jemez so I rode out.

I had to get back to the herd and tell Red that I was going on over to Santa Fe. Something or somebody had wiped out a whole pueblo of Indians, maybe three pueblos. I did not know if the disappearance of the Indians had anything to do with the bandits. But I had stumbled into something big that I did not understand, and the governor needed to know about it.

As I burned the breeze down the road out of Jemez, I felt uneasy, like I was being watched. The feeling hunched my shoulders as if to shirk off a bullet between the shoulder blades.

If I had killed one of the bandits, disguised as a padre, the others would follow to kill me. They could not afford to let me get away. They had too much at stake. If I had killed the padre of the pueblo, the Indians might chase me and seek revenge.

I prodded Rojo hard and rode fast with unsettling thoughts. The outlaws knew how to get ahead of the convoys and ambush them. I could not for the life of me figure out how they could do it. But they had. I felt like the prime target for another of their ambushes.

CHAPTER TEN

"Red, I can't figure it out." I snapped twigs off a stick and flicked them into the fire. "All three pueblos're shut down. A gent dressed up like the padre at Jemez tries to gun me down, damn near kills me. And there's a band of fifteen outlaws roamin' around in groups of three." I hurled the rest of the stick at the fire. "What t'hell's goin' on?" I pushed my hat back and scratched my head.

Red spliced a new rein to a bit. "You got the midnight watch, Eli. It'll give you time t' think. Let me know in the mornin' what you plan to do." He left me squatting by the fire.

I ought to get some sleep, but I was too wound up to relax. Cookie always kept Arbuckle's brewing wherever there was a fire. I poured a cup and walked out by the *remuda* to pester myself with more questions.

I smelled rain on the breath of the breeze as it glided past. I looked over my right shoulder at the thunderclouds building in the southwest. The day had been warm, had felt like late summer instead of mid-fall. The breeze picked up a bit, but not so much as to blow dust.

The horses stomped restlessly, milled around, took bites at each other. The big dun stallion, Buckskin was his given name, thought he ran the place tonight. He took a kick at Rojo as the roan was about to settle and roll off the sweat I had raised on him. The rest of the horses shied. The roan bolted and bucked.

I decided I would take Buckskin out tonight if he hadn't been picked. I'd work the spunkiness out of him.

Pete Montoya walked over, dropped his *quirly* in the dust, ground it under the toe of his boot. His eyes rounded up the *remuda*. "The horses are ver' restless. Perhaps they feel a storm coming." He turned his eyes on me. "It is the storm that makes you restless, Amigo?"

"Pete, when I get this job for the governor done and we've delivered the herd, why don't you and me split off from the VR, partner up, start us a ranch?" When Pete's face did not light up like I had hoped it would I added, "We could stake a claim down on the Animas between Cabezon and Mount Taylor. A little hard work and we could build us a future. It'd beat workin' for cowboy wages." I waited for his answer.

"To leave the VR... you think you have a future? Amigo, look around you." He swept a circle in the air above his head like he was about to throw a loop at a calf. "There are a thousand cattle here. Any one of them can kill you between here and Corrales. The bandits will kill you, if you find them. Patricio Sanchez will kill you if he finds you. I think you have no future." Then Pete flashed a broad grin. "But if you survive all these dangers, I will consider a partner."

Pete stuffed his hands in his pockets and watched silently as the storm clouds climbed the heavens. After a while he pointed at the clouds with his chin and said, "Like the sky, you have your hands full, Amigo. Can I help?"

"You handle the drive, *Guason*. I have to handle this myself. We'll see if I need an extra ace. You think the drive can do without me for a few days?"

"What is the difference? The cattle they do not know your voice, your face. How can they miss you? Run off and be the hero, if you live." Pete's sarcastic tone was tinged with concern. He was a good friend.

We strolled back to the chuck wagon together. Cookie had a bag of apples, and I'd finished the last of my horehound candy this morning. My sweet tooth itched. "Pete, is it likely that several of the pueblos would be havin' ceremonies at the same time?"

"Not likely, Amigo. Perhaps a harvest dance at Zia. Maybe a buffalo dance at Santo Domingo, but not at the same time." He skinned his apple with his long knife. "There are no big ceremonies until the Shalakos dance over at Zuni. It is early for the Shalakos. The other pueblos do not use the kivas much."

I left Pete and went to my gear. I pulled out my slicker and tied it in apron strings where it would be handy. Pulling my blankets, I spread them and stretched out. I felt tired from galloping all over the country. I needed to rest before riding herd. But my brain kept popping damn questions. Who was the man I had killed? Why was he trying to kill me? Where were the Indians? How could I find the bandit groups?

Then my mind flooded with all the questions because there were no answers to take the questions away. Feeling the pressures from the build up and of the situations facing me, I tried to push thoughts aside. I needed a clear head to make the hard decisions that needed deciding tonight. Things that only I could do needed to be done. I had to decide how and when. With great effort, I forced a restless sleep.

Thunder woke me up well before midnight. Night thunder this time of year meant trouble. A warm day, moist air, the heat rising from the sun-baked sand had boiled those clouds coming in from the southwest into thunderheads that survived the cool of the evening. I had seen this kind of storm dump two inches of rain in a half-hour.

No lush growth, to slow the runoff, grew on this arid plateau. The arroyos could be dry one minute and the next minute a head of water ten feet tall could come rushing down the gorge. I did not need to be told to get out to the herd. The cattle needed to be driven out of the arroyos to higher-up ground or they could be lost to a gully washer.

Lightning flashed. I spotted the big, dun horse and dabbed my loop over his head. He seemed a might skittery. Before I rode out, I stopped by my gear and pulled the Winchester out of the saddle scabbard. I wrapped it in my blankets and hauled all my gear to the chuck wagon to stow it under the tarp. With lightning flashing around, I wanted no extra metal near me. Besides, I would be the tallest thing around. I didn't like the prospects.

The shouts of the other cowboys located where they were working cattle. I headed for a wash where I had seen thirty head grazing. A lightning flash turned the clouds green. That green color indicated hail sometimes.

Once, I had seen what large hailstones could do to a herd. The ice rocks had killed the young stuff and beaten the rest of the cattle to the ground stunned. A couple of big stone hits on the head could kill a man.

Luckily, I had seen that hailstorm coming and had time to strip the saddle off the horse I rode. I remembered holding the saddle over my head. Still, one stone had hit my foot. Felt like a bull stomped on it. I was crippled up for a couple of days. Lord knows, we didn't need hail tonight.

I started rousting the cattle out of the wash. They were reluctant to go. Maybe they knew about lightning. They sure as hell did not know about flash floods. I whooped and popped my chaps with my rope to move them to higher ground.

The rain started suddenly in a heavy downpour. Lightning struck no more than a mile away. I moved my bunch up to the rest of the herd. The cattle were bellowing and moving slowly to the north, was my guess. I had nothing to steer by and could not see more that a hundred feet in any direction.

Cold water ran down the back of my neck, down my back under my slicker. Wind driven rain always got down to my skin somehow. I turned Buckskin to go after a bunch I had seen off to the left.

The rain seemed to ease a bit. Then a strong gust of wind hit, damn near took my hat from me. The rain came in behind the wind, heavier than before. The storm reminded me of a hurricane I had sailed into once, off the coast of Georgia. I was thankful to be off a heaving deck and on solid land tonight.

Lightning danced close by on my right. I saw by the light that maybe ten head had drifted back into the wash I had just cleared. I turned Buckskin to go after them.

Lightning struck in the middle of the herd. Swear to God!

The herd exploded into a thundering run. I couldn't see which way the stampede headed. Buckskin had more sense then me, or better ears. He turned to his tail and had made one step when I saw the whole damn herd coming through the rain right at us.

I wished right then that I wore spurs. Seemed I always tripped or hung a rope up on them so I went slick-heeled. But now, I was digging that dun horse in the ribs like I wore big Mexican rowels. I felt like I was about to die and kicking was all I could do.

I didn't have a chance in hell. The ground was wet and slippery. The dun could step into a hole. Blinded by rain, he could run into a *piñon* tree. I hoped he was as scared as I was and would run like hell from his fears.

No telling where we headed, but I whipped the dun on the rump with my rope to get him there faster. Chances were we might run into another part of the herd coming at us from up ahead.

Just as another lightning bolt cut the darkness, I looked back and saw the entire herd behind me. The lead cattle were gaining ground on Buckskin. I leaned low over the dun's neck and bellowed into the night, "Run, Hoss! Charge for Glory, yee-haaa!"

The cattle ran full speed in panic. Some pulled along side the dun. We got swept up in the herd. I knew I was a goner. Tall as Buckskin was I could expect him to get gored in the side and let me down. Instinctively I drew up my legs to get them out of the way of the slashing horns.

There was no way to veer off to the side. I had no idea what lay to the left or the right. I thought about praying. Had there been a God, he would never have made me a cowboy.

I had picked the dun from the *remuda* for his spunkiness, not his speed. It had been a mistake. Some wrinkle-horn would come up behind him soon and push him aside. Buckskin would go down, and I would be bloody pulp in a split second. I hadn't figured on dying this way, but it would surely be quick.

Lightning flashed, and I saw that the thinnest part of the herd ran to my right. I hoped Red would forgive me for what I was about to do, but I had to do it. I pulled my Colt and shot the cow on my right flank between the eyes. Her corpse caused a pile up of the cattle behind her. I veered the dun to the right into the space her death created.

I shot five head of Red's stock. I gambled with the cattle's lives, but I was winning. No telling how many other cattle died as a result of the pile-ups the shot cattle caused. I kept making room to the right to move into. I managed to get Buckskin to the outside of the herd.

Thumbing shells into the Colt, I started firing in the air to bend the herd left in on itself. It might bunch the herd up and start to slow it down.

I kept working the cattle in on themselves. They began turning. I figured I rode the point of the herd. It sounded like four thousand hooves were pounding behind me. I kept shooting and whipping and riding and hollering.

The herd ran full out for maybe five more minutes. Then the cattle started to get winded.

Fat cattle could sprint, but not run for long. The panic began to give way to fatigue.

About as fast as it had started, the stampede came to a rumbling stop. Like some general had given a command, the cattle all seemed to halt on the same foot. They just stood in place blowing with steam rising off their backs into the rain.

I patted the dun on the neck and let him get his wind. I felt beat, too, mostly from fighting my own fears. And I felt mighty thankful to be alive.

I sat in my saddle, hunched against the cold rain. I had no idea where I was in relation to the chuck wagon. I did not know how many head were in my bunch. I heard none of the other cowboys. The cattle were settling, so I let them be.

The lightning played out. The rain dried up to a drizzle. The cattle stood in a sea of mud. I pulled out my pipe and lit up. I figured I would rest the dun a bit more and then move out to start gathering in the cattle that had split off from the stampeding herd. The rain would let up pretty soon and I would be able to see what I was doing better.

I sat smoking when Red and three of the boys rode up.

"Was it you turned this herd?" Red shot at me. "Good work, Waller!" Red seemed genuinely pleased. "There's a deep arroyo not a quarter mile ahead. We'd 'a lost the whole damn herd had she hit it." He laughed, "Remind me to get you out in front of the next stampede."

"I know a lady barkeep I'd rather marry than get in front of a stampedin' herd again." I knew how Red felt about marrying and death. "I may reconsider this cowboy profession, take up drinkin'."

Red chuckled, then started barking orders. "Eli, Johnson, stay with the herd. Keep 'em settled. Donner, find Cookie. Come light, bring the chuck wagon here. Rhodes, circulate. Tell all the boys to find the scatter, bunch the herd. We'll make a head count first thing come light. Get after it, boys. We got a contract t'make!"

All hands and the cook worked through the night rounding up strays and bunching the herd. If we didn't bunch the herd now the chances were good some cattle would just wander off. We fought the dark, the mud, and spooky cattle.

Come daylight we started the count. As it turned out most of the herd had stayed together.

Mid-morning Red rode over. "We can still deliver over a thousand head, if we get the luck from here on in." Red swung a leg around his saddle horn, eased back, offered me his makings. "We lost about fifty head's all. The usual pile-ups. We'll be eatin' son-of-a-bitch stew 'til it comes out our ears."

I shook tobacco out of the bag into my pipe, handed Red his makings back. I took my time tamping and lighting up, trying to delay what I had to say. "Red, I had to shoot some of your cattle last night, had to work my way to the outside of the herd. Some of those pile-ups are my doin'." I figured he would dock my pay, which would put me in debt mighty deep.

"Forget it, Eli. Had the herd hit the arroyo we'd all be wiped out. Your bendin' the herd pulled my bacon out'a the fire." He rolled a *quirly* one handed. "We got plenty of time to make delivery. I reckon we're in good shape." He lit up. "I'll hold the herd here today, let 'em rest and graze. They run off some pounds last night." Red cocked his head and squinted to keep smoke out of his eye. "You decide what you're goin' to do?"

"Bein' this close to Jemez, I'll go scout the pueblo until I find out where those Indians went. Dependin' on what I find, I may search the mesa country between Jemez, Zia and Santa Ana, see if I can get a lead on the bandit's where-abouts." I watched Red's neck for color to see if he was getting riled. "If you can spare me the time, I'll ride on over to Santa Fe and report to the governor, find out what he's doin' about the robberies."

Red pulled the *quirly* from his lips, squinted at the ash, flicked the ash with his little finger. A little color rose on his neck.

"Red, you know I ride for the VR first, but the damn governor had me over the barrel. Twenty-four people have been killed. It has to be stopped." I reckoned Red could go either way. Maybe he'd give me the time off. Maybe he'd pay me off right now. I tamped my pipe and waited.

Red took a drag, sucked the smoke deep. He exhaled the smoke with his words, "If you can get back to the drive, I'd appreciate the help. Otherwise, meet me in Corrales." He took another drag then flipped the butt into the mud. "If you still have outlaw troubles by then, I'll ride gun with you." He raised his leg back over his horse's neck, put boot to stirrup. "Make that meetin' in Corrales or I'll come lookin' for you." He turned his horse around. Over his shoulder he said. "Montoya told me about that Sanchez fella. You watch your ass, Eli."

"Meet you in Corrales, Red." I pulled my horse around and headed for the chuck wagon to collect my gear.

*   *   *

Rainwater, trapped in a pitted rock, was the only reminder of the cloudburst last night. The wind had swept the clouds from the sky and dried the surface of the thirsty sands. I stuck my face into the pool, sucked up the sweet water and thought about the time Patricio had left me thirsty.

Squatting back on my heels, I let my eyes roam the terrain. I soaked my bandanna and dabbed the sweat out of the bullet burn on my neck. Then I let Gray have the rest of the water in the catchment.

The glare of the sun irritated my eyes. I felt the fatigue and soreness of getting shot at and riding all day yesterday, punching spooked cattle all night, and pounding leather all morning without a break. I crawled back into the saddle.

Gray pawed at the empty catchment, coaxing.

"That's all, Gray. Let's go!" I pulled his head up, booted his ribs. He grunted and stepped right into his rocking-chair lope.

I topped a ridge and caught a fleeting glimpse of a herd of antelope as they bolted over the crest of the next ridge. Then I saw a coyote slink through the sage and follow the antelope. He hunted something, maybe a crippled pronghorn.

Like coyote, I hunted. Unlike coyote, I did not know what I hunted, exactly. I prodded Gray off the skyline so I'd be less conspicuous.

A man dressed like a padre had tried to shoot me in the plaza of a deserted pueblo. The shooter's presence and the Indian's absence were the riddles I hunted the answers to. Maybe if I solved these two puzzles, I might find information that would be useful to the governor.

I was curious about the man I'd killed. I felt bad about the shooting. For all I knew, I might have shot another agent the governor had pressed into the investigation. The man I'd shot might have figured me for a bandit.

The gold nuggets stowed behind the dead man's belt could have been booty, or they could have been evidence he'd taken off a bandit. If I'd killed an agent, I had new trouble coming. If I'd killed a bandit, then the outlaws would be warned that someone was on to their operation.

I prodded Gray down the bank of an arroyo that headed north towards Jemez. I intended to skirt around the pueblo and stay hidden in the foothills to the east. From there I hoped to spy without being detected.

With the sun beating down and no breeze in the bottom of the arroyo to cool me, fatigue shut my eyes. My chin hit my chest. To wake up, I dismounted and walked with the gray stallion for a while. Walking cleared my head.

I needed a place to hide Gray and still get close enough to the pueblo to see what was happening there. I tried to remember exactly how the terrain around the pueblo fell away from the mesas into sand hills and settled into the valley of the Jemez River. Frustrated by my own forgetfulness, I ground hitched Gray and pulled the governor's field glasses from the saddlebag.

Jemez Pueblo lay out of sight maybe five miles ahead. I scoped out the route I'd take to a vantage point that appeared to offer the hiding place I needed. Before I mounted up I checked the loads in the Colt and Winchester. I didn't want trouble, but I would be ready for a surprise this time, if I could stay awake.

Taking the long way around and using the terrain to remain hidden, I worked my way to a hill about half a mile east of the pueblo. I tied Gray with a slipknot to a deadfall in a hollow in the hill. I took a good look around and memorized my escape route.

I crawled to the crest of the hill, picked a bush for cover and raised my eyes over the top of the rise. A quick look showed me the pueblo lay deserted. Easing back down the hill a bit, I bunched some long grass. Returning to my observation post, I used the grass to build a small blind under the bush. I felt safer about using the field glasses without being seen.

Smoke rose from only one chimney. A lazy dog slept in the sun. A dozen horses were penned on the north side of the pueblo. A little further out, the cattle I had delivered for Red had pushed through a rail fence and were eating the remains of a bean plot.

I searched the roads in and out of the pueblo, and the hills and gullies on both sides. I studied the pueblo and the entire area for about an hour and nothing changed.

The sun warmed my back. My eyes ached from using the field glasses. Sleep became hard to fight off. I eased back down the hill to stand and stretch. Checking on Gray, I moved him to a spot of grass and left him ground-hitched. Worried that I'd miss something, I went back to my post.

I searched carefully for a movement, a color, an unusual shape, a shadow, a shadow within a shadow. Nothing caught my eye. Another hour dragged by.

Then a door opened in one of the houses on the west side of the plaza. It was the house where the smoke rose from the chimney. Two women emerged, carrying large baskets in both hands. They went to an adobe with no doors or windows that I could see. A ladder lay against the wall of the structure.

One of the women climbed the ladder and handed her baskets down a hole in the roof. The other woman handed her baskets up and they disappeared down the hole. The two ladies returned to the house they had come from.

About five minutes later the two women reappeared carrying more baskets. They went to another structure that was round, maybe sixty feet across, and built about waist high. Steps climbed the side of the structure. Two poles stuck up from an opening in the roof. The poles must be the ends of a ladder down to a floor below.

My guess, this structure had to be a kiva. When I had searched the pueblo before, I had not looked into these structures because they had no doors. Pete had mentioned kivas, but I had failed to ask him about them.

I had no idea what kivas were, or what they contained. Maybe the Indians were in the kivas. Maybe I had almost interrupted religious ceremonies when I stormed in and searched the pueblo.

Indian ceremonies did not explain the killer padre, to my way of thinking. Not unless he was a real padre involved in the ceremonies. His intention might have been to scare off an intruder. I might have reacted too quickly to his drawn gun. I didn't like the idea.

The two women passed their baskets down into the hole in the roof and returned to the house they'd come from. A little more time went by and then the two women came out again. They carried baskets around behind some houses where I could not see them. In a minute they came back without the baskets.

As the women were about to go inside the house, I caught a faint flash of light in the right side of my field glasses. I shifted my field of vision to cover the old mission church. Nothing strange came into view.

Then a second instantaneous flash came from the bell tower. I studied the tower to see if there was something blowing in the breeze and reflecting the sun. It couldn't be a church bell. Someone had told me once that all the mission churches had bell towers, but the pueblos were too poor to afford the bells.

I wiped the sweat and fatigue from my eyes and refocused the field glasses. In the corner of the arch in the tower I saw what looked like a pair of field glasses and a hat. The flash must have come from reflected light off the glasses. I ducked down, afraid I had been seen.

More afraid that I'd miss seeing something, I eased back into position and turned my full attention to the bell tower. The tower was the highest structure in the pueblo and commanded a full view of the valley. It was the perfect place to position a lookout.

The field glasses and hat had disappeared. If a lookout was there, had he seen me and gone to report to the Indians? I lowered my field glasses and used my full field of vision to watch for movement.

I glanced over my shoulder to see if Gray was still on the patch of grass, and search over my escape route. I wanted water to ease my dry mouth, but decided I had to watch the pueblo. Irritated, I swatted at the black flies that had discovered my hiding place.

Pete Montoya had told me about the Mexican *penitentes*, warned me that they would shoot if you interrupted a crucifixion. I didn't know if the Indians were that touchy about having their ceremonies observed.

I searched the terrain behind me, added another worry to those knotting my guts. I wondered if the Pueblo Indians were as skilled as the Apache at sneaking up on a man. I speculated on what they would do to a man caught spying on their secret doings.

Torn between watching my backside or watching the pueblo for a party of irate Indians, I bet that I had not been spotted and chose the pueblo. Just as I lifted the field glasses and focused, a man ran out of the church to the center of the plaza.

At this distance I could not tell if the man was an Indian, but I could make out the shotgun he carried. He seemed to be yelling at something.

Another man stepped out of the same house the two women had come from. The lookout started pointing to the west and must have said something. The second man turned and went back inside. The lookout returned to the church.

I searched the land to the west of the pueblo. It took me a minute, but I spotted an Indian, about half a mile out, running towards the pueblo through the irrigated fields. He ran easily and covered the ground quickly. All he wore was a loincloth and a light leather shirt that was soaked with sweat. He was not carrying anything that I could see

A moment later the tall padre that I knew and the old Indian that gave me the medicine bag stepped out of the house. The man the lookout had summoned followed them. He carried a shotgun. The three men waited without talking for the runner to cross the fields to the plaza.

The runner stopped in front of the old Indian and gave him something he had pulled from his sash. The old Indian handed the object to the man with the shotgun. He unfolded a piece of paper and read it.

The man with the shotgun seemed to think for a minute. Then he said something to the padre. The padre said something to the old Indian. All four men walked over to the round, waist-high structure. The old Indian called something out and two young men rose up out of the hole in the roof. The panting runner descended into the hole.

The man with the shotgun pulled out paper and wrote something on it. He handed it to one of the young men. Words were spoken among all the men. Then the young man with the paper took off running to the west. The man with the shotgun wrote another message. He handed it to the second young man who took off running to the east.

The man with the shotgun turned and yelled something to the lookout in the bell tower. Then he herded the padre and the old Indian at gunpoint back inside the house.

I had seen enough to set off a burning anger. I eased down the hill to Gray and cinched him up. The runner heading east would pass not too far from where I hid. I had to move Gray and remain unseen.

Some sons-a-bitches held the pueblo hostage. A shot-gunner threatened the padre and the old Indian, the chief, I bet. The two women had been hauling food to the rest of the people held in the kivas.

I could have saved a lot of trouble had I searched the kivas the other day. On the other hand, I'd have probably lost a handful of brains to a shotgun blast when I stuck my head down the hole in the roof to look.

I heeled Gray into the hollow in the hill. After the runner passed I would follow him.

How many men would it take to capture a pueblo? How could you hold that many people hostage? Capture the head and you captured the body. The chief had a shotgun to his head was my guess.

Why capture a pueblo? For what reason? The reason would run right past me in a moment or two. The bandits had captured Jemez, probably Zia and Santa Ana too, to take control of the Indian runners.

It made perfect sense. The bandits were using the Indian runner system to communicate. The runners could not outrun a horse in a short-distance race, but they could out-last a horse over the long haul. The runners would run relays non-stop.

One runner could travel fifty miles, night or day, without stopping. The gold convoys would stop and camp at night. The runner system might be faster than the gold convoy. That would explain how the outlaws had both news of the shipments and time to set up an ambush.

The men holding the pueblo hostage must be one of the five outlaw groups. Another group must be holding Zia, another Santa Ana. I could not account for the other two groups, but I suspected a pattern. San Felipe and Santo Domingo pueblos lay east of here.

There had to be an operator in Durango who sent the initial messages by runner. A very clever man, he had remained hidden to all the people I had talked to. Maybe Sandy Thompson, the boss of Durango, had lied to me. I didn't think so. But maybe.

I prodded Gray out of hiding and picked up the trail of the runner heading east. Zia and Santa Ana lay south of here. Unless I missed my bet, the runner would lead me to another bandit hideout, most likely another pueblo.

East lay the course I had to ride to get to Santa Fe and the governor. I had real information to report.

CHAPTER ELEVEN

The Jemez runner trotted over the crest and down the back side of a low hill, a mile ahead. I hung back, tracking and observing. I did not want to be seen by him, nor did I want to lose him. I had a pretty good idea where he headed. A few more miles would prove my theory.

I stepped off Gray and stretched to relieve kinked muscles. Untying the canteen, I took a long pull. I had time to speculate.

Somehow sixteen outlaws had heard of the Indian runner system and figured out how to use it to their advantage. Based on the runner system, they had set up an intricate operation to hold up the gold shipments from Durango. There had to be an inside man in Durango.

The leader of the gang must have divided his men into the five groups and taken five pueblos all at the same time. That way there would have been no warning for the Indians. Unable to unite in defense, the pueblos had been taken hostage.

Taking the pueblos hostage might have been easy. Three heavily armed men might handle it. All they had to do was capture the padre and the chief, then threaten to kill women and children. Taking hostages was an old formula that had worked many times before.

Besides, the Pueblo Indians were peaceful people. The last time they had united in war was against the Spaniards almost two hundred years ago. General De Vargas had brutally beaten any ideas about being warriors out of them then.

Like De Vargas, the leader of this gang was brutal. He had to be one hell of a disciplinarian to control men spread all over the countryside. He was a shrewd planner and had already proved his skill as a tactician and ambusher. I faced a formidable enemy.

I had to admire the brilliance of using the pueblo messenger system. We had used runners in the war but never very effectively. You could not force a soldier to run fifty miles. Very few people even believed that a man could run that far, their limits set by the legendary death of the man who ran from Marathon.

Over the long distances of the holdup operation, the system gave the outlaws a tremendous advantage. Only a man trained in the military would know how important fast communications were to the success of troop movements.

The telegraph system had impacted the War Between the States like no other war before it. One of the first things we did to impede the enemy was cut the telegraph lines. When the time was right, I would have to think up a way to cut off the runner system.

I mounted up. Gray laid his ears back, tossed his head to loosen the reins. He wanted to gallop. Not wanting to get too close to the runner, I held Gray to an easy trot.

I assumed the five bands of outlaws held five of the six pueblos that formed a half circle around the southern base of the Jemez Mountains. I knew for sure they occupied Jemez, Zia, and Santa Ana. If my guess was right as to the destination of the runner, I would find Cochiti occupied. I would ride on down to check out Santo

Domingo, the fifth pueblo in the half circle, if Cochiti proved right. Maybe the runner would lead me to Santo Domingo and San Felipi.

I had some doubt that three bandits could hold Santo Domingo. At least five hundred Indians lived there. That seemed like an unmanageable number of people for three men to control. If Santo Domingo was not occupied, then one of the other pueblos might have six outlaws holding it.

Maybe Cochiti was not occupied and there were six outlaws holding Santo Domingo. That would be enough men to guard the kivas and keep the Indians captive. It was possible that the leader headquartered there with his greater force. Time would tell.

Doubts started ripping at me like vultures on a corpse. I was not convinced that the man I had killed in the plaza at Jemez was one of the outlaws. Possession of the gold nuggets might confirm that he was, if the assay office in Durango could identify the gold and it was from the convoy.

If I had killed one of the outlaws, that would leave only two men to control Jemez. When the gang leader got word of the killing, he might send other men to equalize his forces. That possibility left me unsure about the distribution of the gang. I needed to know how many men were in each pueblo before I could form a plan to liberate the Indians.

With fifteen men in the field and one informant in Durango the gang seemed to me to be spread too thin. I knew fifteen men had attacked the last convoy. If all the bandits were in the field at the massacre, how had they controlled the pueblos?

The only thing that made sense was that only four, maybe just three of the pueblos were occupied. That way a man could be left behind to keep a gun to the chief's head. But I had seen five trails lead out of the ambush. Maybe I was up against more than sixteen outlaws.

If just the three pueblos I had seen were occupied, where was the runner headed? A fourth pueblo had to be occupied. If not, I was on another wild goose chase.

The bandits had to be waiting for word of the next gold shipment. They would strike once more and then abandon the operation. It was too good a plan. But maybe they were pulling out.

Perhaps the runner carried news of another shipment. I reckoned it was too soon. Besides, with the second loss of a shipment, the miners would seek a different way to get their gold to Denver.

Confused as hell by all the variables in the situation, I gave up speculating and pulled an apple I had taken from Cookie's larder from my saddlebag. It tasted sour and dry. I pulled Gray to a halt and gave him the rest of the apple. He chewed while I pissed. Feeling relieved and hopeful again, I mounted up and got after the runner's trail.

If I was right about the situation at Jemez, and if the gang leader didn't reinforce the two men there, then it might be fairly easy to take the pueblo back from the outlaws. Two men could be taken without too much risk to the Indians.

A long shot would kill the lookout in the bell tower. The other man might be taken before he did too much damage, if he were surprised. The risk, of course, was that he would kill the chief. I hated the idea. I wanted to get to know the old Indian. Still, there had to be a time when both outlaws rested or failed to keep watch. Maybe an opportunity would present itself.

If I killed the outlaws, there would be no way of finding where the gold was hidden. I doubted that the gold was kept in the pueblos. Should the situation explode at the pueblo, getting the gold out would be impossible. The bandits would have hidden the gold where they could come back for it.

I wondered if the young Jemez runner that I found shot had come up on two of the outlaws as they were hiding their treasure. He might know where the gold was hidden. My stomach churned with regret as I realized the outlaws would not let the boy live. I might have brought him to the pueblo to his sure death. The bandits had been in control of the pueblo when I rode in that night. That explained why I had been treated so curtly.

I thought of the medicine bag. The chief had given it to me and said I would be welcome when I returned. Was that a message? Was there a message in the medicine bag itself? I pulled it out of the saddlebag.

The medicine bag in my hand brought back memories of the night I spent staring into the fire. This powerful medicine bag had changed me that night. My future had become important to me again. Since then I had been moving forward, embracing what came, planning what I wanted from my future. Hell, with what I faced I had a slim chance of getting into the future.

I looked at the symbols on the bag, a medicine wheel with a snake across it. Four blue dots circled the snake's head. Did the medicine wheel represent the pueblo, or the people? Was the serpent good or evil? If I read the ancient medicine bag in light of the circumstances, the snake could be the leader of the outlaws. The snake dominated the medicine wheel. Was that the message?

I studied the bag carefully. The medicine wheel design was painted on the bag long ago, probably when it was first made. Wrinkles in the leather had cut through the circle randomly. The paint of the serpent and the four dots around its head looked fresh. The serpent was painted in what looked to be dried blood. There were no wrinkles running through it breaking the paint. The dots looked freshly painted. These symbols had been recently added to the medicine bag.

The dots were not in a circle but more in a rectangle. It was like the snake poked its head into a box outlined by the dots. Then I saw three small dots on the snake's head that I had not seen in the firelight. A pattern I knew very well jumped out at me.

The dots formed the four bright stars of the constellation, Orion. The three small dots were perfectly positioned as Orion's belt. The dots were stars and the snake was pointing to Orion.

For a moment I scanned the country ahead of me for the runner and to get my bearings. I estimated he was behind the ridge ahead. I felt safe crossing the open land to it. I slowed Gray to a walk.

I turned the medicine bag in my hand so that the snake pointed in the direction where Orion rose this time of year. The mouth of the bag pointed north and the head of the serpent pointed east by southeast. I knew that the top star of Orion's belt, Mintaka, lay on the celestial equator which lay east by southeast of my position. It seemed like I was holding a compass.

Maybe I could interpret the symbols to mean that the pueblos were held by the outlaws, the snake. Perhaps the outlaw leader, the head of the snake, was in the pueblo that lay on a line from Jemez towards the constellation, Orion.

Then I noticed that the beads on the ends of the drawstrings were not silver, as I had guessed by firelight. They were double-ought buckshot, cut and pressed on to the thongs. I had seen two of the bandits at Jemez carry shotguns. I became convinced the chief had managed to get a message to me. He had meant to give me the spirit powers, the fetishes, to help him free his people.

The eagle fetish came to mind and how the eagle saw the world from above. From an eagle's point of view, I formed a map in my mind's eye of the terrain around the five pueblos.

I imagined that the snake pointed over the map like a compass needle. If I put the tail of the snake on Jemez Pueblo, the head lay on Santo Domingo. Cochiti was due east of Jemez and north of Santo Domingo. Santa Ana was more south. Maybe I had been given a fix on the leader of the bandits. My admiration for the old Indian chief grew.

The symbols on the bag made sense, in light of what I had observed. The runner up ahead would prove or disprove my interpretations soon.

He had been running due east, which made me think he was headed for Cochiti. Not far ahead, the mesa we were on fell off to the southeast. I guessed the runner would either stay up on the mesa and continue due east, or he would drop off to the southeast and head for Santo Domingo.

His decision point lay on the western tip of a triangle. Cochiti lay the same distance to the east as Santo Domingo was to the southeast. It would make sense to have another runner waiting there. The message would get to the two pueblos at roughly the same time with two messengers running.

I wondered if the messenger system was that well organized. Maybe. These were ancient people. Or perhaps the bandits had arranged it so.

I hoped the Jemez runner reached the fork in the trail before it fell dark and I lost sight of him. He would continue to run in the night until he got to his destination. I respected his endurance.

Hell, I was tired and I rode a horse that did all the work. A couple hours sleep before the stampede was all I had in the last two days. I doubted the runner got much sleep, penned-up in a kiva with a crowd of scared Indians.

Gray seemed to be putting up with the slow pace but did not like all the extra travel caused by staying out of sight of the runner. I heeled Gray into a little gully, halted, and pulled the field glasses out of my saddlebag.

Walking up a little rise, I searched ahead for the runner. He had not stopped running since he started hours ago and was running strong as he dropped off the mesa to the southeast. He headed for Santo Domingo.

I decided right then that I had had enough for this day. I picked up dry firewood as I walked back to Gray.

High, thin clouds in the west gleamed a coppery gold. Dusk had captured the eastern sky. The low Cerrillos Mountains were just a purple silhouette. Sandia Peak, to the southeast, still reflected lingering color off the crest. Except for the chirping birds taking a head count just before dark, the land around lay silent. I needed food, coffee and sleep. Tomorrow I would spy on Santo Domingo.

Gray, rid of the saddle and me, found a likely spot and rolled to dust himself. I hobbled him and speculated about whether he would buck in the morning. I had taken him out from under Hollis this morning when I left. I hadn't used Gray since the Santa Fe trip.

I hid a small fire in the gully. The dry wood gave off little smoke. In the dark of night I felt safe from being seen. Stretching my legs out I leaned back against my saddle and waited for my whistle berries to cook. Some grub and sleep would feel real good.

What message did the runner carry? Was another shipment coming?

The questions jerked me bolt upright. If a shipment was coming, the outlaws would move out, pronto, and I'd miss the whole shebang. I could not gamble that it was not so. No time for sleep, I had to get on down to Santo Domingo and see what happened when the messenger arrived.

Still, there might be time for a hot meal and coffee. It would take the runner another hour to get to Santo Domingo. Gray would be in for a run in the dark. I caught him up, rubbed him down and saddled him while the beans boiled and the bacon fried.

Cutting down the slope off the mesa, still chewing the last of the bacon I had gulped, I headed towards the Rio Grande where Santo Domingo lay. A slim half-moon lit the way. I prodded Gray hard until we got to within two miles of the pueblo. Then I slowed him to a walk. If this were the bandit headquarters, there would be a lookout.

Santo Domingo had built up over the years on the river bottom, back from the high-water mark. The river bottom gave way to sand hills on the east, that were the edge of the plateau that lay below the lava flow plateau, that stretched north and east to the Sangres and Santa Fe.

Well south of the pueblo I prodded Gray into the Rio at a wide place in the river. The fording went well until Gray stepped in a hole and plunged into water over his withers. I'd stayed dry till then.

On the other side of the river I slid out of the saddle and pulled off my boots to empty out the water. I checked my guns and wiped them off. I didn't know if I could trust the powder in the cartridges to be dry. I didn't know enough about cartridges. My old Navies would have had to be reloaded. Water usually seeped in around the caps, wet the powder.

I circled to the east to climb the sand hills and worked around on top towards the closest hill east of the pueblo. From the tip of the sand hills, I could spy from above on the east side of the pueblo.

Gray stopped suddenly. He jerked his head up, snorted and sucked air like he was about to whinny. I yanked his head around and grabbed his nose to stifle the whinny. He grunted but not loud enough to cause me concern.

Gray had warned me there must be another horse close by and maybe a lookout. I backed Gray up and then turned him. When I found a gully that cut the sand hills, I found a hidden place to tie him.

Taking the field glasses I walked back on top of the sand hills. Just before the crest I dropped to my belly to snake forward. Searching and crawling, I moved out on the plateau. About a hundred yards ahead I spotted the glow of a small fire. I worked my way over towards it. Then I circled around until I could see the light of the fire. It had been built among boulders, to conceal it. No one tended the fire so I sat down to wait and search with the field glasses.

I spotted the horse that Gray had smelled tied to a bush a hundred feet the other side of the fire. Finally, the silhouette of a man appeared against the half-moon- lit sky. He sat out on the point of the sand hill closest to the pueblo.

What could I do with this outlaw, supposing he was one of them? The other bandits would be alerted if I shot him. I could not take a prisoner. If he failed to show up in the pueblo, the others would be warned. If he were a bandit lookout, when would his relief arrive?

One thing I thought I could bet on, the runner had arrived and the outlaws were not riding out. They would have called this man in. Still, someone might be headed this way right now to fetch him. Or he might be watching the pueblo for a signal.

I crawled on my belly to a bush between the man and the fire and stretched out flat to wait. The fire burned to coals. Cold on the half of my body soaked by the river, sweating on the other half, I lay waiting uncomfortably. Even so, sleep kept trying to take me under. Maybe half an hour went by before the lookout finally rose and turned to walk back to his fire.

Just as he passed the bush where I hid, I stepped behind him, laid the edge of my long knife against his throat. "Don't move," I whispered in his ear. I eased his pistol off his hip, jammed it into his ribs.

"This ain't funny, Jeb." He didn't move. "You got crazy notions about what's funny. I been waitin' here all..."

I bent the barrel of his gun over his head and caught dead weight as he fell. I dragged him behind the rocks by the fire. He was expecting relief so I worked quickly to tie him with his belt, gag him with his bandanna. I hadn't thought to bring rope.

His horse whinnied. A second horse whinnied off to my left. I appreciated the warning, and snaked to some cover between the fireplace and where the second warning had come from.

"Hello, the fire. You there, Tim?"

"Jeb?" I gambled and eased deeper into the shadow of a juniper tree.

"Yeah. I'm coming in." A shadow formed where the voice had been.

Lucky for me, the rider swung out of the saddle and tied his horse to a bush. I had not figured out a way to get to the man without rising up out of the dark and buggering his horse. I did not want to risk the noise of a shot.

Jeb started walking towards the fire. I let him pass me by then took two stalking steps and struck at him with the butt of Tim's bent pistol.

Jeb heard my foot suck in my wet boot and started to turn.

My blow glanced off the side of his head. Stunned, he swung a right punch that landed low on my cut side.

I fell back hurting something fierce from the old wounds.

Jeb slapped his side for his gun.

I couldn't shoot with Tim's bent gun. I jumped and struck down hard with it.

Jeb's pistol spun out of his hand before it came level. He threw a roundhouse left.

I blocked the left and struck at his head again. He went down this time. I pulled up my shirt and felt my scabs for blood. I was dry. Damn, I hated close up fighting.

Quickly, I tied and gagged Jeb. Then I ran to the edge of the sand hill to look at Santo Domingo. Even in the dim moonlight I could see it was deserted like the other pueblos had been. Hell, it was night. The pueblo could be occupied, or just closed down for the night, like a red ant-hill.

I watched the road out of the pueblo coming this way until I became convinced no one traveled it. Then I returned to the men I'd dumped by the burned out campfire in the rocks. Both still lay unconscious.

It appeared like I had captured two of the outlaws. I wasn't sure. Stacking just a bit of kindling, I blew on live coals until I had a small light. Then I searched the men.

Jeb had a long knife, pocketknife, and a couple of letters in his pockets. I found a two-shot Derringer stuffed in his boot and stowed it in mine. Then I found a bag of nuggets behind his belt.

Tim carried nothing much of interest, but had a bag of nuggets also. The leader of the gang seemed to be paying his gang wages in gold. I figured those gold nuggets would get these two bandits hanged, depending on the assay.

Snuffing out the fire, I stepped back to think and let my eyes adjust to the dark again. Then I ran to Gray. I lead him and the other two horses to the fireplace.

Neither man had anything tied to their saddles except a blanket and a slicker. I pulled my good lariat off my saddle and ruined it to cut short ropes. I bound the men, hands and feet. Their bodies were too heavy and limp to hoist them into the saddle and fork them upright. I slung them face down over their saddles like grain sacks and tied them down tight. I didn't want any trouble from these two boys.

I took the field glasses and ran to the point of the sand hill. As organized as this bunch was, I figured they would be operating this pueblo the same way as Jemez. I spotted the dark shape of the bell tower on the mission church.

Sure enough, I saw the faint glow of a *quirly,* maybe a cigar in the bell tower. The deserted pueblo, the guard in the tower, and the gold nuggets behind the belts of the two men I'd captured were proof enough for me.

Tim would be expected to report in soon. If he did not, there might be signals and then a search. It was time to cut and run with my evidence to the governor.

I felt confident no one would pursue me until morning light. Even then, I doubted other outlaws could be spared for the hunt. Holding the pueblo hostage occupied all their time, and I had just cut the force by a third, maybe a half. I didn't want to hang around to find out which.

It took starts and stops before the bandits' horses figured out they had become packhorses. They weren't rebellious, just confused. The loads they carried smelled the same but didn't move like the riders they had carried up the sand hills. I cussed the fact that I had to yank on lines hauling a pack train.

Prodding Gray, clucking and chunking rocks at the packhorses, I worked my pack train toward the trail up La Bajada towards Santa Fe. Riding in the dark and leading the horses made for a slow pace.

Some time during the steady climb up La Bajada the men came to. I could hear them grunt when their horses jerked and stumbled. Riding face down would soften the bandits up a might. They would be less trouble to handle later on.

I wondered if the gang leader would pull out and abandon the operation when he discovered he had lost two more men. The gang was spread pretty thin already. They had held over a thousand people hostage for several weeks now. It would be harder to control the pueblos.

Fewer men had to carry the load. Something would go wrong. A bandit might rape a woman. Over worked, a man might lose his temper and kill someone. Either event could force the Indians to revolt. I marveled at the discipline in the gang, that it had held together this long.

If I led the gang, I'd consider abandoning the operation. The loss of three men could indicate that the law was closing in, or that other outlaws were horning in on the deal. Maybe the Indians were finally taking matters into their own hands. There was plenty of gold to divide up.

The unknown factor that could keep this gang leader on his present course was greed for more gold. I had never felt the gold lust so strong as to drive me to take the risks he took. I'd seen other men lose their minds to gold fever. But I had no way to gauge the power of the lust. My guts felt the gang leader would hold out to strike again.

My neck, back, butt, and legs felt like they could go no further. I found an arroyo to hide in and called a halt. I judged from the stars that there were two hours of darkness left before sunup. I guessed I was sixteen, eighteen miles south of Santa Fe, on top of La Bajada hill. I hoped I was far enough away from the bandits if they rode in pursuit. But I needed rest, no two ways about it.

I pulled Tim off his horse and let him lie on his back. He grunted when I tightened his bindings. I pulled Jeb off his saddle and let him hit the ground hard. He grunted. My cargo hadn't died from riding head down.

I dragged Jeb up against a big rock. His knots were tight. I dragged Tim over to the rock and tied them both to it with their backs against it. They weren't going anywhere.

I tied a short rope to their ankles and jerked their legs out straight in front of them. In the center of the short rope I twisted a stick, stuck it in the ground. I took the blankets and slickers of their saddles and threw them over the men.

I scooped a hip-hole in the sand so I wouldn't roll and spread my blankets. Taking the stick out of the ground, I pulled the short rope tight. I lay down and locked the stick in the elbow of my left arm. I shucked my Colt into my right hand.

"You so much as twitch, Boys, I'll come up shootin'."

CHAPTER TWELVE

A jerk on my arm yanked me out of a dream. I rolled left, shot right. As I eared the hammer back to fire again, my eyes shed the sleep and focused on the prisoners. Both men sat tied to the rock. Tim flinched with his eyes bugged wide open, his head wagging no. Half-asleep or wounded, Jeb moaned.

"Jerk in his sleep?" I dropped the stick locked in my left elbow, looked around, flexed the kinks out of my arm.

Tim eased up on the flinching and nodded yes.

"I shoot the sum-bitch?" I eased the hammer down, holstered the Colt. Tim nodded "no".

"Damn. I hate guardin' prisoners."

To wake Jeb up fast, I kicked his leg hard. He came around slowly, mumbled something behind his gag that sounded like a whine. Sleep to him must have been near death. The gunshot and the splat of lead on the rock beside his head hadn't brought him around. Maybe the upside down ride over his saddle had beaten him up pretty bad.

I caught Gray, took the hobbles off, and led him up the arroyo, out of sight of the prisoners. I didn't want them to witness Gray's first-thing-in-the-morning bucking routine. I usually won the bucking contest more times than Gray when there weren't any spectators. Gray loved to put on a show.

I cinched Gray up tight. Then I looked him in the eye. A rude wake-up, no fire, no coffee, no food, and hauling prisoners added up to a black mood. I felt ready to kick the frost out of him, stepped into the saddle and glued my butt down like a fly on a glass windowpane.

Gray stood still, waiting. I gigged him in the ribs to launch him. He farted. I gave him some rein and knee and he walked back down the arroyo, sweet as can be. The snub line trick must have broken Gray's morning bucking habit. In a way, it made me sad. Gray's bucking routine had cost me pain and pride, but I'd miss working the kinks out in a cool morning.

I rounded up the other two horses and got back to the rock that held the bandits. I bound my prisoners' arms behind their backs, above the elbows, so their wrists could heal and they could get some circulation in their hands. I tied their feet in the stirrups and ran the line under the horse's belly. I wanted those boys to sit tight if we had to make a run for it. Last thing, I took off their gags and gave them water.

We rode out of the gully into one of those New Mexico mornings I prized so much. The sun had just cleared the horizon and shot the air full of orange-golden light. Long, purple shadows stretched over the land towards the other horizon. Just above the sun the sky shimmered, turquoise color. It reminded me of the Blue Gem Turquoise the Navajo silver smiths coveted.

To the west, the fresh sunlight gleamed on the east face of the Jemez Mountains. Mostly pine covered above the mesas, the mountains boasted deep-green pine forests that had a golden glow to them now. The air was so clear you could see a squirrel on a branch thirty miles away, or so it seemed.

"Sure as hell, you boys're goin' to hang for murder on a golden mornin' as glorious as this." I let the statement dangle in the air. "Santa Fe jail's just over the hill." I yanked the lead ropes and dragged the bandit's horses into a lope behind Gray. "Keep kickin'em horses. Let's ride."

"The boys'll bust us out first," Jeb said.

Tim hissed, "Shut up, Jeb. He's just baitin' us."

"I killed another one of you fellers over at Jemez. That only leaves twelve to help you, and one over in Durango. As easy as it was to take you two, it'll be a Sunday walk takin' the rest of the gang by myself." I pulled out my pipe. Turning in the saddle I searched the back trail and watched Jeb as we loped along.

"Nobody's comin' for you Jeb." I turned around and cupped a match to light my pipe. "Your *compadres* have their hands full of Indian trouble at the pueblos. Besides, they get to split up your take of the gold." I laughed. "You got a price on your head, so to speak."

We loped along in silence for a while. The sleep had done me good. The sunrise lighted my black mood. I began to look forward to Santa Fe. If I could get my business done with the governor, there might be time left in the day for a Mexican dinner and poker. Could be, I would get to finish a Rivas beer at Maria's. I hoped she had some on ice for me. I could almost feel it bubbling in my throat making my eyes water.

"You boys ever drink a Rivas beer? Best in the world, Rivas. It cuts the dust out of your throat like no other treat. If you never had one, don't let the sheriff serve you a Rivas beer, by mistake, with your last supper. It just wouldn't be fair to you. You'll die believin' there's no justice in the world for sure. To have one Rivas tantalize your throat and then to die strangling under a hemp necktie? Who-ee!"

"Beer, shit!" Jeb said. "When I get home I'll be drinkin' Kentucky Bourbon and showin' the ladies a good time. I'll own racehorses an' bluegrass farms. I'll be livin' a life you never even dreamed."

"Jeb, your dreamin' days're over. I'd turn my thoughts to dyin'. If I was you, I'd start gettin' my courage up so as not to cry and wet my pants when they lead me up the gallows stairs." I yanked on the lead lines. "Jeb, you're goin' to die soon. There's no doubt about it. I'm goin' to stand at the foot of the stairs up the gallows and wink when they drag you, kickin' and cryin', by. I'll see the rope crush your throat, then I'll go sip a Kentucky Bourbon and celebrate."

We crested a rise and I slowed the horses down. From here you could see the *piñon* smoke haze hanging over Santa Fe, at the base of the Sangre de Cristos.

"Tim, what were your dreams?" I knocked out my pipe, stowed it.

"I ain't no dreamer, Mister. I'm a practical man if you know what I mean. What kind of a man're you? I don't see no badge. You independent, the kind that looks around for opportunity?"

"Depends, of course." I chuckled. "You goin' to offer me the gold you don't have?"

"I figure I'm plumb out of the gold business. You're sure as hell right. Them boys're countin' my gold right now. That's the deal. If you don't make the final split, the gold sure as hell wasn't goin' to your next of kin." Tim kicked his horse up close to Gray. "Looks like the noose meant for my neck is in your hands, Mister. I'd rather fill them hands with somethin' else. What've I got you need? Information?"

"Christ-a-mighty, Tim! You tellin' me to shut up?" Jeb booted his horse up close. "I'll kill ya, you start talkin'! Me and the boys will."

"Who's the leader, Tim? Where's the main force?"

"What do I get for tellin', Mister?"

"Nothing for that information. Give me somethin' of value, Tim, somethin' that makes it easy for me. Then we'll talk about livin' or dyin'." Seemed to me hanging would be better than life in the Santa Fe prison. I'd seen the inside of that hell-hole. But maybe Tim saw some opportunity in staying alive. "You rather do hard labor than hang?"

Jeb butted in, "I'll tell you all I know, if you let me ride out of here."

"Jeb, you're a dreamer. You're tied to a horse. I've got the gun. The jail's just up the road. No way in hell I'll let you go back to murderin'. You're a hanged man. Now Tim, here, he's a practical man. Said so himself. Me and him're talkin' about prison instead of the rope. If he tells me somethin' worth my time, maybe I'll help him." I knew both men saw Santa Fe not far in the distance.

"Sergeant Ben Horton, late of the Quantrell Raiders," Tim said. "Learned his warrin' with the best of them. Pulled this gang together after the war. Horton knows his stuff. Runs the outfit with a cat-o'-nine-tails. Jeb an' me have felt his lash before."

"That's not the Ben that works for Sandy Thompson over in Durango, is it?" It didn't make sense to me that the leader would cut himself off from his men.

"Naw, that's Ben Ronzio. How'd you uncover him?" Tim asked.

"Had a run-in with him. Didn't know he was the point man 'til just now. Does Sandy Thompson know about Ben Ronzio?" I wondered how far Tim would go. He was signing his own death warrant with the gang. Maybe he figured all the outlaws would get shot or hanged first before they got to him for talking.

"Naw, Ronzio's found an' bought-out last minute," Tim said. "He had the easy job. All he had to do's send a message after the shipment left Durango. We done all the rest." He paused, "Horton's at Santo Domingo. There was six of us there."

"I saw how he held the pueblos hostage. How does Horton keep the Indian runners in line?" The problem I mulled over was how to root out the outlaws without harming their hostages or the runners.

"Figured out the runners?" Tim clicked his tongue. "Horton's cagey, ain't he?"

"How's he control'em, Tim?" I yanked on Jeb's horse's lead rope. It had a tendency to try to wander that got on my nerves.

"He's keepin' the runners and their families in one kiva at each pueblo. The kivas're loaded with dynamite. Keeps them Indians mighty tame. I got'a hand it to the Sergeant. That messenger service's a whale of a idea."

"Horton holdin' out for another shipment?" I asked Tim as I jerked Jeb's horse back into line. Seemed like Jeb was holding his mount back somehow.

"One more, he says. He thinks the operation's workin' accordin' to plan. Least ways that's what he's sayin' before you took us captive."

"Where's the underbelly of the operation, the weakest point I can strike?"

"That's the key to your troubles, all right. What I've been tellin' you just fills in some blanks. What do I get for the key, Mister?"

Tim's question put me up against the decision I'd been putting off. Did I want to help this killer out? I'd deliver him to Sheriff Moore in less than an hour. I could let Tim hang. He deserved it. Like the fake padre at Jemez, he would have killed me without a second thought, if he had seen me first last night.

Could I figure out where to strike the heart of the snake? Maybe I had enough information to figure it out. Still, Tim might have an angle I would not think of. And he might be smart enough to set a trap for me.

Delaying my decision a minute longer, I pulled out my pipe and stuffed it. Out of the corner of my eye I caught Jeb kneeing his horse out of line. The best Jeb could do, in this deadly situation, was try to irritate me. Well, we would see. I chuckled to myself, lit my pipe.

"Tim, the head of the snake lies in Santo Domingo. That's Horton. The snake curves over Santa Ana and Zia with the tail of the snake at Jemez. You give me the vital spot on the snake and I'll stand up for you at the trial. Make it good, Tim, or my offer doesn't stand."

"Well, you're wrong about the number of men. There're four more. One in each pueblo. They get left behind durin' the raids to hold the pueblos."

"You said there're six in Santo Domingo."

"Sergeant Horton had to send a man to Jemez after Bob Sands got killed. You kill Sands?"

"He pulled a gun."

"Maybe you was lucky. But you're up against seventeen veterans. You ain't goin' it alone are ya? Hell, that's suicide."

"Maybe. I figure if a posse rode into one of the pueblos, there'd be a battle. Too many Indians would die. The chief and the padre'd be first. The sergeant's ruthless. If he's cornered he'll kill his hostages."

Tim shrugged, cocked his head like he thought I was crazy. "Horton keeps five men close by. I'd guess he'll shift around to give'im five men at Santo Domingo, four at Santa Ana, three in Zia, three at Jemez. I'd cut the snake up in pieces startin' with the tail at Jemez. Ben, up in Durango? He's easy pickin's later."

"That's not good enough, Tim. I figured that out." I halted my column of three and dismounted. I had found what I was looking for and stooped to pick up three sand burrs. I walked back to Jeb and lifted his knee. I placed the burrs under his stirrup strap.

"Jeb, I wouldn't knee that horse again if I's you." I loosened the cinch on the saddle just enough so that if the horse went to bucking, the saddle would roll under the horse's belly. "Your feet're tied under this horse, remember?" I looked up at Jeb, grinned, and walked back to Gray.

"Tim, Quantrell was brutal. You said Horton learned his craft well." I swung into the saddle and started the pack train towards Santa Fe. "He'd kill hostages to force his attackers back, or buy time for an escape. What I need's a weak point where one man can cripple the snake and kill it before it can kill innocent people. If I fail, the law can use force, but the first strike's mine. Think again, Tim. I ain't buyin' your plan."

We loped along in silence except for the muffled thunder of hooves on the sandy loam of the plateau. Tim seemed to be thinking. Jeb squirmed in the saddle as his leg cramped up from holding the stirrup strap away from the burrs on his horse's hide.

I thought about getting back up to Durango after I talked to the governor. It made sense to arrest Ben Ronzio. That would blind the snake and cut the communications system. The miners could ship gold again.

I had no idea how to break the body of the snake. To attack the force in Santo Domingo was out of the question. I didn't want to run any chance of Horton getting away. Horton had thought out his defensive position well. I could see no place to attack a weak point or to infiltrate.

All I had going for me was knowledge of Horton's strength, his deployment, and maybe the element of surprise. Most likely he would be expecting trouble from a large force, like a posse. His small units could hold off a large force using the hostages until the rest of Horton's men could arrive to relieve them.

Horton was military-trained. He might sacrifice some of his force to save the rest. I was sure Horton figured that there were not enough lawmen in the territory to strike all four pueblos at once. It would cause a bloody massacre of the Indians. Only the army could muster enough force to retake the pueblos all at once. But this was a local law enforcement situation. Maybe.

Tim had probably saved my life with the information about the four extra outlaws. At least he had saved me from a bad surprise. There was another problem I hadn't figured out. Maybe if he told me where the gold was I could cripple Horton's operation somehow. If I got that information, maybe I'd bargain with the judge for Tim.

"Tim, where's the gold hidden?"

"Wondered when you'd get 'round to it. That's the joker, all right." Tim turned in his saddle to look at Jeb and his burr predicament, then turned back. "You sneak in somehow an' kill the men, you never get the gold. There'd be buried treasure all over'em mountains. It'd take all the miners in Durango a lifetime to find it again. You ain't given me nothin' yet, Mister. What're you offerin' me?"

"Like I said. I'll stand up for you in court, if what you give me's good enough. It's life or a hemp party, Tim."

"Each squad hides their own gold. That way nobody can get greedy for the whole pot. Don't kill Sergeant Horton. He's the only man with maps to all four treasures. He calls them maps his insurance. I never seen'em all."

Jeb snorted in disgust, "Shit! Why don't you jus' tell'im everything, for Christ sake! Give him a map. Walk him to the gold, why don't you! Swear to Christ I never seen a traitor like you. Bastard! I don't know how I ever called you Friend."

Jeb was still dreaming he would get saved, could spend that gold. Tim wasn't helping him any. I was afraid Jeb would get carried away with himself and accidentally knee his horse. I loosened up my hold on the lead rope not wanting to get pulled into the bucking fracas Jeb's carelessness might cause.

"I aim to give it to him, Jeb. If it'll keep me from hangin'. You ever see a man hang? Eyes bulgin' out, tryin' to scream with a crushed voice box, lungs full of air bustin' to get out. Face turnin' purple with the mouth suckin' to get air in, body kickin' and runnin' in the air if his feet ain't tied. You die with shit in your pants, Jeb. It ain't no way for a man to die. I'd rather be shot full of holes facin' an enemy. Hell, I'd rather die bustin' rocks, if that's all the choice I get," Tim spat.

"If the squads get split-up and everybody runs, where'd Horton head? I need to know, Tim. Horton's the only one who can end up with the whole pot." I would chase Horton to hell. Ann had gold in the first shipment and had lost her husband to this man's greed in the second shipment.

"Horton's got allies over southeast Kansas. That's where most of us're from. I've seen 'im send money back that way over the years since the war. It might be family. I ain't sure. The Horton name's common enough over'ere." Tim raised himself in his stirrups, looked back over the way we'd come. He settled and studied Santa Fe just up ahead.

"Mister? I got to broodin' about Sergeant Horton bein' the only one with all'em maps. Seemed like I ought to have some insurance, too." Tim squirmed in his saddle. His shoulders sagged then braced back. He shrugged. "It was me that drew the Santo Domingo gold map. It ain't right." Tim leered at me.

"The map you gave Horton is wrong?"

Tim nodded yes, said, "Just enough. Give me your word you'll stand up for me in court an'

I'll give you the right map. You may not get all the men or all the gold, but you won't come up empty-handed neither."

"You think the men in the other squads figured that way, too? How good're the rest of the maps Horton's holdin'?"

"I've no idea, but that's the weakest link in Horton's plans. Most of the men, like Jeb here, put their complete trust in the sergeant. I'm offerin' you the recovery of two fifths of the treasure. Will'ya stand up in court for me?"

"How accurate's your map, Tim?" I asked twisting in the saddle to watch him answer.

"I drawed maps for Quantrell durin' the war. He got where he wanted to go with'em. I know how to draw maps." There was a touch of pride in Tim's tone.

"There won't be a trial until the lid's blown off this whole thing. There'll be time to prove you out before the trial. If the gold's where you say it is, I'll stand up in court for you. Where's your map, Tim?"

I would do the best I could for Tim, but it was up to him. If the map was correct and forty percent of the gold was recovered, the jury might let him live instead of hanging him for murder. But you couldn't tell about a jury.

"How do I know you won't kill us and chase after the gold yourse'f? I don't even know who you are, Mister. That map's my insurance all 'round."

"Forget it, Tim. You run that risk with anyone you give the map to. Hell, when I tell Sheriff Moore, he'll beat the map out of you. Or, you can wait until the trial and try to buy your way out of hangin' then. That jury's goin' to have hemp fever. Or, you give the map to me." I fished around in my pockets, came up with the tin star the governor had given me with the commission. I showed Tim the tin star. "I'll testify that you gave me useful information an' that you're the cause for the recovery of the gold. As the arrestin' officer, the jury'll at least listen to me." I paused. "The way I see it, Tim, I'm the only chance for leniency you have. I'm your insurance now."

"Map's in Jeb's pocket right now, if you didn't take it out already." Tim grinned. "Probably been in your pocket all along." He laughed a high cackle. "I got your word, Marshal."

"I'll stand for you at the trial." I pulled the two letters I'd taken from Jeb out of my duster pocked.

"One of them letters is to my woman in Kansas. I give it to Jeb to post if anythin' happened to me. Jeb's one that stays behind to hold the pueblo. I figured nothing'd happen to him, and I could always get the letter back from'im whenever I wanted. Map's in the letter." Tim cackled his high-pitched laugh again.

I opened the letter and studied the map. "The map's clear."

"You're one son-of-a-bitch." Jeb grunted.

"Like the marshal here said, Jeb, you're a dreamer. It's goin' to get you hung." Tim's voice was suddenly flat, tired sounding.

I folded the map and put it in my breast pocket.

Santa Fe lay no more than two miles ahead. I needed to figure out what to tell the governor. Most likely, the governor would want to use force. I was convinced that the use of force would cost too many Indian lives. I wasn't sure how, but I thought I could break up the operation alone. If I failed, then the governor could pick up where I left off and solve the problem his own way.

Tim had all but guaranteed the return of a large portion of the stolen gold, but his information about the operation had been sketchy. I still needed more facts before I could figure out a plan that might work, or that the governor would accept.

"Tim, I'm goin' to sweeten the deal. I'll see the judge today and ask him to turn you into a witness for the territory, with extra protection, before the trial. I'll argue for a ten-year sentence. You give me good information that proves to be accurate about the names and descriptions of all the outlaws. You tell me all you know about the communications system, codes, everything. What do you say?"

Tim took his time and gave me the names and detailed descriptions of all the men. He told me where each man was stationed last he knew. He detailed how each man fought, his weapons, and what kind of warrior he was.

"The messenger system's simple. Runners're set up to run relays. They carry written notes. Ain't much to it." Tim said.

"Can all the outlaws write?" I asked.

"Naw, but Sergeant Horton keeps at least one man who can write at each pueblo. If I get your drift, Horton knows each man's handwritin'. He can tell who sent the message, which pueblo he's at by the hand writin'. No names's ever mentioned. Nobody ever signs the notes. Other than that, there ain't no code. Will you talk to the judge today?"

I thought for a while. "Yeah, Tim. If you haven't set me up for a trap, I'll be at the trial for you."

"You ain't goin' to make it." Jeb said. "You're up against the toughest men to survive the war. Hell, one man hadn't got a chance. I'll get free. You jus' watch. An' Tim, I'm goin' to kill you myself, slow and painful."

We passed some of the houses on the outskirts of Santa Fe. Three small boys ran out to trot behind my pack train, like a parade. A couple of barking dogs accompanied them. A woman stuck her head out of her door, looked at us, and called an old man to come look.

The day had warmed up and offered a comfortable mid-day. I didn't feel comfortable, wondered where Patricio Sanchez was. I didn't want to fight him now. I had too much to do. If I saw him, I would try for a delay, another pretty day. If I could end his revenge without bloodshed, I would. But I wasn't sure Patricio would give me the choice.

My plan for stopping the outlaws's operation was fairly complete. With some luck, the governor would give me the go-ahead. My guess was that I was the only one who knew anything about what was going on. I would probably be calling the shots.

Avoiding the plaza, I rode up to the Santa Fe jail with my prisoners.

CHAPTER THIRTEEN

Deputy Beckett quick-stepped out of the office of the Santa Fe jail as I tied my pack train to the hitching rail. "No need to bellow so's the whole, damn town can hear," he crabbed as he gimped off the boardwalk. He shucked his gun when he saw the men behind me were bound hand and foot. "What we got here?" His eyes shifted through a squint between me and my prisoners.

"Lock 'em up in separate cells, Deputy. Tim here gets special care. Don't let anyone near him." I scratched out the sand burrs under Jeb's stirrup strap before I untied him from the saddle. "Jeb here, threatened to kill my witness, Tim. Hold 'em both for robbery an' murder."

Jeb's cramped up leg wouldn't hold him up. I let Beckett yank him up by the collar from his fall while I turned to Tim.

"I hear the charges. By what authority're you lockin' 'em up? I can't just go lockin' up anybody." Beckett manhandled Jeb to the jail door, inspected his leg for bullet holes. "Who's goin' to pay for their grub?" Beckett spat at a sleeping dog's nose just before he pushed Jeb inside the door. "I swear, if I's to lock up everybody on some broken-down cowboy's say so, this 'ere jail'd be full to the brim."

"Take it up with the governor, Beckett, but hold these men until you do. Where's the governor?" I untied Tim, hauled him inside the squat, adobe jail.

"The governor's otherwise occupied today. This here's Fiesta time. He's out'ere politickin', hobnobbin' with everybody who's in from out-of-town. By the way, the whole, damn Sanchez family's in town. You better lay low 'til I can get you a army for escort." Beckett chuckled to himself.

Slamming the iron bar door on Jeb and watching Beckett throw the lock gave me a sense of relief. Depositing Tim in the last cell with no window and bolting that door left me feeling like someone had lifted a weight off my shoulders. I hated hauling prisoners.

I reached my long knife through the bars and cut Tim's bonds. I cut Jeb free. Beckett holstered his gun after he ordered the prisoners to step back from the bars.

"Feed and water 'em." I pointed at the water bucket next to the thundermug in the corner. "You can expect trouble. They'd as soon kill you as not, Beckett, an' they have friends outside who're killers. Their trial won't be for a while. Watch 'em close." I had to find the governor, turn over my prisoners, and get on with this matter, Fiesta or not. "Where'd you say the governor is?"

"Try the bar at La Fonda. That's where the rich folks're stayin'. What do I tell Sheriff Moore?" Beckett asked, as he hung the keys on the gun rack.

"Tell'im what I told you. These men're the governor's business." I pulled a couple of boxes of .44 shells off the rack, turned, and walked out.

A gentle breeze shuffled some dead leaves in the dusty road. Out over the tops of the low, adobe buildings, the mountain peaks glistened, covered with a fresh snow. On the slopes the gold of the aspen leaves had been replaced by the gray of bare branches. I noticed the smell of *piñon* smoke for the first time. Santa Fe stirred an excitement in me.

The plaza bustled, too busy for siesta time. The army band played a march from the bandstand. Canvas, stretched between poles, covered cooking stands that lined the streets. The smell of fried, Mexican food filled the air. Red, orange, and yellow banners flapped listlessly from the lampposts. A recently clapped-up platform blocked the entrance in front of the governor's mansion. Flags dressed all four corners.

The evening crowd, out early this holiday afternoon, promenaded around the plaza in an ambling parade. The young men circled the plaza in one direction. The young ladies walked in the other direction. Occasionally the flirtations of the promenade ended in an agreement and a couple paused to get something to eat, or headed for a quiet place away from the crowd. Fiesta fever bloomed early in the day, well before dark.

The young daughters of the rich Mexican families, *Las Ricas*, clustered in the southeast corner of the plaza, giggling, hiding their faces behind brilliantly painted fans. Their chaperones stood guard nearby.

The young ladies were all dressed up in their finest short, red skirts, white bodices, and fringed shawls. Even in the cool breeze, they managed to bare their slender necks and shoulders. They watched the young men of the wealthy Mexican families smoke, brag, and plan their conquests. Like the men, each young woman hoped to find her lover today.

In fact, the young ladies of the rich families were sent to Catholic schools when they reached puberty. They remained carefully cloistered away from any suitors until the family could arrange a suitable marriage. Any other woman was considered available for romancing. The Spanish blood that flowed in their veins ran hot.

The Spaniards that conquered this land two hundred years ago and settled the watered valleys had been cut off from the rest of the world and had not changed their ways. Fiesta remained an ancient, medieval ritual.

The Anglos, soldiers, teamsters, and traders all planned to have a fine time this Fiesta. There would be fights with the locals and someone would be killed. I had heard a killing always happened at Fiesta.

It would be fun to join in, to dance, to drink, to find a willing señorita. Instead, I had business with the governor. I tied my horses in front of La Fonda and attempted to brush off some of the trail dust and mud I'd picked up crawling around, river-wet, on the Santo Domingo sand hill. I switched the loads in my Colt with the new cartridges I took from the jail and hitched up my gun belt.

The boisterous crowd in the lobby made it difficult to push my way to the bar. A mariachi band played and six couples danced a Mexican fandango in the corner. The governor stood at the bar, surrounded by several men dressed in black suits, wearing broad-brimmed hats. They looked like ranchers from over Texas-way.

I moved to the edge of the group and caught the governor's eye. He showed no sign of recognizing me. I wasn't about to wait.

"Governor, I must have a word with you, privately." I called over the noise of the crowd.

"Not now, Sir. See my aid for an appointment!" His sharp tone indicated his irritation at the interruption and pissed me off.

"Now, Governor!" I said it so that there was no doubt I meant it. Noting the scorn from his entourage, I turned my back before any unseemly comments could be made.

We pushed our way through the crowd to a small room, off the barroom. The governor asked the occupants to excuse us and we were left alone. I shut the door.

"Now what is ... Ah, Mr. Waller. This better be important. Those men I left waiting are from the railroad, right? You know, of course, how important it is to convince them to bring rails into the territory, right?"

"Your reappointment as governor by the President, and those men bringin' the railroad here depend on how you maintain the law in this territory, right?" I shot back. "I think what I have to say is very important to you politically, Governor. You're sitting on a powder keg, and the fuse is lit. If it blows, it'll be heard all the way back to Washington." I paused for him to answer. I needed a lead from him in order to know how to proceed. His face turned to stone, but he reddened around the ears.

"What could you possibly have to do with my career?" His tone rang with anger. His head snapped back so he looked down his nose at me.

"Well, Sir, how about preventing the massacre of a thousand Indians, for a start?" I spoke slowly, evenly and waited for his anger to ease up.

"That's preposterous! The Apache in the Northwest are staying on the reservations, for the most part. There're some renegade bands raiding to the southwest, but Major Watson assures me that he'll have them cornered soon, right? The Comanches are in Mexico and have not come over the border in months. The Navajo are under control." He glared at me, appeared to be about to leave the room, but made no move towards the door.

It was clear to me that the governor had no information about the situation at the pueblos. He was not thinking of the gold robberies, and had probably forgotten about the job he had given me. He had barely recognized me. Must be that my commission meant nothing to him. I thought for a moment about letting him walk out of the room.

I could probably drop the whole thing right here and be shut of it, but I was in too deep. Twenty-three men had been murdered. The Indians were being held hostage. Apparently, I was the only one who knew anything about what was going on. I would have to see the job through, with or without the governor.

"Are you aware of the holdup of the second shipment of gold from Durango?" I paused. The governor didn't answer. "Thirteen men, including the Mayor of Durango, were killed from ambush. What're you doing about it?" Like him, I began to get angry.

The governor turned to breast me. He stared intently at me for a moment, then he motioned to two chairs.

"We received word a few days ago. The Mayor, you say? Very unfortunate, right? I haven't received any other information from any of my sources. The bandits have vanished. I'm assuming that the outlaws have left the territory, right?" He leaned back in his chair. "Durango's outside my jurisdiction. I can do nothing but send my condolences." He clasped his hands in front of his chest. Then unclasping his hands and leaning forward he asked, "What've you got?"

I told him everything I had discovered. I turned over my two prisoners officially and reported the death of the third outlaw. I outlined my plan for taking the rest of the outlaws and requested his authority.

"Do you really think they'd kill all those Indians, if I used force? This sounds like a matter for the army. How can you possibly think you can subdue seventeen men?" The governor looked like a frightened and confused man I had seen once on the deck of a sinking ship. He appeared overwhelmed by my account of the circumstances.

"They have dynamite in the kivas and they've proven themselves killers. Sergeant Horton's an experienced tactician. He has it set up so that force's the last thing you can use." The governor listened and my anger cooled some. "I'm thinking he'll wait for one more shipment and then disappear with the gold. Governor, my plan's the only sensible approach. Horton's strength is his hold on the hostages. His mistake's the division of his forces. I can destroy him bit-by-bit." I sat back in my chair. My words seemed to take effect on Connelly. "If I fail, you can try force, but it'll cost you the governorship. Even if I don't get them all, I'll break up the operation, and some of the gold'll be recovered. Your problem'll be over and you'll come out lookin' pretty good." I waited impatiently for his answer.

The governor sat back in his chair and gazed at the ceiling. I think he appreciated the dilemma of his situation. He couldn't risk the massacre of the peaceful Pueblo Indians, and he had to rely on me, an unknown entity. He reached into his breast pocket absentmindedly and pulled out two cigars. We lit up and smoked in silence, as he thought over his situation.

"Governor, I have to get moving," I said urgently. "I'll need a blank requisition form for two, fast, army horses and some equipment from Fort Marcy. I'll get to Durango in two days, if I ride straight through. Any further gold shipments have to be stopped!" I slammed the arm of my chair to stop his internal debate. "My first move's to cut the messenger system that starts in Durango. Do I have your authority, Sir?"

"Yes, yes anything you need, right?" He leaned forward again looking at me as if seeing me for the first time. "Why're you doing this? Surely you'll be killed, right?" He rose to pace the confines of the small, smoke-filled room.

"You gave me the job when you made me a deputy marshal, Governor. Like you, I plan to build my future in the territory." I pulled the badge from my pocket. "You want my badge, or do we play it my way?"

The governor regained his composure. He took a long draw on his cigar, exhaled. "Keep the badge, Deputy."

I rose to leave. The governor waved me back to my seat, poking a thumb at my chair. A tight smile flickered over his face.

"Mr. Waller," he said smoothly, as he wrote out the requisition, "I'm thinking about our futures, right? If you live through this, you'll become a famous man in the territory. A hero, right? I want you on my side, politically. Tonight's the Governor's Fiesta Banquet and Ball. It's the high point of the Fiesta, right? I want to introduce you to my friends and the influential people who'll be there. Come to the governor's mansion at eight, right?"

"What? Beggin' the governor's pardon, but I have to ride hard for Durango. The lid could blow off this thing at any moment. Horton's lost three men and could pull out. We could miss our chance at him." Disgusted, I rose to leave. "The miners could try another shipment and get more people killed. I'll get social with you when I get this job wound up." I stepped towards the door.

"Deputy," the governor commanded, "I'm givin' you an order." The governor extended his hand. "A few hours, right, Mr. Waller? The people you meet will be very important to your future successes."

"Governor, I've no formal clothes." I protested as I took the requisition. He left his hand out. I shook his hand absentmindedly.

"See my tailor here in the hotel. Put whatever you need on my bill, right?" He clapped me on the shoulder. "By the way, I hear you shot Patricio's favorite stallion out from under him. Seen any of the Sanchez family lately?" The hint of a smile played around the corners of his mouth again.

"I hope I don't run into any of them. It's not my intention to continue this feud, if I can help it." We walked out of the little room together.

The governor steered me back to the group of railroad men. "Gentlemen, this's Mr. Waller. You'll be hearing about him in the future, I'm sure."

One tall man, with a bushy, black mustache, extended his hand and introduced himself as Thorn Jenkins. "You a railroad man, Mr. Waller?"

"I've blown up a few railroads, Mr. Jenkins. I's always impressed with how fast you all could get them back in action." I shook his hand. "I'm sure I'll be shippin' cattle in the future. Now if you'll excuse me, Gentlemen." I pushed through the crowd and headed for the governor's tailor.

The tailor showed considerable irritation, said he was very busy while he measured me, but indicated that he would have what I wanted by evening. I ordered the works and a new black hat. My sweat stained and worn out old John B. had seen its best days long ago. The governor would be very surprised when he got this bill.

*   *   *

Fort Marcy, the garrison for most of Northern New Mexico, lay a little north of town. Two hundred and fifty men were stationed there, under the command of Major Watson, who also commanded all the federal forces in the territory, under General Carlton, I believe. The fort itself comprised little more than barracks, stables, blacksmith shop, supply warehouse, and a parade ground. Troops drilled on the dusty quadrangle when I rode up. I proceeded past them to Major Watson's headquarters.

"Major Watson, I'm Eli Waller, Deputy Marshal for the territory, under cover for the governor. I'd like to bring you up to date on the Durango gold robberies." I found myself standing at attention and shifted to relax.

"Good to meet you finally, Colonel. I first saw you under the worst of circumstances at Appomattox." He came from behind his desk to shake my hand. He offered me a drink. "What've you found out, Sir?"

The major listened with interest as I filled him in on the situation. "Major, if I fail, whatever you and the governor decide to do, don't use strong force. Horton may seek revenge. Don't goad him into it. Unless I have rotten luck, the operation'll be broken-up. If not, I'll leave some word as to how to proceed. Now, what've I overlooked? I want your advice." The bourbon he had given me tasted fine, and I took another with him when he offered it.

He thought for a while, stepped to a map of the territory on the back wall and studied it. "I have nothing to add. While you draw supplies from the quartermaster, I'll have Sergeant O'Hara get my two fastest, personal mounts. They're tested, fine warhorses. I'll miss'em, but you should have no others. I'll wait for further communications from you, Marshal Waller. Good luck!"

I equipped myself at the quartermaster's. I took another Colt like the one I had given Pete and stuck it behind my belt. A short-barreled shotgun looked handy. On a back shelf, I found a fleece-lined duster fit for cold weather. I pulled a stack of blankets from the pile. I could use them for trading for items I needed that were not in supply here. I replaced my rope. Finally I talked the supply sergeant out of a hundred dollars pocket money. This deputy marshal business paid off handsomely, at the governor's expense.

Gray and I led the bandits' horses, and Watson's two horses, out of the fort. Both the army mounts were big-boned, long-legged, deep-chested stallions. I could see why the major felt bad about lending them to a stranger.

Returning to Santa Fe, I stayed to the east of town until I got to the livery stable. I did not want a chance encounter with a Sanchez brother. At the livery I made arrangements for them to tend my growing *remuda*. I forked over some of my new pocket money.

I needed one more item for my attack on the outlaws. I rode Gray over and tied him to a tree behind the cathedral. I took my stack of blankets from behind the saddle where I had tied them.

The cathedral, a magnificent church, was the life's work of Bishop Lamy. Pete Montoya had told me that Lamy had come to the territory a relatively young man and had worked long and hard to build this monument to God. It was still unfinished. He and the parish had run out of money.

Recently, Lamy had obtained the money he needed from the Jewish merchant community. The only concession demanded for the money was that some Hebrew letters be placed over the main entrance. I walked through the church to the main entrance to see the letters. They weren't carved in stone yet.

I went back inside to look for a priest. Several old women, with black shawls over their heads, prayed and lighted candles for the dead. No one else was present. I went to the rectory. An old priest, lost in contemplation, strolled in the garden. I cornered him.

"Padre, I want to trade these blankets for a monk's robe, just like yours."

"You want to convert, My Son?" He sounded incredulous, but his eyes sparkled with a playful devilishness.

"No, Padre," I chuckled. "There's a priest at one of the pueblos who deserves a gift. He's my size. Can you help me?"

He went inside the rectory. When he returned, he produced the robe, a braided rope belt, and a rosary to complete the gift. I bargained some more and obtained a pair of sandals. I thanked him and returned to Gray.

I rode past Santa Fe to the stream that flowed south of town. I hobbled Gray where he could graze and found another grassy spot to stretch out on. Sleeping in the warm sun by the water, like a turtle on a log, would feel mighty fine.

There would be no rest tonight. I would have to stay late at the governor's ball to be polite. In the old, Spanish tradition, one had to always be more polite than his host. Politeness could be carried to ridiculous extremes, even in comparison with the manners of the Old South. After the ball, I had the long ride to Durango ahead of me.

I lay by the stream debating whether or not to go to Maria's for a Rivas beer. I still had not had a Mexican dinner in Santa Fe. On the other hand, I had run into bad luck at Maria's and Beckett had said the Sanchez family was in town for Fiesta. By now they would know I was in town. Why take a chance?

Just after sunset, I found a pool in the stream and took a cold bath. Then I packed my gear for traveling fast. When I was set up right for the trail, I rode over to the livery stable by La Fonda and checked on the horses.

The stable boy groused around feeling grumpy, a might upset that he couldn't celebrate Fiesta with his friends. I paid him extra to feed the major's horses grain and rub them down. Then I went to see the governor's tailor. He waited impatiently for me. Seemed like Fiesta had every body rankled.

The black suit, cut in the most modern style, waited for me. The pants fit snugly around the waist and narrow in the leg, but were cut to fit over my boots. The coat hung long with narrow lapels. The vest sported silver buttons, made by a Mexican silversmith of local renown according to the tailor. I had ordered two boiled shirts and a black belt with a silver buckle.

The outfit, topped-off with a light-blue, string necktie, fit like a doeskin glove. It had been a long time since I had been this well dressed. I felt elegant, the way I had felt when I captained the *Croft*.

The tailor seemed pleased to point out how he had adjusted the cut of the coat and vest so that I could carry my Colt out of sight, behind my belt. He warned that no man should go unarmed at Fiesta, no matter what the occasion. I thanked him and signed the governor's bill.

I had time for one Rivas beer before the governor's ball. I strolled from La Fonda into the plaza, now crowded with jubilant celebrants. A ten-piece, mariachi band had the crowd lathered up. Besides the usual promenade, people danced with abandon.

As I passed by the bandstand, a young señorita brushed by me, then stopped to look teasingly at me over her bare shoulder. Her eyes and the proud jutting of her chin invited me to dance.

This was Fiesta de Santa Fe and one of those cool, fall nights with music and hot passions in the air. The Rivas beer would have to wait.

CHAPTER FOURTEEN

I arrived at the governor's mansion late because it had been difficult to leave the arms of so-willing-a-señorita. Dancing in the cool, night air, to the music of the mariachi, at Fiesta de Santa Fe, the moment had to be savored, enjoyed.

Fiesta descended from pagan ritual, but fit right into church dogma. One sinned and confessed sins later. Without sin, there was no confession. With confession, one could sin. It was the ancient belief of the church that the two went hand-in-hand because of the weaknesses of all God's children. True believers therefore sinned and confessed with equal ardor.

After checking my new Stetson and gun belt at the door, I was ushered to the end of the receiving line. Some one had to be the last to meet the governor, his wife, various state officials and senators. I took my time.

"I was afraid you would not come, right? Welcome, Mr. Waller." The governor smelled of heavy drinking and cigar smoke, the rigors of politics. He had been enjoying himself. "This's my wife, Gloria Connelly. Gloria, this's Eli Waller, the man I told you about who won the duel with Bustos Sanchez, right?"

"Ah yes, Mr. Waller. I hope you've recovered from your wounds. You must tell me all about the duel. Rumors have it that you're quite a man with the knife and very brave." She patted my arm and spoke confidentially. "Your duel is all that's being talked about these days. You've become quite famous in Santa Fe society," she gushed.

Since I was the last person to arrive, Mrs. Connelly took me by the arm and introduced me to the other guests and dignitaries. She had a bright, gay smile and spoke softly. The governor wandered-off politicking so Gloria stayed on my arm. By the time dinner was served I had met half the people there.

When I sat down at the linen covered banquet table I was surprised to discover that the man on my right was the old priest I had made the trade with earlier today at the cathedral. He appeared to be much younger now, maybe in his mid-fifties. He smiled warmly. His body seemed more animated. I was astounded by his physical transformation from this afternoon and impressed by his rich, black vestment, trimmed in scarlet.

"Good evening, My Son. It is a pleasure to meet you for the second time today." He flashed his warm smile again. "Seldom do I get to meet a man who trades with the church rather than donating to the church. I think there is some hidden value I do not yet perceive in the robe you acquired." The same devilish eyes as this afternoon dominated his friendly smile. The combination in this holy man's face unsettled me.

"I hope that the monk's robe has special qualities, Father. All of the power of the church is needed where it is going. Does it have your blessing?" I asked.

"This is no small thing," boomed a voice from my left with a heavy, rich Spanish accent, "to ask for the blessing of the Archbishop of Santa Fe, the Monsignor Lamy,"

I was surprised by the intrusion and turned to look into the deep black eyes of the man sitting on my left. Obviously a *Rico,* strands of silver were woven through the fabric of his jacket. His curly, black hair, streaked with gray, framed his broad aquiline face, deeply seamed with wrinkles and darkly tanned by the sun. His bearing seemed proud, but not rigid. His voice held a note of condescension. He looked vaguely familiar, but I had not met him before. I had the strong impression that he was gently chastising me.

"When it is I who seeks the blessing of the Archbishop, he makes me get down on my knees. I must reach deeply into my pockets." The wrinkles in the corners of his eyes deepened briefly. "I have yet to meet the man who can make an even trade with the Archbishop. And then, to seek his blessing to boot? I should like to know what power you hold over him, this head of our holy church?" The *Rico* looked past me. "Tell me, Bishop, who had the better of this trade of which you speak? Am I in the presence of a new saint or merely a Yankee trader of great skill?" The *Rico* obviously bantered with the Archbishop at my expense.

"I fear my old friend, El Don Manuel Sanchez," the Archbishop looked me directly in the eyes when he said the name, "is eavesdropping again on the business affairs of others. Is it your habit to run the temporal affairs of all men, Don Manuel?" The Bishop's tone sounded affectionate. He cast his eyes on mine again and said directly to me, "I bless the monk's robe, if it is to be used in the service of God."

Governor Connelly had promised to open the future for me and here I sat between the two most powerful men in the territory, besides himself. Suddenly I became convinced that the governor might have also promised me a very brief future.

On my right sat the head of the Catholic Church, Archbishop Lamy, ruler of all men's souls and most of their wealth. He had more power over the beliefs of the people than any temporal ruler ever could. He could also recommend my soul to heaven and would probably have the opportunity to do so before the night was over.

On my left sat El Don Manuel Sanchez, *Patrón* of the Hacienda Sanchez, undisputed owner of more land than some of the monarchs of Europe ruled. His power dominated the actions of men. He, too, had the power to introduce my soul to heaven, and he had good reason to. I had killed Bustos, his son.

I sat between two counter-balanced forces. I felt safe for the moment, because El Don would never embarrass his host. The Archbishop would moderate any hostility that might arise. I began to appreciate the governor's sense of humor, even if it was at my expense, right?

It occurred to me that El Don might not know who I was, but that was most unlikely. El Don would be informed about everyone here. The situation I was in had been created with great care and design. I decided to sit back and enjoy the unfolding of the plan, whatever it was.

I started to introduce myself to El Don but was interrupted when Senator Lucero proposed a toast. We stood and drank to the great Territory of New Mexico, the governor and Fiesta de Santa Fe. When we sat down, El Don became occupied by the lady to his left.

The Archbishop turned to me and gesturing with his chin in the manner of the Mexicans indicated the governor. "He is a cunning man and a superb politician. The governor takes great risks with people. His power is derived from the fact that he is seldom wrong in his estimations of their worth." The Bishop was about to say more when he was interrupted by another toast to guests and friends.

El Don turned to me as he deftly slashed the steak on his china plate. "I have been told that you owned plantations and many slaves before the war with the Yankees. What is it like, Señor Waller, to lose all you own to the government of the country in which you are a citizen?"

"That's all behind me, Señor Sanchez." I paused as a waiter refilled my crystal wine goblet. "However, Sir, I imagine making this fine Territory of New Mexico a state will have the same effect on certain property owners. Having suffered the losses to my own government once, I'll work against it being done to me again, here, by my own government." I admired the color of the wine against candlelight then savored it. "To be an American and to fear the power of the federal government puts a man in an awkward position. This territory still has the chance to exert its sovereign powers." I caught El Don's eye. "I'll resist statehood, but when it comes, I'll fight to retain as much state's sovereignty as possible. I believe your son, the Senator, holds similar beliefs. I should like to meet him and discuss the matter fully with him one day."

I had made my opening for a peace-talk with the family. I wondered which way El Don would move on my offer. The circumstances of this dinner party falsely indicated that no feud existed between us, but I had no idea where El Don really stood on the matter.

"I shall arrange it, Señor Waller, but only if I may partake in the discussion." He looked at me intently.

I met his gaze steadily. "By all means, Señor Sanchez. The matter must be of great importance to you. Will I meet Señor Patricio Sanchez at this discussion?" I wanted to get things out in the open. This cat and mouse conversation with its dual purpose could easily be misunderstood. I would rather talk about a matter, than talk around it. I had found it safer to be direct, even in delicate matters.

"Ah, Patricio. My son has a mind of his own. He is not the politician like his brother. *Vamos a ver*, Señor Waller." Uncertainty played across El Don's brow, but did not slip into his eyes.

I translated the old Spanish saying he'd used, "We shall see." Because of his tone of voice, I added, "Perhaps."

It seemed, from the conversation with Don Sanchez and the comments of the governor's wife, that the killing of Bustos was being treated as the sad result of an honorable duel. In such matters the survivors of the victim carried on as if the deceased had met with an unfortunate accident. But, Don Sanchez's last statement left me with doubts as to how Patricio treated the matter.

It would be impolite to raise that issue directly with El Don. We had cleared the air between ourselves and had agreed to meet again on matters of state. El Don had made it clear he did not speak for Patricio. I hoped that, over time, an acquaintance with Don Sanchez might mature, allowing directness in our conversations.

I also felt some relief. Patricio would not strike from behind. Most likely he would contrive some insult and challenge me to fight to the death. Or, possibly through his father, I might get to know Patricio. Maybe I could figure a way to convert his revenge to friendship. Again, I could be making the whole thing up. Revenge might not be important to Patricio anymore. Still, I killed his prized stallion and set him afoot, a personal insult, in addition to knifing his brother. As El Don had said, "*Vamos a ver.*"

After dinner came brandy and cigars for the gentlemen. The ladies departed to another sitting room. Servants cleared the great hall of dining tables and made ready for the ball. The orchestra arrived. Ground, white sand was spread over the dance floor. More lanterns were hung on the bannered walls. The great doors were opened to clear the air. The excitement of Fiesta seeped into the grand ballroom on a cool mountain breeze, which carried the sound of a Mexican trumpet, clear, staccato, plaintive.

More guests arrived for the ball. I excused myself from the smoker and stood by the door where I could observe the arrivals. Carriages clattered up to the main entrance, escorted by mounted *caballeros* in their finest attire. Major Watson and five officers, dressed in blue with gold epaulets, galloped up. I watched for Dora Luz and wondered if she would be here this evening. I meant to have the dance Bustos had denied me.

Music called the banquet guests to the dance hall. The governor and Mrs. Connelly led the grand march to open the ball. I noticed that the Archbishop prepared to leave. I stepped to intercept him on his way out.

"I'm indeed honored to have met you in both your capacities, Bishop Lamy," I said as I reached his side. "I'll look forward to bringing the humble padre good news about the monk's robe. And, I shall anticipate a time when I'll not need the protection of church to balance the power of state at the dinner table." My smile brought forth his smile. "Perhaps, one day, I can have philosophical discussions with the man that is Archbishop." I had genuinely enjoyed meeting him.

He climbed the steps to his carriage then paused to watch another coach arrive. He turned, descended and said, "Perhaps the power of the church, as you put it, shall administer matters of state for a moment longer. I shall introduce you in the proper manner to La Doña Sanchez, Dora Luz, Patricio, and Edwardo." He studied me for a moment before he continued speaking. "Should your heart mislead you where Dora Luz is concerned, come and see me. I shall instruct you in the ancient manners of these proud, Spanish descendants. There are strict, rules with harsh penalties for their breach, and there are accepted ways to break the rules. I have some influence with the family. It may save your life." He turned to receive the adulation of the Sanchez family.

I greeted La Doña Sanchez with a sweeping bow. A strikingly beautiful woman, she seemed almost regal. Undoubtedly she still took lovers, as was the accepted custom in the *Rico* class.

Edwardo spoke politely but did not extend his hand. Nor did I. He turned and escorted La Doña Sanchez into the ballroom.

"Señor Patricio Sanchez, this is Mister Eli Waller." Archbishop Lamy took a step back from us so he could watch us both.

Patricio stood medium-tall, broad-shouldered, barrel-chested. His legs were too short in proportion to the rest of him. Thick, black, curly hair fell over the forehead of his broad, flat face, which was bisected by a thick mustache trimmed in the current style of the *Ricos*. His jowls hung flabby, like those of a man who drank heavily. His black eyes were deep, like his father's, but seemed to lack his father's liveliness. A deep, purple scar, too broad for a knife or saber wound, disfigured his left cheek. It looked like the mark of a bullet from his dueling days in New Orleans. Patricio reminded me of Bustos, except that Bustos had been leaner.

"So this is the man who ambushes horses. I would not have expected a gentleman so elegantly dressed." Patricio was careful to balance his slander with a compliment. He knew I could not take offense here, nor could he risk giving offense at the governor's ball.

"Señor Sanchez. May I buy you a drink later?" I turned anxiously from Patricio to meet Dora Luz.

The Archbishop introduced Dora Luz and her aunt, her chaperon. He continued to watch the event unfold with a fatherly eye.

"Señora Mondragon, Señorita Sanchez." I bowed, but did not step forward. "It is indeed my great pleasure to be formally introduced, and by the Archbishop of Lamy." I smiled broadly at Dora Luz. "Perhaps he will preside over a more formal event in our future." Glancing at Patricio, I saw hot anger flash in his eyes.

Above the edge of her fan, Dora Luz pierced my heart with her eyes. She lowered the fan gracefully to reveal a warm smile. A magnificent woman, she could not be over eighteen. Women of her age were usually already married. The fact that she was not spoke of some independence in her. I wondered if El Don had as much difficulty controlling her as he had controlling Patricio.

"Señor Waller," she spoke softly, "I hope you will save a dance for me this evening." Covering her face again she turned to enter the hall on the arm of Patricio. Her aunt followed, but turned to give me an appraising look. Her eyes were not friendly.

The Archbishop spoke at my side. "Patricio is bound by his father's will. But, I expect he will come to kill you the moment after Don Manuel's death. I pray we can find a way to end this need for killing. Think on it, My Son." He turned to enter his carriage.

"Bishop Lamy, the formal event I referred to was not a funeral." I assisted him up the steps of the carriage. "Good night, Sir."

The Archbishop's carriage pulled away and was replaced by another. I moved back into the shadows and lit one of the governor's cigars.

Dora Luz, beautiful and the daughter of the richest man in New Mexico, did not hate me. Patricio was not a present concern having been pulled off his hunt for revenge by his father. What did El Don have in mind? I was just another cowboy of no value to him. His son's killing me would be of little consequence.

I liked what had happened so far this evening, but there was more going on than I could puzzle out. I became very curious. Was I the pawn in the governor's, El Don's, or even the Archbishop's game?

Dora Luz would probably be married to the son of another rich family soon. Land meant more to these Spanish descendants than love. Women were treated as property by the rich land barons. Marriages were arranged to maintain the power of the families. After the marriage, both the men and the women were free to seek pleasures with others. These affairs were always discreet, but expected. I did not like the idea of Dora Luz taking lovers.

She was Catholic, from a family that could not consider itself separate in any way from the church. The church dominated and dictated their way of life. Before the war, my family had been Episcopalians, but during the war their church and beliefs had been blasted to rubble.

It seemed foolish for me to consider marriage in these circumstances. Dora Luz must know that she would lose everything if she married outside the Catholic faith. She simply indulged in a flirtation with those beautiful eyes of hers. I was nothing more than a notorious toy to her.

I flicked away the cigar and watched the sparks explode on the cobblestones. "*Vamos a ver*," I muttered as I strolled into the ballroom.

The orchestra finished the waltz and I returned Mrs. Connelly to the governor. She smiled warmly, insisted we dance again before the evening ended.

I enjoyed being in the presence of women. It brought out a better side of me. When I was alone or working, I found little to laugh at. But around women, one had to have a sense of humor.

I danced with several of the ladies, wives of the *Ricos*, or of the politicians. Linda Murdock was the wife of the army doctor stationed at Fort Marcy. I picked her for a polka after watching her dance with a young staff officer. We breached the usual manner of the polite, Spanish *Ricos* and chatted while we danced. She came from a Kansas family, over by Wichita.

The time came for me to make my move towards Dora Luz. We had watched each other from across the room. She had given me a questioning look the last time our eyes met.

"Señor Sanchez, may I have the pleasure of the next waltz with Señora Sanchez?" I gestured politely towards the Don's wife and took great care not to look at Dora Luz.

"Of course, Señor Waller. La Doña favors the waltz." His tone sounded casual. He did not appear displeased by my request.

I felt the situation was bizarre. The governor had invited me to his ball. A barroom fight, ending in a killing in self-defense, had been pronounced an honorable duel. Now I danced with the beautiful mother of the man I had killed. I wondered if it was all part of an elaborate trap.

The mother of Dora Luz danced as if trained in the art. She would be offended, think me most impolite if I spoke to her while dancing. Her face showed absolutely no emotion, as was proper. Yet there was a message in the way she moved her hips. She was of hot-blooded Spanish decent.

As we walked from the dance floor in silence our eyes met once for a moment. She gave me the kind of look that can drive a man mad trying to figure out what emotion lay behind it. I thanked her gallantly for the dance.

"Señor Sanchez, may I have the pleasure of the next dance with Señorita Sanchez?" I turned to face her. Only her sparkling eyes showed from behind her fan.

This was the one moment this night was meant to deliver to me. If I danced with Dora Luz, all war with the Sanchez family might be over, at least until El Don died. If I danced with Dora Luz, I felt my future would be changed forever. El Don paused only a moment. Courtesy demanded that he not refuse.

"You may have this pleasure, Señor Waller." He handed me his daughter's hand. There was a twinkle in his eye. Swear to God, I had the feeling I had just been bear-trapped.

I became aware of her perfume, like lilacs in early spring. My focus narrowed to only the woman I held in my arms. Her slim waist flared gracefully into womanly hips. Her dark eyes fixed themselves on mine and never broke the gaze. She moved to the music as if she were the instrument that created it.

She smiled. Her lips parted gently. Her long hair, piled upon her head behind a silver tiara, left her long, slender neck revealed. Bare shoulders framed her bosom. She wore a single, large ruby on a gold chain that lay deeply between her breasts. I was sure she had chosen the position of the jewel to offer the wandering eye an excuse to pause.

Holding her close in my arms I could feel no weight. She moved as I moved to the music, anticipating dips and twirls. I felt the warmth of her body when I used an old Virginia step to wrap her against me in a graceful spin. She moved gently against my body and stayed a moment longer than was proper.

Was it just the natural passion of these hot-blooded women or was Dora Luz stirred by me? My heart captured my head. I wanted the waltz to go on forever.

Then a deep sadness struck me. There was no rational explanation for these events tonight. I was but a toy to her, a flirtation. I had no land, wealth, or position to offer her. What could she possibly see in an over-dressed cowboy like me? Perhaps only the passions of La Fiesta worked their magic.

She must have sensed my feelings because she took over the lead in our dance just for a twirl or two, just enough to break me free of my sadness. I appreciated her intuition and gave her a broad smile. We danced together in a moment devoid of anything but our movement, her eyes, and her fragrance.

Reluctantly, I returned Dora Luz to her chaperon. I bowed deeply and thanked them both. Then I invited Patricio to join me for a drink at the bar. The joker in the deck, I needed to find out just what he stood for.

We talked about the ball, Fiesta, some of the prettier women dancing. Finally I asked him directly what he intended to do about my killing his brother, Bustos.

"It is simple." Patricio drained his glass. "I will kill you when my father is dead and can no longer command me. He has dreams of uniting the Spanish and Anglo peoples in New Mexico. He believes we will not survive if we do not mix the blood and the ways of our people with those of you invaders." He gestured a curt command to the bartender to fill his glass then turned to face me. "I do not agree and will bide my time. He is an old man." Patricio's look was cold, hard. "I think you owe me a horse. Perhaps I will spur you to death instead, *qué no*?" He strode off to join the family.

The bar served Rivas beer. I appreciated the governor's good taste and switched from the brandy I had been drinking. Apparently I might get to finish a Rivas in Santa Fe without a violent interruption.

I hoped Don Sanchez would live a long life and proposed a toast to him as I watched Patricio walk away. A formidable enemy, he would not let up and would pursue his hatred until he had his revenge. I would have to kill Patricio someday.

I ordered a second Rivas, drank it in honor of the sergeant and Pete, and watched the dancers glide and dip to the music for a while longer.

This was one hell of a ball. I had an engagement with El Don and Edwardo to discuss the statehood of the territory. I had shot the horse from beneath the *caballero* Patricio, but discovered he was as docile as a house dog, right now anyway. La Doña Sanchez had danced with me with the blessing of El Don. I had held Dora Luz in my arms. But I could not figure out nor trust the turn of events. It seemed like Bustos had never existed or that I had nothing to do with his death.

Dora Luz had danced with me flirtatiously. El Don had given me her hand courteously. I still had the scent of her on my hands. I burned her vision into my memory as she danced with Edwardo. If I looked at the situation one way, it appeared as if I were perceived by her family as a suitor for Dora Luz.

The difference in our ages meant nothing to me. What worried me was the church and its hold on her and the Sanchez family. Bishop Lamy had said that there were ways to break the rules. I would have to find out what he had in mind. It might be possible for Dora Luz to go against the family, if I were to win her hand. It seemed doubtful she had the free will to go against the church.

It had been quite an evening. I knew one thing. After I finished the jobs for Connelly and Red, I would court Dora Luz, hat in hand. Or was I dreaming under the influence of music, brandy, Rivas, and La Fiesta.

Midnight closed in. I had the long ride ahead of me to Durango and straight into danger. To make my manners and depart, I worked my way through the dancers and the observers to the cluster where the governor and Mrs. Connelly entertained their guests.

"Governor Connelly, I appreciate all you've done for me here tonight. I hope to be back with good news soon."

The tone with which the governor wished me luck made Mrs. Connelly look at us both curiously.

I bowed to Mrs. Connelly.

Concern etched her forehead, stole her pleasant smile away. She reached for my arm to restrain me, give her time to ask the question that perturbed her.

I turned away to get after the job at hand.

CHAPTER FIFTEEN

I relished the feeling of the stallion working between my knees. Major Watson's warhorse had an easy, rolling gallop. He shifted nimbly to miss brush and boulders, jumped gullies smoothly, climbed inclines with a steady, powerful pace. Leaning back in the saddle, I let him carry me mile after mile. I would switch horses in another hour, but now, I admired the horse and enjoyed the ride.

The night air felt cold and loneliness chilled me as I stood under the deep-indigo sky and stretched. I untied the fleece-lined duster from behind my saddle and shucked it on before I switched my saddle to the second mount.

The stars cast light on the ground so bright I looked up to see if the moon had risen. No moon, but Venus had arrived above the eastern horizon. Her brightness put Mars to shame as he stalked Aldibaron. Even Serius, brightest of all the stars, paled in her presence. All was silent except for the pounding of the horses' hooves and the memory of the rhythm of the music.

I had left the governor's ball at midnight. The fever of Fiesta still infected the air as I had approached the plaza. The music of the mariachi and a night of mescal had frenzied the dancers.

I had told the señorita that I danced with before the banquet, that I would return at midnight for another dance. I had wondered if she would be there. Perhaps some lucky local had wooed her away.

She had picked me off the bench, where I sat in the plaza watching the endless promenade of young suitors, and hoped. She had greeted me with a broad smile. We had danced again in the cool, fall breeze.

She warmed and invited me. In a cool, dark *placita* we found, away from the crowd, we satisfied each other's passions. The sweet tryst reminded me of nights before a battle, when some tender southern belle might grant me the graces of her body as if the gift were to be received for the last time ever.

As the major's stallions charged further into the night, away from Santa Fe and from Fiesta, my head cleared. Women always cast a spell over me. I realized I had been thinking of marriage at the ball, hinted at it boldly, if I remember rightly. The absurdity of that behavior and my circumstances struck me. I lay back in the saddle and belly laughed. Then I howled sadly at the stars. I rode not to meet a bride, but to challenge death.

Not wanting to jigger the horses, I pulled up and found a sheltered place to build a fire and boil coffee. As the water heated I switched my saddle and gear back to the roan stallion.

A cup of coffee always brought a bit of peacefulness to me. Troubles seemed to stop tormenting for a moment. I concentrated on just the movements of the process of tending fire and making coffee. Time slowed to the pace of the water taking its own time to boil. There was no way to change that measure of time. Water boiled when it was ready, and all else waited until then. I paused in that elongated time then drank black coffee. Memories of Fiesta faded away. My mind shifted to the dangers ahead.

I decided to stop bushwhacking and ride south a bit to intercept the main road from Santa Fe to Durango. Well used, it would be easier to follow in the dark of night and less risky to the horses. In tomorrow's light I might encounter travelers and would seek any news they might carry.

The road bypassed the pueblos, which lay in the backwash of the territory. Their isolation had made Sergeant Horton's plan so effective.

The roan horse picked up his easy gate where he'd left off. Time and distance rolled by. I fought off sleep. My senses numbed. Calculating time by the swing of the Big Dipper, I estimated that the sun would brighten the east in an hour. Its glare would make it harder to keep my eyes open.

I promised myself a short sleep just after sunrise. I thought about the feeling of stretching out, letting the saddle pounding relax away, if only for a short nap.

The stallion broke gait, paused, then leapt the gaping ditch that grew into an arroyo further south. Caught napping, I was pitched back over cantle on to his croup. His stiff-legged landing bounced me back into the saddle. The ache in my battered balls kept me awake for some time. Finally, I could no longer resist sleep.

Bright sunlight woke me into a nagging feeling that time was running out. The horses pranced, ready to run, and I felt refreshed. I estimated the ride to Durango would take another thirty hours and decided to forego coffee. Pulling dried beef out of my saddlebag I mounted up and booted my steeds into a gallop as I gnawed at my

breakfast, worried about my plan to stop the outlaws.

*   *   *

Tired bone-deep, I rode into Durango just
as dusk settled on the land. I had covered over
two hundred miles since the ball two nights ago.
From the pomp and gentility of the governor's ball
I had ridden into a cruel world, one where I stood
alone against hardened, trained killers.

I had a rough plan, based on incomplete
information, but I felt calm, past fear. There had
been battles many times before. I felt ready.

The general store was closed for the night
when I went to find Ann. A dim light glowed in
the back window where her kitchen was. I
knocked, then rapped hard again at the back door.

"The store is closed." Ann called through
the closed door. "Come back in the morning."

"Ann, it's Eli. I have to see you, now." I
did not like standing in the alley yelling my business at a closed door.

Ann half opened the back door and stood
blocking it. She wore a black dress and looking
haggard. "It's you?" she whispered. Her face hung
flat, drawn tightly over her cheekbones. "What
do you want? Can't it wait?"

"My condolences, Ann. I know this's a bad
time for you, but I need your help to capture the
men that killed your husband." I pushed her back
from the door and stepped inside past her. My
brusqueness startled her.

She recovered quickly and led me into the
kitchen where we had enjoyed her peach pie before. She poured hot coffee into two cups as I
told her what I had uncovered and what I planned
to do.

"Ann, I'm deputy marshal for the Territory of New Mexico. I'm out of my jurisdiction, but the trouble starts here in Durango. I know who killed the convoy guards and your husband. I need your help to prove it." I piled on the table the three bags of gold nuggets I had taken from Tim, Jeb, and the bandit-monk who tried to gun me at Jemez Pueblo.

"I want you to take these samples to the assay office in the mornin'. Get a report from the assay master pinpointin' the locations, the exact claim these samples came from." I pushed the bags across the table at her. "I'm sure they'll prove to be from Durango claims. I need this evidence to convict the outlaws."

Ann reached for a bag then withdrew her hand. Her eyes filled with tears.

"Ann, send the report to the governor of New Mexico as soon as you get it. Will you do this for me? Ann?"

Her mood shifted and she settled in her chair holding herself less rigidly. "Nothing has been done around here. I'm glad to see someone has some interest in the murder of my husband, uh, late husband." Her mouth pursed as she fretted. "How am I supposed to say that, Eli?" Her eyes clouded up again and almost spilled over tears.

Ann cleared her throat and not waiting for an answer continued, "Fortunately, no more gold has been shipped." She lifted a bag, furrowed her brow as she measured the weight of it. "The town's completely disorganized. Sandy Thompson's being proposed for sheriff. That takes the cake! The citizens of Durango's turning to a crook to catch the crooks?"

"I'm goin' to see Sandy next. I don't think he's directly involved, but I think one of his men is. You know anything about Ben Ronzio?"

"He works for Sandy, a bodyguard I think. He lives in a cabin about two miles out of town, on the road to La Plata. He comes in the store and buys supplies enough to take care of three or four people. I have never seen his family." She rose and stepped to the iron stove and the coffee-pot. "He came in the store late this afternoon," she said as she refilled the cups.

"May I keep my horses in your barn, Ann? I need the freedom to come and go without stirring up interest." She nodded assent. "After I take care of things here, I'll ride hard back to New Mexico. You have some grain I can give the horses?" I knew I was imposing, but I did not think I was putting her at risk.

"Sure, Eli." She looked at me from under long eyelashes. Her face softened around the eyes. "You look tired out. Would you like to rest upstairs?"

"No, Ann, thanks. Time's runnin' out on this job. I have to get on with it." I drained my coffee and studied the bottom of the cup. "I'll be back for more of your fine pie an' coffee when this is over. It'd be nice to sit with you by your fire for awhile." I rose to go. At the door Ann touched my arm and looked deep into my eyes when I turned. "I want you to come back, Eli."

Thompson hadn't come to the Red Garter yet. Nobody knew where he was. Ronzio wasn't around either. I went to the livery stable and hired a fresh horse. After finding the road to La Plata, I headed for Ronzio's cabin.

Most people don't ride out much at night. Coming up to a camp or a cabin in the dark was risky business so I rode past Ronzio's cabin to scout it out and look for a likely place where the runners might camp while they waited for a message to deliver.

A small canyon opened on to the road, about a mile past the cabin. On a hunch, I turned up the canyon. I remembered the last time I had ridden to Vallecitos on a hunch that had not paid off.

I pulled my Winchester and left the livery horse tied. Going on foot along the dim trail up the canyon would be quieter. I hadn't gone more than a few hundred yards when the night breeze flowing down the canyon brought me the smell of drift smoke. I left the trail and eased forward, careful not to make a sound. I searched for the campfire's light.

In a small cave, almost covered from view by a fallen slab of rock, I spotted the campfire's glow. I shifted position to get a better view inside the cave. Ronzio hunched in the cramped space and gave sacks, probably of food, to two young Indians. I pulled back and headed for my horse.

The messenger system was still in place. I reckoned that if the Indians needed that much food, they intended to stay put for a while. Sergeant Ben Horton must be holding out for more gold and one more ambush.

I speculated about Sandy Thompson as I rode back to Durango. Where was he? I needed a man I could trust to hold Ben Ronzio in check. With the sheriff of Durango killed in the first ambush, Thompson was my best bet. Ann had said the town's people wanted to put Thompson up for the sheriff job. Apparently they trusted him. Still, I had some doubts about Sandy Thompson.

Around midnight I found Thompson behind the bar at the Red Garter. He smelled of cheap perfume and looked rumpled, tussled like he had been sporting with one of his painted ladies. "Where's Ronzio?" I looked around.

"Town's mighty quiet, I sent him on home. You need him?" Thompson jabbed my chest with a stiff finger, "I'll call him to protect you." Thompson broke out in laughter. "You expectin' trouble? I can send for him," he laughed heartily again. "Let's go to my office." He grabbed a couple of beers from behind the bar.

He turned to walk ahead of me. I slipped the thong off the hammer of my Colt and followed. In his office he handed me a beer and offered a cigar. He gestured towards a chair as he settled behind his desk.

"How long've you known Ronzio?" I held a light to my cigar.

"Been with me a couple of years now. Cleans up messes for me from time-to-time. Says he's goin' to kill you with his bare knuckles next time he sees you." Thompson's face contorted meanly as he imagined the results of the encounter. He ran fingers through the fiery hair on his head, then laughed. "I'd like t'see that. Don't know how I'll bet."

"You goin' to get elected sheriff of Durango?"

"It'd sure keep the suspicions off me. The robberies've riled up the people pretty bad. They want action, and I can't deliver a thing. I can't promise'em nothin'. So who knows?" He chewed at the end of his cigar. "You must have somethin' or you wouldn't be back here. You find my gold?" He leaned forward to rest on his forearms, turn his beer bottle absentmindedly between both palms.

"Some of it. What'd you do if you found out one of your men was gettin' paid by another boss to steal your gold?" I watched Thompson closely. He sat back in his chair and played with his cigar this time.

He rolled the cigar between his fingers. "I'd kill him!" He crushed the cigar into shredded leaf. "You pointin' a finger at Ronzio?"

"What do you know about him?"

"He's around when I want'im, does what I tell'im to do." Thompson reached for another cigar. "Ain't no reason to distrust'im."

"Ronzio's out of my jurisdiction. I can't arrest him, but he's the inside man here in Durango. You can kill him for all I care. For sure, keep him tied down for the next ten days. Don't let him go to his cabin durin' that time. Not for any reason. You do that, and I think I can get all your gold back." I was offering nothing if Thompson was mixed in this with Ronzio.

"Have any proof, Marshal?"

"All I need for a jury. Will you hold him for me?"

Thompson rose, paced to the window and thought for a while. "I'll do it," he said turning to face me. "I'd like to see this town settle down again. Business's off on account of instead of em robberies. I'm a businessman, not a sheriff or politician. If Ronzio don't meet with a fatal accident, what do I do with him after ten days?"

"Send him under guard, maybe with the next gold shipment, to the governor of New Mexico. Tell the governor that Waller sent him to be held for trial on charges of murder and robbery. The governor'll take care of him after that. Don't let a gold shipment head out for a while."

I studied the ash on the end of my cigar and weighed what I thought I needed to do next. Then I rose from my chair and shifted the cigar to my left hand. I stood facing Thompson across the room by the window. "Sandy, if Ronzio isn't out of business, I'll know it. I'll assume you and him are in this together. I'll step out of my jurisdiction long enough to kill you."

The muscles in Thompson's shoulders flexed. Color rose in his neck, spread beneath the freckles on either side of his nose. I tensed, ready for trouble.

Then a broad grin spread over Thompson's face and he raised his hands to rest on his hips. "There ain't much trust in this world, Marshal, 'specially for a man like me. I'll disregard the threat." He turned back to the darkened window and talked over his shoulder. "A threat to kill me and a promise to recover my gold're the only chips you had to play. But, that ain't the whole game now is it, Marshal. You need to know where I stand." He turned back around to face me straight on. "Well, Sir, I like this town. She'll be good for a few more years if the gold don't play out. By that time I'll be rich. So, I'll cover your backside from Ronzio. You bust up the outlaws and recover my gold." He lowered his head to frown at me from under his red eyebrows. "Don't threaten me."

I left the Red Garter and headed for the livery stable to return the rented horse. It being so late, I saw no use in rousting out the livery boy. I tied the horse in an empty stall, pulled my gear, slung it over my left shoulder.

As I stepped out of the stall, into the dim light of the lantern hanging on a nearby post, I heard the crunch of a man's boot in the gravel outside. I froze in my tracks. At the same time the silhouette of a big man loomed in the barn door. Then Ben Ronzio stepped into the ring of light across from me.

Ronzio held the reins of his lathered horse in his left hand. He let them drop and with his left hand he started to unfasten the buckle of his gun belt.

"I wondered who come sneakin'up my canyon. Took some doin' ta track that horse yonder." The left side of Ronzio's face twitched and set his mustache to dancing. "Works out nice this-away. I get ta kill a man fer spyin' on me and a cocky jackass I hate all at once't." The twitch spread to the other side of his face and forced his top lip to curl back. "Take off your gun," he fairly purred. "Let's see if you're a man without it," he chided. "I'm goin' ta kill you with my bare hands."

Ronzio had not yet let his gun belt fall. His right fist hovered, clenching and unclenching hypnotically, over the butt of his pistol.

"Guns, Ronzio." I felt cold and empty inside. "We fight with guns. Now!" I barked the command to jerk Ronzio into action.

His top lip snapped flat over his teeth. He palmed his gun. As the muzzle cleared leather, heavy lead ripped open his heart. He staggered back into his spooked horse.

Ronzio's shot ripped into the timber of the loft above my head.

My second shot pounded Ronzio backwards into the darkness. I heard him crash on the gravel. The gun in his fist exploded in the dirt.

I didn't hear thrashing, moaning, or labored breathing. I stepped into the bright light to douse the barn lantern, then slipped out the back door with my gear and melted into the shadows where I waited for trouble.

Nobody came to see what had happened. Nobody even lighted a lamp in a window nearby. By ambushing all the leaders of this community, Sergeant Horton had taken Durango hostage and subdued it by fear of violence. Or hell, maybe people in a boomtown were used to shots in the night and didn't care.

With Ronzio dead I had cut off the rattles of the snake that lay over the pueblos. No messages would be sent from Durango. I had bought some time, and maybe the element of surprise, unless Thompson sent a message out to Horton.

I had no proof that Thompson was in cahoots with the outlaws and felt it unlikely. Tim had named only Ronzio, which meant that his hand on the note was the one Horton recognized. My gut feeling told me that Thompson did not know about the Indian runners. But I sure as hell wasn't positive.

Maybe Tim had set a trap for me here, with Ronzio the bait, Thompson the killing mechanism. Yet without proof I could not confront Thompson. I had tried it once this evening and had to back down. I would have to take a chance on him after all.

Staying well hidden in the deepest shadows, I hauled my saddle through the silent town back to Ann's barn. I found the low door on the side of the barn away from the house. After listening and watching for pursuers, I slung my gear inside the barn, struck a match for light, and stepped in.

Ann startled me into shucking my gun. Unexpected, she stood just inside the door wrapped in a blanket. I stomped the dropped match before it kindled the straw on the floor, holstered my gun and struck another match to light a lamp.

"I heard shooting. I just wanted to know you were safe." She sounded afraid and relieved. "Here, I made something for you to eat on the trail." She held out a bundle.

"Thanks, Ann." I accepted the bundle and packed it away hastily. "Ann, if you hear that I'm killed, or if the robberies don't stop, get word to the governor that Sandy Thompson's the place to start his search. He'll understand the message," I reassured her as I cinched up my saddle.

Suddenly Ann stood very close beside me. As I turned to her she let the blanket slip from her shoulders to the straw covered earth. She turned her face up to mine. I took her in my arms.

We both needed the warmth of each other. Her breathing quickened on my neck telling me all I needed to know. I kissed her hard but gentle against the moment of saying good-bye.

Ann pressed full against me, made soft mewing sounds deep in her throat, then pulled me towards the blanket.

She was newly widowed. I had to ride. For all I knew, half of Durango could be after me by now for killing Ronzio.

"Ann, not like this, Honey." I tried to pull away but felt compelled to kiss her again. "I want to take my time with you, to be gentle."

"No... Be rough! Eli..."

*   *   *

I had the whole damn ride to do over again, most of it anyway. The major's horses, watered, fed, a little rested, seemed ready to make the long trip or die in the effort. But my butt was dragging from fatigue.

Timing was the key to everything now. I had to strike the body of the snake while it had no warning. If I could retain the element of surprise, I had a chance. Without word from Ronzio in Durango, I had a chance. Even if Thompson sent a message, if I rode straight through, I had a chance.

I had left Santa Fe two nights ago at the same late hour. This time I headed straight for the constellation of Orion. Venus hung to my left. Her brilliance reminded me of Dora Luz, but I saw Ann's face instead.

I tried to put Ann out of my head and concentrate on Venus. But what might have happened with Ann only moments ago filled my brain. I cussed myself for not accepting what she had so strongly offered, praised myself for denying my lust for a change.

Venus seemed to climb from the horizon more slowly than usual. The fatigue of the long ride slowed down my world. I felt each step of the horse jar my bones and eat away my flesh as he galloped.

I dashed for the pueblos until red lights exploded in my head. Finally I realized the sun had climbed above the horizon and shined in my eyes. Out of my head with fatigue, I would fall out of the saddle and kill myself if I didn't get rest.

Time to rest would cost me my edge on Thompson, if he turned out to be one of the outlaws. I would lose my lead on the runners, if they were coming. But I could not go on. I rode off the trail and picketed the horses. I fell asleep before I could pull my blankets over me.

I woke up stiff and sore. My wounded side hurt from pounding leather for days on end. Coffee did not make me feel any better. I did not relish having to charge on. Then time leaned hard on me. I had to push it now or pay a high price later for dallying.

A dry wind kicked up from the southwest. Up high, mares' tails soared quickly across the sky. It didn't take long before the wind stopped lifting dust and started throwing sand. Off to the south I could see the sand storm building. I kept driving the horses at a killing pace.

When the blowing sand cloud struck, it felt like a load of buckshot in the face. This dust storm meant to sand everything down to a smooth finish. I turned the horse's rumps to the wind and sat out the blasts. I didn't think she would blow for long. This was the angry burst of wind, preceding a mass of cold air, blowing in from the west.

This kind of weather could spin into a blizzard this time of year. It could be one of those early, quick-hitting, fast-melting snowstorms. It could be a killer, if it caught men or stock unprotected.

I wondered how Red and the herd were progressing. They would be out on the high plateau west of Corrales. The storm might reach that far south. I started thinking over the country I rode in and decided I would head over to an arroyo and seek shelter from the grating sand.

As quickly as the wind came up it died down. Dust fell out of the sky like rain. The temperature fell out the bottom as the cold air arrived. I turned the horses toward the road and drove them into a lope.

Sunset brought real cold. My new fleece-lined duster protected me. About midnight, the air warmed up a bit and it started to snow. The storm laid down three to four inches of dry crystals, and then the sky cleared and the night turned cold again, with brilliant starlight bouncing off the fresh white earth.

The weather might be my ally. The snow might not have melted by the time I arrived. Before I rode into Jemez Pueblo, I could scout around the west side to see if any runners had beaten me home. I would know if I still held the element of surprise. I never thought I would be grateful for a dusting and a snowstorm, but I felt that way.

I rode until dawn, then broke off my dash south for a fire, coffee, bacon and beans. The horses needed water, munched snow.

I had not thought to look at what Ann had sent with me to eat. I had just stuffed it in my saddlebag. Opening the cloth sack revealed half-a-dozen cornbread muffins and a small jar of apricot preserves.

My spirits brightened up a bit as I remembered Ann. A woman's touch in this lonely camp lent a comforting feeling, before the impending battle.

CHAPTER SIXTEEN

Snow still hung on the *piñon* and juniper trees, the low sage and prickly pear. Here and there clumps of grass stood-up straight, but most of it bent over under the weight of a snowcap. The cliffs of the mesas in the distance seemed more red in contrast to the white blanket at their feet. Above it all, a cold sun hid in a cloudy, gray sky and refused to come out to melt the snow. I appreciated the sun's reluctance for a change. The snow on the ground gave me an advantage this time. San Ysidro lay a couple miles ahead. I would arrive around noon, perfect timing for my plan. I eased up on the near spent horses, reined them back from an easy lope to a determined walk. The slow pace and sleep conspired to close my eyes. I dozed in the saddle.

When I rode into Señora Martinez's yard the house appeared to be deserted, no tracks outside in the snow. Yet a wisp of smoke rose straight up in the still air from the *curandera's* chimney. When I knocked, she came to her door and spoke through a crack until she recognized me.

"You come for the healing powder? You ver' soon come back. No matter. She is ready for you." She left the door to get my mixture.

"Señora, *por favor*. I have another request," I said, as I handed her coins for the medicine. I added an extra coin with a flourish. "I want to borrow your burro for a day or two and to leave one of my horses in your care."

We made the arrangement. I roped her old burro and dragged him off behind the roan stallion. This desert canary balked and brayed like I meant to lead him to slaughter.

I had seen burros carry a load that would stagger a horse. They could carry forever, seemed like, but only at a walk. The sight of a running donkey was an unusual thing unless you carried a catching rope. When they did not want to work, there was nothing that could convince them. The major's roan horse applied brute force to get the burro up the trail on the end of the rope.

I headed out from San Ysidro to Jemez Pueblo. About three miles from the pueblo, I cut west off the trail. Finding a suitable place, I tied the burro. Then I rode the roan stallion in a sweeping search around the west side of the pueblo, about two miles out. I remained very careful not to fall into the line of sight from the mission's bell tower.

I searched the snow cover for the tracks of an Indian runner. Here and there the heat stored in the earth had melted patches of snow. Still, the white blanket, though tattered, covered the land sufficiently. I became confident that a runner had not passed over it.

Maybe Sandy Thompson could be trusted after all. The evidence indicated he, or Ronzio, had not sent a runner. If Thompson had sent a runner, he had not arrived yet. If a messenger was running now, the snow might have slowed him down. Suddenly I felt a compelling urgency.

The first strike on Jemez was the key to my plan to cripple the bandit's operation. So far it appeared that the communications system had been cut. I held the element of surprise.

If I got my way, Sergeant Horton might be beaten a step at a time. If I was lucky, I would get him and the gold. To tell the truth, I didn't feel optimistic. I knew I could stop the robberies, but I wanted to win the whole, damn war. I had a promise to keep to the governor, and to Ann.

The burro, waiting to give me grief for dragging him away from home, lay where I had tied him. I grabbed his ears and hauled him to his feet. Then I tied the major's stallion where he could paw grass from the snow.

From my gear I assembled my weapons. Making a sling, I slung the sawed off shotgun down my backbone. I pulled the monk's robe on over my head, over my clothes. I cut slits in the sides of the robe so that I could get to my Colts.

Taking the most worn out blanket I had, I made a pack to throw over the shoulders of the burro. Then I cut a burro stick from a bush. After checking my loads and slipping the holster thong off the hammer of the Colt, I took off my hat and put on the monk's hood. If Bishop Lamy could see me now... I put the sandals on last. My feet danced to the cold as my toes curled away from the wet snow.

Burros didn't wear halters or bridle and bit. I rode this one by sitting way back on the rump and steering him by stinging him on the neck with the burro stick. It didn't take long for the burro and I to get to an agreement. He would go where I directed, but it would be at his pace. He moved like he was as worn-out as I felt.

I pulled the hood of the monk's robe over my head to hide my face and for the little warmth it provided. Thinking of myself in this get-up, astride an ass with my feet dragging over the tops of the snow, made me laugh. Maybe there was some humor in my life away from women after all. Trouble was, I was laughing at myself.

Bishop Lamy had not laughed when he gave me his blessing. I recalled the look in his eyes. I forced myself to become more serious and face the dangerous task ahead, but the coyote fetish the Jemez chief had given me came to mind and I chuckled again. The image of the pagan prankster, dressed in religious garb, tickled me. For a man building a new future, a new identity, I had picked an identity as far from what I believed as could be imagined. The atheist dressed in God's uniform? Trusting the disguise?

The burro knew the way up the trail to Jemez and after a while he needed little urging. Finally the bell tower of the Jemez mission came into view. I slumped over and tried for all the world to look like an exhausted priest at the end of a long journey. The act came easily enough.

As the burro and I approached the plaza at his slow walk, the sun broke free of the clouds and bathed the snow-covered pueblo in dazzling light. Perhaps soon, the captive Indians would be free to go about their business in the sun again. And this might be the sunny day I died, trying to imitate a child of God.

I hesitated, afraid to sneak a look at the bell tower for fear of tipping my hand. I'd been here before. Someone might remember my face. Danger prickled fear down my spine under the shotgun as I came into rifle range.

I knew an outlaw hid in the bell tower and had observed my approach. He hadn't shot me yet. So I rode up to the steps of the church and stopped. After sliding off the rump of the burro, I stretched then walked up the steps.

Pausing at the church door, I bowed my head, steepled my hands in prayer and closed my eyes so that they would adapt from the glare of the sun off the snow to the dark I would find inside the church. Tensed, I took a deep breath and crossed myself to fortify the disguise, maybe to test my belief by taunting the Catholic God.

I had not expected to get this far without being shot at or at least hailed by one of the bandits. I was still an easy target for the men in the chief's house across the plaza, or where ever they hid now. My shoulder blades itched like they expected the sting of a bullet. I pulled the hood low over my face and stuffed my right hand into my robe. Left handed, I pulled the door open and stepped into the gloom.

A shadow struck at me from my left.

I ducked. The blow glanced down my back off the shotgun under my robe. I would have been clubbed senseless had I not expected the attack.

I spun left, caught the attacker off balance with a strong right jab to the guts. I shucked my Colt as he doubled over then straightened.

Gasping from the gut jab, he attacked with the shotgun butt again.

He should have pointed and fired. He'd have cut me in two.

I chopped the side of his head with my gun butt, dropped him in a heap.

Listening, I heard nothing but his labored breathing. Cutting a length off the monk's rope belt around my waist, I tied the outlaw and gagged him with his kerchief. I dragged him into the confessional and returned to the church door. Still no sounds came from the pueblo.

I put on the bandit's hat and ran up the bell tower ladder. Pulling the hat down low I exposed just my eyes as I looked out of the bell tower window. Nothing moved below me in the plaza.

Suddenly the door of the chief's house opened and a man carrying a shotgun stepped out. He waved at the bell tower. I waved back. He said something over his shoulder and started for the church with the shotgun in the crook of his arm. It looked like things might be going my way. I climbed down out of the bell tower.

Hiding in the deepest shadow of the entry, I waited. I heard the man's boots crunch snow as he came up the steps. He paused and then pushed the church door open.

He stepped out of the bright light into the dark. I counted on his momentary blindness, took two steps, and stuck the Colt in his face. His eyes adjusted to focus on the big-bore muzzle. He froze. I relieved him of the shotgun.

I jerked him in the rest of the way and shut the church door behind him. I cocked the shotgun in my left hand and jammed it into his ribs. He raised his hands.

"How many bandits're in the chief's house?" I jabbed his ribs again.

"One. But you lose, Pardner. He'll kill the priest over there if I don't brin' you back right away. Then he'll kill the chief." The outlaw spoke calmly, but his eyes darted alertly as he searched for the lookout. "He'll keep on killin' till you give yourse'f up."

"Let's accommodate him then."

I shucked his pistol, unloaded it, and put it back in his holster, with the thong on the hammer. As I searched him, I told him what to do. I assured him that if he so much as twitched out of line, I would shoot out a big chunk of his backbone, first thing.

Emptying the loads out of the shotgun, I tied it in the crook of his right arm in such a way that his arm looked natural enough but was rendered useless.

When we emerged from the church it appeared that the outlaw held me up with his left arm under my right shoulder. My right arm reached behind him. I held my Colt up against his backbone. I staggered as if stunned and let him drag me part of the way. The snow bit coldly at my sandaled feet. I fought to keep from jerking them up.

About midway across the plaza I jabbed him with my Colt. Like I'd told him, he yelled, "Come out here an' he'p me with this bag of bones."

I felt him suck air and tense as if to say more. I jabbed him with the Colt. He had second thoughts and continued pulling me across the plaza.

"Call again!" I hissed. "Convince'im."

"Get the hell out here and he'p me!" he shouted. No one answered his call. He dragged me up to the chief's house.

I stood at death's front door holding a live rattlesnake by the tail. I broke out in a cold sweat, felt time slow way down, almost to a dead stop.

The feeling had come over me many times before in combat. All the planning and maneuvering were over. Now it was face-to-face with the enemy. In the next split second, someone would die and I might be the one to get the call to Glory.

Lives were on the line, and death seemed to take forever to choose which to take. My body felt like it moved in cold tar. All the muscles seemed to hold a movement rigid. My brain raced ahead of movement, saw the consequences about to unfold, and ordered more movements from a body barely launched in its first motions. I twitched in the dance of the dying. In the absence of time, urgency became the demon from hell calling the dance steps.

I stood suspended, waiting for the first threatening movement to react to. All my senses peaked. I felt that addictive surge of energy that drove me to violence, that rush of power, which would leave me weak and worn-out when it departed after the shakes let up.

The door swung open. A big man in a faded, red-checked shirt stooped to step into the low opening. He held a shotgun in his left hand and started to reach for me with his right.

To free my gun hand, I lunged hard against the bandit holding me up. He twisted in front of me, clamped down with his arm as he started to fall. He pinned my gun hand to his side.

The man in the door jumped with his first recognition of the situation. He jerked his shotgun across his body into position to fire.

I rolled with my pinned hand and the bandit pulling me. I gave an extra kick to push myself into him and roll to get under him as we went down. In the fall my gun hand came loose. I fired.

The boom of my shot and the roar of the shotgun blended in a single thunderclap.

I fired again through the gun smoke, pushed hard to get shut of the bandit on top of me. I shot again at the man in the door.

He just stood there, looking down at his chest with hands hanging at his sides. His shotgun lay by his feet in the packed snow.

I hammer locked the bandit on top of me, put the muzzle of my Colt to his head. He stopped thrashing, just twitched.

The man in the door dropped to his hands and knees. One arm buckled and he rolled on his side.

I wrestled the man I held off of me and stood up. Then I felt the pain of buckshot in my right thigh.

The bandit on top of me had taken most of the load of buckshot in his back. He started to moan.

I ducked to the side of the door and leaned against the adobe wall.

"I have taken three outlaws, Padre. Any more around?" I yelled. No answer left me in a quandary. "Padre, Chief, you all right?"

I pulled the medicine pouch from my pocket and threw it into the room without exposing myself. I heard movement in the room and then the chief said something. The padre answered the chief. I heard more rustling around in the room.

"No more!" the padre yelled. "It is safe to come out? What has happened?"

The padre poked his head out of the door and squinted into the brilliant sunlight reflecting off the snow. He seemed surprised to see my monk's robe. After a hesitation he stepped out over the dead man. He called over his shoulder to the chief.

The chief emerged, then started grunting orders to men inside the room. They ran out towards the kivas. The chief approached me and put both his hands on my shoulders. He kept nodding his head as his eyes searched mine. A broad smile flooded his ancient face.

The plaza began to fill with silent, staring people. They had been badly mistreated, were gaunt, hollow-eyed. The padre stood transfixed.

"Padre, Padre? Tell these people to start their cookin' fires, get food and water. Tell them the outlaws're finished. Hell, tell'em to kill a couple of the bandit's horses and feast on'em," I ordered.

I pulled off the snow-caked monk's robe. It seemed to have an effect on the padre. He came to life and began to speak to the people.

The chief took my arm and led me into his house. He barked more orders. Water was brought. An old woman began to fuss over my wounded leg. I waved her away gently and drank the water. My mouth was as dry as the dust storm had been a day ago.

I went to the light in the doorway, ripped my pants leg enough to see the leg wounds. Two double-ought pellets were lodged in the big muscle. I squeezed one out between my thumbs like lancing a boil. The other pellet had pierced too deep. It would have to come out soon or it would fester. I tied the wounds to stop the bleeding with a woven sash the old lady handed me.

The dead man in the checkered shirt had been struck by all three of my shots. I wasn't proud of the pattern, but under the circumstances, I felt relieved to have killed him before he cut me down with the shotgun.

I searched the body and found the usual bag of gold, some pocket items, a hidden gun. I searched the wounded man, took his bag of gold and found little else. A women tended his wound. She did not look hopeful.

"Where's the gold hidden?" I knelt down beside the bandit, untied the shotgun from his right arm, tried to give him some comfort.

"Out of reach." He moaned. "Help me. Don't leave... savages."

From the way his blood flooded the snow beneath him, I reckoned a main artery had been severed.

"You're dyin', Mister. Where's the gold?" I stuffed the robe under his head, opened his coat collar.

"No one'll find it. No one'll find..." He passed out.

I had one chance left to secure the Jemez band's gold. I limped on a stiffening leg to the church to fetch the last outlaw. He had come conscious and was flaming mad. I jerked him to his feet roughly and threw him up against the wall.

"You're it, Mister, the other two're dead. No one else to help you. Not Horton, no one. You hear me?" He jerked his head back, stared defiantly down his nose at me. I moved right up to his face. "I'm the law. You're my prisoner. I'll give you one chance, only one, to tell me where the gold is hidden." I slammed him up against the wall again. "Or, I'll leave you with the Indians to roast it out of you." I ungagged him. "Where's the gold?"

Anger welled up inside him. He puffed out his cheeks as if to explode out words. I backhanded him to shut off the words, drove a hard left deep into his guts to churn up a better answer.

"The first words I hear better be about gold. You got that?"

"I copied a map," he gasped, sucking for air. "It's in my Bible. In my saddlebag. Swear to God. You gotta get me outta here!"

From what I had seen of the poor condition of the Indians, I could understand his fear of being left with them. I hauled him out of the church and told him to lead me to the Bible. It and his bag of gold nuggets were in his duffel in a corner of the chief's house. I tore out the page with the roughly drawn map and made him explain it to me until I thought I knew where the gold was buried. I stuffed the map and his bag of gold into a pocket.

Turning to the padre, who had come in with the chief, I asked him if there was any place where the prisoner could be held until someone came to pick him up. The padre said there probably was but asked if I thought it was wise to leave the outlaw at the pueblo. "I am not sure I can protect his life." The padre warned.

"Can you keep him from escapin's all I want to know, Padre."

"Yes."

The chief said something to the padre and then stepped in front of him. He handed me back the medicine bag I had tossed into the room.

"The chief says you are a powerful man but must keep this medicine bag with you. He asked, do you understand the message. I do not know what message he is talking about, Señor." The padre looked puzzled, gestured with a shrug, both palms up.

I grinned at the chief, nodded yes, and drew a snake in the air. He shook his head exuberantly then said something else to the priest.

The priest frowned. "The chief says you cannot stay and rest. He says, there will be a ceremony for you when you return with the head of the snake. What is the chief talking about, Señor?" The padre now looked perplexed.

"He'll explain when he's ready, Padre." I held the medicine bag up for the padre to see the symbols, then stuffed the pouch into my pocket. "Thank the chief and tell him I'll be back. Padre, did the wounded runner I brought in live?"

"Yes. He will want to thank you. You must stay, to be polite."

"Padre, I must go. You know that three other pueblos need to be taken back from the outlaws?"

"Ah, *por Dios*! We knew our brothers suffered captivity as we did. We did not know the reason."

"Gold, Padre. The outlaws have been killing and stealing gold."

He crossed himself, mumbled a prayer for the dead.

"By the way Padre, the Archbishop of Lamy sends his blessings." I turned to leave the room.

The padre crossed himself, twice, then again and changed the tone of his prayer.

I picked up the monk's robe and put it on. The sun was too low now to cast any heat. I was wet from rolling in the snow and the breeze felt much colder all of a sudden.

I looked around the pueblo, which came to life slowly. Smoke began to rise from chimneys, as it should. I heard the ring of axes. Small boys were sent to the fields to gather and pen the loose stock, the cattle I had delivered. I noticed that life proceeded in regular time now. Death had struck and moved on without taking me.

"Padre, don't let any runners pass through here," I yelled over my shoulder as I headed across the plaza. "And if any come up from the other pueblos, hold'em here. You got that?"

My burro stood obediently by the steps of the church. He seemed unconcerned with all the proceedings. I picked up my burro stick and climbed on board his rump. He carried me slowly back to the stallion.

It felt good to put on my heavy duster and boots. Still, I shivered as I repacked my gear and headed for Señora Martinez's adobe. The burst of energy from the fight had started to wear off. In a bit I would shake and feel hollow and low-down. Then I would need sleep.

The first strike against the bandits had gone pretty well, considering. The map to the gold, if it proved accurate, gave me sixty-percent recovery, if I got a hand on it before the other bandits fled with it. Three more bandits were out of action. The runner system had been cut off. Jemez Pueblo had been liberated. Maybe I could claim that the backbone of the outlaw operation had been broken. Future gold shipments might be safe.

I still had the rest of the gang and Horton to bring to justice. I wondered if the monk's robe disguise might work for me again. I would have to cover the blood stains.

Remembering the blood stains made me regret that I had killed another man. One had died at the hand of his partner. A third man would probably not survive being held by the Indians. I had to face the fact that I was in the killing business again. Where I went, death followed. The hollow and low-down feeling took over. I was too tired to contemplate the role God, in disguise, had played today.

It was dark when I rode into Señora Martinez's yard and untied her burro. She came to the door when I called out and motioned for me to come inside out of the cold. I did after I tended my horses.

She held up an oil lantern to look me over. Her eyes settled on the blood on my thigh. "You to kill *los ladrones* in Jemez?" She squinted as she raised the lantern to look into my eyes.

I nodded. "Will you dig buckshot out of my leg?" I moved toward her fireplace for light and heat. "We'll try out your healin' powder, Señora. You knew about the bandits in the pueblo?"

"I to guess it, Señor. Jemez friends stop comin' round. After the first killing? I to take the burro for to look. Nothing is right there." She collected things from boxes and stacks and put water on the fire to boil. "*No hay nada* we can do, the farmers here." She laid out a thin-bladed skinning, knife on top of clean rags. "The padre here, he is humble. After I to tell him, he say he to send word to the Holy Father in Santa Fe. Maybe so," she said sarcastically. She cocked her head and looked through her squinting eyes again. "After you to take the burro, I know for sure."

With her chin Señora Martinez indicated a chair. I pulled it close to the fire and sat down. "*Solo un'hombre y mi burro...*" she mumbled. She bent at the waist, opened the rip in my pants, got after the buckshot with the skinning knife. "How you do it, Señor?" She looked up from her surgery. My teeth were clenched. She chuckled, "I will better to ask the burro, *qué no?*"

She dug for the buckshot with gentle, experienced hands. I handed her my pouch of healing herbs. She waved it away, reached for a small Indian pottery bowl she had placed by the rags.

"I to put special herbs to this. Perhaps she work more better. You will to tell me, *qué no?*" She pinched some powder from the Indian bowl and applied it to the two holes in my leg. Then she packed and bound the wounds.

I walked outside to suck in fresh cold air, shake the pain from my body, shiver off the last of the rush of power that had now subsided.

The horses were tied where they could reach water. I fed them some of the burro's haystack. I paused to admire the evening, get reacquainted with the stars and time. The smell of juniper smoke filled the air. A breeze whispered over the snow, froze it into ice crystals that reflected the starlight.

Ann, gentle, passionate, sifted into my mind. She was the kind of woman a man could build a life with. She might offer support for the kind of future I wanted. Future?

Thirteen more outlaws blocked my future! If I killed them all before they killed me, I could step into my future. Or, I could start my future by heading back up to Jemez, collecting my prisoner, finding the gold, and riding with them into Santa Fe.

I would have stopped the bandit ring from holding up any more Durango shipments. I'd have recovered the biggest portion of the gold. I would be a live hero, could probably walk away from the governor's job and get back to Red and the herd.

The idea of leaving the rest of the outlaws to chance had its appeal. But that left the job I'd started unfinished. I remembered the sight of the Indians as they rose up, half-dead, from the kivas.

All the outlaws had to be captured and punished. Besides, I was a man to finish a job I'd promised to do. Knowing what I had to do squared my shoulders, put determination back into my stride.

Returning to Señora Martinez, I asked if we could eat and then if I could sleep for a few hours inside, out of the cold. I fetched the rest of the cornbread muffins and jam from my saddle-bag and handed them to the *curandera*.

She admired the jar of jam, holding it to the lantern light. She gave me a snaggletooth smile and said, "I to trade a place by the fire *por un tarro de conservas*." She turned to the plank table piled with covered wooden dishes.

I could not tell if she saw the value in the use of the jar or if she had a sweet tooth. Either way, we had struck a deal.

We ate hot mutton stew, corn bread, and apricot jam. Halfway through the meal I could barely hold my head up. Fatigue stiffened me relentlessly. The small room felt warm, made me sleepier. Maybe five days of pounding leather with little rest, and the gunfight at Jemez, were finally taking their toll on me.

"Señora, where can I find a burro outside of Zia Pueblo?" I mumbled.

"It is not possible, Señor. Take the old *pendejo* with you. He good war burro, *qué no?*" She chuckled as she lay out a pallet for me by the fire. "I to put the herbs in the stew. You to sleep ver' good now."

I needed to think about a plan for tomor-row. To tell he truth, I had not expected to live through this day. But my head stopped working when my butt hit the pallet.

I stretched out full length, comfortably for the first time in weeks, it seemed like. My body felt as if it drifted in warm water, free of all pain. Every muscle let go. Sleep took me far away.

CHAPTER SEVENTEEN

The smell of coffee woke me up. Firelight flicked dancing shadows into the *vigas*, where herbs hung in bunches to dry. The old woman moved silently to the cluttered table, made room for a wooden mixing bowl. She started clapping tortillas flat.

I stretched and felt fit all over. No soreness taunted me to refute a strong sense of well-being. I stepped outside to check on the horses and measure the time. Dawn was two hours away.

I returned to the warmth of Señora Martinez's hearth. "What did you put in the stew last night? I feel like I just slept late of a Sunday mornin'."

"I to put the bud of the hemp *y la pulpa de* willow bark. You feel ver' good, *qué no*?" She handed me a cup of coffee and a rolled tortilla stuffed with mutton. "I to give you some. Do not to take it before the fight. It is for after. When you can sleep safely. Let me to see the wounds." She motioned me into her one chair by the firelight. She untied the bandage.

"Have you put anything in the coffee this mornin'?" I chuckled around a mouth full of mutton adovada and tortilla.

She looked at me seriously. "No, but I to have some herbs... You must to get used to them first. *La medicina* slows down the time. When you to take it, you be faster than any man who not to have it."

"Seems like that happens anyway, time slowin' down when I'm in a battle." I inspected the buck shot wounds. "Looks like the healin' potion's workin'. There's no redness, no swellin'. We ought to get into the patent medicine business. We could sell this for a fortune." I usually did not feel this leaky-mouthed this early in the morning.

Señora Martinez washed and dressed the wounds with some more of her powder. We ate. I packed up to go. She gave me a little bag of the pain killing, sleeping potion and a warm smile. I gave her another coin.

I stood by the fire a little longer, drinking hot coffee, trying to think up a plan of attack. The monk's robe had worked to get me into Jemez Pueblo. It might work again. Trouble was I did not want to drag the señora's damned burro all the way to Zia Pueblo.

I didn't know the layout of Zia that well. I had known what to expect at Jemez, knew where the chief and the padre were kept. Tim's information about the number of men at Jemez had been correct. His descriptions of the men had been accurate. But things might have changed at Zia. I needed information before I could make a plan.

I decided against taking the burro. He would have to be returned which would cost too much time. I would spy on Zia Pueblo until I got the layout and an idea.

After all the time that had gone by since the last gold shipment the outlaws might be expecting messages. It was possible that messengers ran on the trails between the last three pueblos right now. Sergeant Horton could be shifting his men. I needed to know, could only guess.

Perplexed, I heaved a great sigh and stepped away from the warmth of the fireplace.

"You have a plan, Señor?" the señora responded to my movement. "Why you not to take others to help you? Is ver' danger, this thing you do." She sounded motherly and puttered at mixing cornmeal for more tortillas.

"If the outlaws saw men comin', they'd kill the leaders of the pueblo. And no, I don't have a plan yet, Señora. I'll have to see what's goin' on at the pueblo. Then I'll decide." Not wanting to leave the peacefulness of her home yet, I held out my coffee cup for more.

"Ah, *sí*, like the eagle. He to watch. Then he to choose the time to strike." She filled my cup. "*Pero hay* the lizard that changes his own color. He no see by his prey. He no see by his hunter *tambien*." She said no more as she cleaned up around the place.

*   *   *

I left in the dark just before dawn, when it was always the coldest. Frost formed then as the cold air squeezed the last of the moisture from itself. The remainder of the snow had a frozen crust that crunched under the horse's hooves. The brittle sounds carried vast distances in the crisp air. I felt as if I intruded, interrupted the peaceful sleep of the night, disturbed the spirits of the dead.

My youngest brother came to mind. I missed Johnny suddenly. He was the last of us in the Old Virginia tradition. I wondered how he had met his death. In that moment had he faced his fate head on, full of pride?

I felt sure of it. Johnny had been strong, would have had strong sons to carry on the Waller name. He had been born of a strong father. As I rode on a cold, dark trail I wondered how I would die.

Morbid feelings pestered me tenaciously. I had not mourned Johnny. For that matter I hadn't mourned the loss of any of the family. Mother, Dad, and my brothers all died during a time of such massive killing that I could have been overcome by grief, if I'd let myself in for it. Still, Johnny had been the hope of the family.

I was the hope of the Waller future now, but I was headed into another battle. I started to contemplate my own funeral, then decided against it. Instead, I threw a zealous Rebel yell into the dark silence, and then another. That ought to wake up the coyotes!

My father was a hero, to my way of thinking. At sixty-five years of age he had died as a Colonel leading a supply corps in the Battle of the Wilderness. The battle was fought in forests so thick that opposing troops passed within yards of each other without knowing it. In all the confusion, Dad and his men had been taken by surprise when a Fed cavalry stumbled onto his wagon train. A survivor of the battle had told me that Dad had gone down shooting from both hands. My guess, he took more than a handful of Feds with him to Glory.

It seemed to me like all us Wallers were going to die by the gun. I shook myself to get free of the morbid feelings. It was an old habit, feeling sorry for myself before a battle. Next I would have a bout of fear and doubt. Then I would get cold and calm inside and wait for something to react to, to strike at relentlessly and destroy.

Maybe all warriors went through such feelings. Maybe some heartless ones didn't.

The sun poked up over the distant mountains to blind me. I pulled my hat brim low and contemplated having a family. If I survived to become something other than a warrior, I might have the future to raise kids in. I had been thinking about my future a lot lately. I had been a long time running from the past, had a lot of dreams to catch up with.

Wonder what kind of sons Dora Luz and I might have? They would be full of fire and dash. Kids with Ann would be different, seemed to me. They might farm or ranch. Maybe there would be a doctor among then.

My horse stumbled and broke the pattern of my thoughts. Besides, I had nothing to show for all my work as a cowboy, no home, no land. Some bucks in my pocket and what I carried on two borrowed army horses were all I owned. It wouldn't feed a family and by rights I shouldn't even be considering one, with the danger I was in. I rode on with my doubts and fears. I had forgotten. Doubts and fears came along with having a future.

A mild wind from the south warmed the day and melted the snow rapidly. Pure water soaked the earth into mud and I had to slow the horses down a might. I turned my thoughts to finding the best approach to Zia Pueblo.

When I got close to the pueblo I turned north and rode up on the mesa that guarded the pueblo on the north. I had driven cattle off that mesa a time or two, knew the terrain well.

An ancient trail lead off the mesa on the east side, away from the pueblo. It followed along an arroyo that passed not far from the pueblo, on the east side, before it dumped into the Jemez River. I might use the arroyo for cover. If I remembered right, I could get within a couple hundred yards of the old Zia Mission. I expected a guard to be there. Maybe there was a gully that flowed into the arroyo that would lend me cover. I couldn't remember exactly.

I picketed the horses on top of the mesa and walked, then crawled, to the cliff edge with my field glasses. Same as before, there wasn't a soul around. I settled down to spying.

Before long the guard in the bell tower showed himself. Mid-afternoon, women carried food and water to the kivas. I couldn't imagine being cooped up under ground for weeks at a time. It would take a heap of fear to hold me in dark confinement that long.

An hour later, two men carrying shotguns came out of the third house on the west side of the plaza. One stretched, the other lighted a smoke. They talked for a minute then one went back inside. The man who had stretched walked to the church. Sure enough, the bandit I had seen in the bell tower came out of the church and strolled to the third house.

The new guard in the bell tower took a good look around, stretched again, then moved out of sight. It was time for me to make my move.

Fetching my horses, I worked my way down the old trail and into the arroyo. A bend in the gulch where the side had caved in offered a hidden place to tie the horses.

I shucked the Winchester from the saddle boot, checked its load. Then I leaned across the saddle and studied a shallow gully that might hide me until I got to about a hundred yards from the buildings at the northeast corner of the pueblo.

Figuring I'd be crawling before long, I tied my new Stetson to the saddle horn. I checked the loads in my Colts and decided against hauling the short-barreled shotgun.

I duck-walked up the gully, then dropped to my belly. Taking my time, I crawled further up the gully. Adobe mud stuck to me all over my front side. Cussing the sticky discomfort of it gave me an idea.

I rolled on my back in the muddiest wallow handy. Covered with mud I would look like a lump of dirt and blend with the color of the earth. My chances of sneaking up undetected felt better, although I had to fight the clammy mud to keep my weapons clean.

I thought of Señora Martinez and the chameleon she'd mentioned. Maybe she had given me her blessing in her own way. She had given me the idea for the disguise.

When darkness offered cover, I crawled up out of the gully. I slithered then froze to the earth. I watched the bell tower. I crept forward again with my eyes locked on the bell tower. The guard looked in another direction or slept on his watch. He never appeared in the window facing me, for which I was thankful. I kept crawling on my belly.

I reached the buildings and blended into the shadows created by a dim quarter moon. Slinking silently along a wall, I inched forward until the plaza and the churchyard came into view. I could watch the bell tower and the third house at the same time. My fingers felt, then crumbled, dried mud off the action of the Winchester.

If Tim had not lied and Horton had not reorganized his troops, I reckoned four outlaws manned Zia. Horton had not changed his men at

Jemez. But a day had gone by since the Jemez battle. No telling how many men I faced here now.

I knew one outlaw stood guard. I'd seen two others enter the house across the way. The fourth man's location worried me. He might be out somewhere, maybe coming back soon. I eased back into dark shadows and listened to the night sounds.

There might be a time when the two men in the house stepped out for air again. Two quick shots would solve a lot of my problem, but killing them would put the hostages at risk. There was dynamite in the kiva with the runners, according to Tim. And the lookout might get a clear shot at me. I dumped that plan.

But, maybe I could bag three outlaws when the lookout showed himself in the bell tower to take a shot at me. That left me exposed to the fourth outlaw. I didn't know where he would pop up. Besides, all the fancy shooting I contemplated had to be fired in the dark. Targets, distances and gun sights had a tendency to blur out after the blinding flash from a muzzle. The first shot might kill, but after that, night shots got too chancy.

Better, if I could get inside the church, I could wait until the bandits changed guards again. Maybe I could capture two of the outlaws at once. It seemed more like a hope than a plan, but it was all I could come up with that wouldn't warn the outlaws in the house and put the hostages at risk.

A hundred feet of open space spread between the wall I hunched against and the church. Plain-spoken, I had not expected to get this far into the pueblo. Now I was here, I had no idea where to go next. Unsure, I studied the church.

Leaning against the side of the church facing me was a low shed that looked like it might be the padre's quarters. A crooked stovepipe stuck out of the low roof, but no smoke rose from it. I wondered if the door into the shed was locked. I decided it wasn't. After storming Jemez that night I kicked open doors, I was convinced there were no locks in any of the pueblos. There wasn't much worth stealing.

Dropping on my belly I elbowed and kneed slowly over the open ground. The hair on the back of my neck stood up prickly. I could almost feel hot lead ripping into me from the bell tower above. I made it across the deadly gap without being spotted.

The door to the lean-to had no lock. I listened, then eased inside. The place stunk inside. I heard coarse breathing and froze against a wall, pistol in hand. Nothing happened. Then the breathing changed to a pained moan. I laid the Winchester up against the wall and lit a match. A man lay on a fouled pallet in the corner.

"Ah, *Madre de Dios*, you come for me." A feeble hand reached towards the match light. "I surrender my unholy spirit to God in Heaven." The padre's voice sounded weak, dry.

A lamp hung by the pallet. I lit it as the match expired. Across the small room, a door led into the church. There were no windows to open for fresh air. I moved to the pallet to examine the sick man. His eyes could not focus on me. I found a bucket of stale water and put a cup to his lips. He sucked at the cup like a baby.

"Evil men here. Help my children." He rasped, in short bursts between gulps. His hands shook too violently to hold the cup for himself.

"How many men, Padre?" I whispered and held his head up so he could drink. Hot to my hand, he burned with fever.

"Four...fight among themselves." He fell back, too weak to continue.

Snuffing out the lamp, I skulked to the door into the church, opened it silently and listened. The padre moaned, but no sound answered his groaning plea for help. I crept into the darkness of the church and sought a place to hide and wait.

An hour passed, maybe more. The guard in the tower hummed a monotonous ditty to keep himself awake. Occasionally he made up words to the tune, mostly sleazy. Another hour took its time passing.

"That you, Shep?" the guard spoke into the night from the tower above me. "About damn time I got relieved. I'm starvin'."

Boots scuffed up the steps outside the entry. The guard clambered down the ladder from the bell tower. I fisted both Colts and waited in the dark of the cove.

Shep walked in carrying a lantern. The guard met him in the entryway.

"You better get back over there, Bob. Them two're at it again. Swear to God, they'll kill each other over them cards." Shep held the lantern out in his right hand to give it to Bob who shifted his shotgun so he could take the lantern in his right hand. At the same moment I stepped into the lantern light with two guns up and cocked.

"Keep hold of that lantern!" I relieved Shep of his shotgun. "That's right, Gents. Don't let go." I took the lookout's shotgun.

"Together now, put the lantern on the floor. Lie face down. Slowly now." I was calling the dance, and so far they were willing partners. "Now put your hands behind your backs." I moved the lamp from between them. "You boys're under arrest for murder and robbery."

This time I had thought to bring pigging strings with me. I hog-tied the bandits. A quick search revealed the usual bags of gold and some personal stuff but nothing useful. I stacked their guns after I unloaded them.

Toeing the bandits over to lay on their sides, I set the lantern where I could see their faces. "Where's the gold hidden? I know Horton has a map, but you make it easy for me, and I'll take you in alive." I unsheathed my long knife and tested the edge. "Otherwise I'll leave you to the Indians to skin alive. What's it goin' to be?"

Both men, hardened veterans, mocked me through stone cold eyes. "Well, Boys, I'm goin' to go free those Indians. You think on my offer." I gagged them, rolled them back on their bellies and tightened the pigging strings.

I paused to pin the marshal's badge on my mud caked duster and declared my identity as lawman. Then carrying the lantern left-handed down low by my knee, I stepped out the church door into the night. I shucked a Colt to hand.

I walked, in the small circle of orange lamplight around my boots, to the third house. When I got to the door I stopped to listen.

Two men inside argued angrily about something. They bellowed and whined back and forth like the cheated and a cheater. Then one started to give the other Jesse, like he had turned suddenly demented.

I set the lantern down. The Colt behind my belt slipped easily to hand. My shoulders rolled of their own accord to stretch out the knots of fear that bunched the muscles. I took a deep breath, breathed it out as I cocked the Colts. The rush of power flooded my nerves.

Time slid away from me like snow off a steep, tin roof. Death waited behind that door. Courage was all I had to shield my heart behind the tin star on my duster. I remembered courage now. Felt it accelerate the beat of my heart, not from fear, but from care, concern for what had to be done. A man with a future needed courage so he could step forward boldly into risk. I kicked the door open, stepped in.

Foul air pinched off my breathing. Cedar smoke hazed the dim firelight that spilled into the room from the corner fireplace. Another screech directed my eyes to focus on two white men across the room.

A heavily bearded man strangled, with his left fist, another man in a faded-blue shirt. His right arm was cocked for a hard chop to the gasping face he clutched. Blue Shirt flinched and flailed his arms to protect his head. He squealed.

Startled by the slam of the door against the wall, both men froze and cut their eyes in my direction.

I volleyed fire and thunder into the room. Two hot balls of lead shattered the ribs of the bearded man below his left armpit and tore out his heart. His startled eyes blazed then clouded. His cocked right arm quivered, but the punch never got thrown.

Side step! Shoot again! But I could not move. Framed in the door, I had boxed myself in.

Bad decision! I crouched. The thought of being an easy target jarred me, threw off my aim. Blue Shirt twisted to his right and slapped for his gun.

Very fast! I stared down the .44 caliber muzzle of his Remington.

My bullets struck him. I'd misfired one high. I'd intended two shots in his heart. The stray bullet in his brain kept the bandit from mashing down on his trigger.

Screaming, moaning, and the thunder of my guns deafened me. Then stony silence and the acrid smell of gun smoke captured my senses. For the first time, I saw ten Indians lining the walls of the cramped room. They sat, mouths open, stunned on low benches. Nobody moved.

I stepped into the room. "Where's the chief?" I holstered one Colt, thumbed two bullets into the other.

An old man rose unsteadily from the corner by the fireplace. "Two more bad men." He gestured urgently behind me at the door.

I spun away from the opening, dropped to one knee facing it. "More than four?"

"Four bad men!" The chief held up four fingers. "You kill'em all?" Hope enlivened his question.

"Yes, Chief." I switched pistols and replaced the other two, spent rounds. I holstered the Colt and reached to shake the chief's extended hand. "Call your people out of the kivas." I waited until he had reassured the people in the room and sent them out to free the rest of the pueblo. "Will you come with me to the church?"

MICHAEL C. HALEY

As we walked across the plaza, I told him
to stop any Indian runners, and asked him for
information. All he knew was that he and his
people had been held and starved for a long time.

The chief stopped me, raised the lantern
to light my chest. He put his thumb on my badge.
"We think our white brothers in Santa Fe have
forgotten this pueblo. It is good you come now.
Many are sick."

We walked into the church. I lit the other
lantern.

Shep's eyes bugged wider when he saw
the chief. Bob squinted in disappointment. I
ungagged both men.

"The Indians're comin' up out of the kivas.
I have a choice to make, Boys. Save you? Or
satisfy them. Where's the gold hidden?"

Both men glanced from me, to the chief,
and back again at me. Neither spoke.

"That's it?" I waited a minute. "Seems
crazy to me. I'd rather die fast at the end of a
rope than fight havin' to beg for death to end Indian torture."

"You ain't goin' to leave us, Marshal." Shep
sounded smug. "You ain't goin' to get us to jail
neither. We got men comin'. I'm bettin' you die."

"Bob? How're you bettin'?" He remained
stony-faced. "Chief, any message runners come
through here the last two days?" I turned to the
chief who had not answered me. He appeared to
be deep in thought.

"Gold is here," the chief said firmly. "They
all time fight over gold. Five days they keep horse
packs in house. They fight over horse packs."

"Any message runners, Chief?"

"No."

I prodded the prisoners at gunpoint back to the chief's house. The gold lay stacked in the packs. Shiny, it was the first of the Durango gold ingots I had seen. Even in the dim lamplight, the luster of the gold bars set me to longing, to speculating. My hands itched to touch it.

Gold fever had just got two men killed. I shook off the fever that tried to infect me. "Chief, can you hold the gold and these *ladrónes* until someone comes to haul'em in to Santa Fe?" As I turned from the horse packs to leave I saw the chief nod then give his men sign-talk orders.

"Hold on there, Marshal!" Shep barked. "Ya got the gold. Ya..."

I walked out on Shep's begging.

After retrieving my Winchester from the church, I walked into the pardre's lean-to. He was conscious. When I held the lamp up close I saw that he had been beaten, brutally. I checked him for broken bones. He might live to stand between the Indians and their outlaw prisoners, if the fever broke. I wouldn't bet on any of the three men surviving for long.

I promised the padre I'd give him some of Señora Martinez's pain killing, sleeping potion before I left. I conveyed Bishop Lamy's blessing. The padre seemed relieved and turned to the wall to seek strength in prayer.

The chief had followed me to the church, but waited for me outside. A bonfire had been built to light the plaza. I waited until the chief finished giving orders to his people. A woman was sent into the church to tend the padre.

"Chief, you have two men, good bowmen, who can kill a man? I need help."

"I have such men." The chief frowned, pondered before he added, "We are peaceful Indians." His face sagged into a scowl as if he regretted his decision. "I forbid killing." In the light of the bonfire I could see he was torn.

"Even if your bowmen kill outlaws holdin' Santo Domingo hostage like here? I'll make 'em deputy marshals."

"Even if Indian kill bad white man, other white men will not forgive. We cannot leave our farms to run like the Apache. We all die on some reservation. I must forbid killin' to keep the peace in this place."

Peace meant more to him than helping me. I understood. Hell, I wanted to live in peace. Also, I had no authority to force him, or any of his people, into more risk. I told the chief I would return shortly with the medicine for the padre and then depart.

I fetched my horses and rode back toward the church and the padre. The pueblo had come alive, like a red ant-bed freshly kicked open. The chief met me by the bonfire in the plaza. I gave him the medicine for the padre and rode out of the pueblo into a cold, clear night.

Moonlight cast an indigo hue into the shadows around me. I waited for my eyes to adjust to the gloom. The horses were rested and ready to gallop. I held them back until I could see where I wanted to go.

I began to shake violently. The rush of power that jolted me when I kicked in the door, bolted into the room shooting, now ebbed from my body. I felt weak as an acorn calf.

At the time, charging into the room seemed like the only choice I had for getting at the outlaws. Now the attack seemed foolhardy. It appeared to me to be the act of a man who had nothing to lose. I had a future to lose and felt lucky I hadn't caught a face full of buckshot. I would sure as hell meet the muzzle of that .44 caliber Remington again, in my bad dreams.

After a while, the shakes left me. I turned my horses eastward. "Two more pueblos. Nine more outlaws." I chanted the words to the rhythm of the loping horses to keep my mind from thinking, my fears from rising.

Sadness began to creep over me, despite the numbing chant. The sadness made me feel hollow inside, like there was nothing left to rely on, like all the moral laws of the world had changed. Sadness carried hopelessness with it. I sought the comfort of my pipe. Lighting up didn't help any.

The sadness came because I had killed men again. Like the chief had said, there was no forgiveness for killing men, even evil men. I would be known as a gunman in the territory where I had come to live peacefully. Other men, good and bad, would call me out to test my reputation as a gunman. That was the fate of a fast gun. I wanted no part of that immorality.

The only way I could see to stop the gunman's life was to leave the territory when the governor's job ended. Maybe I could start over in Colorado, maybe cold Wyoming. I could see no other way to reestablish a peaceful life and build the future I wanted.

The thought of having to flee New Mexico made me feel even worse. This was my home. I did not want to be run out of my country again. Losing my home in Virginia was enough. The thought of having to run again to find a good life, the thought of being run-off, bowed my neck against those who would violate my rights to choose where I would live out my future.

Anger flowed into the hollow place of sadness, and churned my guts. Damn Bustos, the governor, Horton and the Durango gold for putting me in this battle against the outlaws in the first place. To hell with anyone who sought to run me off. Anger and determination clenched my jaw. I clamped down on the bit of my pipe too hard and snapped it off.

Shadows moved off to my right, caught my eye. Five or six coyotes, curious about a night traveler in their land, loped along on my flank with the pace of the horses. They veered off shortly and set up a howl to send me on my way.

I thought of the coyote fetish, wondered if I had anymore luck left. I'd used up more than my share. Maybe the singing coyotes were a good sign. I was not a superstitious man, but I did not feel like I could rely on anymore good luck. I needed cunning. Hell, I needed an army.

I stowed my broken pipe, leaned back in the saddle, and rode doggedly into the night to meet death again at daylight.

CHAPTER EIGHTEEN

As I switched my saddle from the roan to Major Watson's black stallion, I reflected on my campaign against Horton and his gang. My tactics resembled Grant's flanking strategy against General Lee in the battles to capture Richmond.

I wondered if Watson, now my ally, had fought in the battle that destroyed my old Virginia life. I had stood on a hill, less that a mile from home, and watched Federal artillery level Mama's grand, Waller House.

Maybe Watson had helped Grant plan the relentless, systematic attacks on General Lee's flanks. The Feds had pushed the General back, in a series of bloody battles, and forced him to retreat to his Richmond stronghold. The strategy had worked for Grant then. So far, attacking Horton's flanks had worked for me.

Horton was no General Lee. Nor did I have a greater force to rely upon, like Grant had then. There was just me, working on a strategy to pick off the outlying forces. Still, I had cut Horton's forces in half like Grant had cut General Lee's. But I had not encountered Horton's main strength. Nor did I know his location for sure. Horton might be on the move by now.

I snugged the cinch, mounted up, and whipped the major's warhorses into a gallop towards Santa Ana.

I faced a choice. I could try to take Santa Ana and cut off more of the snake's body and further reduce Horton's forces. The tactic had worked twice now. Or I could attack Horton at Santo Domingo. I was afraid that Horton might take his gold and run.

If Horton had ordered a retreat out of the territory, neither choice made sense. I decided that since Santa Ana was on the way to Santo Domingo I would scout it. If the outlaws still held Santa Ana, I could assume Horton had not folded and fled yet.

In my guts, I doubted that Horton had pulled stakes and run. Yet I was not sure what the effect of cutting his messenger system had been. I was sure that Horton had not received messages from the West in days. I had told the chiefs not to let any runners through. That silence alone might force Horton to shift his position.

Still, without information that he had lost his men at Jemez and Zia, Horton could be holding his position. A seasoned, military leader stood his ground until he confirmed information that would force a shift in position. Horton was of a military mind. I had to rely on that. The situation at Santa Ana would resolve my speculations.

The Big Dipper told me there was time for a rest before sunrise. More worrying about my tactics now seemed futile. I would have to uncover the situation when I encountered it and react then. Food and coffee became my main concern. Halting on a grassy slope, where all the snow had melted, I let the horses graze. I rested, squatting on my heels by a low fire, stretching my lower back muscles.

Shifting a scalding, tin cup of coffee hand-to-hand, I thought about the disguises I had used to get into Jemez and Zia. I needed an idea that would help me now. The monk's robe had worked fine, but without a burro it seemed to me the disguise would fail. Crawling in the mud at Zia like Señora Martinez's lizard got me into the pueblo, but I was less familiar with the terrain around Santa Ana. I drew a deuce when it came to new ideas. I gulped the rest of the coffee, threw a blanket around my shoulders, and stretched out to sleep.

I kept jerking awake out of a series of fitful naps. My muscles were wound up too tight with anger and fatigue. My guts churned with too much worry. I gave up trying to rest and broke camp. If I pushed the horses hard, I could reach Santa Ana just before sunrise.

The waxing moon had set and abandoned the earth to cold darkness. Regulus twinkled brightly through the clear air. Leo stalked the eastern horizon. I preferred to watch the old lion prowl overhead, in early-spring, evening skies. It would be fine with me to live into another spring. As I headed the horses towards Leo, I resolved not to take any unnecessary chances rounding up the rest of the outlaws.

Red light tinted the bottoms of scudding clouds in the east as I passed by Santa Ana, a couple of miles to the south. The location I sought lay on the east side of the pueblo so the sun would rise at my back. I didn't want to risk a flashed reflection from my field glasses as I spied on my enemy.

The major's black stallion jerked up his head suddenly. His ears pricked forward, twitched, listened. I yanked the bit in his mouth to stifle a whinny. I slid from the saddle to tie my bandanna over its nose. Then I looped the lead rope around the roan's nose. I shucked my Winchester and field glasses, shinnied up the rise ahead to hide and search.

Dawn's light made more shadow than bright. Nothing moved in the gloom that I could see. Maybe I had misread the horse's warning. My gut didn't feel so. Anything live out here now could be a threat. A minute snuck by then I caught a movement.

The heads of two men bobbed above the skyline of a low hill, not more than a hundred and fifty yards away to the northeast. I watched as two, mounted men rose up from behind the hill. They lead two packhorses behind them.

Shielding the lenses from the growing light in the east, I studied the two riders. From Tim's descriptions, I recognized the older man, Stone. The younger man was Cox. Tim had said that they would be manning Santa Ana, if nothing had changed. I suddenly felt obliged to Tim for his information. I'd stand up for him in court if I lived through the danger coming my way.

The packs on the trailing horses looked familiar like the ones that had held the gold bars in the chief's house at Zia. I figured the two bandits had gone out to collect the gold. What I didn't know was whether or not all the outlaws were already on the move or getting ready to move out.

The riders came directly toward me. I eased the Winchester into position and waited for them to drop off the hill into the little valley that lay between us. I studied each man again carefully through the field glasses. I picked Stone.

When the two outlaws rode to about seventy-five yards away, and the light was right, I squeezed off my shot. Stone plunged out of his saddle, over the rump of his horse. Stone's two horses spooked. One jumped into Cox's horse and set him to bucking.

Cox, fighting with a wild horse, tried to see where the shot came from. He couldn't control his bucking bronco. On the next buck he bailed out of his saddle and dove for the bank of a gully. Cox chose the wrong side of the ditch to hide behind. He lay exposed, back to me with his gun aimed in the wrong direction.

"Don't move, Cox!" I levered another round into the chamber of the Winchester, squeezed down on the trigger. "I'll kill you!" He took my advice. "Let go your gun and stand up slow."

Cox stood quietly, head down, hands in the air as I approached. The spooked horses settled down a bit, but were uneasy with my presence and the smell of the fresh blood of the dead man. I talked to calm them more. I sure as hell did not want one of them to move between Cox and me.

Cox stood real tall, skinny, a young man with real bad skin that he tried to hide with scraggly chin whiskers. If he had served in the war with Horton, he'd have been just a pink-cheeked horse pestler. Less than a minute ago he had probably figured he was a rich man. Now he stood alone and captured. His left leg started to shake.

"You boys movin' the gold or stealin' it from Horton?"

"You goin' to kill me?" The sharp edge of fear broke through Cox's voice. He was obviously rattled by Stone's sudden death.

"Where're you movin' the gold to, Cox?" I shifted the Winchester left and drew the Colt. His eyes widened but he said nothing. I eared back the hammer.

Cox had relied on the strength and protection of the gang. I could see fear and turmoil ripple around his face as he tried to be brave facing his own death alone. Then he hung his head again and sagged on his backbone.

"We was to head for Santo Domingo today." Cox barely whispered.

"How many men left in Santa Ana, Cox?" I turned him to search his pockets. I relieved him of his sack of gold nuggets and a pocket-knife.

"Two."

Cox dragged Stone's body up under a little ledge in the gully. He pulled off the dead man's coat and hat, like I'd told him to. Stone's bag of gold was behind his belt. I ordered Cox to cave the bank in over Stone. The coyotes wouldn't get his flesh until the next gully washer, or maybe never. Then I tied Cox's hands in front of him to his feet.

I walked back for my horses, slipped the muzzles off, rode over to Cox. I caught up with the bandit horses then hobbled my mounts. Stone's packhorse had tangled itself up pretty bad in the lead rope. I was afraid it had injured itself in the bucking fracas. That wasn't the case. Grunting some at the weight, I got the packs reorganized, adjusted, and cinched-up tight again.

Stone had been my choice for killing because we were about the same size. I put on his coat and hat.

Cox did not resist as I tied him to his horse, hands in front to the saddle horn. I pulled off his bandanna, wadded it up and stuffed it in his mouth. Taking the thong off his hat, I tied the gag in place. Then I turned up his collar and pulled his hat low, to hide his face. I removed his spurs and tied his feet so he couldn't boot his horse.

"Cox, let's ride on into Santa Ana and pick up your *compadres*."

Shooting Stone from ambush for his hat and coat bothered my conscience until I justified it by remembering my resolve not to take unnecessary risks with the outlaws. Facing two, armed bandits, in the open, was asking to get killed. They would split up when they saw me coming and make two killing shots hard to get. Maybe I would have killed one, but the other would have shot lead into me for sure.

Besides, these men were killers, had used ambush themselves. I viewed the situation now as I had viewed the war. If you got involved in the killing, you assumed the risk of getting killed. Stone, like six others in the gang, had gambled on that risk to get gold, and had lost his life. I shoved Stone from my mind and turned to the situation at hand. I rode towards two more killers fortified in the pueblo.

The idea seemed chancy, but I had formed a plan. I assumed the two men in the pueblo still followed the routine laid down by Horton. I hoped I would look like Stone returning with Cox and the gold. All I needed was a chance to get close enough for a sure shot at the guard in the bell tower.

Several variables increased my risk of failure. First, the men in the pueblo had heard my shot. Maybe when they saw us approaching, they would think things were okay, would figure we had taken a shot at game for food. Second, I rode with one of the outlaws at my side. I would have to split my attention, guard against anything Cox might dream up to pull. I kneed my horse so as to be to the right of Cox. Riding abreast, I shucked the Winchester which I laid across my saddle, muzzle only inches from Cox's belly. Third, I didn't know where the two other killers hid.

"Cox, a wrong move'll get you killed. Sit tight. You understand, Boy?" Cox nodded. We rode the last half-mile to Santa Ana.

As we approached, I pulled Stone's hat down low, but not so low as to keep me from seeing the bell tower windows. I slumped as if I dozed in the saddle. I let Cox's horse drift a bit ahead. The four horses, headed home, kept up a good pace.

The bell tower guard showed himself when we were about three hundred yards out. The distance was still too great for a guaranteed killing shot. I kept pretending to doze in the saddle. So far, it appeared, the guard did not suspect anything. He disappeared from the bell tower window. Cox's horse kept leading us straight on in.

I shifted the Winchester to the crook of my arm, where I could get it into action with a minimum of movement. The guard did not reappear. It occurred to me that he might have left the tower. That worried me. I had no idea where he might reappear, or if he would be alone when he did show up.

At about fifty yards from the bell tower, almost to the first of the adobe houses, I eased my horse in front of Cox's and halted the pack train. I stepped out of the saddle and positioned my horse between the bell tower and me. I laid my Winchester over the saddle and ducked low behind the horse. Making it look like I was adjusting the cinch on my saddle, I held that position until I heard the bell tower guard call down at us.

"Somethin' the matter, Stone?" The guard stood up in the window to talk to us. "You get the gold?"

"Naw, just fixin'..." I swung the Winchester to my shoulder and shot. The guard grabbed his chest. Surprise flooded his face. Blood gushed between his fingers, flowed down his coat front. He staggered, fell forward out the window, thudded to the ground on his head. He died of a broken neck, if the heart shot hadn't killed him first.

Hunching low behind my horse, keeping him between me and the church, I nudged him over and caught up Cox's reins. Staying sandwiched between the horses I trotted them over to the back of the church.

I could not see the plaza from where I stood and had no idea where the last outlaw hid. I felt sure he would come to investigate the shot. I was almost positive that he would not think to hold a hostage in front of himself when he came. I could be wrong.

Working quickly, I untied Cox's feet and pulled him off his horse. I laid him out on the ground, hog-tied him. I ducked for the cover of the wall.

Sliding along the wall, I eased to the northwest corner of the church. I dropped to my belly, took a quick look around the corner. Nothing moved on the west side of the plaza.

I jumped up, sprinted to the other corner. Dropping on my belly again, I eased my eyes just past the corner, to search the east side of the plaza. The dead guard's body still lay where it had fallen and the east side of the plaza was empty. I crawled back to Cox, rolled him on his side, and ungagged him.

"Which house's he in, Cox?" I slipped my long knife into my hand, laid the razor edge up against his Adam's apple. Cox didn't hesitate.

"House's on the west side. Second door from the south end." Cox squirmed back from the knife causing the hog tie rope to cut into his throat. He winced. I let up on him, but gagged him again.

I crawled to the west corner of the church for a quick look. The house Cox said hid the other outlaw had a small window that faced the plaza. If I measured the angles right, I reckoned the outlaw inside could not have seen the guard fall from the bell tower when I shot him. The body lay on the opposite side of the church from the house. If the last outlaw hid in that house, he had no idea what was going on out here.

I took a moment to figure. It might be possible that the outlaw in the house had not seen us approach from the hills. We had come in from the east and might have been blocked from view by the church. I ran back through my memory trying to picture if I had seen a clear view of the bank of houses on the west side of the plaza as I rode in. I wasn't sure. I'd been watching the bell tower.

It was possible that the lookout in the bell tower had alerted the other bandit of our arrival while he was gone from my view. I had to assume that the outlaw inside the house was aware that Cox and I were back and had been warned of trouble by the shot that killed the bell tower guard.

Trouble was, there was no way I could force the outlaw out of the house without risking the lives of Indian hostages or getting myself shot. I could not rely on the element of surprise and barge in like I had before at Zia. Much as I hated it, the outlaw had the next move.

I did not like my position. I was, in fact, pinned down behind the church that sat at the end of the plaza. Open ground surrounded me. The church didn't have any back or side doors to slip into. All I had were church walls to hug.

I wanted to get up in the bell tower that commanded the field of fire over all the plaza. To get to the tower I would have to expose myself to fire, when I ran around to the front to get to the only door into the church. I thought about climbing the wall, but a quick search proved there was nothing to throw a loop over to secure my rope. I wished I had a grappling hook, quickly gave up wishing.

I crawled back to Cox and ungagged him. "Is there a back door in that house over there?"

Cox was beginning to size up my position, which was not strong. I think he began to take hope in the possibility that I might fail.

"Cox, I'll stand you up in front of me, walk in with you as my shield, if I have to. You keep answerin' my questions, you hear?" I shook him angrily.

"There's a back door. Johns ain't in there. He don't like to be cooped-up in a fight. He'll get you, Mister. This ain't over by a long sight." Confidence gleamed in Cox's eye for the first time.

"Don't count on it, Boy. Johns's second-in-command of the gang, right?" I prodded Cox with the Colt this time. He wasn't going to help anymore. Hope had got the better of him. I knocked it out of him with the butt end of my Colt.

If it was Johns, he was a mean and cunning man, almost as bad as Horton according to

Tim. I might have made a mistake about him using a hostage to cover himself and to force me back. Suddenly I did not like how things shaped-up at all.

I couldn't move or see. Every minute I gave Johns gave him the advantage. He would figure out pretty soon that he did not face a big force. He would have planned how to handle a posse attack. I figured he had plans for a situation like this, too. It was all to his advantage.

I did not know the layout here. From what I had seen riding in and from checking the plaza from behind the church, the place seemed pretty much the same as at Zia or Jemez. But, if I had been an outlaw here for several weeks, I would have found the hidden places by now, to give me an edge. My skin crawled.

I moved the horses around to offer some cover. Trouble with that was, they would jump, buck, and kick if some one shot into them. Wild horses could be as deadly as a bullet. I thought about using a couple of them to shield me as I moved to a better position. I could expect to get shot in the legs. In fact it was simpler to shoot the horses and leave me exposed. Any way I cut it, I was pinned here.

I moved like a caged bear from one corner of the church to the other. With every step I feared the bullet that would kill me.

Johns had plenty of time to leave by the back door and move to the section of the pueblo, on the south side of the plaza, that I could not see. Hell, from there he could walk across the plaza and into the church. I started watching the bell tower again. I was in a fix, or so I tried to convince myself.

Maybe Johns had cut and run. It was a small hope that faded when I looked at the packhorses loaded with gold. I needed something more than a small hope.

Cox came to, started to groan. I crawled over to him and gagged him. I hunkered on my heels over him and tried to figure out a way to use him to get at Johns. But Cox had no value. Johns had no use for the kid, would relish the idea of spending his gold.

Suddenly I heard two muffled shots. I dove to my belly beside Cox for protection.

I could not tell where the shots had been fired. It sounded like inside one of the houses. From my position behind the church, I could not get a bearing. I figured Johns had decided to kill a hostage to make a show of force. He would toss a body into the plaza and call me out to negotiate.

Nothing happened for a quarter of an hour. Getting impatient, I ripped off Stone's coat and threw his hat down. The early morning breeze blew by coldly. I didn't feel it.

Frustrated with waiting, I edged to the corner of the church on the west side. If I had to come out shooting, I wanted my right hand to lead.

Gun first, I peered around the corner. Nothing had changed on the west side of the plaza. I ran to the east corner and eased my head around for a quick look. Still nothing different, except the knotted muscles between my shoulder blades. They squeezed pain all the way up to the back of my head.

Since I saw nothing to shoot at, I decided to try easing along the east wall of the church to the front corner. I was getting angry enough to try for the front door and the bell tower. I went back to Cox to get a horse for a shield.

More and more of the south side of the plaza came into view as I moved cautiously between the east wall of the church and the horse. All the adobe houses joined together, to form a solid wall on that side. All the doors I saw were shut. Then as I moved forward, an open door came into view.

A long pole stuck out of the middle of doorway, parallel to the ground. In the shadow of the room I could not see who held the pole. Nor could I see yet what might be at the end of it.

I feared that Johns had tied a hostage to the pole and had pushed the hostage out the door to get my attention. If I took another step to see, I became a target for whoever hid in the darkened room, behind the open doorway. I was afraid to expose myself for a look at what was at the end of the pole.

Abandoning the horse shield, I slunk back along the east wall to safety. Then I ran to the west side of the church. If Johns hid in the door on the south side, he would not be in the house on the west side. Johns might have coerced one of the Indians to shoot me from that window. I would have to risk it to see what was on the end of the pole.

Easing around the corner to the west side of the church, I never took my eyes off the window of the house on the west side until I was sure my next step would reveal the end of the pole.

When I looked, I was shocked to see a white man tied there. He stood with his legs wide apart, arms bound behind him, gagged. He fit Tim's description of Johns.

I ran back for Cox and jerked him to his feet. I put the Colt to his head and walked him around the wall. I watched him as he first spotted Johns. I felt sure from the disappointment on Cox's face that it was Johns tied to the pole. I ungagged Cox.

"What do you say, Cox? That Johns?" I jabbed him with my gun.

"That's him." Defeat weakened his voice. His chin sunk to his chest.

I stepped out of the shadow of the west wall, with Cox in front of me, and walked towards Johns and the open door.

A hundred feet from the door I halted Cox in the center of the plaza. From a hundred feet it would not be an easy shot from the door with a pistol or shotgun. Had a decent rifleman waited there, I would have been dead by now. I turned Cox around slowly, protecting myself with his body between the door and me. I wanted whoever was inside to see that Cox was tied.

"I'm Deputy Marshal, New Mexico Territory. If there's no more than four outlaws here, we've captured them all." I waited.

A short, round padre with a bald head stepped out into the sunlight. He squinted against the glare, raised a hand to shade his eyes. He moved towards me.

"Padre, keep your hands where I can see them. Last time I wasn't payin' attention, one of the outlaws dressed like a padre, took a shot at me."

The padre nodded and raised his other hand to shield his eyes. He stopped some yards from me. "I am unarmed and very frightened. I do not know that you are not an outlaw. Perhaps

Cox is tied up to trick me? I fear I may be the condemned man here."

I pulled out the medicine bag, which I was now in the habit of carrying for luck, pinned the tin star to it, and pitched them over to the padre. In an even tone, I told the padre that Jemez and Zia were free from the bandits. "Show the pouch to the chief. See if he recognizes it's from Jemez."

The padre turned carefully and walked to the open door. I jabbed Cox's ribs with my pistol to remind him he was dead meat if he moved. I watched Johns like a bunny watches an eagle. Johns, keen-eyed, watched every move I made. Then he tried to slip Cox an eye signal. I jerked Cox around to face me. "Stay quiet now, Boy. Johns can't help you. I can kill you."

After a long minute, several Indian men and the padre emerged from the door and approached me cautiously. None of then was armed. Then one of the older men said something. All the Indians seemed to relax a might. They advanced to surround me. I tensed, felt unsure and threatened. I holstered my Colt as a gesture of good will.

Three men surrounded Cox, took him from me. The old man who had spoken handed me back my medicine bag and tin star. He started shaking my hand strongly up and down, like he was pumping water from a well. The other men broke off in different directions to handle Johns and summon the people from the kivas. The chief let go my hand. Then I relaxed a might.

"The chief thanks you and welcomes you," the padre said graciously, but with some effort. The skin on his face hung, gray from fear and fatigue. "You are the man who took Jemez back from the outlaws." Aware of my surprise, the padre added quickly, "The chief knows the story of the medicine bag. A runner from Jemez slipped in here last night, to warn us that you might come."

"Next time I see the chief at Jemez, I'll tell him how powerful that medicine bag is." I felt a grin lift the corners of my mustache.

I told the Jemez chief not to let runners pass between the pueblos. He'd gone against my orders. But the messenger system had worked to my advantage this time, probably saved my life. I'd forgive the chief.

The Santa Ana chief left to oversee the recovery of his pueblo. The padre turned, cast his eyes around the pueblo to look for someone. "The runner from Jemez told us you saved his life when he was shot by the outlaws. He wants to thank you. Many people owe you a great debt, Señor Marshal."

"What about the shots I heard, Padre?" I feared a hostage had been killed. I did not want any Indians to die because of my actions.

"When we heard the shot and saw the dead guard we guessed you had come. A chance presented itself." He shrugged and raised his hands palms up. "We tried to capture Johns when he started after you. We overcame him." The padre crossed himself. "Two of my children were wounded. They will live, *gracias a Dios*." He crossed himself again. His pious expression changed to scowling. "Where is Stone?"

As I told the padre about Stone, we walked to the wall where Johns and Cox sat surrounded by men, women, and young boys. The crowd stood staring quietly. I could not tell what their thoughts were from their faces. I guessed.

The governor ought to invite at least one Indian from each pueblo to sit on the jury at the outlaw's trial. These people deserved retribution for what they'd suffered. Sitting on a jury might help them get to know more about law-abiding Anglos.

The padre recommended the Indian with his long hair tied back by a bandanna around his forehead. I handed Cox's pistol to him, asked the padre to tell him to stand guard. I tied the prisoners again, hand to foot, before I turned away to get on with bringing the pueblo back into the sunlight. As I turned, I noticed other Indian men held the bandit's pistols and shotguns.

As I crossed the plaza to collect the horses and gold, the young Indian man I had saved up at Jemez Spring ran up to me. He pulled up his buckskin shirt to show me his scars so I'd recognize him. With sign language he thanked me for saving his life.

He had risked his life again to slip into the pueblo while the outlaws still held it. With my awkward sign-talk, I thanked him for saving my life, said we were even now.

In a while, I told myself, I would go get the major's horses and some of Señora Martinez's healing potion for the two, wounded Indians. Later, I would arrange for the Indians to hold the prisoners until the governor's men came for them and the gold. After that, I would head for Santo Domingo and Horton.

First, I wanted to watch the pueblo come alive again.

CHAPTER NINETEEN

Women, carrying baskets in their hands, babies on their backs, headed for the corn fields to gather what the crows had left of the harvest. Older girls walked, with *ollas* balanced on their heads, towards the river to fetch water. Young boys chased sheep and goats to pens. Men loped on foot to round up stray cattle and horses. Some mended corrals, gathered hay. Old women hauled wood and kindled the cooking fires. A baby boy, just old enough for mischief, squatted by a dog, teased it with a stick.

The padre stooped and ladled grain from a fifty-pound sack into waiting hands. I picked up the other end of a ladder and helped carry it across the plaza on my way to the padre. "Does the chief speak English, Padre?"

"Yes." The corners of his mouth dropped. His eyebrows rose. He cocked his bald head like he was thinking about a balky mule. "When he chooses to."

I hunted around for the chief, found him by the ladder I'd carried. The ladder stuck up out of the entrance to a kiva buried under my feet. Two men listened to the chief. They turned and climbed down the ladder into the kiva. One of them carried a colorful, ceremonial drum. The chief turned his eyes on me.

"Chief, makes sense to give the outlaws' horses to your men there, so they can round up the stock." I pointed to three Indians chasing horses beyond the cornfields. The horses sprinted away from them again.

The chief's eyes ran down and up me once. He scowled, and then he looked me directly in the eyes. "You killed the outlaws. The horses are yours. You leavin'?"

"Not just yet."

The chief's face softened. "You are generous to lend us your horses."

"Chief, they're your horses to use as you want." After the padre's warning, I was pleased the chief had spoken English with me. "Use'em for food if you like. Fatten up your people. Looks like they've been starved by the outlaws."

The chief shook his head. "I can not repay you for such a gift."

"I'll trade you then. For four horses, you guard the gold and my prisoners, feed them until the governor sends someone to haul'em to jail. Besides, Chief, I have to ride fast. Herdin' extra horses and men'll slow me down."

As the chief pumped my hand again, he ordered men to unload the gold and take the four horses out to work. I watched the padre protest, look over at the chief, frown suddenly, and then let the men carry the gold into his church.

Six men hustled Cox and Johns toward us. The chief grunted. The men forced the prisoners down the ladder into the kiva where the drummer had gone. I bit off the questions my curiosity asked.

"Chief, the outlaw's still holdin' Santo Domingo. I'm heading' there now. You know any way I can get into that pueblo without bein' seen?" I was fishing for something that would help me plan an attack.

The chief's eyes crawled over me slowly this time, then focused behind me. "Navajo and Apaches stopped stealin' our corn an' women when the ancient people learned to build thick, adobe walls. They built out in the open so they could see the enemy comin' an' prepare for war. There is no way to come close without bein' seen." The chief swept the arc of the pueblo with his eyes and extended arm. "We all know our faces. I can not help you," he said flatly.

There had to be ways past pueblo defenses. Hell, there wasn't even a wall built all the way around any of the pueblos I'd seen. I felt the chief's refusal to help more than I bought into his reason. Why had he refused?

Why had the chief at Zia also refused to help me? He'd claimed his reason was to keep the peace.

Maybe Indians didn't lend a hand to strangers like white folks were obliged to. Maybe they didn't trust us. I could understand why, since most whites cheated or killed Indians. Two men who proved we were a violent race had just been hustled into the kiva under guard. Two more lay dead by my hand.

The chief at Jemez helped me by giving me the medicine bag and sending the runner to Santa Ana. But, come to think on it, I had not asked the chief directly for help and the runner had been sent to warn Santa Ana, not to help me directly.

The actions of the three *caciques* confused me. I needed to know more about Indian ways. What did an Indian have to know to make sense of the chief's words 'we know all our faces'? The words made no sense to me. I sure as hell didn't understand how the three chiefs made sense out of their world.

Right now it didn't seem fitting to stand around and argue with the chief about the merits of helping me out. I shook his hand again and left to walk back over to the padre on the church steps. I wanted to ask him what 'we know all our faces' meant.

"Padre, walk with me to get my horses. I got a couple of questions?"

He still scooped and gave away what looked like seed corn. "I can not leave my children now." He straightened up. "Give me your hat, My Son." I handed him Stone's battered hat. The padre filled it to the brim with corn. "For the horses, My Son. *Vaya con Dios!*"

I walked out of Santa Ana with four outlaws killed or captured, a fortune in recovered gold stored in the church, and a hat full of corn. Not bad far a morning's work.

Walking carefully back to the major's horses with Stone's hat full of corn held out in front of me, gave me time to worry about the gold stored in the church. Gold never just lay idly by. First it infected a man's imagination. Then gold and dreams combined in a flammable mixture, like gunpowder and a spark. If the spark flamed into passion, gold fever exploded into violence. Leaving the gold in the church exposed the Indians and the padre to gold fever.

So far the fever for Durango gold had killed thirty-three men. Most likely more men would die because of it. I didn't want Indian lives lost. Maybe I'd made a bad decision, leaving the gold in the pueblos. I couldn't see another way to handle it now.

The major's stallions fed on corn while I rubbed them down. They looked good, but I could feel their ribs and the loss of weight. I had used them hard the last few days and couldn't judge how much more running they had left in them.

Maybe I should return these magnificent horses to the major now and go tell the governor to send men to pick up the gold. That way the borrowed horses might survive and the Indians would be saved from exposure to gold fever.

Maybe I just wanted an excuse to ride on past Santo Domingo and avoid having to deal with Horton.

A sudden gust of wind prodded me out of my wishing, made me look up. High up, strong winds marched thin clouds northward, over the sun that hadn't made it to noon yet. The sun urged the wind to carry bad weather in from the southwest. I reckoned I had time before the storm to water and graze the horses, get a little rest before I rode to Santo Domingo.

I figured Horton was pinned down at the pueblo for a while. He had called his gangs in to muster. He'd wait out the day, and into the night, before he discovered he had a short roll call to make.

I planned to strike at night. It would take me three, maybe four hours to get to Santo Domingo. I fought the urgency I felt and stretched out to rest under the sun.

I woke up swatting at stinging, black flies that sought the sweat raised on me by the hot afternoon. Fear of maggots made me think to check my wounds. I rubbed healing potion into the buckshot holes. Señora Martinez would be happy to hear that her improved potion worked better than mine. That half-baked idea to get into the patent medicine business with her made more sense now. I had a fast healing leg to prove our claims of potency.

I dropped bacon into the frying pan, sat back with my coffee to ease into the rest of the day. Squinting into the intense sunlight, I gauged the speed of the breeze from the dust it kicked up. The wind carried more moisture than this morning. Soon the sun would boil the moisture into thunderheads and rain. Or maybe the weather would blow on by this patch of the territory. I never could predict for sure.

I didn't want to think about the job ahead. I watched the country around me, ate bacon, and lingered in the lull. I cleaned my weapons, broke camp, and packed. Then I dallied around adjusting the horse's gear. I took more time and teased some burrs out of the black stallion's tail.

I recognized the routine I was caught up in. Dally to fill the interminable waiting before the rush to get into position for battle. Wait again with uncertainty and fear. Finally, the violence of fighting struck. Then the letdown and shakes came. The time to move to the next position had come, but I didn't want to move out. That, too, was part of the battle routine. Booting the stirrup, I stepped into the saddle.

The stallions pranced, eager to go. Holding them to a trot, I warmed them up, then let them choose the three-beat gait of an easy canter. The warhorses settled into their waltz over the hilly terrain, towards Santo Domingo. I mulled the situation while my butt pounded leather to the first beat of each measure of the horse's waltz.

Calling in his gangs meant Horton had abandoned his gold robbing plan. He'd be bent on implementing his getaway plans now. How would he react when his gangs failed to show up?

If it was me they stood up, I'd figure I'd lost hold of the gangs, discipline had crumbled, the boys had deserted and run off with the gold. I'd load up my gold and run for the nearest border.

If I didn't panic, and kept thinking with a military mind, I'd hold to a plan to withdraw from the territory in force, with the protection of all my men. I'd hold to that plan until facts dictated the reason to change it.

I hoped Horton didn't know his gangs weren't coming in today, wondered how long he'd wait to find out.

Before Horton tried to escape he had to recover the gold buried outside the pueblo. He'd have a hell of a time finding it if Tim's map was wrong. Most likely Horton would post a guard while they searched. I tried to picture where the lookout would hide. I didn't need to jump and surprise a wide-awake rattlesnake.

Maybe Horton's lost gold gave me an advantage. His men could get mighty pissed-off when they failed to find the gold where the map showed it to be buried. They'd get suspicious of Horton and each other. Gold fever had a way of magnifying suspicion into distrust. Maybe Horton already had a mutiny on his hands.

I was wishing again. Horton knew something had gone wrong with the operation and would be on guard more than usual. He would maintain his cat-o-nine-tails -control over his last four men.

Horton's iron fist over his men and Santo Domingo made this battle the most dangerous. A master tactician, he'd have known to keep his most loyal killers with him. But Horton's discipline could be a weakness if he ran Santo Domingo just like he had ordered the other pueblos run. It would be fine by me to find a lookout in the bell tower of the old mission. I had become pretty good at picking them off. I liked the idea of evening up the odds a bit.

Three times before, I had speculated on what might come to pass as I rode to the battles. The future never had matched the guesswork. Like before, I'd end up riding into the situation, laying siege to the pueblo, attacking whoever got in my way, and seeing what happened. As I gave up speculating, El Don Manuel Sanchez's prediction came to mind. *"Vamos a ver."*

The Sanchez family hadn't crossed my mind in days. Perhaps the three-beat gait of the horses reminded me of the governor's ball and waltzing with La Doña Sanchez. I heard the music. La Doña's swaying hips and deep black eyes struck me again. Truly a beautiful woman, she had passed her mature beauty on to Dora Luz to shine in early bloom. The dancing image of Dora Luz hovered before me. I felt her warm touch and smelled her sweet perfume. That strange feeling filled my chest.

Marrying Dora Luz would be the best thing that could happen to me. I'd have her to love and step right back into the rich life I had known as a young man in Virginia. Only better, I'd be living with her in the new land that enchanted me now. I could handle all that. I loved them both.

Dora Luz disappeared before my eyes as I stopped imagining her and looked at the situation instead. My chances of getting to marry Dora Luz were less than slim. Unless El Don had met with death since the governor's ball, Patricio posed no threat. But position, class, wealth, and religion stood between Dora Luz and me. Still, I felt she was worth the challenges.

More than likely, if I married, raised a family, I'd end up with a good woman, like Ann. If Ann hadn't left the West because of the murder of her husband, I could court her. Maybe she would consider the ranching life with Pete and me, down on the Rio Puerco by Cabezon. Or we could operate the store in Durango, have kids.

The feeling of being a storekeeper jarred against the three-beat gait of my loping horses. I needed action out in the open. Unlike a life with Dora Luz, living with Ann would not be a waltz. I reined in the stallions and my run-away imagination.

I coaxed the stallions into a single-foot. I'd waltzed them long enough, needed to let them cool and dry the sweat before I switched my saddle to the roan stallion. I halted below the crest of a hill to hide the horses while they rested and I climbed the crest to search the terrain ahead. Horton might have a man out scouting for the other gangs.

Before I stretched out on my belly on the crest I searched the dirt for the little cacti I usually felt before I saw. I called them desert surprises and hated their sting, the later festering.

The sun on my back baked and eased the knots between my shoulder blades. It felt good to lay in the sun and warm up.

Looking through field glasses was like looking into the future. They brought a place up to you for a closer look before you had to really go there to see it. Setting the field glasses down, I wondered where I wanted to go in my future. I'd give five-to-one odds against me surviving the next battle, but if I did live, my future could open wide.

If I disregarded the trouble the reputation of a gunman could bring, I could build a future in this territory. The worst that might happen, I'd end up hiding out on the VR range, working cattle for Red. Up until now it had proved to be a good life. Wouldn't be so bad a go-round, if that was all the day money available.

I'd bet the governor would keep me on payroll as a marshal. I'd earn the right to keep the badge if I cleaned up this mess with Horton for him. If I kept the badge, it would take some getting used to the idea that I had chosen to stay in the killing business.

Maybe killing was my province. I sure as hell had done a lot of killing to set things right. This was a hard land and lent itself to lawlessness. The Southwest would need honest men to police it. Hell, I held the job of policing New Mexico right now, if a bullet didn't resign me from the position tonight.

Maybe I could talk the governor into hiring me as an Indian agent. There'd be less killing in that job. The pueblos were getting to know me as a man that could get things done. They needed an honest representative in government to pull them out of the backwash they were lost in. Word would get to the other tribes that I was a man to reckon with. The Indians and the governor could use a man like me between them.

I had real choices out there in the future to pick from. All I had to do was survive a little fracas waiting for me up the road. Horton had ordered his men into Santo Domingo. He had me, and disappointment, coming instead. I raised up the field glasses, took a last look around, then slid down the rise to catch up the major's horses. *"Vamos a ver, Caballos!"*

*   *   *

The half-moon sailed a turbulent sky. Low, scuddy clouds blew across her, turned her light on and off like a flashing distress signal. Deep below her, a chilly breeze gusted, lifted dust in eddies off the bottomlands, stirred up unusual sounds that kept me edgy, moody. The sand hills east of Santo Domingo, reflecting a flash of moonlight, rose out of the gloom before me. I hauled in the stallions, steadied them to a quiet walk.

The roan stallion snorted, fiddle-footed sideways, reminded me that I wanted to ride the black horse in tonight's hunt. I found a likely place, in a steep-sided gully, to hide the roan. I tied him to a cedar root, exposed by the crumbling bank, and saddled the black stallion for war.

I slipped my long knife under my gun belt, cinched it up tight. Reaching back into the saddlebag, I dug out a handful of .44 shells. This time, fording the Rio Grande, my horse hadn't dunked me. I kept my boots dry. But the horses had splashed a might. Caution triggered the old habit left over from the cap and ball, black powder days. I loaded dry bullets into all my guns.

Feeling ready to hunt, I wondered if any bandits roamed outside the pueblo tonight. I had captured Jeb and Tim up on the sand hill over looking the pueblo. Another outlaw might be up there, standing guard or watching for the rest of the bandit gang expected to come riding in with their gold. Maybe Horton had come out with a couple of men to pick up his gold.

It made sense to hunt the sand hills first. I stuffed another handful of .44s into my duster pocket.

The black stallion carried me in a wide circle, around to the east side of the pueblo, before I turned him west, directly towards the lookout post on the sand hill. About a half mile from the overlook, I tied him in the dark shadows of a *piñon* tree. I slung the field glasses around my neck and pulled the Winchester from the saddle boot.

Hunting afoot was slower but less risky. Gusty wind disguised the occasional noises I made, the crunch of dried grass, the snap of a *piñon* twig, the hiss of yucca on my pants leg. Walking limbered me up. The soreness in the buckshot wounds and the stiffness in my body from the hard rides eased up some. Maybe soon I could rest.

I felt time slow way down as I picked my next hiding place, waited for a cloud to dim the moon so I could sneak forward in total darkness.

Not far ahead a lantern bobbed up and down, stopped moving, then took off in a different direction. I hunkered down, brought the field glasses up. The man carrying the lantern took long steps as if he paced off a measured distance.

Tim's faulty map, his insurance policy as he called it, came to mind. I stifled a chuckle. That outlaw was in for a frustrating night if he searched for the buried gold with Tim's map. So far Tim's information had proved accurate. Maybe, in a way, Tim had given me some insurance. The outlaws had split up to search for the gold and would stay split up for a while. If they stayed split up, maybe I'd live to stand up for Tim at his trial.

More than one outlaw should be out after the gold. I searched the darkness for other out-laws. It made good sense to have three men out, two to search, dig and load, one to guard. That would leave two men to hold the pueblo hostage.

Another outlaw appeared carrying a shot-gun in one hand, a spade in the other. They talked. The first man gestured a lot with his free hand, pointed in several directions. The wind covered their words. The second man threw down his spade, stomped around looking at the ground. Then he kindled a small fire in the same fireplace between the rocks that Tim and Jeb had used. In the firelight, the two men studied and argued over a piece of paper. I stifled another chuckle.

In a brief shower of moonlight, I spotted the bandit's horses and a couple of packhorses. I couldn't find a third man, a lookout. I would have stationed an extra man up here. The fact that Horton hadn't began to worry at me, like I was the dry bone a hound-dog gnawed.

Retreating quietly, slowly, I returned to my horse. Those two boys were going to be up on the sand hill chasing snipe for a while. I aimed to go after the guard in the bell tower if one was sta-tioned there. The next move appeared to be mine for a change, and I had a plan. I rode the same wide circle back to the south until I hit the road into Santo Domingo.

A few hundred yards from the pueblo and the old mission church, I pulled off the road into the protection of a motte of cottonwoods. The lookout post, up on the sand hill, lay off to my right. I searched lookout hill and the bell tower with the field glasses.

The bell tower appeared to be vacant until a light suddenly flared in the window. The light flickered for an instant then went out. A lookout had lit a match to a smoke. I eased the stallion out of the trees, moved forward. I had three of Horton's men located. It took a hell of a tobacco habit to force a man to smoke on watch, show his position and risk ruining his night vision. I wondered if the guard was the wrangler who smoked ten *quirlys* while he tended the ambush party's *remuda* in the arroyo outside San Ysidro. If so, I could rely on his habit to my advantage.

A sandy road and the shifting breeze muffled the sound of the black stallion's hooves as I walked him closer to the bell tower. The moonlight, when it poked between the clouds, offered enough light for the guard to see me on the road. If he did, I hoped he would mistake me for one of his own men coming back from lookout hill.

The field glasses picked up the pinpoint of light, the tip of the *quirly,* as it danced eerily in the bell tower. Then the spark floated back out of sight. I eased the stallion forward, stopped and spied, moved forward again. The pinpoint of light reappeared, flared, and then shot out of the tower in a red arc to shatter on the ground in a burst of sparks. I waited for the lookout's next smoke. It didn't take him long to roll his last cigarette.

When he lit it, he faced my way. I kicked the stallion forward and moved up to about fifty yards from the tower. So as not to squeak saddle leather I slid off the black stallion and eased the Winchester from the saddle boot. I took a quick look around and planned my escape route.

Tension prickled in my legs. Except for the cover of night, I stood in the wide open, exposed, and about to point myself out real clearly.

When the red dot of the *quirly* appeared again I crouched to kneel and steady the Winchester. Making adjustments for my target, the darkness, and the moonlight reflecting off my front sight, I shot just below the red dot. Then I fired two rapid shots into the air to finish the three shots of a distress signal.

I made a running mount and beat it out of there, like a Nueces steer. I quirted the black stallion to get him to the sand hills quick. I meant to cut off the men up there, keep them from joining forces with the two outlaws still inside the pueblo. I guessed they were two. One for sure had to hold the Indians captive.

I figured the bandits on lookout hill would head for the lookout post to check out the distress signal. I gambled on a third man not being there now and charged the stallion to the base of the sand hills. I yanked him to a butt-skidding stop, made a running dismount into a wash that cut down the side of the sand hill, south of lookout hill. Leaving the black stallion ground hitched, I took off on foot.

I hoped my distress signal would confuse the bandits. Those inside the pueblo might think the outside men had fired the signal. The outside men might think the signal came from inside the pueblo. Both parties might conclude that the shots were a signal from one of the gangs coming in from the other pueblos. Three variables were enough to create confusion.

Soon, somebody had to make a move to find out what was going on. I stood a good chance to see them when they did. Most likely, one of the men in the pueblo would check with the guard in the tower and discover the truth. All hell ought to break loose then.

I climbed from shadow to shadow, up the wash. Between gusts of wind I thought I heard a man hail the guard in the bell tower. I stopped scrambling to listen. Then I eased my eyes up over the edge of the wash to watch. A knob of rocks halfway down lookout hill blocked my view of the mission. I bolted up the rest of the wash and dropped on my belly on top of the south sand hill.

From where I lay, I could observe the road into the pueblo, the plaza and mission below, and the lookout post across from me. The intermittent moonlight was a mixed blessing. At times I could see pretty well, but so could the outlaws.

I adjusted the focus on the field glasses, searched for the outside bandits. They had snuffed the fire and abandoned the fireplace. I made out the silhouette of only two of the four horses that had been there. I did not locate the men. I flinched at the tension between my shoulder blades, rolled my shoulders.

I searched the plaza for the dark shape of horses against the lighter hue of the packed earth. I didn't find any horse's shadows. I assumed that the outlaws were not yet packed up and ready to ride out of the pueblo.

After a long search all around, the only living things I'd found were the two horses on lookout hill across from me. I had lost track of all the outlaws except for the body in the bell tower. I had lost any advantage I might have gained by firing the distress signal. All I knew for sure, I had stirred up the wasps in their nest.

I had no idea what was going on in the nest, no idea where my enemies circled around me. I felt exposed laying on top of the sand hill. I needed a place to hole up and wait safely for the next development. Careful not to crawl on to any stinging, desert surprises in the dark, I sought cover, eased into a depression, the beginning of the gully.

I grew impatient waiting, figured I could best hunt the bandits in the pueblo. Besides, I was worried about the Indians in Horton's hands. A fair-sized cloud looked like it would keep the moon covered for a bit. I headed for the knob of rocks that jutted out of the slope of lookout hill. From there I'd have a closer view of the pueblo. The moon came out of hiding just as I hid in the shadows of the rocks.

The sound of a galloping horse broke the silence between gusts of wind. I turned to my left to listen. The Winchester came to my shoulder. In two steps I got a view of the road below. I saw the shadow of the rider when he drew abreast me. As he raced on towards the pueblo he hollered, "Groves! Groves! I'm comin' in!"

Adding an allowance for shooting down hill, I fired, jumped backwards. Buckshot splattered the rock I had stood on. A second load splattered closer to me, like advancing hail. Guessing the shotgun above was empty, I poked my head up for a look at the road. I needed to know if I had killed the rider. The horse had run on by, riderless.

I ducked and remembered what I had just looked at. A bulky shadow, could be a man, lay by the side of the road. I had been over that same road to the bell tower and didn't remember a pile of rocks or a log there.

I needed to take another look, maybe make a killing shot, but they had me in a bear trap. The bait lay in the road. The jaws of the trap would spring from in back and above me.

Squirming around in the cracks between the rocks, I found a boulder to protect my back from the shooter up above. I eased up enough to see the road over the bounders in front of me. Matching memory to vision, I guessed the shadow had changed position. If I shot left handed, I had room to shoot the man in the road without exposing myself to the gunner above.

I fired. Buckshot rained down on the rock behind me. Rifle and shotgun thunder echoed back off the walls of the pueblo, the mission church. The shooter above had not seen me, but had fired both barrels at my muzzle blast. While he loaded, I put a clean shot into the other end of the shadow in the road. It rolled over, didn't move again.

I snaked in the rocks to another position. The shooter above would be moving to get a better shot at me. I had to keep an eye on the bell tower, too. A man, good with a rifle, could pick me off from there. I had taken the bait, killed the man in the road below, but I was still in the jaws of the bear trap. Sweat soaked my shirt. I opened my duster to get cool, took a deep breath, and squirmed between two boulders.

Buckshot and the boom of the shotgun reached my ear at the same time. A double-ought pellet nicked my earlobe. The rest of the shot splattered on the rock in front of me. I writhed down deeper into the crack like a snake seeking a hole. Another load of buckshot urged me deeper. From the angle of the buckshot I guessed the shooter above had moved lower off the crest, was between the pueblo and me. Or, there was a second shooter.

While he loaded his shotgun, I sought a boulder between us for protection. Hoping to catch a shadow when he moved, I eased my eyes over the rock for a look. I wondered when he would switch to his pistol and abandon the two shotguns. The fact that he hadn't, told me he hadn't seen me clearly yet. He blasted flashes of light at shadows and hoped.

As I searched for the shooter, a door on the west side of the plaza opened. A man sprinted out of the lamplight behind him. He ran across the plaza towards the mission.

I took a shot. Buckshot cut through the light of my muzzle flash.

I shifted to the right side of the boulder, fired a quick shot into the shadows where I'd seen the shooter's gun flash. Levering a round to chamber, I aimed at the plaza. The moon chose to escape the clouds then, bathed the plaza and me in pail moonlight.

The runner in the plaza crawled towards the protection of a *horno*. I dropped him to his belly with another shot. The shotgun shooter blew my new Stetson away.

I dropped the Winchester, drew and put six, rapid-fire shots into the area of the shooters muzzle flash.

Grabbing the Winchester, I dove for another rock, landed prone. Buckshot buzzed close over my head. I rolled, came up for a killing shot at the crawler in the plaza. He lay where I'd dropped him. Just before the moonlight dimmed, I shot out his lights.

I crammed .44s into the rifle, thumbed the Colt full. The Santa Ana chief said the pueblos were built out in the open for protection. My Winchester proved the pueblo strategy, good in the days of the bow and arrow, had become obsolete.

Just ahead lay a rock my size. I rolled behind it. Colts in both hands, eyes just clearing the top of the rock, I shot from both sides of the rock. Ten bullets cut a straight-line pattern through the shadows where I'd last seen the shotgun flash.

Reloading, I listened. Gunfire and whistling wind left me deaf. Then with both hands pumping lead, I widened the pattern, punched holes in the deeper shadows. The wind sucked the air clear of gun smoke. My hand found an empty pocket when I clawed it for more bullets.

"You Horton?" I shouted into the shadows I'd just riddled with lead. "There were five of you. Now there're two." I emptied the loops in my gun belt to fill the Colts and considered the risk of talking.

If I faced two men out here on the hill, hollering pinpointed my position for them. They would circle around to get me in a crossfire. Hell, from all my blasting, they knew where I lay. I crawled back to the big crack in the rocks where I'd started. From there I searched the darkness for movement, watched the pueblo.

Seemed like the Indians would be coming out if the man I killed in the plaza had been their guard. They could see him laying by the *horno* better than I could. I had to conclude that another outlaw still held them hostage. I wiped the sweat off my hands, bet that I faced one man out here.

"There were twenty of you. Now there're just two." I jerked left, crouched deep in shadow. "If Horton wasn't one of the three I've killed, he'll get the gold." I moved again. "He's got a good map hid away." I shifted to the other end of the crack, listened, watched. Worry dug its fangs into the knot between my shoulder blades. "You've been huntin' snipe up there."

I heard the farting and clopping of a spur raked, jump-started horse, listened to the receding gallop. Ducking out of the crack and around the rock I caught a glimpse of moving shadow as it crested the sand hill to the south. I sent a bullet after the shadow, another into the dark where I thought he might ride. Talk about snipe hunting, I had been yelling at shadows and let a bandit get away.

I waited to hear if the galloping sound doubled back. The sound faded, mingled with the ringing in my ears, finally got swallowed by the wind. Whose horse was that running? The gait sounded familiar. Strong need urged me to go check on the black stallion. But I felt pinned down. I might have been talking to another shooter in the shadows, not the getaway artist. Anyway, it was too late to save the black stallion if he'd been stolen.

I snaked up-hill in the rocks, twisted, slithered on my back sometimes to keep the Winchester handy. The sky blue turquoise turtle fetish came to mind. I didn't know any turtle attributes, other than laying in the sun to warm. Yet, a turtle on its back flailed and fought to stay alive. Wanting to get off my back, knowing how to get on my feet and live, was the attribute I took from the turtle fetish.

One man, the last of twenty, stood between me and living. I had come too far to have this war end just short of getting the job done. The only thing that kept me here on my back was fear.

I bet the last bandit held the Indians hostage in the pueblo. I stood up, looked around, walked down the hill. I had a job to finish.

The black stallion stood ground hitched where I'd left him. I rode him south, away from the pueblo, stopped him so I could listen. Worried that I still had an outside bandit to contend with, I listened until the wind blew a handful of fat raindrops into my face. I reached to pull down my hat brim, remembered my new Stetson lay wounded up on the hill.

I pulled my collar up, booted the stallion. We rode to the roan stallion in the gully, gathered him up, and headed back north, towards the pueblo. Raindrops darkened the shoulders of my canvas duster. Rain running down my back cooled the tension there. The water felt good. The squirrelly gusts of wind smelled fresh, told me it had rained harder somewhere else.

The roan stallion shied when he smelled the corpse in the road. I jerked his lead line to startle him out of his fear of death. Suddenly thinking my bold ride towards the pueblo foolish, I turned the horses into the motte of cottonwoods and sought cover. I tied the roan to a tree then sat on the black and tried to come up with a plan. I dug in a pocket for my pipe, felt its broken stem, and swore.

I couldn't just ride into the pueblo and take over for the same reason I'd told the governor he couldn't use force. Hostages would be killed. I knew I'd back away from an outlaw to save an Indian's life.

I couldn't ride into the pueblo for fear of getting shot by the outlaw I believed was still inside. If he had fled, Indians who believed me to be an outlaw returning in the dark could shoot me.

Backhanding the last of the rain from my eyes, I concluded I couldn't stay out here either. I dismounted, shucked my damp duster, tied it to my saddle. With the Winchester, the field glasses and another hand full of .44s from the saddlebag I took off on foot.

I headed west towards the *rio*, came around to the west side of the pueblo. I wanted to be as far from the bell tower, as possible as I snuck into the pueblo. I pushed through the dried stalks of a cornfield. Rising ground-fog covered my sprint over the open field. House to *jacalito* to *horno* to house, moving, stopping, listening I walked, crawled, dashed, snaked towards the plaza.

Muffled yelling, then a muffled shot jerked my attention left. I couldn't tell which house the sounds came from. I moved to my left.

Wisps of steam rose off the packed dirt of the plaza as the light rain evaporated. For an instant, a drifting wisp turned yellow. Then another. Watching the wisps drew my eye to two, very thin lines of light, reflected light off two poles sticking out of the ground fifty feet away.

The reflected light flickered then disappeared. Another shout came from near there. Then a form rose up out of the ground. Light from inside the ground gave the form shape from below. Two men climbed backwards up a ladder out of a kiva.

They ascended awkwardly. One man hauled the other by the neck in a hammerlock. He pointed a pistol into the kiva with his other hand. He searched with his heels for the next rung up the ladder, found it and boosted his load higher. The choked man kicked with his heels to find a rung and step up to ease the choking.

Unable to get a clear shot, I stacked the Winchester against a wall, shucked a Colt, held the trigger down to ear the hammer back noiselessly. On the damp earth I stepped forward silently.

The outlaw dragged his hostage up the rest of the way out of the kiva entrance. Standing finally with the hostage locked against his front, the outlaw fired another shot into the kiva then backed away. He turned his human shield towards me and danced him right at me.

He must be night blind. Without the reflected light from the kiva I couldn't see the outlaw well either. The rain cloud still held the moonlight captive. In the darkness I couldn't distinguish the outlaw from his hostage. Suddenly the outlaw jerked up short, about twenty feet from me.

"Simmons?"

"Horton?"

"Who's the son-of-a-bitch shot Groves an' Porter?" He nudged his hostage forward a couple of steps. "Get the gold?" He stopped again.

I could see them better now, enough to tell that the outlaw showed half his head from behind his hostage so he could look at me. I could barely make out that he held his pistol to the hostage's head, maybe muzzle to cheek.

"The gold's up on the hill." Slowly I turned sideways to him. "I'm the son-of-a-bitch shot Groves an' has a gun on you. Your choice, drop your gun or use it."

"I'll use it all right. I got the chief here. Back off or I'll shoot him!"

"Then what'll you do?" I raised my Colt to eye level, aimed.

Moonlight erupted from the rain cloud, burst forth with the brightness of dawn, bounced a glint of light off Horton's Colt, and showed me his gun was not cocked. I fired.

With moonlight's help I shot again. Loving sweet moonlight for her help, even more than I loved Dora Luz, I shot again. Then again.

Clutching the right side of his head in both hands, the chief of Santo Domingo hunched beside the body of the outlaw.

"You hit, Chief?"

He grunted something then wambled to the entrance of the kiva, steadied himself, descended into the lamplight.

"Horton!" I kicked the outlaw's foot hard. It kicked back. Then suddenly a flashing gray fist, blurred in the moonlight, slapped at the empty holster tied to the leg that kicked. I stomped the fist, pinned it under boot until all the life drained out of it. Going for the gun must have been reflex, like the blind strike of a just-killed rattlesnake when you poke it.

Bending over the body I struck a match. Tim had said Horton's eyes were different colors. In the gore that had been forehead and cheek, I wiped a blue eye clear with my thumb. The other eye was brown.

My legs gave way. I slumped beside the head of the snake that lay over the pueblos. No more! This war was over. As my body shook off the energy that drove my violence, I realized how much I loved the violence, how much I hated the killing. I laid back on the hard-packed earth of the plaza, stared up at the moon, breathed deeply to settle my guts.

CHAPTER TWENTY

I yawned, stretched the sleepiness out of my muscles, but not so hard as to disturb the well-being I felt. Señora Martinez's sleeping potion had felt like this, that morning at her house after the Jemez battle. I hadn't taken any potion last night. After the shakes left me, sleep had come naturally, peacefully.

Scanning a deep, clear sky, I searched for today's weather. Most likely the rest of the afternoon would remain clear, hot. No wind blew over lookout hill to change my prediction.

I shook out my boots, shucked them on, stood up laughing. I'd slept not more than two feet from a treasure in gold buried beneath the ashes in the fire pit at the head of my blankets. The gold lay buried between the rocks where the bandit lookouts had built their fires. They had warmed their hands over the gold and never knew it. Imagining the two outlaws arguing over Tim's map, by the light of the fire that hid the gold, brought another chuckle.

I scratched at my ear, started it bleeding. I did not mind the hurt. Considering all the battles I had been through lately, some buckshot wounds and a nicked ear didn't amount to much.

"Yes, Sir, this war is over," I said to the day. I'd wound up on the winning side for a change. I stood on the lip of my future.

Tranquility and anticipation rippled through me, as I stretched again.

After coffee I'd head down to the pueblo, fetch a couple of the outlaw horses. Then I'd dig up the gold and head over to Santa Fe and the governor to close out the Durango gold case.

While coffee made on the fire, I caught the major's horses and gave them a rub-down. Both stallions acted spunky, feisty after the long rest. I spent extra time working them over. A fine pair of horses, they had carried me on a long and fast mission. They would breed a strong line of colts. Funny, the comradeship I felt for these animals, good warhorses, both.

Sipping on my coffee, I walked over to where the outlaws had tied their horses the night before. I picked up the tracks of the man and horse that had cut and run in the night. I burned them into my memory.

From Tim's descriptions I had identified all the dead men last night. The outlaw that got away was named Al Simmons. Tim had described him as a man who could get a gun into action mighty fast and did not hesitate to shoot a man before words were spoken. Back shooting was his preference.

I had one thing going for me. I knew what Simmons looked like but he did not know my face. I would cross his trail one of these days, of that I was sure. Before I rode to the pueblo I would take some time to track him. I needed to know if he had kept on running south.

Except for the gold, I was packed and ready to go. I tied the roan by the fireplace to guard the gold. Riding the black stallion, I headed south over the sand hills to pick up Simmons' trail.

Wind had blown the sharp edges off the tracks. Last night's rain had patted them down, but I could follow the trail. Simmons had kept running south. Probably Mexican *Rurales* would have to contend with him shortly. He had fled with nothing, would have to steal to live.

Santo Domingo appeared to be slow to come alive. Under Horton's fist, this pueblo had suffered the most. The Indians I saw looked dazed, moved slowly. They hadn't started the hard work necessary for the pueblo to recover fully and survive the winter without famine. They paid me no mind as I rounded up the outlaw horses.

I bunched a dozen horses in the center of the plaza, then cut three geldings from the herd. As I tied lead ropes on the geldings, the chief came out to meet me.

"How is the ear, Chief?" I pointed at my matching wound. When I'd shot Horton in the face last night I'd nicked the chief's earlobe. "I apologize for my poor aim."

The chief jerked his chin up once to acknowledge my statement. He remained silent. If he had worn pockets, he'd have stuffed his hands in them.

"The rest of the horses are yours." I jerked the lead lines and rode out of Santo Domingo.

I loaded the gold packs on two outlaw horses. I was not about to raise sores on the major's warhorses, using them for pack animals. Santa Fe was not that far away but I would be slowed down by the pack train. I figured I would ride into Santa Fe around sunrise.

Besides, there were no good reasons to hurry. I was a man of leisure, except for Red's cattle drive. I calculated I had five days to get to Red at Corrales. Maybe I could take a little time and call on the Sanchez family before I joined up with Red.

Considering the choice of trails to get to Santa Fe, I decided to stay out in the open. Going up the river trail offered Simmons too many good ambush sites if he had turned back to get the gold. Staying in the open, on the main route between Santa Fe and Bernalillo, I would be at risk for an ambush only for a while going up La Bajada.

Remembering how the outlaws set up their ambushes in what looked like open space, I decided to ride wide of the trail. Riding at night would make it harder to spot me, and I would run into fewer people traveling, if I ran into any at all.

The taste of Rivas beer and fine Mexican food prodded me through the night. The air smelled fresher, the stars seemed brighter. Overhead Mars had dimmed and backed away from Aldibaron. The conjunction of the red war god and the red eye of Taurus had ended. Mars backed away from the bull. Moonlight bathed a peaceful sky. I sang to the moon like I was standing under Dora Luz's window.

*   *   *

Troops drilled on the parade ground when I rode into Fort Marcy, north of Santa Fe. At the sound of barked orders I straightened to attention in the saddle, out of old habit. A sergeant directed me to headquarters when I inquired about Major Watson.

Major Watson looked up from his desk when his orderly spoke my name. A warm smile spread over his face. "Pleasure to see you back, Colonel Waller. What news do you bring, Sir?" He came around from behind his desk, shook my hand, and led me to his private stock of whiskey.

"I brought you more than two hundred pounds of Durango gold to guard, Major, and your stallions are tied outside." I accepted a shot of bourbon. "I'm assumin' the governor'll request that you send a detail to pick up the prisoners at the pueblos and the rest of the gold." I walked him outside. The gold needed tending. I wanted to keep an eye on it until he took responsibility for it.

I gave the major a detailed report and handed him the map to the gold hidden outside Jemez. He ordered men to transfer the gold to the warehouse and set a guard. I felt better seeing the gold in his care.

"Fine work, Marshal. Very impressive. We need men like you out here in the army. Would you consider a commission as an officer?" He spoke seriously.

I looked at him sideways then decided to play it straight with him. "Major Watson, I'm finished with this job, and I'm finished with killin'. However, I'll have another shot of that fine, government-issue bourbon."

Watson asked about details as we drank. I suggested that he send a man up to Durango to notify the people there that they could resume shipments. He said he would work the details out with the governor. We walked outside to the horses.

"I hate to return these stallions. They're fine warhorses."

"They're yours, Marshal, bought from the army and paid for by Governor Connelly. By the way," he chuckled, "The governor mentioned that you'd run up quite a bill for him, right?" The major cleared his throat formally. "After the job you've done, I doubt he'll dock your pay." He rubbed the black stallion's nose, patted his neck. "Poker tonight at Maria's? Maybe you'll wager this fine horse after I've taken your last dollar."

When I led my herd of horses out of the fort a sense of freedom began to settle over me. I would have my independence after I saw the governor. First, I wanted to stop by the cathedral and talk to Bishop Lamy.

Pulling up behind the church, I took a minute to pull the black coat and a white shirt out of my duffel and put them on. I dusted off my buckshot Stetson. Then I took the monk's robe and sought the Bishop. I had to wait a few minutes.

"Ah, My Son, you've come for instruction in the faith." Devilishness played in his eyes like it had when he addressed El Don Manuel Sanchez at the governor's ball.

"Bishop, I've come this time to make a donation to the church, poor as it may be." I handed him the robe, rosary, and the sandals. "I delivered your blessin's at four pueblos. I regret that this fine robe has two holes in it, but it's served well and still retains the power of your blessin'." We walked in his private courtyard while I explained what had happened with his padres at the pueblos.

"Bishop, it's my intention to court Dora Luz Sanchez. You mentioned that you'd advise me in matters of the church. How should I proceed?"

He thought for a moment as we strolled. "I cannot advise you in matters of the heart. But I would advise that you speak to El Don before you see Señorita Sanchez. You may be in for a surprise. Modern beliefs are changing the ancient customs of my children. I assume you're not of the Catholic faith?"

"That's correct, Bishop."

"This matter with the Sanchez family will not be easy, but there are ways, as I have indicated. I shall give it thought, but you must tell me what El Don has to say. That will dictate how we proceed." He paused, turned to face me. "Would you consider embracing the sacraments and becoming a Catholic?"

"Bishop Lamy, I'm a practical man, a realist, probably an atheist. I've seen too many men die horrible deaths to believe that God is concerned with the lives of men. I could learn to behave like a Catholic, but my heart wouldn't be involved." I hoped I did not offend him. "Can you still see your way clear to help me?"

"Of course, My Son. If only to save your soul." His smile was fatherly.

I left the Bishop and headed for the livery with my herd of horses. Old Gray and Tim and Jeb's horses were waiting for me. They were fat from too much grain and disuse. The stable boy recognized me from Fiesta and hung around, waiting for an extra coin, before he turned my stock into the corral, went after them with a brush.

Leaving the stable, I almost ducked up an alley to the governor's mansion when it occurred to me that I didn't have to seek cover or take special precautions anymore. My enemies were dead or captured. Patricio would not be hunting me. El Don still lived.

I could shed the feelings that had come with the marshal's badge. I was not under cover anymore. I was not a spy. Throwing back my shoulders I strode towards the plaza. This was my territory, my Santa Fe.

This day was mine to celebrate. She was a beauty. A cool breeze chilled me when I stepped into a shadow. The sun felt hot when I stepped out again. Bright sunlight danced everywhere, made colors more vivid.

The snowstorm that hit me a few days back had pushed the snow line down the mountains to the east of town. The stark white above the dark green of the slopes made the deep blue of the sky more vibrant. To the west, the Jemez Mountains cut the skyline with bands of dark purple over tans and browns. I was free to roam all this beautiful land again.

Under the portal of the governor's mansion, Indians displayed black pottery and shiny, silver jewelry. I stopped to admire a couple of trinkets that might please a lady I knew. I bought them.

The governor sat in his office and seemed surprised to see me when I walked in on him, unannounced. I pulled the deputy marshal badge from my shirt pocket and pitched it to clatter on his desk.

"The Horton job's finished, Governor. No Indians died." I took great pleasure in the announcement. "Looks like your political career's secure for awhile."

He came from behind his desk and clapped me on the shoulder as he shook my hand. "Good to see you're still alive, Marshal Waller. Tell me about it, right?" Connelly pulled two cigars from the humidor on his desk. "It's hard to believe you're back in one piece," he said, respectfully holding a match for me. "To be perfectly frank with you, I didn't think you had a chance in hell, right? You had lunch yet?" He picked up the badge, stuffed it in his breast pocket.

As we walked over to La Fonda for lunch, Connelly commented on the fine, white shirt I wore and asked if it was one he had bought. I began my report.

"I killed Horton. Only one outlaw escaped. There're five prisoners to be picked up from the pueblos, if they live long enough to get to'em. I told Major Watson you'd request that he pick them and the rest of the gold up. He said he'd see you about the details. The rest of the bandits're dead."

The governor stopped to shake hands and introduce me to Chet Stevens, the president of the Santa Fe Bank.

As we entered La Fonda, I continued, "Major Watson's storing more than two hundred pounds of gold I recovered. Another two hundred pounds're bein' held at the pueblos. I gave Watson a map I took off one of the outlaws in Jemez. That'll account for all the gold. Did you get an assay report from Durango yet, Governor?" We entered the dining room.

"It came in late yesterday, right? The judge's holding it for evidence. With your testimony, the judge believes I have an iron clad case for hanging. I'll order the trial as soon as the other bandits're brought in, right?" He smiled broadly as we crossed the room to his table.

I had covered the last of the details by the time the enchiladas arrived. The boy I'd sent out arrived just in time with the Rivas beers. I took time to savor the meal. People kept coming over to our table to talk to the governor. I didn't mind much, except for the occasional interruption for an introduction. I was polite but brief. Chili-hot food came first, in my opinion.

As we walked back to the governor's office, and while he was in a good mood, I raised a subject that I figured he might be touchy about.

"Governor, I ran up some expenses. A couple hundred dollars ought to cover'em, and some pay for my time." I waited with my neck bowed, ready for an argument.

"I'll pay you when we get to the office, right?" He looked at me out of the corner of his eye. "Buy a new Stetson. That gut-shot critter you're wearing looks mighty shabby, right? It isn't the image I want for my marshal." He paused mid-stride, grabbed my elbow to stop me. "Why don't you go on the payroll, stay on as my Marshal? I'll get you a permanent commission, right?"

"No thanks. I'm not a wounded and hunted man this time, Governor. I'm feeling good, looking into my future. You lost your hold on me."

"Take the badge, Eli." The governor held it out to me.

"No, thanks." It was easy to stand firm. Unlike the first time I met Connelly in the Santa Fe jail, I was on my feet, could cinch up my belt, and didn't have to carry my gun in a pocket.

*   *   *

With new money in my pocket, a full belly, and time to waste, I headed back to La Fonda to get a room for the night. I wanted a hot bath, could use a shave and a haircut. I would send my clothes out for cleaning and get my boots shined. This gentleman was going courting.

Soaking in the tub, I enjoyed another Rivas and saluted the Irish sergeant. The Rivas made me think of Pete Montoya. Thinking about Pete reminded me I had a job to do for Red. I had to get back to the herd and close the cattle deal I'd made with Sam Bartlet. But all that waited a few days off.

After the cattle deal closed I had a choice to make. I could quit working for Red or anyone else for that matter. I could strike out on my own. Or, I could choose to go on cowboying, stay with the outfit.

I liked it at the VR, but I had horses and enough money to start a rawhide outfit with Pete. We could stake claim down by Cabezon, gather up a herd, build up a ranch.

If I struck out on my own, I could head on up to Durango. Pulling gold out of the ground seemed easy enough. Or, maybe they still needed a sheriff up there. Maybe in time, Ann and I would hit it off. For that matter, the quiet life of being a store owner held some attraction today.

I could be a marshal in the territory, if I wanted. Turning down the governor's offer had been just for the pleasure of the turn down. I was still angry enough at the way he had black-mailed me to still want evens with him. But I could go back and get the job.

The dream that kept turning around in my mind held Dora Luz in it. I could offer her nothing but myself. Maybe I could make that enough. I could read law, become a lawyer. I might find a future in politics. I would consider doing anything because I wanted that beautiful, spirited woman. This dream held the most stimulating challenges.

Clearly the major's bourbon, the Rivas beers, and the hot bath were getting to my head. Maybe I was just getting better at dreaming about my future. What was clear, not a dream to me anymore, was that from now on I worked for myself. In a few months I would turn thirty-five years old. It was about time I built something for myself.

Late afternoon, after siesta, all slicked-up in my Sunday best, I rode my black stallion out to the Sanchez's Santa Fe residence for a social call. I pranced the black up to the main gate and yanked the bell chain. A *pistolero* came to the summons, stepped out of the smaller guard door cut in the main gate. He wore a silver inlaid, double holster rig, rested a hand on the butt of a Remington.

"*El Patrón*, he is not here," the *pistolero* intoned haughtily with a flourish of his other hand that indicated I should be gone. When I stood my ground, he added, "He and the women go to La Hacienda de Cerrillos." He turned his back on me. "Maybe they return *por La Navidad*." He kicked behind him, booted the guard door shut in my face.

The slamming door dashed my hopes, left me feeling foolish, sitting up high on my black horse. It had not occurred to me that Dora Luz would not be waiting in Santa Fe for me to come courting. Once again, my dreaming and predicting had little to do with how things really turned out.

An ugly mood settled into my chest. Suddenly nothing I wanted to do in Santa Fe appealed to me anymore. I might as well head on back to Red and the hands on the cattle drive. I jumped up a lot of dust heading back to La Fonda to collect my war bag.

As I rode into the plaza, guitar music from the cantina strummed into my black mood, soothed it some. I reckoned I'd find the poker game Watson had mentioned, spend the night

MICHAEL C. HALEY

playing and then get on back to Red and the herd. First, I wanted to ride on over to the Santa Fe jail. I had something to say to Tim.

Sheriff Moore sat behind his desk with his boots up on it. The worn-out newspaper he'd been reading lay in his lap over the hand that rested on his pistol. He picked his teeth with the other hand. "Hear tell you been out on quite a shootin' spree here lately." He slammed his boots to the floor, crumpled the newspaper on to the desk, eased up on his pistol and toothpick. His cold eyes locked on mine. "Built up quite a name for yourself." His flat face showed no emotion.

Word spread fast. Must have been the damn governor talking around. My mood took a turn for the worst. The last thing I wanted was the reputation of a *buscadero*. I sure as hell did not want to have to deal with an envious or spiteful sheriff. Thoughts of a new life in Colorado or Wyoming crossed my mind, appeared likely again.

"Doin' a job for the governor, Sheriff. I've come to talk to his prisoner. What the hell's Tim's last name?" I felt real short-tempered.

"Spragens? He's in the last cell where you left'im." Moore waived me by. His eyes addressed my holster rig, out of habit more than likely.

"I got'em all but Simmons," I said to Tim Spragens. "How they treatin' you here?"

"Tolerable, Marshal. The food ain't good, but it's regular." He hung from both hands on the iron bars.

"The army'll be bringin' in five more of the gang. I'll ask the judge to quarter you up at Fort Marcy for protection." I handed him a sack of Durham, papers. "All your information proved accurate. I'll stand up for you at the trial." Looking Tim in the eyes, I said honestly, "I owe you my thanks."

"Stay above ground for the trial, Marshal. Simmons's a vengeful man, may hunt. Hunted, he's mean as a cornered badger." Spragens turned from the prison bars, took a step to the bunk, slumped down on it. He folded over with his elbows on his knees, his head in his hands. "It's about stayin' alive, ain't it Marshal?"

As I headed back to the plaza, Tim's words haunted me, kept me thinking. Simmons had stayed alive, survived his murdering spree. Simmons being out there, unpunished and free, was going to rub me sore. My job for the governor was not yet finished. I took pride in being a man who got the job done. The whole damn job, kit and caboodle.

If Simmons was a vengeful man, he might come after me, save me the job of hunting him. Either way, defend or hunt, I would not rest easy until I had the badger cornered, caged, hung, or shot dead.

Feeling guilty like I had work to do and was shirking it, I tied my black stallion outside Maria's cantina and went in to drink and play poker.

Maria's hummed with the usual rowdy, working crowd that had come to kick back, drink, sport with the soiled doves. I liked the feel of the place, although a señorita sang a little too soulfully for my mood. A chilled Rivas beer teased my palate, put some perspective on my mood when I remembered the Irish Sergeant. I watched the men playing poker over in the corner by the guitar player and his evening thrush.

Mexican dinner left my mouth on fire, my tongue numb, and sweat popping out around my eyes, the way I liked it. On the governor's recommendation I had requested the *habanero* chili shipped up special from Yucatan. I asked Maria to sell me some *habaneros* to take to Pete Montoya.

After cooling my mouth with another Rivas, I carried another bottle over to the poker game I'd been watching. "Major. Patricio. Gents." I stacked my stake on the table, pulled up a chair.

During my Mexican dinner, I'd watched Patricio play good poker. He pitched them when his cards didn't make and bet heavy when they did. There was no bluff in him. When he stayed in the game he held winners. If he stayed, it became a heavy betting game. I liked the way he played, and he was sitting behind the biggest stack of gold coins on the table.

Major Watson sat to my left. He had been drinking whiskey and having fun with the game. When he checked the bet, he would slam the table with the back of his hand in a grand gesture. When he bet, he would toss the money on the table with assurance, flamboyantly. His bets always pushed the limits higher. He loved to bet in the blind, and his luck had saved him most times.

The other three men had been losing. The rancher in a calfskin vest was trying to run bluffs, but he signaled them by the way he turned pink in his cheeks, just under his eyes. The others gents read him and picked him clean every time he bluffed. The other two players had been trying to work their way back into the money and had taken risks that did not pay off.

The man directly to my left dealt seven-card stud. I pulled two aces in the hole and a ten showing. The major slapped a big bet on the table, to back his queen of hearts. The rancher called on his nine. Patricio raised the bet. I figured he held a high pair or three of a kind, with a six showing. One gent folded. I raised the bet and a lot of money got pushed to the center of the table.

The next two cards up did not improve my hand but I felt I could not abandon my hidden aces and kept betting on them. No one showed anything to beat them, although the major's three hearts were worrisome. After the round of betting, four of us remained in the game.

My sixth card paired my ten, gave me two pair with one pair showing. The red of the heart flush built to my left. The major bet like he already had the flush working for him.

The rancher didn't have any power showing, but his first card up was a nine. He had kept betting that nine. I figured he had three of then. The forth nine hadn't turned up yet. The rancher raised the bet, didn't turn pink under his eyes.

Patricio had a pair of sixes showing. He raised the bet. He must be holding two pair, could be holding four sixes. No other sixes had appeared. No aces were showing to cut my odds. Patricio could fill a full house. So could I. The rancher could take the whole pot with four nines.

If the major was bluffing, he had to stay in to make his flush and hope the rest of us drew cold cards. Right now he looked like top hand.

Looking at four hearts with another card coming could make your heart pound. I figured the major had tried to buy the pot. His hand would make or not on the last card, just like the rest of us. I raised the bet.

Poker was prime when a big pot hung on the last card down.

The seventh card went down all around. I watched Patricio as he looked at his last hole card. He gave no sign. The rancher stacked his hole cards, looked around the room. Betting three nines from the beginning had been an expensive game for him.

I looked at my third ace in the hole. I had a full house and the power did not show.

It was my bet on the pair of tens. I pushed my usual bet into the pot, knowing that if the major was in with a flush, he would raise the bet. He raised. He had to since a flush had everything beat that was showing.

The rancher folded, sat back to watch who got his money.

The bet went to Patricio. He raised. He had to have a full house or the four sixes to beat the flush.

The bet back to me amounted to cowboy wages for three months. I had any other full house beat with my aces. The gamble was on the Patricio's four sixes. I bet against sixes and raised.

The major raised, pounded the table with his bet money. He'd played with Patricio long enough to learn that the he didn't bluff, but the major couldn't fold now and discover this was Patricio's first bluff of the night. The major must have thought that I thought he was bluffing his flush and he could buy me out of the pot with one more expensive round of bets.

Patricio raised the major's bet with no change in demeanor.

I raised Patricio's bet with the last of the money the governor had paid me.

Watson finally figured we had his flush beat. He folded.

The crow's foot in the corner of Patricio's right eye deepened, just for an instant. A slight hesitation in Patricio's hand interrupted his reach for his money. He called my bet.

"It'll take four sixes, Patricio." I introduced my three aces to my pair of tens. "Got'em?"

CHAPTER TWENTY-ONE

I put seven hundred dollars in Chet Steven's Bank of Santa Fe before heading south to meet up with Red and the herd. It had been a hell of a poker game. The cards had been good to me and the betting heavy. I still owned the black and the roan horses, and a lot of Major Watson's money. I appreciated the fact that the game with Patricio had stayed friendly, even after the larruping I gave him a-going and a-coming.

It felt good to have money in the bank again. It had been six or so years since I had had an account anywhere. With the equipment and horses I had requisitioned from the army, my outlaw horses, the money I'd been paid by the governor, and my winnings, I sat pretty high, felt mighty proud. I had a sufficient stake to start my own cattle operation.

Heading south to Corrales, I pushed my *remuda* hard. I rode old Gray who needed a workout. He had resumed his first-thing-in-the-morning bucking routine, and my buckshot leg ached from working him out. I'd enjoyed the go-round. He was a ripper, set a fast pace for the *remuda*. We jammed the breeze.

Dropping off the Santa Fe plateau down La Bajada, I headed to the southwest on a line I figured would get me to the herd. I would either hit the herd or cut its trail. Finding a thousand herd of bunched cattle was easy enough.

Night came on as I passed by the little settlement of Algodones, mostly a cluster of small, irrigated farms along the Rio Grande River. I dropped on down to the river to water the horses.

After picketing the horses on grass and rubbing them down, I turned to making camp under tall, cottonwood trees. A light breeze rustled through the dried leaves still hanging in the trees. Before I built a fire, I savored the smell of the river, the plants growing along it, the mulch of dead leaves building up along the riverbank.

After a dinner of beans, coffee, and tamales, bought from a lady on the plaza, I kicked back with another cup of coffee and stared into the fire. I didn't think about anything. My eyes rested on smoldering coals. My skin absorbed their heat. I listened to the river and the life around it, but I didn't give a name to any of the sounds. After while I could not draw a boundary between the feel of my body and the feel of the ground. I slept soundly.

Mid-morning, I spotted the dust the herd kicked up and headed for the brown cloud. A little before noon, I swung my horses in with the trailing ranch *remuda*. I shifted my saddle to my new roan, picking the army mount to see how he worked around cattle.

I threw all my gear in the chuck wagon and tossed a hello at Cookie, along with a sack of horehound candy from Santa Fe. Then I rode out to the plodding herd. It felt real good to be back in the cattle business again.

During the afternoon, I run into some of the boys, but did not see Red until I came in for some of Cookie's chuck. Steaks fried over his fire and I had developed a powerful hunger.

"You workin' for me again?" Red spliced a *honda* into a new lasso over by the firelight.

"Red," I touched the brim of my second new Stetson in salute. "Another couple days and we'll have this herd in Corrales. From the look of it, that snowstorm a few days back didn't hurt the cattle any."

Red snorted. "A dustin'." He coiled his lasso, tied it to his saddle, stomped over. "Start yarning, Waller." He rested his fists on his hips. "Well?"

"Hold on a minute Red, just hold on." I got up and walked slowly over to the chuck wagon.

Since I was traveling with so many packhorses, and since I was so rich, I had thought to stock up on lots of Rivas beer. Besides, me being gone so much I needed to get back on the good side of the boys. Even though Red had a law against drinking on the job, I pulled a bottle for each of the men in camp.

I was turning to go over to the fire when Pete rode in. I pulled another bottle. It was the first I had seen of Pete in a while. Wouldn't you know he'd arrive in time for a Rivas?

"This that famous beer you and Pete crave?" Red held out his bottle, admired it. "Thanks. Just one beer, Boys! I'll bend the rule tonight." Red's hard eyes cut into me. He was as impatient without tipping over into anger as I had seen Red get. "Now, what happened the last couple of weeks?" Red took his first long guzzle, but kept his eye on me as they watered.

I watched Red get a kick out of the Rivas and come up smiling.

"I won a few hundred and some dollars playin' poker in Santa Fe the other night. Thought about you boys out here, dry and all." I got a kick out of stringing Red along. He started to get red around the gills, like he did when he was angry, so I stopped horsing around and spun out the story.

*   *   *

On the twenty-ninth of November the herd grazed a mile outside Corrales. Red and Pete rode over to me. "Come on, Waller. We'll go find that buyer of yours. What's his name?" Red wore a fine-looking blue shirt and black coat. He rode Chance, the Sunday horse in his string.

Feeling mighty proud and looking for Sam Bartlet, we rode into Corrales on prancing horses. Bartlet had seen the herd approaching and met us in the street. He untied his horse from the hitching rail and we all rode back out to the herd for a survey and count.

Close to noon we all joined up around Cookie's campfire. "I counted a thousand a hundred and fifty-five, give or take, all fat cattle," Bartlet said over his cup of coffee. He sounded pleased.

"That's good by me." Red said.

"Let's head back to Corrales," Bartlet proposed. "I'll buy the first round of whiskies. I shall write out a Bank of Santa Fe draft for eighteen thousand, the rest in cash so you can pay your cowboys. That ought to cover it?" Bartlet stuck out his hand.

"That'll do fine." Red shook on the sale.

Red, Pete, Bartlet, and I stepped up to the bar in the dingy cantina. A dozen or so men loitered around drinking and playing cards. Probably Bartlet's cowboys, they would take over the herd from us now.

Bartlet ordered the best whiskey in the house and clean glasses for the four of us. "To the cattle business, Gentlemen." Not to be compared with Major Watson's bourbon, the whiskey, rotgut alcohol with iodine in it for color, burned the throat going down, but sealed the deal.

As I reached across the bar to fetch another whiskey glass, I thumbed the thong off the hammer, loosened the Colt in my holster. I turned to the man on my right, set the glass in front of him.

"Like to buy you a drink in celebration," I said to Al Simmons.

I spotted the outlaw when I first walked into the cantina and surveyed the room. The murdering gold thief, once rich, looked shabby and poor. The orphan of the gang, he had run from Santo Domingo with nothing but a horse and saddle, shotgun and pistol. I had found his poke of Durango gold in his war bag when I searched the bandit's gear in the pueblo. He must have stopped in Corrales to get work when he heard Bartlet had a herd heading south and needed cowhands.

Simmons turned slowly to face me, stuck his chin in the air to look down his nose. The scar, the main feature Tim had described, ran from the corner of Simmons' mouth to jaw-line, glistened with reflected light, and bleached the whiskers around it white. His right ear, freshly scabbed, looked like the lobe had been shot off. Blood had dried to stain the collar of his canvas duster.

"Do I know you, Mister?" His eyes crawled over my face as they tried to match my image to a memory.

Thinking about his ear, I chuckled. "We've met before, Simmons." Time slowed way down for me as I remembered the two shots I'd taken at the running shadow, skylined on the south sand hill. One of my shots had nicked him.

"What're we celebratin'?" Simmons spoke slowly, cautiously, still unable to place me.

Reaching for the bottle in front of Bartlet I poured Simmons a shot then another one for myself. Setting the bottle down, I raised my glass in my left hand, signed for him to pick up his glass. He raised it in his right hand.

"I propose a toast," I said, "to a couple of inches."

"I don't get your drift, Mister." Simmons stiffened. His eyes narrowed down to slits.

"Two inches left, you'd have blown my head off."

The cantina fell stony silent. Then I heard my three friends behind me move away from the bar.

"Two inches left, I'd have blown your head off, saved myself the trouble of arrestin' you for murder."

Simmons and I stood facing each other holding drinks in the air. His right side hugged against the bar and his gun was pinned to his side under the bar. My gun hand hung free. I remembered fighting Bustos, using the bar to protect my side from his knife hand. The man who outlived this lead swap would be the man who could survive the most lead poisoning.

Simmons threw his drink at my face, ducked left, slapped for his gun.

Before it cleared leather, my shot smashed into his chest. I laid the hammer back as the Colt bucked back in my fist.

Reeling backward, Simmons brought his gun level.

We crushed triggers at the same time.

Simmons' heart pumped one gush of blood through two bullet holes. He felt his last heart-beat at the same time he felt the last kick from his pistol. He stood hunched forward. The front of his duster smoldered where burning powder ignited it. His heart ruptured and part of his spine blown out of his back, he felt nothing. His knee jerked and buckled, toppling him left onto a table.

The body slid to the floor, left a scarlet smear on the tabletop.

I had practiced long and hard for this fight. Palm, clear, fire, shift, fire. The shift had been enough. Simmons' bullet had cut two holes in my new boiled shirt and burned a welt on the brand Bustos had carved on my side. I holstered my Colt, patted out the sparks in my smoldering white shirt.

The barroom slowly filled with voices again as the gun smoke lifted then hovered below the low ceiling.

"You hit?" Red said behind me.

I turned. "He's the third damn bandit to put his a mark on me. I'm okay, Red."

"Those were the fastest two shots I have ever seen," Bartlet said.

"He's an outlaw, not a cowboy, Bartlet." I reached for my toppled glass on the bar. "Hope I didn't leave you short-handed for your cattle drive, but I had to cull a bum calf here."

Grabbing the whiskey bottle off the bar where Simmons had faced me, I filled the empty glasses of my friends. "I'm buying, Boys. Drink a toast to the governor of New Mexico and the end of the dirty job he gave me." My hand did not shake when I held up my glass.

Bartlet signed over the bank draft and counted out the cash. He turned to his cowboys and started organizing the takeover.

Red, Pete, and I stepped out of the cantina into the bright sunlight to get our horses. Red stuffed two bottles of whiskey into his saddlebag. We rode out of Corrales to collect the boys and turn over the herd.

Mid-afternoon, Red gathered his cowboys and gave out orders. "Kid, Johnson, and you, too, Pete, take the chuck wagon and the *remuda* back up to the VR, then take a week off." Red counted out wages in stacks on the chuck box lid, Cookie's working table. "I want the rest of you men to head on into Bernalillo or Albuquerque and blow off steam." A rare smile shattered Red's usual serious foreman's face. "Unless you're fools enough to get yourse'f kilt or married, get on back to the VR after a week of carousin'. If you get back home, start on the winter chores. I'm headed to Santa Fe." Red shook each man's hand when he paid him. "It's been a good year boys." He broke out a bottle and passed it around.

Red hadn't given me orders yet. I started hauling my gear out of the chuck wagon.

"Ride up to Santa Fe with me, Eli? You'll have to report this killin' to the governor. I'd feel a might better carryin' all this money, if you's along. We can have a high old time." Red jerked his chin at me requesting an answer.

I nodded yes. I had to go. Red hadn't paid me wages yet.

Since I was headed to Santa Fe with Red, I gave my last five Rivas beers to Pete, who was headed home with the *remuda* and my new string of individual horses.

Pete hefted the beers, loaded a saddlebag. "Gracias. My father will savor one of these by his fire with me." Pete leaned over his saddle, pointed at my gun. "You are ver' fast with the pistol, Amigo." I think you will have to carry it from now on." Pete straightened up, reached to tighten the cinch. "There are men who will want to test you. The reputation will get around. It is a sorry thing, but true. *Vaya con Dios*, Amigo."

"I'll see you back at the VR, *Primo*. Enjoy the beer with your father." I swung into the saddle, backed the black stallion away from Pete with a sweeping tip of my hat to him, then reined the stallion around. I had the feeling Pete was saying good-bye for good, as I rode over to join Red.

Red and I chose a campsite on the Rio Grande a little before sunset. We both lazed around a bit, took our time getting camp chores done. After supper Red broke out the other bottle of rotgut. We had a couple of pulls before we settled back against our saddles with our feet to the fire.

Red got that look on his face like he got when he offered a cup of coffee and gave out an extra job. Only this time he looked like he would spit and whittle a little, socializing over whiskies first.

"Eli, you 'member the papers you picked up at the land office in Santa Fe a while back? Same time your troubles with Governor Connelly started, 'member?" He hit the bottle a good lick. "I got them with me," he growled as the rotgut burned his voice box. He handed me the bottle. "There's a contract and a deed to the VR. When I get to Santa Fe and the bank, I'm goin' to make the last payment and the VR becomes my ranch."

"Congratulations, Red." I took a long pull on the bottle. "You bought yourself a fine spread." I felt some envy as I wiped whiskey tears from my eyes. The VR was as big as a man could make it. The ranch controlled several hundred thousand acres and good water. It occurred to me that I had never known who the suitcase owner was. I had been content to work for Red without asking. I handed the bottle back.

"You 'member how you bent the herd the night of the stampeded, Eli?" Red took a sip this time. "You saved the herd and my deal." He doffed the bottle at me. "I thank you for that, Eli."

"Nothin' to it, Boss." I laughed, remembering near death in the mud.

"I've been thinkin'." He handed over the bottle. "I'm goin' to need some workin' money and a good man to run the business end of things. There's timber to cut and mill. I've seen coal trace in a couple of places."

Red pulled out his makings, started the job. "Now, I'm good with cattle. I'll handle that." He handed me his tobacco sack. "You know a good man with investin' money that can handle the rest?"

I had never talked about Red's business with him before, hadn't thought much about operating the VR. "Can't say as I know anyone, Red." From my pocket I pulled a reed I had found by the river, started to whittle a new pipe stem. Red watched while I fit it to my pipe. I tried the bite.

Red licked the paper and snugged up the roll. "You sure slicked ol' Sam Bartlet when you talked him out of seventeen dollars a head." Red admired the shape of his *quirly*. "The way I figure it, you got three-thousand-some-dollars comin' to you from the cattle deal."

I bit through my new pipe stem. "Damn. Red I..."

"Before you go dreamin' about spendin' it, I'll make you an offer." He dug in his pocket for a match. "You leave your money in the new VR account and we'll partner up, fifty-fifty. I'll put your name on the deed. What do you say, Eli?" He struck the match with his thumbnail, held the flair to his face, and illuminated a warm smile. Then Red laughed at me.

I must have been batting my eyes, with my mouth hanging open, like a southern belle who just heard an indecent proposal. I shut my mouth.

When Red had said he was buying the VR and had started talking around, I had figured he might be leading up to offering me the foreman's job. I'd given up that hope when he asked me for a recommendation for an investor. His offer came as a real surprise.

"Grab holt of yourse'f Eli!" Red eased back his laughing. "Think on it! I'm pickin' up a lease on the Valle Grande at the same time. You always spoke highly of her. She's half yours if you come along. Hell, we can gather a couple thousand head on that grass. With your help, we can bootstrap them cattle into minin' and lumber operations. Big time!"

I grabbed the bottle and corked my mouth with it. I took a long pull to give me time to think.

I felt like I stood in front of another door, like the door at Zia before I kicked it open and stepped in shooting. Only this time nobody would be shooting at me from the other side when it opened. Still, part of me would die if I stepped in this doorway.

I said good-bye to the cowboy, Eli, hello to the cattle baron, Mr. Waller. "You got a deal, Partner." We shook on it.

We killed the rest of the bottle while we talked about the things we could do with the ranch, the cattle to be gathered, the markets we could supply, getting the railroad into this territory, shipping coal and timber. We made plans until the fire burned low.

"Red?" He looked half-asleep. "I want to make Pete Montoya top hand."

"Okay, so long's he calls us 'Mister Charney,' 'Mister Waller,' and not 'Boss.'"

As I set up the kindling and coffeepot for my morning fire, I had one last thing to say to my new partner before we turned in for the night.

"Red?" I waited for him to grunt and open his eyes. "After we finish up at the bank tomorrow, I'm goin' to take a little time off and ride over to Cerrillos. I want to call on a young lady I know over there."

"You're goin' to get yourse'f killed yet, Eli Waller."

THE END

ABOUT THE AUTHOR

Michael C. Haley was born in Albuquerque, New Mexico and grew up in the Los Alamos area. His youth was spent in the mesa country seeking Indian artifacts in the caves and ruins from Bandelier to Puye and along the Rio Grande River. He spent his summers and vacations wrangling horses on the VR Ranch.

Haley has always been fascinated by the Indian, Spanish, and frontier histories of the region. He has traveled the back country of the Southwest extensively, gathering historical and technical skills for writing quality western adventure. Haley uses this intimate knowledge of the region to vividly and accurately describe the terrain and western lore in his novels. Haley supplements his knowledge with research to give his novels an historical foundation.

Haley began writing fiction in 1990. By this time it had become clear that the estate of Louis L'Amour did not intend to publish anything new, that Louis, the great storyteller, was gone for good. Starving for a good western, Haley decided to write his own. "I'm different from Louis because I develop the hero more. My hero not only 'does what a man's got to do', but he suffers and is transformed in the doing of it," says Haley about his writing style. "My intention is to entertain, impart knowledge of western lore, and leave the reader slightly changed through the transformation of my characters."

Haley currently lives in Parker, Colorado, with his wife, Linda. His next novel, *The Gold of El Negro,* is due to be released from Poncha Press in 2001.

Portrait by David E. Sheldon

MICHAEL C. HALEY
Author

Watch for the next novel
in this series by Michael C. Haley,
The Gold of El Negro,
due to be released
by Poncha Press in 2001.